Clipped In

The Ride of a Lifetime

By Steven Cohen

Clipped In: The Ride of a Lifetime by Steven Cohen

Copyright © 2015 by Steven Cohen

Cover by Steven Cohen

368p. ill. cm.

ISBN 978-1-935795-39-1

LCCN 2015912020

———————————————

Michael Ray King Publishing

PO Box 353431

Palm Coast, FL 32135-3431

Printed in the United States of America

Foreword

I first met Steve when he was eleven-years-old. He was a little shy but he was also focused and determined to be a BMX Champion. Steve wasn't the fastest kid in his age group, but he was the most focused, ran the most practice laps, and possessed the most desire to win. He wanted to be on the JAG BMX Team and I wanted him to be on the team too.

He made everyone on the team practice more, even our #1 Team Rider Anthony Sewell, World Champion. Anthony asked me one day, "Who is that kid?"

"That's Steve Cohen," I replied. "If everyone on our team worked out like Steve Cohen they would finish first in every lap and every main event. That kid is awesome."

Yes, Steve Cohen is in fact "awesome." He's also creative, and caring, a great father, a hard worker, enthusiastic, positive, determined, and relentless in his quest for excellence. Steve Cohen knew what it took to be a champion and worked hard at achieving the best his mind and body could do.

When Steve told me he was writing a book, I was anxious to read it. Nothing has changed. Steve is still awesome and creative. Follow him through this world of competitions. This book will weave you through the turns and over the jumps of life and competitions. It is an adventure that is ongoing, fast-paced, over the whoop dee do's, around the banked turns, with words that paint an incredible picture.

This time Steve definitely put the pedal to the metal because I couldn't put the book down. It was as if each page I turned took me closer to the finish line. Steven's characters are real, and I found myself associating with certain people in this book.

Steve literally took me for an incredible ride through a period that I loved to have been involved with. Take the ride down a tall hill, maneuver through and over the jumps and find yourself thrilled with the ride and the lives of those characters created for our enjoyment. This is HOT! Exciting! And GREAT! Thank you for the ride Steve.

Renny Roker

European BMX Hall of Fame Inductee

This book is dedicated to anyone who competed with the desire to never give up and to all the parents, coaches, or any person who supported athletes anywhere in this world.

"You miss 100 percent of the shots you don't take." – **Wayne Gretzky**

Chapter 1

Its 2:15 in the morning and the alarm is sounding. Its early spring with a light chill in the air for this time of night or some would say early morning, for me its morning. The alarm seems to be getting louder at every pulse of its sound. I rush to shut off the alarm as to not to wake my beautiful wife of over 20 years.

Too late, I hear the sound of an angels voice saying to me, "Sweety, see you in a couple of days, I love you. Be careful on your way to the airport." I reach over from my sitting position to give her a kiss on the cheek. I can faintly make out her smile as she turns and swiftly falls back to sleep.

I see my suitcase is packed and my uniform hanging in the bathroom with my tie and under garments. I arise from my slumber feeling as if I only had slept 30 minutes instead of the 5 and half hours I abruptly awaken from. I make my way to the bathroom, shower and ready myself for about an hour commute to the Philadelphia International Airport. I have my bag, wallet and my jacket downstairs. I grab all my belongings and walk into the garage, start my car and make my way out of the driveway with no lights as to not wake my angel who is still sleeping. Headlights on and I am on my way.

As I make my way towards the airport, I reflect and think of my life. I feel like the luckiest man in the world. I have a wife who loves me, an awesome family and children who look to me as their hero. None of this came easy; there was a lot of work and support from my friends and family. Nevertheless, I worked through many difficult times at which sometimes felt impossible and over bearing. But I alone with self-perseverance struggled and my hard work has paid off in unimaginable experiences.

Life is a challenge and only produces what you allow it. There is the old saying, "if life gives you lemons, then make lemonade." I say phooey. What if I don't like lemons? Someone gives me a lemon, I simply say thanks. It's a matter of perspective and interpretations. My life's become what I allowed it to be by my own demise. I refused to allow an unchanging heart dictate my fate. I will always choose the path of least resistance if the outcome allows me to decide my fortune. Life gives us many decisions, it's important to choose the correct one.

My car thermometer indicates the temperature of 56 degrees F and I add a small amount of heat as I drive. I recall all the past decisions I have made in my life and the outcomes. I have always been a competitive person and I lived my life the same.

If I was playing football at a field next to my house, I always wanted to win. Dodge ball in high school, I wanted to be the last one standing. Always, I have had the drive and determination to want to be the champion. I am that person.

Understand, I believe in teamwork and togetherness, but teams are made of individuals who strive for the same goal. I never got mad or upset when I lost fairly. I'm the first person to shake hands and say, "nice game." This is what motivates me.

I understand that I'm not always going to be the best and somewhere out in world somebody will always be better. I accept it as my initiative for discord.

In my competitive nature to be successful, I built this life I am living. Bicycle racing, or known as BMX, created the man I am today. My desire for accolades is a personification of my surroundings and people who I allowed to influence me. My youth built on layers of life events allowed me this opportunity to be successful.

I credit back all my successes to my youth and the people I allowed to surround me in my life influencing my decisions. I loved riding my bike. I loved traveling the country. I loved meeting people of different cultures and beliefs.

This all happened essentially in my back yard. This was a great time of my life. It changed me. It changed me and I didn't even know it. I was making critical decisions in my life and I didn't know it. I was influenced towards directions I would take in my life and I didn't perceive it.

I pull into the employee lot and gather my belongings. I lock the doors and hear the chirp of the alarm and catch the blinking of the lights on my vehicle as I walk off. I walk towards the glass bus shelter and patiently wait for the bus to arrive.

I look up into the heavens. I think of my destiny. I look at the beauty of the stars in the heavens as the cool breeze blows chilling me a bit. Although it is way too early for anybody to want to be awake, I am feeling happy and content.

I am now fully awake. The employee bus rounds the corner and stops directly in front of me. I pull my bags into the bus with me and set them on the shelf directly in front of me. I say hello to the driver. He does not reply. Maybe he is tired. I say nothing and quietly recall my thoughts.

I think back of all the people I can remember from my BMX days. I think of where they are now and if my preconceived thoughts of their future were correct. I think of how some of them are still friends and others just memories.

It still gives me chills remembering my racing days. I can still hear the cadence of the gate, the lights, and the sounds of the gate hitting the dirt. I still remember my first race as vividly as my last. This was good ride for me. I feel gratified in my thoughts.

The bus stops and I gather my belongings and head into the terminal. I bypass security for the most part showing my company ID and head into work. My flight leaves in nearly an hour and I need some preparation before boarding the flight. I travel for a living and enjoy it most of the time. I miss my family when I'm gone, but it's usually not more than four days at a time.

Chapter 2

Its mid-August in Valle Hermoso Mexico and the year is 1970. Valle Hermoso is a medium sized town in the state of Tamaulipas in Mexico. It is approximately 25 miles south of the Mexico/United States border.

Valle Hermoso, translated Beautiful Valley, is a modern city with office buildings, modern roadways, and a solid infrastructure. Valle Hermoso is not the stereotypical border Mexican town that is usually portrayed as desolate, dusty, tumbleweeds blowing, and a shelled out ghost town with very few occupants.

Valle Hermoso is modern for its time period with slate roofs contrasted of the tar roofs used in today's construction. This town has traffic lights, walkways, and suburbs. It is surrounded by typical family style homes common for this region.

It's 105 degrees Fahrenheit and its 12:30 PM, lunch just ended for Maximo Santos. Maximo is not a highly educated man, but has a technical background in HVAC (heating, ventilation, and air conditioning systems). He is a shorter man of 5'7". He is in his mid 30's and in good physical condition. He works as a maintenance technician for one of the office buildings in downtown Valle Hermoso.

He is a respected man by both his coworkers and the individuals who work in the building. He is directly employed by the management company who is contracted to facilitate the maintenance of the property. Maximo has been employed by this company for almost 6 years.

He rarely misses work and has a superb attitude. He never comes into work with an attitude or the preverbal chip on his shoulder. Many times when you walk up on Maximo, he is performing his job and even singing. Maximo has a very limited understanding of English and struggles if spoken to in other than Spanish.

As the building maintenance technician, he is required to fix things or perform small repairs. He assists on the larger repairs when vendors are called in to perform such tasks. Maximo has perfected the air conditioning system in his office building.

It is murderous to the other occupants in the building on a summer day when the heat index is over 120 degrees Fahrenheit. Although the heat does not affect him as others, he still takes pride that he can fix things from air conditioning units to doors and windows. He is basically your Mr. Fixit man and no task is impossible for Maximo provided he has all the tools to perform his job.

Many occupants in the building bring him appliances to be fixed. Many things include toasters, TV's, and sometimes children's toys. He brings them home and fixes them in his garage. This brings joy to Maximo and he is revered for his servitude for wanting to help others. He is a quiet kind-hearted man who does not say much, listens to everyone smiling as if he has no cares in the world.

Maximo lives approximately fifteen miles from work. He has a small house with 3 bedrooms and garage. The house is the same house he and his brother grew up in. Although he was not the only child, he was sole survivor of his kin. The house is well kept and maintained. Of course one would expect this of Maximo and his valued work ethic.

The inside of the house is well maintained by his wife Florencia. Maximo and Florencia have been married for nearly 9 years. Although married very young, Maximo being 19 and Florencia age 17 have had a blissful life together. He always worked and attended vocational school for air conditioning repairs while courting Florencia.

He asked for her hand in marriage when he was seventeen. Her father said he would bless their relationship when he finished and graduated his vocation school for HVAC. He obtained his diploma and was awarded Florencia's hand in marriage.

They married and he immediately found work as a handy man with a small company before taking the job downtown. They lived in a one-bedroom apartment before moving into the house they live in at this time.

Florencia never worked and Maximo preferred it this way. He was old-fashioned in his ways and never felt that she couldn't work. He preferred her to not work. He enjoyed coming home with dinner ready and the house always immaculate.

After working in the heat of the day, it was refreshing to see a nice meal and his wife whom he revered awaiting him. There was small talk at times of Florencia wanting to work, but Maximo never gave it any thought. If she needed money for shopping or for the house, it was never an issue.

She had full reign over the money as did he. She would on occasion buy herself new clothes or treat herself to a dress at times. It was briefly discussed with Maximo. He made it a point to discuss what he spent as well. There was never a doubt, he felt they were a team and they worked together towards one common goal, each other. It brought him joy to see his wife happy and secure in their marriage. Florencia found joy knowing Maximo was happy.

They both had their strong religious beliefs. Although they lived in Mexico, they were not Catholic. They practiced their faith in a non-denominational church. Within one year Florencia was pregnant with their first child. They would have a total of 4 children total approximately one and a half to two years apart. They moved into Maximo's family home shortly after their oldest son Carlos was born.

Maximo's family home was nearly big enough to accommodate them. Luckily for Maximo there was a basement in the home. Although it was a dirt floor, this would present no problem for Maximo. On his days off with help from friends and family in the area, he was able to pour a cement floor and install windows in order to provide extra living space for his children over a period of 3 months.

Although there was only one bathroom in the residence is was not an issue. There were those times as the kids started getting older and school times differed. Needless to say, Maximo and Florencia nearly always reckoned the matter with little or no conflicts.

For the most part, the Santos's were a close family with strong core beliefs. Maximo with resilient persistence from Florencia ensured they attended church on Sundays. When Church was over, they always went to eat together. It was a non-traditional type of lunch. This was not your typical go to the diner and wait for someone to seat you. It was often followed by going to a park and finding a man selling empanadas or tacos and sitting down under a tree enjoying their meal.

For Maximo it was heaven. He enjoyed the fact that he was outdoors with his family feeling the breeze and enjoying the sunshine. This wasn't always the case, when the heat reached the 100 degree Fahrenheit mark; he was very content to find a restaurant with air conditioning.

They never struggled for money per se, but it was closely monitored. They were not rich by any means. Maximo and Florencia made it a point to try to save money and only take from savings as absolutely needed. Maximo would work late some nights and earn extra money when needed. He often would take on garage projects for people as a repairman.

You couldn't park a car in the garage because of workshop Maximo had created. Also the garage was full, it was very organized and his suede man cave. He had a workbench and tools neatly hung over it. He was very proud of this area, even when it was blistering hot in the summer months. This is Maximo, this is his personality. There is nothing he couldn't fix.

One day he was visited by a friend asking for assistance starting his car. He told Maximo that the car had been sitting for a couple of years. When he arrived at his friend's house, there was a 1940 Chevy pickup sitting under an old army looking tarp with holes in it. Maximo was not familiar with this type of American vehicle but was willing to take the challenge and make this thing start.

He asked the pertinent questions. How long has it been sitting? How old is the gas? Is the battery charged? Maximo had his friend get a battery and installed it. He cranked the engine and it turned. It did not start but he was able to deduct what caused the engine to not start.

He was able to rig up a gas line to the carburetor with a funnel and a rubber hose. He poured some gas down the carburetor and the vehicle started on the second time. It ran for 2 minutes before it stalled. He explained to his friend that he needed to buy some parts in order for the truck to run and be drivable.

His friend did have enough money to buy all the items needed. Maximo came back the next week and took inventory of the items he told his friend to buy. Maximo left and came back with a generic fuel filter and fuel lines. He removed the fuel tank and cleaned it out thoroughly. He installed new spark plugs and wires and fired up the engine again.

It purred like a kitten. He figured the engine to be a 216.5 cubic inch engine and timed it per the specs he was given from the parts dealer were he bought the engine parts. It was a six cylinder engine known as a Stovebolt Six. He not only got the truck running, he helped his friend change the brakes and change the lights that were burned out. Maximo took pride in fixing things.

It's not the work, it's the challenge. He had the gift of fixing things and they lasted. His children inherited part of his work ethic. Although very young, they found joy in doing things for others.

Chapter 3

Its mid-August the weather in NJ is pleasurable. It's around 88 degrees Fahrenheit with limited humidity. Angelo Carlucci is at work on a job site. He is a mason by trade but later decided to work for himself.

He continually worked in the heat of the day perspiring rivers of sweat moving heavy blocks or in the winter months working in the hostile cold with the wind figuratively blowing through his winter garments. Compound this with extreme deadlines on jobs he was performing for his previous employers. He was a gifted mason with many years of experience. He is characterized as prideful Italian with strong connections to his native Italian ancestry.

Angelo Carlucci grew up in Southern NJ. He was an average sized man 5'11" of stature. He is in excellent shape and slightly over developed arms. He met his wife Maria in High School. They courted for nearly two years before they were married.

They lived in a moderate home surrounded by farms and trees. Houses were scattered in their small town anchored against the protected forestry of the pinelands. Maria worked part time with her sister in the summer canning spiced vegetables and fruits selling them to the local markets in their small town and the outskirt neighboring communities. They both enjoyed their time together.

Normally Angelo arrived home between 5 or 6 pm. Maria, working with her sister had the flexibility to leave and be home for her awaiting husband. Maria was an amazing cook and rarely opened a can for her sauces or gravy's. Angelo caught the brunt of her excellent culinary skills. His co-workers would make humorous remarks of the fact that he had put on a few pounds after being married.

After nearly one year of marriage, Maria was pregnant and gave birth to a son. They had a total of two children. Both children were boys born nearly two years apart. In the typical Italian family tradition, there was an impressive celebration event for each child including baptisms in the huge cathedral churches of that day. Thus, this was the catholic tradition.

After many years of working for other employers, Angelo made the decision to start his own Mason Company. His wife Maria supported him through the transition answering phones, making appointments, and doing the books while he was on a job site. It would be several years later that they had saved enough money to buy a building allowing Angelo to store the blocks and his company trucks.

He had an office that was considered very affable for this time period. His deduction is that if his wife was going to be in the office, he wanted it to be as comfortable as possible for her. Many clients arrived to pay bills in person in those days. There was no ATM's or instant money wire transfers. Bills had to be paid by check or cash.

It would come to pass that Maria would have to bring the children to work with her until they were old enough to go to school for a full day session. Angelo made it a point to separate the children to a back office during the day. This office was more like a child's playroom.

They had a TV, their own desks, carpeting, and a refrigerator. There was a large glass window allowing for Maria to see the children as she continued to work. They had plenty of help from Maria's parents and his parents when needed. Although this was convenient for them, there was the joy of the children in the office when Angelo would pull into the parking lot and immediately see his children. This always brought him great joy.

Angelo's business became very successful and he had the means of upgrading the family home. He grew the business from just himself and a laborer and his wife to a company of over 20 employees in the summer months. He took on large commercial projects to include, apartment buildings, bridges, and overpasses.

He expanded from not only blocks but into concrete. He had built a small empire. Maria no longer needed to be in the office all the time. She continued to occupy her time with her sister in the summers along with the children. Her sister also had 2 children. The children would play together all day at times. Winters were somewhat boring for Maria; she found joy being in the office during these periods. She was very knowledgeable with the business and was a great asset for Angelo.

The business thrived over the years enabling a very beneficial life for Angelo and his family. The children grew over the years and were exceptional students. There were times boys would be boys, but there was never a behavior issue with school. They more feared their father then their faculty.

Needless to say, they were above average students with good dispositions. The oldest son, Dominic is best described as a character. He had a strong competitive nature. He excelled in his studies because of this competitive disposition. He had a strong drive to excel in all endeavors, be it school, sports, or organized competitions. This would later motivate him and become a part of his strong moral character.

Chapter 4

Its 1977 and Maximo made the decision to move to the United States. He and his wife both agreed that they wanted a different life for their children. Not a better life, a different one. Maximo knew they could not afford to send all their children to college at the same time.

Although they had the means for a good life now, it would definitely change as the years moved forward. He was striving for a better job making more money. He was willing to give up all he had for a dream of moving North. He had the knowledge and skill set of finding employment in the United States. It was a matter of making the move and taking on the task of making it happen.

Maximo filed all the appropriate papers and was granted passage for him and his family. Now it was a matter of finding work and a place to live. He and Florencia made the decision to sell their home and use the money to finance their way with the required Visa's for the entire family.

After a while they had acquired the needed documentation. Maximo found work originally working as a laborer with a contractor for cash. He was extremely limited based on his limited understanding of the English language and his ability to communicate. It wasn't very long before they sold their house and Maximo was able to move north of the Border.

They relocated four and half hours north to San Antonio, Texas. All the children attended school and were placed in special classes in order expedite their English speaking and comprehension skills.

Maximo and Florencia rented an apartment for one year based on the lease they had signed. They agreed not to move the children out of the schools they were attending and continue to live in that school system district. Although there was a large Latin community, Maximo strived to learn English. It was not long before he had the limited knowledge to apply for different career opportunities allowing him more salary and the ability to earn a larger paycheck.

He finally was awarded a position at Lackland AFB, Texas. He worked as a construction worker and was given the opportunity to advance with his HVAC knowledge. It would be nearly a year before he was awarded his license in the United States and exercise his ability to perform this type of work.

As time elapsed for him working and living in the United States, he gained the respect of his fellow workers. He and Florencia purchased a home large enough to accommodate him and the family. Along with the savings and the money from their previous home, they purchased their home in a moderate neighborhood.

There was not a large Latin Community in this area, but for them it was home. It was perfect. All four children nearly had their own rooms except for Juan and Rafael. They had to share the biggest bedroom.

Carlos the oldest son procured the smallest room but it was his own personal space. The youngest sibling Julieta also procured her own room. There was no basement, but there was a detached two car garage with a small space above it. It was more like a storage area and could not be constructed as a separate living quarters.

The children had learned to speak English within six months. In their school environments learning English was easy. There was no spoken Spanish in the classroom and it was considered a hindrance in the comprehension of obtaining and mastering English. Spanish was often heard when on the play grounds or outside the scholastic academia of an organized classroom.

All the children had the ability to read and write English within a years' time. Maximo had a full understanding of English. He had the ability to read and write English. He never would lose his accent but had full knowledge and a command of English.

He needed this ability when performing his job. He needed the ability to read manuals, construction diagrams and order parts in English. Florencia took a part time job as a check-out clerk at a local supermarket. It was not for the money, she felt that if she needed to learn English, she would immerse herself in the culture and only speak Spanish if a customer could not speak English.

Life was going well for Maximo and his family. The children were doing well in school. He and Florencia had the ability to speak English. They owned their own home. They even had the ability to buy a newer car with air-conditioning. In the Texas heat of the summer, it was an incredible convenience when driving in the hot summer months.

It was in time that the neighbors that had surrounded his 2 acre property got to know him. The neighbors found Maximo and his family a great addition to their community. Maximo had gained noble respect from his co-workers and superiors. He rarely turned down overtime and performed any tasks he was assigned. Maximo's determination and Florencia's willingness to achieve was a mentoring influence of how they were raising the children.

It wouldn't be long before the first social issue would arise. The youngest son Rafael came home extremely upset. Rafael was not being bullied but in the nature of some children was being called a name by one individual and had no idea what it meant.

Apparently one of Rafael's school mates called him a dimwit and he had no idea what it meant. It wasn't until another student friend of his described in detail the true definition and meaning of this word. Rafael felt comfortable speaking with his father. It was one of the many things that made him feel close to him.

He conveyed what had transpired with his classmate. Maximo always had a kind way about him. He listened to his son as Rafael continued. He conveyed to his father that he was called a dimwit. He further explained that he was called this because he did not understand some of the slang terms that children and adult often use.

His classmate felt it appropriate to call Rafael a dimwit because he did not understand the concept of the slang, "tear 'em up" while playing in the school yard. Maximo explained this situation using a metaphor. Understand, they are talking in Spanish.

He continued on with Rafael, "People are very judgmental. Many people make deductions based on incomplete facts. The fact that you don't know slang makes you a dimwit in his eyes. The actuality that you never heard of this phrase doesn't make you stupid or ignorant. It makes you aware of a new word. Let me give you an example," Maximo continued, "Your late uncle taught mathematics at the university. He had a Master's degree in physics and was a brilliant mathematician. He was vacationing in Canada one summer and someone walking along the street asked him for directions thinking he lived there. He looked at them and made a gesture to imply that he didn't speak French. They asked him if he spoke English. He shook his head to indicate no. They walked off making facial expressions as if he was dumb and clueless. Truth be told, he probably had more education and thinking ability of both of them combined. Because he didn't speak the language doesn't make him less smart. The fact is, your uncle didn't speak French or English. That's all. He wasn't dumb, he wasn't clueless. He simply didn't speak their language. People are quick to judge based on first impressions. If you give in to their judgments you become just like them. Imagine if they spoke Spanish! Imagine if they asked your uncle to explain quantitative physics as a theory!"

Maximo looked at his son and said to him, "remember what I am saying to you. You're only a man once and a boy twice."

Rafael looked at him confused and asked, "What does this mean Papa?"

Maximo answered him, "when you figure it out one day, you will know that you are a man."

Chapter 5

The years continued. Angelo's business had become a small empire. He had niche market in concrete design and designer of masonry blocks. Angelo had a building on his property built to accommodate the resources for making his own blocks. He perfected the art of adding a sparkle like glimmer to specific types of blocks. Many newer buildings were using this as an accent design and at the same time providing integral space.

His two sons, Dominic and his younger son Joey were working for him at the plant. They didn't do the most strenuous jobs, but they enjoyed operating some of the machinery. They felt as if they were earning their keep. Angelo would tell them over the years, "one day all this will be yours and you need to learn all the jobs and take orders. You have to learn to take orders before you've earned the right to give them."

He further explained, "There will be people who will always be with you in this business. Look around here, some of these men have been here from the first day I opened the doors. They were with me when we were out digging holes by hand before I bought the machinery that digs it for us. They were here when we struggled and worked long hours in order to be successful. They will respect you the harder you work. When you have earned their respect and take over, they will make you successful. They will never let you fail."

He continued, "There is no bigger champion than your mother. She struggled with me and without her help I would not be where I am today."

Dominic remembered these words as did his little brother. Their father was well respected and had a strong reputation of always completing jobs on time and producing quality products. Their parents were both very active in their youth. Any organized sports they competed, their parents were always there to cheer them on.

Dominic was a very strong competitor. Before the summer his father bought him a bicycle enabling him the freedom to hang around with his friends in the neighborhood. Dominic had a small group of friends he always hung around with and liked being around.

Rex, Jimmy and Larry were benevolent children. For their ages they were well behaved, not causing any mischief. They were all around the same age and attended the same school. Rex was one year older than them all. Rex was reflected as the ring leader of the group of boys.

Not far from the house and not deep into the woods was an open gravel pit area. Dominic and his friends would ride there all day occasionally riding back to their respected houses for lunch and dinners. They did not have dirt style bicycles but loved riding in the pits.

The most fun was riding down from the steepest part and gaining tremendous speeds. Tremendous speeds equating to 15 to 20 miles per hour on a good dry day. They made a pseudo race track with many twist and turns. There was even a jump before a long winding right hand turn.

They would ride there for hours. Many other neighborhood kids made their way back to the pits. The pit, as it was nicknamed, was a social gathering area for all the neighborhood kids with bicycles. They often talked about going to watch a BMX race. They had seen the BMX magazines in the stores and perceived that there had to be a place near them to watch the races.

As they talked over the weeks, continuing to ride in the pits, Dominic had become untouchable. He had no fear of any jumps or speeds when negotiating the turns. Over the weeks of riding, they shoveled more jumps and incorporated longer straight-aways enabling more speed for the jumps they had made.

Rex, being the oldest, was the strongest of the boys but not the fastest. There was a sense of competition between Rex and Dominic. Although they were competitive, it was friendly.

It wasn't long before Larry found that there was BMX track less than an hour away. Dominic begged his father to take him and his friends to watch. Rex obtained all the information from one of the local bicycle shops in town. They knew the races started at eleven in the morning on a Saturday.

Angelo agreed to take Dominic, his brother and two other friends. There wasn't enough room in the truck for all of them. It was agreed, Larry and Rex would accompany them. Jimmy wanted to go but even if there was room, he had a family barbeque to attend. Needless to say, he made all efforts to go to the BMX races.

Saturday morning the gang is at Dominic's house. They agreed to meet at 9 am. It was a brutal hot day. Nearly 100 degrees. Like clockwork, Angelo had the truck started and ready to go at nine twenty nine. Angelo was militant about being on time and the boys were already sitting in the scorching 105 degree truck with windows open.

They were more than enthusiastic knowing they were actually going to see their first BMX race. Angelo fired up the truck and they were on their way. After about a mile down the road, Angelo had the boys roll up the window as he set the air conditioning to its coldest level. They were off to the races. It was not a quiet ride by any means but an exciting one. Angelo heard so much about it he was anxious as to what this was all about.

On the way to the track, the boys discussed their trials of their bike racing at the pits. They discussed all their endeavors. Poor Jimmy wasn't there to protect himself, needless to say he was the slowest of the boys. He might have been the slowest but still was fast considering the banana seat bike with the ape like handlebars he was riding.

They discussed the quickness of Dominic. His father never heard any of these conversations and was quite surprised of his son's abilities. They were telling Angelo of Dominic's heroics. Larry was describing a race they had. "Mr. Carlucci, Dom is a mad man when he rides. He rides so hard into some of the turns his knee actually hits the dirt from the ruts we made. He jumps everything, he never slows down."

Angelo continued to listen, "We started calling him Dom Dom." This being a play on words for dumb dumb. "But this wasn't a good nickname so we started calling him Killucci. He kills the track when he rides."

They all started to laugh and make jokes as Angelo shook his head in disbelief and continued down the road. They boys continued to discuss their ventures as they neared the BMX track.

They turned off the main highway to a smaller road that looked as if it should be a one vehicle thruway. Feeling more anxious, the boys were now in deep thought trying to find the track entrance. As they made their way down the road, Dominic called out, "There it is!"

There was a small little sign stuck in the ground with an arrow pointed to the left with the words, "BMX Track." Angelo made the turn down the dirt road and drove about a half a mile back into the woods to an open field. There it was. Their Mecca.

The track was there with a bunch of kids riding their BMX bikes. Angelo parked the truck and they got out. The heat of the day caught them by surprise but it didn't matter to them. They were there.

They made their way around the property. The bikes looked different and there were many banners, Schwinn, FMF, Redline, and several others. The bikes were smaller. They looked flimsy like tinfoil. They had smaller, skinnier tires.

There were the other bikes that were bigger with heavy wheels and larger spokes. The bikes were colorful. They had padding across the frame, goose neck and handlebars. The bicycles had no foot brakes.

All were freewheels and utilized hand brakes. Some of the bikes were aluminum. All the boys were perplexed. They all believed that a true BMX bike would be heavier and built much beefier.

There was a starting gate. It held eight riders. It was a gate about one foot high. All the riders lined up and there was a cadence, "pedals up, wheels on the ground." After that the gate would drop and off they went. The boys were overwhelmed by the speeds kids their age were reaching in a short distance.

The track was constructed with hard packed dirt with tires aligning the edges. The track wasn't incredibly long but it had some length. It was three times longer than the pits they were used to riding.

They all walked around as a group. A kid rode up on his bike directly to Dominic, took off his helmet and said, "Hey Dom, whatcha doing here?" It was a friend from school.

Dom replied, "Hey Pete, I didn't know you raced? How long have you been doing this for?"

Pete replied, "This is my second year. Last year I started in the middle of the season, kind of about now." They talked for a short time and Pete went to the start gate. He raced in the 12 novice race group. He had a very nice bike. It wasn't brand new but it was nicer than all of theirs.

Pete made his way to the gate and lined up. They heard the cadence and off he went. He was with a group of younger kids and was gone as soon as the gate dropped. He was fast, really fast. He hit the first jump and kept on peddling. It was amazing. They never saw this before.

There was an announcement and practice was over. The group made their rounds to all the vendors. They looked at some of the bikes. The cost for a decent bike that was considered competitive was nearly $350.00. In 1978, that was an expensive for a bicycle. There was all the accessories needed like helmets, bike pads, and a racing jersey with long sleeves and elbow pads.

Angelo was recognized by a few of his past customers whose children were racing. One of the customers went over and said hello. Angelo explained to one of them that he took his sons and friends to watch the races. He talked with a man for a long time.

From a distance the boys could see him laughing and pointing to parts of the track. It was burning hot and they moved into the shade and continued talking. The boys walked back to Angelo as he shook the man's hand and met the boys halfway. They continued to walk about looking at all the bikes on display at the vendors and they noticed many of the competitor's bicycles.

It was close to 11 AM and the announcement rang out, "Motos are posted." There was a mass exodus to these flat boards nailed to some four by fours. There were sheets that allowed the riders to know what heat they were in and their position on the starting gate.

For example: if a rider was designated to moto 5, this is the heat or what is referred to as motos. This designated what number race you are in. Moto 5 indicates that the rider would be in the fifth race. Also, the moto sheet showed who you were racing against and what your positions are on the starting gate. If you are in moto number 5 and you see the numbers 2-8-4. You are in lanes 2, 8 and 4. Normally there are 3 Motos for each race series.

If a rider finishes their three races or Motos in first place, then first place in the second moto, then he finishes third. The finishing positions are added up and the lowest number wins first place. In the event there is a tie. The third moto finishing place would be the tie breaker. In this example the rider would collect a total of six points. If the rider ties another rider with a total of five, the third moto would indicate the winner.

They all waited for the races to begin. The first to take the starting gate was the six year old kids and under. They watched with great enthusiasm. It was surreal to actually watch what they have been pretending while riding at the pit. It was incredible for them. The racers during the motos started getting older till they finally got to watch their friend Pete. The track was not overly long. It had some jumps, long turns, and various straight-aways.

As Pete entered the gate the boys stood up from their cozy shady spot they seized. There were 6 kids racing the 12 year old novice class. The gate dropped and the race was on. Pete grabbed the lead in the first straight, over the three foot jump a small straight to a left hand flat turn.

Pete was in the lead. It was a ninety degree turn to the left. They came out of the turn with Pete still leading by one bike length for a short straightaway over the second jump to a sharp one hundred eighty degree left turn. Another ninety degree right turn to a small straight to a forty five degree right turn.

Then there was a small jump to a long sweeping left turn to a straightaway then the finish line. Pete led the pack the whole way. He steadily pulled away. The announcer was making jokes calling him Pedaling Pete. Pete eventually came across the finish in first place.

Finally the eighteen and over experts take the gate. It was the fastest race they ever saw. The boys were elated. This group of riders were blazing the track. They hit the jumps as if they were not there and tightly packed.

Not one of them fell. They stayed tightly packed the entire race. There was very little separation as this moto continued. They could not believe how much fun this was for them. They were in heaven this day. This was their motivation to want to race.

The races ended around three thirty and they discussed the races the entire way home. They talked about how they would change the pit to mimic what they had witnessed. The air-conditioned truck overwhelmed them with comfort and they were all sleeping within 15 minutes after leaving. Angelo looked over at them and laughed to himself with delight as he drove back home.

Chapter 6

Maximo and his family have been living in Texas for nearly a year. The summers are brutal just like in Mexico. Waking up at five in the morning and the heat index nearly one hundred degrees will get anyone's blood pumping. Maximo makes his way to work as his wife and children remain sleeping in the cool comfort.

Florencia awakes around seven thirty AM and starts her routine. She begins with breakfast. The smell of bacon awakens the children. Carlos normally awakes first to claim his prize of eggs, bacon and flat bread. Then he is followed by his other siblings. Rafael is always the last to awake from his slumber.

Typically his sister Julieta has to shake him as life bleeds slowly back into his body. He knows that if his sister is unsuccessful, his mother is more stringent in waking him. Rafael makes a priority of waking because the brother he shares the room with won't wake him as a cruel joke of allowing their mother to instill turmoil on him.

Carlos, the oldest of the four children makes his way around the neighborhood gathering recyclables. It wasn't long before he had a shed full of junk bicycle parts. Rafael being intuitive like his father was able to build a bicycle. It wasn't a ghastly build. Shockingly the bike he produced was exceedingly appealing.

He needed new tubes for his tires. The ones he was able to piecemeal together had slow leaks. Maximo came home and noticed what Rafael had manufactured. He was very pleased with his son. Not only was he pleased, he was impressed that all his tools made it back their proper place.

Maximo made it a point to inform Rafael because he returned all the tools, he was going to buy him new tubes. Rafael was increasingly excited. Not only did Maximo buy him tubes, he also purchased a new chain. Rafael was in heaven. He had a bicycle and limited amount of freedom to ramble about the neighborhood.

One day while riding his bicycle, he came across some friends from school. Rafael was close to his house. He was down the street near a field with a dirt road. All the boys were racing each other on their bicycles. Extending kindness towards Rafael, they challenged him to a race. They were using a rock pile as a marker and raced to a huge dip in the road with a rope extended across the road.

There were four boys total including Rafael. They all decided to race and Rafael wanted to watch at first. Still a little shy he wanted observe the other kids as they performed their race. Someone said go and they were off. They raced down the dirt road crossing the rope as the race winner.

Rafael accepted their invitation and raced with them the second time. He trounced them. He was the last person to start pedaling and hurtled his way past them in a fury. The other boys were ecstatic at the end of the finish line where the rope lay.

All the boys took notice of his bicycle. He described how his brother found all the parts and he himself put the bike together. They were impressed. Rafael was establishing friendships and making acquaintances with his classmates.

Their bicycles were all nearly the same. All were twenty inch size bicycles with big ape like handle bars and large seats. Some bicycles had fenders and the others had a gear shifter. Rafael's bicycle had one speed and he pedaled furiously when they raced.

Rafael and the other boys rode their bicycles on the dirt road all day. There were many farms far off the roadway. There was always a property that was more prominent among all the other estates. There was one home in particular that was gated and was not like the other farms or properties.

It was exclusive and always made one wonder of what is happening within the closed walls. Moreover, the boys commented of who might own this palace-like estate. Many rumors escalated but never with circumstantial evidence of the owner. The boys captured glimpses of large earth moving equipment they sought while building their track.

The boys swapped bicycles with each other and stated their affections. It was getting late in the afternoon and Rafael needed to return to the house. The sun was blistering down on them all day. Rafael decided to leave and make his way home.

He arrived at the house and told his mother what had occurred. She was happy for him. In her mothering nature, she warned Rafael about being careful of the boys since she didn't know them. He convinced her they were respectable. He pointed out how they played on the school grounds during lunch recess and he never had any issues. She expressed her happiness for him as she kissed him on the forehead.

For several weeks Rafael and his new friends would ride up and down the dusty road for hours. They would take breaks to get water and return to their respective houses for lunch or more beverages. The boys continually made it a point to meet each day at 10 AM for their daily racing event.

One day when riding on the road, they saw an old tractor coming towards them. They continued until it got close. An old man driving the tractor asked the boys what they were doing. The tallest of the four boys explained to the old man what they were doing and portrayed sincere politeness. The old man looked at them for a moment and asked, "Are yaw decent folks?"

Together they all answered, "Yes."

With the low buzz of the diesel engine running, the old man told the boys "follow me."

He turned the tractor around and the boys followed him. They followed for nearly five minutes until coming upon a clearing. To their amazement, it was a large open field with giant mounds of dirt arranged in different locations. Some dirt mounds were from eight feet to a few colossal ones nearly twenty feet high with a large plateau on top.

The old man warned them, "If you get hurt, it's on yaw."

They laughed and stood looking in amazement. They all discussed what they wanted to do. On that day, they created a path down the largest mound and took turns peddling down it at tremendous speeds. It was not physically close to the main road but they didn't care. For them, they struck gold.

On one of the days of riding, one of the boys discussed about going to watch the BMX races in Austin. Rafael asked, "What is BMX?"

The other three boys laughed. Tommy, The oldest of the group, explained the entire BMX racing series that they were discussing. He said they should go next Saturday. It was just over an hour away and there are races on Saturday mornings.

As they discussed the race, Bobby said, "I can ask my parents. We have a station wagon."

There it was. It was final. Bobby was going to ask his parents about the races. The boys were eager to watch a genuine race and not the make-pretend adventures they were constructing.

Rafael raced home on his bicycle. He pulled in the driveway and made a beeline for the back door. He came in the house excited. He asked his mother if he could go with his friends to the BMX race in Austin.

As she was asking him about it, Maximo entered the house and was met by both his wife and Rafael. Rafael kissed his father on the cheek and asked him how his day was. Maximo looked at him with resolute confusion. He immediately looked to his wife. She smiled and remarked, "Sit down" and laughed.

Rafael explained the events of the day. Maximo looked on with skepticism. Florencia sat quietly as Rafael continued. He alluded to the fact that Austin had an organized BMX race and he enjoyed riding his bicycle. Rafael spoke for nearly ten minutes nonstop.

Maximo interjected, "OK, you can go but, I want to go with you. Maybe we can go together."

Rafael was confused and figured, what the heck sounds like fun. He called his friend Bobby. Bobby had just finished speaking to his parents as well. It was going to happen. Rafael explained that his father wanted to go. It would be a long three days before Saturday morning arrives.

They met the next day at the dirt road nearly 10 AM. All the boys were allowed to go. Rafael offered a ride to the others if room was needed. They all agreed to wait and see as the day neared. All the boys made their way to the dirt mounds and started laying out a suede track in anticipation of the Saturdays BMX event. They all agreed Rafael was on fire, validated by the way he was riding.

Chapter 7

In the summer of 1978, BMX was making its impression on both youth and adults. The infancy of BMX was making its claim on society. It was a new sport that was proclaiming its future. California was the birthplace of BMX and introduced it to all mankind. The sport was rising in popularity, exponentially growing through the years.

There were several factory teams staking their claims and fortunes on the sport. There were a few magazines that covered nothing but the sport of BMX. The sport was new and less than five years old, gathering the curiosity of both spectators and riders on an equal basis. Families would come to the track to watch the races as many families came to the track to participate.

There were two major sanctioning bodies to which a rider must belong. It was a license allowing a rider to race in that sanctioning organization. It was a tossup of which organization to join. There was the National Bicycle League (NBL) or the American Bicycle Association (ABA).

During the initial stages of the sport, many factory teams joined both organizations and raced in both events. The riders would gain popularity by gathering national titles in their respective age groups and the ability to be called a two-time champion or dual champion.

During this period there was a man named Reggie Stokes. Reggie was a very educated black man. He was approximately six foot tall and projected a positive persona. He was a gentleman and a flourishing team owner of a BMX factory franchise, "Team Panther."

Reggie was the newest factory team on the BMX scene. He acquired some of the fastest riders. Not only were they fast, the team competitors were peculiarly obedient and well-mannered in their adolescence. Reggie built his team over the past few years with a strong sense of moral and honest natured individuals.

Reggie owned a bicycle factory manufacturer's license and produced frames and accessories solely targeting BMX racing.

Team Panther was on tour during the summer of 1978. The team consisted of two professional riders, six bracket riders, a team manager and the owner Reggie Stokes.

The team was on a cross country tour participating in all the national events in both organizations. It didn't matter if it was ABA or NBL, but the NBL had a tour that was being shadowed by Team Panther. There were other teams that were stringent about participating in only the NBL tour in an effort to gain their riders top number plates.

This was in lieu of state number plates. In both organizations, you could ride as a state rider or a national rider or both. State number plates could be used at local tracks. If you finished in first place in a particular state, you were awarded the state number one plate.

If you were awarded a national plate number, you were able to race that plate at any track in the United States in the respective organizations' series.

The tour series was making its way through California. Compounded by the tour and popularity, many factory teams, suppliers and vendors supporting the sport had become popular. BMX was exploding on to the scene.

Tracks differed from each other with no consistencies or commonalities. One track might have large jumps and large berms in the turns. Other tracks would be flat with flat turns. Starting gates commonly were being electromagnetically controlled. Magnets would hold the gate in the up position and when released, gravity takes over.

Gates fell at different rates. The heavier and steeper the starting hill, the faster it would fall. There was no assist mechanism to lift the gates; it was all manual for now. In the future and today, all the starting gates are pneumatically operated and electronically controlled.

Reggie was a brilliant promoter and champion for his brand. He marketed team Panther as the brand any one could own or afford. It wasn't just a powerful competitive racing bicycle; it could be utilized as a daily rider for all ages. Reggie didn't have the largest motorhome or RV when his team arrived at the tracks. But, Team Panther had one of the finest paint schemes and graphics.

The motor home displayed a Panther from the front of the vehicle ending at the rear with a trailer in tow resembling a tail. Reggie ensured his label resembled class. Imagine this rig traveling down the highway. You almost had to ask, what is team Panther? There was the trailer with the team logo and a young man riding a bicycle. The words BMX were labeled over the entire paint scheme.

Team Panther continued to tour the California circuit and then finally making the proverbial right turn east. Reggie enjoyed travelling with the team and children listening to their stories. On the way east Reggie continued to market his bicycles and scheduled several Team Panther demonstrations.

Spectators were amazed by the ability of the younger children as they demonstrated their remarkable skill sets. The pro riders were extraordinary. The biggest thrill for the spectators was watching the number one pro rider, Tony Scholls, bunny hop on to a picnic table. This was a spectacular feat.

With no ramp or assistance of any kind he was able to lift his bicycle up off the ground and land on the top of the table. This was simply an amazing skill. Reggie would narrate on the microphone like a DJ. He had the gift of gab and possessed a command presence when he spoke.

Reggie was a positive man surpassed by his ability to be successful and driven by his determination to be profitable. Reggie made others successful with him. He knew how to motivate himself along with others. He carried himself as a professional business man and demonstrated this ability with his sharp skills of marketing his brand.

Chapter 8

Saturday couldn't come fast enough. Rafael was up and out of bed at 7 AM. He paced up and down the hallway in hopes to see his awakened father. His adrenaline propelled through his body as if he just got done racing his friends at the dirt road. He was excited to see real BMX racing. Rafael never visited Bobby's house, but he knew the road he lived on. He had the house number and all he had to do was find it.

Maximo came out of the bedroom at nearly 7:45 AM that morning with a tee shirt and old pair of sweatpants. He appeared wide awake. This was like sleeping in for Maximo, considering the time he normally wakes up for work.

Nevertheless, as he passed through the hallway, Rafael was there to greet him. Rafael told his father that they were all going to meet at Bobby's house at 9 AM. Maximo shook his head as to acknowledge he understood. Rafael continued to speak about the day's events. Maximo listened as he made coffee for himself.

Florencia was still fast asleep, so he thought. Maximo could hear her in the bedroom moving around and decided to make a full pot of coffee. Rafael continued on about how he and his friends would race and he was the fastest. He boasted how fast he could spin his pedals. He continued on ceaselessly about BMX racing. Maximo was astonished by his son's enthusiasm of racing his bicycle.

Rafael was dressed with shorts, a tee shirt and a pair of converse sneakers. He was trying to look the part of a BMX racer. He wanted to be comfortable; it was going to be a normal hot Texas day. He sat with his father and ate breakfast.

Maximo made some eggs with cheese and white toast with butter. There were beef strips from last night's dinner. Maximo placed this in the frying pan where the eggs were cooking. They sat eating steak and egg sandwiches. Maximo drank his coffee while Rafael continued to talk with his mouth full of food.

As they sat and ate, Florencia came into the kitchen and sat with her son and husband. Maximo poured her some coffee and offered her some breakfast. She smiled shaking her head no. As they were finishing breakfast Florencia told her husband, "Go get ready, he's so excited." Maximo laughed and made his way from the table to the bedroom.

Nearly fifteen minutes later, Maximo came out of the bedroom fully dressed with a nice pair of shorts and a collared pull over shirt and a pair of sandals. He went outside and started the car to allow the engine to heat up and the interior of the car to cool down. It was 8:30 AM and the mercury was already nearing ninety degrees. Maximo asked Rafael, "Are you ready son?" Rafael leaped to his feet and said, "Yes." He ran out of the house to the car.

Maximo approached the car and Rafael gave his father a piece of paper with the address of his friend Bobby. Anxiously he asked his father, "Do you know how to get there?"

Maximo looked at the paper and replied, "Yes son."

They were off to Bobby's. As they approached Bobby's house, they couldn't help but notice how far back off the road it sat. The house was surrounded by a large fence with many horses and cows. They made their way down the stone driveway astonished of the size of the property. The house was in the style of an old farm house. It was 3 stories high surrounded by a few trees as one approached. It was not an enormous house but it is had a bulkiness about it.

They arrived at the house. Before Maximo had even stopped the car the three boys came out of the house to greet Rafael. He introduced them to his father. With a slight accent Maximo greeted the other boys. He also noticed that there was a Gran Torino Station wagon in the driveway running.

He thought to himself that Bobby's parents had the same intention as he about allowing the vehicle to cool down. Maximo let the car run as he exited and walked with Rafael to the house. He was met on the porch by Bobby's father. Bobby's father said hello to Rafael and shook Maximo's hand and joked about the BMX race.

"I hope you got to sleep in."

Maximo laughed and said with heavy Spanish accent, "I actually overslept."

Bobby's father laughed and asked, "You ready for this?" He then walked towards the car and asked, "Which one of you is coming with us?"

Tommy shouted, "I got the whole back seat of Raff's car." He then jumped in the back of Rafael's car making a prodding jester of wanting to leave. Maximo advised Bobby's father that he would follow him to Austin knowing it was just over an hour drive. The cars made their way out of the driveway and slowly onto highway 35.

On the way, both cars were bursting with excitement. Approximately one hour and twenty minutes later they were at the track. It was nearly 11 AM and practice was nearing its end. They parked the cars next to each other in a makeshift parking lot in the middle of a field. Nearly jumping up and down, the boys made their way to the track's edge with both fathers in tow.

They all watched in astonishment as the riders moved off the starting gate with extraordinary acceleration. They were witnessing the eighteen and over riders make their last runs with a few younger riders filling open slots on the gate. Both Maximo and Bobby's father were flabbergasted watching the practice. The track was well groomed and the entire event was very organized.

Maximo stayed close to his son as the boys made their way around the track area. The boys were surprised by how the competition bicycles differed from their bicycles. To the boys, the bicycles seemed somewhat fragile as if they were not very durable. To their amazement not only were the bicycles lighter, they were much stronger. The type of metals used was a new science to all of them except the parents.

Some bicycles were aluminum and others were made from Chromalloy steel. The boys, along with Maximo and Bobby's father, gathered with a spectator whose young son was racing in that day's competition. He explained in detail of how the motos were organized along with the lane choices. He followed up with the organization sanctioning the day's event. They all understood the membership of the sanctioning body and how the races were systematically organized.

Although it was brutally hot, this did not bother the boys. Maximo and Bobby's father found a nice shady spot next to a local bicycle team. They were both impressed by the manners of the kids. They ranged from six years old to nineteen years of age. One of the most exciting things for the boys was that they were allowed to walk the track after practice ended.

There were a few things that overwhelmed the boys. The sizes of the jumps were striking. Not oversized but big enough to make one think about how fast they were going. There was vulnerability and a risk about the track but it was competitive for all age groups. There were three jumps in a row coming out of one of the turns. They were not very high but you needed to be cautious when negotiating this obstacle. You could undoubtedly fall. They were nicknamed woops or commonly known as woop-de-doos.

The track had 4 banked turns called berms. The berms were not too tall. They were wide enough for about three riders across to access at the same time. The first turn was the highest bank. The berms allowed for the speed through the turn into the jumps and obstacles.

The boys and both parents were astonished when the races started. The races began with the youngest riders first followed by the next age groups. They were excited when the twelve and thirteen year old riders took the gate. This is the class they would have to race if they were a participant in the day's events.

After a short time passed the twelve year old novices took the gate. The gate dropped and the race commenced. They were fast and the boys found it exciting to watch their age group tear up the track. The race finally ended with the group spaced far apart from first to seventh places.

It appeared the first and second place riders broke away from the rest of the pack and this was the only competitive race within this age group. Next to take the track were the 12-13 year old Experts combined. It was a noticeable difference just in color.

All the riders had uniforms with decorated number plates. The group of riders lined up on the gate awaiting it to fall. The boys lined the perimeter of the track and waited anxiously. The gate dropped and they were off. It was clear that there was an immense difference between the novice and expert class.

The group of riders fiercely pedaled off the gate. Tightly bunched they made it to the first ninety degree left turn followed by the first four foot jump. All the riders took the jump landing successfully peddling into the next bermmed one hundred and eighty degree turn.

Immediately after the turn there was a set of whoops. The first and second place riders jumped this section with a few riders back accomplishing the same. They immediately peddled the straightaway to a long winding flat right hand one hundred and forty degree turn.

There was a long straight before making the sharp tight bermmed one hundred and eighty degree turn to the last straightaway to an all-out sprint to the finish line. The riders thinned only a little but for the most part it was tightly packed heat race.

The boys were cheering and screaming with excitement. They found themselves in awe. Everything they thought they knew about riding bicycles was just crushed in a twinkling of an eye. Rafael looked at his friends and said, "you know what this means right?"

Jokingly they answered, "We're gonna need jobs!"

Chapter 9

I arrive at the aircraft, boarded and took my seat. I reflect on the achievements in my career. It's been a long hard trip to what I have become as a man to myself and family. It was the influences of having the right friends and support structures I allowed to transform my life.

I recollect my past experiences and thank God Almighty that he led me down the accurate fork in the road. It is said that the narrow path is the toughest and respectable path to take in life's everyday challenges. I believe this to be true only sometimes.

There are those moments that the narrow path is a mere short cut in life but a little trail blazing is required. One needs to get a little sultrier and work a bit harder when taking the narrow path. There are more dangers versus the larger path with its more forgiving roads.

Thinking of my past, I was wondering if my decisions rendered would predict my future. This is a metaphor of many past mistakes corrected before they commence again. This is to be my life changing moment. The many reasons I was formed.

As I sit in my seat I wonder, was this to be my destiny? Do I give all my thanks to those who influenced me or do I look at myself in the mirror and say, "It was you!" Although I was influenced by many life events and friends, it was me that worked towards my goals and conquered my ambitions.

I was the one who was studying late into the morning hours. I was the one who lived on edge making my aspirations my dreams. It was I who manifested my future path by my own decisions.

I sit in my seat and connect my seatbelt and wonder. If not influenced by the people I surrounded myself with in my inner circle, where would I be? Sometimes I feel that I don't have a choice and people end up where they are by chance.

We all know right from wrong in some type of capacity. We know if we are doing the right thing. We get the electric shock feeling that pierces the back of your neck when you know something is immoral, dishonest or sinful. It's the choices you make to correct it that defines your character. I am content with who I am and my decisions. I always suspected it was my influences that defined me as a person and gave significance to my life.

I continually think about my old friends in the BMX arena. Where are they? What are they doing now? What has their life given them or what have they made out of it? I am grateful for my many friends from days past. BMX was a part of my life that founded many friends and acquaintances to this day.

I have friends from those days with whom I still associate, those whom are successful entrepreneurs, construction workers, manufacturers, ministers and many other walks of life. I regress. I created my circle and many of my old comrades are a part of it.

This has become the best decision I have ever made. I surrounded myself with successful positive people with upstanding character and being influenced by them made me the creature I am today. It's very easy to get caught up in nonsense and not know it. It's a matter of grounding one's perceived thoughts of grandeur of what is and what should be.

I know we are getting closer to taking off. I hear the First Officer making the weather and destination announcements. I hope the weather is nice in Germany. It's a short stay. I'll only be there for about thirty six hours. Although I am going to be there alone and on the job, I will think of my family and make the best of it. I enjoy beer. Germany has beer. Seems it won't be that bad of a trip. It's a perspective of moderation. I am definitely of age and know when enough is enough. Like I said, "it's about making the right decisions."

Chapter 10

Its 4:45 AM on a Monday morning. Dominic is woken by his father who is dressed and ready for work. He called to him, "com'on son, were gonna be late for work!"

Dominic, thinking to himself, "Ah man, what did I sign up for?"

Dominic made an agreement with his father just the day before conveying that he wanted to work and earn money for a new bicycle. Dominic got out of bed and proceeded to get dressed. He was going to work for a few weeks with his father at the plant.

He was excited about this new endeavor. After he was dressed he grabbed his work boots in hand and walked out to the kitchen. Angelo asked, "Are you ready?"

Dominic answered, "I'm hungry."

His father told him that they were going to stop on the way and get a breakfast sandwich and coffee.

Dominic thought to himself, "Coffee?"

On the way to the plant they stopped and got their breakfast sandwiches. Angelo drank his coffee black with no sugar. Dominic gathered his breakfast sandwich and his large carton of Orange Juice. He enjoyed the fact that he and his father were able to spend this type of time together.

Although he was very close to his brother, he relished the alone time to bond with his father. They got back in the truck and made their way to work. They pulled in the entrance and parked at the front of the office. They were the first ones to arrive approximately 6:20 AM. Although the first shift to start was 7 AM, Angelo always was on time and never missed a day except for rare occasions when he was sick or on vacation.

They were followed shortly by the Plant Manager, Nick. Nick was called by his nickname, Pino. Pino walked in from the back lot where he parked his company truck. He walked to the front office complex with coffee in hand. He strolled into Angelo's Office and went over the day's deliveries and the days agendas. They talked for nearly twenty minutes seriously and then jokingly afterwards.

Pino asked, "What about Dom?"

Angelo queried back, "What needs to be done?"

"Where do you think we need to put him for the next few weeks? Making product or on the road with the deliveries?"

Angelo thought a moment, "I don't want to kill him in the warehouse, maybe on the road assisting with deliveries."

"Ok, but I'm not going to allow him to operate the boom without one of the drivers there directly next to him."

"I Agree. I'd like to get him back here for lunch. I want to grab a bite to eat with him for the first few days. Let the driver know to come back. They are not too far out of town. I'm sure he'll understand."

Angelo shrugged his shoulders with a confused look on his face. Pino looked at him and laughed. He told Angelo, "I know who to put him with and it won't be a problem."

Pino came out of the office and told Dominic, "Kitty up, grab your work gloves and let's go."

Dominic answered, "I don't have any work gloves." As he said this, his father poked his head out of the office and threw a pair of new leather work gloves at Dominic hitting him in the head.

Pino laughed and uttered, "You're going for a ride."

Dominic was excited. He walked to the back of the plant where he was introduced to Oscar. Pino explained that he was going to help him for the next few days with deliveries and make sure he stayed safe. He further explained that his new helper was the boss's son. Oscar smiled and in his thick broken Latin accent said, "Ok Hefy."

There they were in a huge flatbed truck lifting pallets full of bricks into the back with a huge hydraulic arm. Oscar made small conversation as they worked. Dominic was basically a guide man. Not realizing his significance to the operation, he was very productive. About two hours later they were off.

Dominic jumped into the cab that was a little dusty but very orderly. As they accelerated down the street, Dominic asked, "Where is the air-conditioning button on this thing?"

Oscar laughed and remarked, "Back in the office."

Dominic had received his first dose of work reality. He said nothing and understood that they were going to sweat all day. They drove and made their delivery nearly an hour away. Dominic had done everything Oscar asked of him. They made their way back to the plant by 11:30 AM. Dominic reached his father's office close to noon. Angelo looked at him and smiled. They went to lunch and spoke of the day's experiences.

Dominic worked for nearly three weeks straight except for Saturdays and Sundays, getting done early on Fridays. On the last Friday, his father told him that they normally get done early on Fridays as an incentive for the morale and hard work of his employees. He further explained that many employees don't work Saturdays unless he asked them for overtime.

It was nearly 3:30 PM and Angelo waved Dominic over to him as he and Oscar arrived at the plant. Dominic was pleased and could not wait for the weekend. He just wanted to get home to ride his bicycle with his friends. He enjoyed his time with Oscar. He was a nice man and a hard worker.

He took young Dominic to his house a couple of times in the last few weeks. When they were close to Oscar's house making deliveries, they would stop in and eat lunch as Oscar shared time with his wife. Dominic would call his father from Oscar's home phone and let him know where he was.

Angelo was a very understanding man and was gracious for allowing Oscar to open his home to Dominic. Oscar's wife was a terrific Latin cook. Dominic never had Latin food and he loved it. He could not get enough of it. It was the best. He genuinely worshipped it.

Dominic said goodbye to Oscar for the weekend and walked to his father. Angelo asked, "How was your day?"

He answered, "Hot. Very hot. You need to get Oscar some air-conditioning."

Angelo expressed that he had a surprise for him.

Dominic shook his head in disbelief and asked, "Yeahhh?"

Angelo pulled out a wad of cash and peeled off four one hundred dollar bills and handed them to Dominic.

Dominic was in shock. What's this for he thought to himself? He asked his father, "Dad, what is for?"

Angelo looked at him, "you're not working for free son. Now let's get out of here. Where do you want to go?"

Dominic, ecstatic, answered without hesitation, "Mack BMX." He was jumping up and down with absolute excitement.

His father joked, "We only have your mother's car. We have to wait until tomorrow."

Dominic, frantic said, "Dad, I see your truck right there. OK. I'll ask Oscar to take his truck."

Angelo looked and him laughing, "That's my truck son." He then said, "Ok, let's go."

They were off to Mack BMX. It was a small shop filled to the brim with bicycles. They arrived and Dominic ran inside leaving his father behind. His father felt great joy for his son. As they passed through the doorway, the bells on the door mechanism rang out. A man around the age of 22 came from around the back with an apron around his waist and chest. He asked what he could do to help them.

Dominic answered, "I want a new bike." He was nearly jumping up and down.

The young man asked him what kind of bicycle he wanted, a bicycle for jumping, a road bike, and a street bike with gears?

Dominic answered, "I want to race BMX!"

The salesman looked at Dominic's father and asked, "how much you looking to spend?"

Dominic answered, "$400." The salesman looked up at Angelo as he shook his head nodding as if to say yes.

The salesman gave his pitch. "Well, here is something's to consider. If you want a true BMX racing bike, you're gonna have to take into consideration the following. You are going to race as a novice. Do you plan on continuing if you have to turn expert? Or, do you want a bike you are going to jump around the neighborhood and race only sometimes?"

Dominic answered, "I want to be the one to beat. I want this more than anything."

The salesman brought them to a few BMX bicycles that were near the end of a line of other dirt bicycles. The salesmen conveyed that the most expensive bicycle was less than four hundred dollars not including tax.

The salesman gave his sales discourse of few features and differences of the bicycles they were surveying. One of the features that seized both Angelo and Dominic was the sealed bearings. They never had to be greased and they were a truly competition level construction. He explained that the entire bike from front to back was built with sealed bearings as a true BMX competition bicycle. He then asked about his riding style.

For example he asked, "When you ride now, do you spin your chain fast or do you feel that you are pushing hard and still are able to obtain and hold your speed?"

Dominic answered, "I feel like I pedal really fast. It's like I run out of gearing and can't spin any more. It feels comfortable to me."

The salesman further explained that gearing is very important when racing. He suggested a gear ratio of 43x16 with the 170 millimeter cranks that are already installed on the bicycle.

Angelo asked, "What is a 43x16?"

He explained to Angelo that the front gear has 43 teeth and the rear hub on the wheel has a 16 tooth gear sprocket. The salesman pitched that the older kids normally don't go above a 45 tooth gear and Dominic should practice with a 43x16 gear. He felt that this would be perfect.

Dominic examined all the bicycles and finally found his BMX Bike. He asked how much it cost. The man answered him, "its three hundred and sixty-five dollars not including tax. He also expressed that if he was going to race he needed to have pads on the handles bars, goose neck and the frame.

He would need a number plate and a helmet. Dominic looked at his father. Angelo looked at the sales man and shook his head yes. Dominic was overwhelmed. This was his dream and it had come true. He had a bicycle custom built with all high end components and race ready.

His frame was an aluminum racing frame with all the best components and ready for the track. Angelo spent nearly four hundred and sixty dollars this day. But it was money well spent. He was excited to see the decisions his son made.

Dominic rode his BMX bike outside in the parking lot before bringing it back to the salesman to inspect. He went over Dominic's new bike to ensure all was OK. He pointed out that the brake cable was going to stretch and it would need continuous adjustments. He told him to bring it back and he would show him how to do it himself after the bicycle had a short time to break in.

He set the seat height and the position of the handle bars for Dominic. He put the pads on for him and mounted the number plate with no numbers. That's it. Dominic was ready for the raceway. All he needed to do was practice and show up at the track and obtain his license.

Chapter 11

Its mid-August and the American tour is complete. Team Panther was strong. They won it all. In the team competition they had the most riders finish in the top spots. It's now time for the brilliance of Reggie to market his brand. He knows that he needs to capitalize on the success of his team.

Most of the BMX Nationals are coming to a close as the school year peeks its head from around the corner. Most of the kids will be back in school, but the summer in southern California never ends. Reggie has given numerous interviews with the popular BMX magazines of this time.

He has made every arrangement with manufacturers as a new sponsor for his team. He has gone over every marketing strategy to enhance what he has built. He has the quality leadership and a well-mannered group of kids and adults alike representing Team Panther.

Reggie called his leadership and management personnel to his office during the week. He advised them of the radical changes that are about to take place within the organization. He was smiling, and all can tell this was going to be good news. Reggie was one to not hold back any news even if it was unpopular.

Good news or bad, Reggie felt the obligation to be honest, direct and truthful with his staff. They all waited with great anticipation. He first announced that they have been awarded some new sponsors. He announced that they have picked up a clothing line for racing pants, shirts, and shoes. They all would be given helmets and facial protection as a side bonus.

There was clapping, shaking of hands and high fives around the room. Reggie sat there quietly but with a big smile on his face. The staff knew he wasn't done. Reggie stood there almost anxiously wanting to finish. He further explained, "Well guys I have better news. We have also partnered with a bicycle manufacturer and we are going to sell our bikes as a complete unit. Not just frames any longer."

More cheers could be heard. He continued, "We are going to have two entry levels of bicycles. One everyday bike that anyone could afford that comes in two styles. We are also going to have the true BMX bike that is race ready minus the number plate. I'm talking competition rims, tires, handle bars and pads. This again was followed by more Cheers and excitement.

Reggie introduced his manufacture representative who followed up Reggie's announcement with slide presentation and posters of the new line of bicycles. He involved the entire staff for their inputs. He asked about color schemes and product advertisement. Reggie had a creative way of motivating his staff and was brilliant for giving them a sense of ownership.

They sat for nearly an hour discussing ways of marketing the sponsors. In the middle of all the discussions, Tony expressed the winning idea. He simply said, "Why can't we wear all their patches on our team jersey's and decorate our motor home incorporating their logo with ours? Or, have some of the company's sponsors show up at our races and be part of our family?"

"Brilliant," Reggie was pleased. He looked at the representative and asked, "Do you want to take this back or do I need to sell it to them?" Reggie smiles as he said this to the young man.

He looked at Reggie and stated that he would present it to the board when he returned.

After this, they all decided to take a break and get some lunch. Reggie invited his team manager and Tony to join him. They made their way to a little corner restaurant about a block and a half away. It was hot and they made it to the cool air-conditioned café without hesitation.

They made their way to a nice place to sit far enough away from the window in the back of the café. They discussed the meeting they just had before getting their glasses of ice water and lunch menus. The waitress knew Reggie and said hello to him as he ordered for them all. He joked with her for a while and continued discussing the sponsorships.

They all received their lunch and began to eat. Nearing the end of the meal, Reggie brought up the topic he has been eagerly awaiting to discuss. He waited for a pause in the conversation and stated, "Well there is no better time than the present. I trust you all and we need to think about a few things. We currently have eight factory riders. Today we total six kids and two pros representing Team Panther. We need to come to common ground on a few issues and I asked you two to come with me for the following reasons. Number one, I trust you. Number two, I believe in you both. One of the issues is the number of riders we want to take on as a Factory Sponsor. I am feeling good about the number twelve. Only twelve riders total including pros. Of the twelve riders, were do we stand? Do we want a female? Do we want more pros? Do we need more pros? Things like this", he explained.

There was some silence around the table. They simply looked at each other for a moment before Tony finally broke the silence. He asked, "Reggie, do we really need twelve riders or is this a number you determined you want? I would say no more than twelve riders and only those you feel would fit into the Team Panther family. I personally feel that if we find a talented young or older female who rides well, then yes, by all means offer the sponsorship. But looking for quality is better than any number. I don't know what to say. You are the one with the final authority and you are going to be the one who has to make the call. When the season begins I become tunnel visioned on competing. I'm looking forward to new riders as you are. I also know we are going to lose some riders this year also. I'm focused on racing but not blind. I know who we need to keep and I also know one for sure who is going to quit and one who didn't compete that well this year."

Reggie sat there with his arms folded looking at Tony as he spoke. When Tony was done speaking, Reggie sat there silently looking at him for a few seconds. He laughed and then spoke, "I really want to do this for kids. I sometimes rather watch a kid fail to only grow and learn from what they did. But on the other hand, this is a business with business decisions to be made. I think having a female is good business only if she is productive. But I don't want to give a full sponsorship to her only for the sake of having a female on the team. This is not fair for her or the other riders on the team. This doesn't begin to blanket the fact that I am looking for specific types of individuals that are a good match within the organization. I would love to have all champions, but I would rather have a type of person who personifies what we are about. Winning, but with dignity and sportsmanship. No one likes a show off or big talker when they are a winner. People respect the quiet unsung heroes. This is what I built this team on. Tony, when I sponsored you, you were winning but not every race. When you did win, you shook their hands and I witnessed you walk back to your shady spot under the trees with your mom and brothers. Not once did I see you make a fool of yourself. This is why I sponsored you. You were already a winner both inside yourself and on the track. I now call you a champion and I don't see any differentiations."

Again there was silence, his team manager simply looked at Reggie and said, "You let me know what size shirt and pants to order. I'll work on the other particulars as it pertains to their school grades, home town track representation and their responsibilities to the team. I'll converse with the parents and gain their support with sponsorship agreements."

Reggie shook his head yes and sat for a moment. Reggie looked at Tony and his team manager and expressed, "Next year there is no specific tour dates. There are going to be cities that are strategically set up for the big teams including us, to make it to them. There is no specific outline of how we are going to make each stop. We might even skip a smaller national race in order to make it to the bigger races with bigger crowds. We are going to set up bigger clinics at armories and bicycle shops. We are going to be National, not a selective city frame manufacturer. We are going to donate bicycles to organizations that benefit children. We're going to go to hospitals, schools, parks and give clinics to children. We are going to visit many diverse locations and become nationwide. Tony, you are a ranked pro now, you're the one who is going to bring attention to Team Panther. Tell me what I need to do for you."

Tony looked at Reggie and said, "Nothing. I just need time to practice and a part time job." Reggie told him, "Show up tomorrow ready to assemble bikes for a while. Later I'll find a paying job that will allow you the time to practice and still get paid."

Reggie thanked them both for coming to lunch with him. Tony excused himself because he needed to catch the bus home. Reggie asked Tony as he was leaving, "You still going to race the locals until the season end?" Tony looked at him and smiled, "Locals? There's a regional in Van Nuys this weekend."

Chapter 12

Rafael was awakened by his father early Monday morning. He looked up at him and asked, "What Dad?"

He responded, "I have a surprise for you when you get out of bed."

Rafael looked at his father with confusion and said, "Now Dad?"

Maximo shook his head yes. Rafael got out of bed a bit confused and followed his father out to the kitchen. Rafael and his father sat at the table and ate breakfast. Maximo asked his son, "Did you want to race son?"

Rafael answered, "Yes Dad, I really want to try and see how I do."

"Ok," he answered. He then told Rafael to take a walk with him. They made their way out to the garage. There, against the wall, was a brand new shiny bicycle. Rafael was ecstatic. He could not believe it. He had a new BMX bicycle. It had all the trimmings including the pads.

Rafael was more confused by how his father knew what to buy and when he bought it. Rafael simply asked his father, "Dad, when did you buy this for me? How did you know what to get? This is amazing. How did you pull this off? We went to the races on Saturday and now its Monday and I have a new bicycle."

Maximo smiled and told Rafael he would explain it when he came home for work. He further told Rafael that he could ride his bicycle after 10 AM. Rafael sat there for nearly an hour wiping his bicycle down with an old rag keeping it clean. His father purchased him a Mongoose bicycle with racing wheels and the complete works.

His bicycle was wanting in regards to the front chain ring, cranks and pedals, but it was a race ready bicycle. All Rafael needed to do was obtain a number plate and license. As his mom and other siblings awoke, he steadily watched for the ten o'clock hour. His mother allowed him to leave early and he made his way to the dirt road to meet his friends. He was anxious to see their faces when they arrived and he was on his new bicycle.

Nearly an hour later, Rafael could see his friends approaching him in the distance. As they neared, it sunk in that Rafael had a new bicycle. They rode up to him and high fived him. They all looked his bicycle over-describing what they saw.

Rafael was excited and headed directly to the pits. All the boys followed in tow. When they arrived, they all immediately made a beeline to the top of the highest hill. They gathered and decided what they wanted to do. Rafael came up with a great idea.

He wanted to ride down the hill as fast as they could and use other hill side as a berm to make a hard left turn and ride to the next hill and make a right hand turn with a makeshift finish line. All the boys agreed. They rode up to each hillside and used logs and other debris as rakes to smooth the turns. They set broken logs standing straight up and down as the finish line.

One at a time the boys took turns negotiating the track they had designed. It was apparent that they had become comfortable and faster with the track. After several hours of riding they began to race each other two by two. Rafael was untouchable.

He was the fastest of them all. The turns were a little shaky for Rafael but he was blazing fast on the straights. The other boys discussed making jumps. They all agreed to wait and continue with the track as is for now. Shortly after 1 PM, they decided to make their way home and get some lunch. It wouldn't be long before they all met back at the pit again.

Rafael made his way home. He arrived and his mother had his lunch waiting for him. He discussed the day's events with her. She smiled and listened. He asked her how his father got him the bicycle. She said that he would explain it to him when he comes home. She told him to make sure that he was home by 6 PM.

Nearly an hour later he was off to meet the boys. They met as usual and made their way back to the pits. They rode for hours and hours. They all decided to leave at 5 PM. They were all exhausted and it was nearly ninety five degrees. Again, as they departed the pits, they all commented on the huge house sitting far back off the road. Rafael arrived at his house just after 5:15 PM.

He cleaned his bicycle for nearly twenty minutes before entering his house. He locked his bicycle in the garage with a padlock and a cable. He went inside waiting for his father to arrive. He awoke on the couch nearly an hour and a half later. Feeling refreshed, he entered the kitchen where he could smell the food his mother had just prepared. He sat at the table and looked at his father and didn't say a word.

Maximo looked at Rafael and said, "OK son, let me tell you how I pulled this off. I was going to buy you a new bicycle nevertheless. You do everything I ask and you continually help your mother when I'm not here. As you and your friends were at the track roaming all over the place, I spoke with several people about the type of bicycle you needed if you decide to race. I wasn't going to spend a lot of money on a bicycle but I wanted to buy you something that would last. Finally, I made my decision to purchase your bicycle from one the dealers at the track who also owns the store here in town. I explained that I wanted to surprise you this Monday. He dropped your bicycle off late Sunday night while you were in bed sleeping. I told him that I would meet him down the street. I paid him and I walked your bicycle into the garage. I knew you would be surprised and your mother and I wanted to do this for you." Rafael was surprised and figured his father to be a genius.

Rafael's brothers and sister weren't that jealous. He figured that his father continually gives his brothers money for gas and buys them soccer shoes when he receives nothing. His sister is the apple of his eye. She was spoiled in Rafael's eyes. He loved his sister but felt she got most of their mother's attention and his father's, especially when she helped Florencia cook dinner.

He thought about it and decided, "I like it when she cooks also, so I am not going to say much about it." He was happy for the fact that she liked to cook. Moreover, there were times when he was riding at the pit and she would meet him at the door when he arrived with ice water. He thought to himself, life is good.

Chapter 13

Dominic woke up and made his way directly to the kitchen. As he walked in, his mother stood at the stove cooking. She asked him if he wanted to eat some breakfast.

Dominic answered quickly, "Yes, but please make it fast. I want to go ride my bike again."

She looked at him with delight and prepared him some eggs and sausage with Italian toasted bread. He wolfed down his food and made his way out the door. He grabbed his bicycle and rode down to the pits to be with his friends. He was the first to arrive. Dominic rode for nearly thirty-five minutes before Rex showed up briefly followed by the others.

Dominic had a crude track for them all to ride. It was wide enough to fit three riders at a time. There were some challenges on the track. For example, the boys had shoveled out berms that were tight but very fast. There were some substantial jumps to negotiate.

There was a drop off and they would amass tremendous speeds before enduring another huge jump before making a sharp right turn to the finish line. The group of boys rode all day. There were some other neighborhood kids who showed up to join in the fun, but they were no contest for Dominic and his group.

At the end of the day they all agreed, Dominic needed to race this Saturday. He was untouchable in the straight-aways and had no fear of jumping. He had the miraculous capability of having the ability to either jump or stay on the ground enabling him to pedal if needed.

He was the kid to beat in the neighborhood. Rex spoke to him the entire day. He strongly urged him to race this Saturday. The others agreed. All Dominic had to do was convince his father.

Later that evening Dominic was home before his father arrived. As Angelo got out of his truck, Dominic greeted him as he always has in the past. Angelo asked, "I know you're up to something. What do you need son?"

He looked at his father. Before he could say anything his father interjected, "What time do they start?"

Dominic was entranced and immediately went back inside to call his buddies to convey the good news. He was bouncing all over the house. He had only two days to prepare mentally for his new endeavor.

It was now Friday and Dominic was excited and nervous at the same time. How does one prepare for this type of thing? Pedro, Rex, Jimmy and Larry all agreed that he needed to do sprints on the dirt road next to the track. This will enable him to spin his legs as fast as he can in preparation for the race. He practiced for nearly four hours before calling it a day. Dominic had the need to rest and be ready for race day. He didn't want to show and be tired for the very first race he was about to endure.

It was Saturday morning and Dominic was ready. He slept like a log and gathered all the rest he needed. The phone rang and Dominic answered it. It was his friend Rex. Rex explained that he was going to enter the race as well. Dominic was excited.

They agreed to meet at Dominic's house in the next ten minutes and the parents would follow each other. Dominic explained this to his father who shook his head yes as he was fumbling for the words. Rex showed up with his father in the driveway as Dominic came out of the house. They introduced themselves and made their way to the truck.

Dominic's younger brother and mother accompanied them to the track. It was to be a family day and he was excited they were all going.

They made their way to the track. When they arrived it was still somewhat early. Angelo was able to procure a nice shady spot under some trees near the track along with Rex and his family. Dominic, Rex and their parents in tow made their way to the registration area. They paid for their licenses and both had to endure a bicycle inspection. The inspector was nice.

Both parents agreed to buy number plates and helmets. Dominic and Rex were both wearing long pants and long sleeve shirts. It was nearly ninety degrees and muggy. They brought a change of clothes and shorts to wear in between races or better known as Moto's.

The number plate system was easy. As a new and unranked rider, your number was the last three digits of your license number, or during this time a rider was given a random number followed by a letter. Rex was issued number 999 and Dominic was issued number 000.

Both boys suited up and took the track. There was no starting gate ready at this time. The boys took their time riding around the track at first. Dominic decided it was time to put the hammer down. He took off halfway down the first straight, took the turn and negotiated the first jump. He was perfect. Rex followed in tow.

He took the jump and launched off the jump way too far nearly missing the next turn. The boys were on to something. Dominic was racing in the 10-11 Novice class. Rex was racing the 12-13 Novice class. Since they were so early, the person operating the starting gate was very helpful on how to get the best starts.

He explained there was nothing to time; it was a randomly dropped gate. Both boys were somewhat bothered by wearing a helmet and trying to get used to this new apparatus. They practiced for nearly an hour before heading back to their camp area.

Practice was ending and the Moto's were nearly posted. In BMX, the area a team sets up is nicknamed a camp. It is normally referred to as a camp and common vernacular is excepted when others refer to it as a camp.

Dominic was pumped; he was ready, nervous but well prepared. He had the right bicycle, the right helmet, and he was mentally and physically conditioned for this event. The announcement was made, "Moto's are posted."

They ran over and there it was. They were to race back to back. Dominic was first racing moto number 11 with gate positions 8-2-4. Rex was moto number 12. Each boy had seven riders in their race.

They made their way back and waited for the announcements. Finally it was time. The announcement was made and the boys made their way to the staging area. While waiting, they met with old friends and watched as the younger riders took off on the first moto of the day.

Finally it was Dominic's turn. He was all the way to outside sitting on the gate. He was more than ready. The gate operator made the call, "OK guys here we go. Riders ready! Watch the gate!" Dominic waited with his foot on one pedal and his left leg close to his back tire ready to push as instructed the gate operator showed him earlier.

The gate fell and Dominic took off like he was shot out of a canon. He pedaled as hard and fast as he could making his way to the left hand turn. As he approached the turn he was in first place. He could see a rider to the left of him but slightly behind him. He made his way around the first left hand turn followed by an immediate jump.

This not a problem for Dominic, he took the jump hugging the ground as close as he could before the next couple of left and right turns with berms to keep the riders snugged in tight.

Dominic could hear the announcer make comments about him. He was not sure exactly what he was saying. Dominic could also hear the cheers of the crowed. He made his way to the last straightaway and

Dominic continued to accelerate towards the finish line. Just like at home in the pits, Dominic was untouchable when came to straightaway speeds.

He was a rocket with a red streak behind him. He pulled away from the pack as if it were no contest. Dominic was unstoppable. He raced as if he had been doing it for years.

As he came across the finish, he stopped to watch his friend Rex. Rex didn't fair too well. He finished all his heat races (motos) in third or fourth place. On the other hand, Dominic finished with all first places. His family was up and cheering the entire time he was on the track.

After his last race, Dominic made his way back to the truck and lazed out on the grassy area under the trees. He was exhausted; he changed into his shorts and tee shirt. He nearly drank an entire gallon of water in thirty seconds. His family patted him all over, overflowing with delight.

Angelo looked over to Dominic and said, "Next Saturday?"

Dominic nodded and smiled at his father.

Angelo said, "Common son get up; let's go buy some racing clothes."

Chapter 14

It's a Friday night and Rafael approached his father. "Dad, I want to ask you a question. Do you remember the BMX race we went to?"

His father nodded and replied, "Yes."

Rafael continued, "I am begging you, can I please race tomorrow. I found a place around here called Rabbit Run. I really want to race."

Maximo laughed and looked at his son and muttered, "I don't care son, but you need to speak with your mother."

Rafael jumped up immediately and ran into the kitchen, "Mom, can I race tomorrow. Please, please, please."

His mother looked at him for a few seconds and replied, "I suppose."

Rafael was elated. He was going to race. He got on the phone and called his buddies to tell them his good fortune. Rafael was out of his mind. He could not figure out how he would get to sleep that night.

He sat with his family at dinner and told them all the good news. They already knew and they all had to go and watch. It was going to be a family affair. His mother even prepared extra food that evening for the next day.

It almost seemed they had it planned. There were extra cool-aid packets on the counter and the large five gallon drinking thermos was already out and cleaned. Rafael thought to himself that this was peculiar. Nevertheless, he was ready for the next morning event.

The morning came fast. The alarm sounded at 8 AM and Rafael jumped out of his bed. As he rose and came out of his room, he could see that his father had the car packed and loaded.

His brothers busted his chops as they arose from their slumber. They joked that he better win for making them wake up early on a Saturday morning. Although they all had to wake early, the smell of bacon was prodigious throughout the household. It was a mini-feast in the morning.

Bacon, eggs, toast, tortillas, and potatoes lined the table for the family. Rafael was afraid to eat too much in fear of getting sick. He had to make a fast decision; his brothers were on their second helpings and the once oversized heaping pile of food was quickly dwindling to a pile of crumbs. Rafael gave in to his temptation and took his second helping of eggs and the last piece of bacon.

His sister had made herself a fruit bowl that she shared with her mother and father. Rafael grabbed some long pants and shirt before leaving the house. His older brother Carlos came back into the room with an old motorcycle helmet he had for years.

He gave it to Rafael and told him to take care of it and don't ruin it with his thick head. They both laughed and walked towards the car. They piled into the car and the brothers continued hazing Rafael. They had about a twenty minute ride to the track.

They arrived at the track. It was evident this was an organized event. There were banners, vendors and a well exposed track. It was a wide open area and it was going to be hot. They all bucked down and bared the rising heat index.

They were sitting in folding beach chairs and only sat in them until Rafael was about to race. Rafael obtained his license and made it through bicycle inspection. He made his way to the starting gate and noticed it was a steep downhill straightaway into a ninety degree left hand turn with no jumps or obstacles.

Rafael was not intimidated by the track. It was wider than what he was used to, but the pits were steeper and the turns were much harder to negotiate. Rafael caught on quickly by watching the other riders on the gate starts.

He made friends with another rider who described the moto's and the starting gate positions. His particular track used the chit process. All riders took a token out of a jar. It had a number on it and that was your starting position. There weren't that many riders but there was still a total of twenty three moto's.

There were six riders in his class, 10-11 novices. It was finally his turn. He got up to the gate and readied himself at the gate as it was pulled up. He listened for the cadence and made himself ready. The gate dropped and he was off. He peddled as hard as he could and found himself in a tie for first place.

He was on the outside and continued to peddle into the turn. He was in the lead. As he was making the left hand turn still heading down the hill, he could hear the sounds of crunching behind him and riders were falling. He made the cardinal mistake of looking back. As he looked back, he inherently stopped pedaling and was passed.

He could hear his mother and brothers yelling for him and he chased the rider in front of him. There were a few places he tried to make moves but it was no avail. He was a bit wobbly over the jumps but the more experienced rider was too far ahead of him. He finished a solid second on this moto.

He walked himself back to his parents only to be met halfway by his sister and father. There always seemed to be a crowd around his sister. He knew that she was very attractive even for a nine year old. She was very mature and always was the best student of all the children.

They were excited for him. His first race and he finished in second. He had to further explain to them all that there were two more races and could finish in first for the day.

It was time for his second race, he lined up and this time he was in lane one. The gate dropped and he exploded off the gate. Like before, he was slightly ahead but he had tremendous pressure from the same rider on the outside. They came into the turn and he found himself drifting into the outside rider.

They bumped hard but both were able to control their bicycles and continue riding. As they approached the finish line, there were some jumps that they had to traverse before entering the finish line.

They both made it over the jumps and Rafael came across the finish line first. The other rider was not a good sport and deliberately ran into the back of Rafael. It was so obvious that even the announcer made a comment of his poor sportsmanship.

Rafael had a passive personality and he shrugged it off as he continued to ride away meeting his family halfway. His older brother walked past him in the direction of the other rider.

Rafael was able to grab his brother by his arm, "forget about it, I'll beat him next moto. Besides, you're over eighteen and he's my age. It's not worth it. Plus, Mom's here." Carlos looked at Rafael and laughed.

It was time for the last moto. If Rafael could finish in front of this sore loser he could get first place for the day. Again, they made their way to the gate. Rafael pulled lane six and the other rider pulled the chit for lane one. Rafael knew he had some work to do.

The gate dropped and Rafael had the best start of his life. He was clearly out front and made his way to the inside. As he was making the left turn, he could feel his back wheel slipping from under him. He didn't know if he was being hit or just not catching the grip he needed.

As he continued into the turn he finally slipped enough to where he had to put his foot down and stop himself from falling and drifting to the outside. The other rider was able to get in front of him and Rafael could not chase him down. As they crossed the finish line the other rider looked back and made some type of hand jester as if to say, "oh Yeah." Rafael thought nothing of it and simply rode back to his family.

He placed second this day. His family was excited and his brothers promised a no weggie evening. They joked about the other rider. They were brutal. Rafael now knew what he had to do. He now understood how he needed to practice. It was getting late in the day and he was spent.

The sun took its toll on him. As they made their way back to the house, Rafael fell asleep along with his brothers. There was no hazing or weggies that evening as promised.

Chapter 15

Several weeks passed since Dominic's last race and he had become a force within the 10-11 Novice Class. School was getting ready to start and the BMX season was coming to a close. Dominic had won first place in the last four races. If he won his next race, by rule, he would be moved up to the 10-11 expert.

Dominic continued to ride in the pits near his house with his friends. It was no surprise that he quickly outgrew the track they had built. Rex only raced a few more times before hanging it up. His feeling was that it was not fun any longer. He liked to ride his bicycle but mostly with his friends. Competing lost its allure.

Dominic's skills were peaking. The group of boys all agreed to step up their track. They all got together during the week and added more jumps. It was remarkable the amount of dirt the boys moved with just shovels. The jumps became bigger and there was at least one jump in every straightaway.

It was very technical. The downhill portion of the track had a jump on the bottom into a sharp turn. It was a matter of timing and braking in order to navigate the turn. Again, Dominic was untouchable and he was only 11 years old.

The pits became a very popular place at this time, not only for Dominic and his friends but for all the neighborhood kids. There was always someone riding in the pits. Most of the kids riding the track could not make it around at full speed. There were a few exceptional riders but they were considerably older than Dominic. By the end of the summer, this was the place to hang out.

Saturday morning was a big day for Dominic. He was about to race one of his last races for the season. He was becoming very popular and was recognized by many other riders both old and young. He and his family arrived at the track and set up camp. By this time, Dominic's father had bought a tarp-like tent to provide more shade for him and his family.

They brought a grill and coolers full of drinks. It was a fun family day. They all enjoyed it. His younger brother talked their father into buying him a bicycle but not as nice as Dominic's.

Dominic took the track for practice. As he did, one of the local bike shop teams approached Angelo about Dominic possibly taking on a sponsorship. Normal sponsorships on this level included a fifteen percent discount on all items in the store.

Included was a free racing jersey and sometimes a matching helmet. The only drawback was that he had to race the open class every week and travel to other tracks as a team. The open class included the eleven through thirteen year olds.

Novice or experts were not segregated. It was just as it was called, an open class. Angelo thought about it for a couple seconds and answered, "I would like you to ask him and give him your terms. I think it would be better if he heard it directly from you. I am happy for him and he seems to like this sport. He's doing really well. We're proud of him."

Dominic made his way back to his family's camp. He saw a man speaking with his father and knew exactly who he was. He turned from his conversation with Angelo and looked at Dominic and said, "Hello Dom, I was talking with your father about you possibly taking on a sponsorship."

Dominic's eyes lit up and he became unsettled with excitement.

The man continued, "Well, I want to ask you a few questions before you make any decisions. I would like to extend you a sponsorship with our team with some conditions. Along with a sponsorship, you also are required to race the open class. Also, you will be required to travel as a team. We meet at the shop and travel in a convoy to the track hosting the event. You will be given a free jersey and discounts at the shop. Lastly, you are invited to move over to our reserved area along with your family. I spoke to your parents and they asked me to speak with you directly."

Dominic was frenzied about this opportunity. Dominic asked, "What do I have to do in order to get this sponsorship?"

The man answered, "Win!"

Dominic asked, "Sir, what is your name?"

He looks back at him before he walked away and answered, "Brent Lock."

Dominic replied, "Thank you Mr. Lock."

He replied, "thank you Dom, please call me Brent, it's ok, I appreciate your manners."

It was fate. Dominic was going to race his fifth race and possibly an expert and he was going to race the open race for his age group. His family was proud of him. Dominic was about to race with the big boys and possibly be an expert rider.

Dominic practiced hard and constantly asked all the riders on the gate how old they were. He was sizing up his open class to no avail. He got his moto's and prepared for the open race. His age group of 10-11 novice only consisted of 5 riders for this day. As always he was out front by the first turn and checked out finishing first place.

It was only fifteen minutes later before his open class. As he entered the staging area, the reality of this race was magnified by the size of the other racers. Dominic suddenly felt like the young man he was.

He was towered by the other riders. He never had this sinking feeling before but something inside of him gave him the instinct of his drive and determination. They all lined up on the gate.

The starter gave the cadence and the gate dropped. For the first time, Dominic did not find himself pulling into the front of the pack. On the contrary, he was in the middle of the pack tightly squeezed and given no room to maneuver. Dominic was not in the lead, he was in fourth place. This was respectable considering that there was full gate of eight riders.

They rounded the left hand turn and the jump was approaching them. Dominic thought to himself that this would be a game changer and he would be able to make up some ground. This was not the case. All the riders in this moto were just as technical as him and they were bigger, stronger and experienced.

Dominic was not only in fourth place, he was being pushed by the rider behind him looking for a way to pass Dominic. This was a unequivocal eye opener for Dominic. He was racing the big boys and reality had shown its true course.

There was no shame for Dominic racing in this class. He was the only eleven year old in the open class. There were two heats of riders. Since there were a total of fifteen riders, only four riders would advance to the main. The main consisted of the two motos combined.

The main event consisted of one moto and however you placed across the finish line was the trophy you were awarded. Dominic finished all three moto's and placed in fourth place. He qualified for the main event. He was excited about his endeavor but he was really nervous.

Dominic finished his age bracket in all first places. He was now considered an expert rider by a BMX sanctioning body. Dominic was an Expert. He was pumped. As he rode back to his family, they greeted him with great excitement. His father picked him up off his bicycle as it fell to the ground and hugged him.

He conveyed how proud he was of his efforts. Angelo told his son, "You have one more race today before we go. I don't care how you finish. I'm proud of you. The fact that you try as hard as you do and don't give up makes you a champion. Go race the last race and try your hardest. We're proud of you already."

Dominic lined up for his main event. There was slight hazing from the other riders in the staging area. There were no comments directed at Dominic but a jovial traditional embracing. All the riders were bewildered that an eleven year old novice rider made the 11-13 open main.

They all lined up on the gate. The normal start cadence was called and the gate dropped. They were off, Dominic pushed as hard as he could towards the first turn. He was squeezed to the inside by the entire pack. He did not have the girth or developed strength to push back. He was in lane two and was towered by thirteen experts on each side of him.

As they exited the first turn he could hear the announcer call his name as the new eleven year old expert currently in third place. Over the first jump and heading into the second turn Dominic was passed by two riders.

He did not have the strength or power of the older riders and he felt himself peaking. He chased the other riders through the entire race track. He finished in fifth place. He could not make it past any of the other riders. He was being pushed by the sixth place rider and held on to fifth place by one bike length.

He made his way back to their camp. As he entered his father shook his hand over the top of his head as a proud gesture. Dominic was exhausted. He looked at his father and smiled.

Angelo said, "C'mon son, let's go meet your new sponsor."

Dominic agreed. They made their way to the team he would be a rider for named, "Power Shot BMX." They had only eight riders and he was now number eight. He received his jersey and was introduced to his new teammates.

Brent introduced Dominic as their new 10-11 year old expert rider. He told the team to be ready for next week's regional championship in North Jersey. He thanked Dominic and told him to stop by the shop this week for his helmet and some goodies he had for him.

Chapter 16

The weeks were also moving on for Rafael. He continued to race every weekend accompanied by his father and mother. Sometimes one of his other brothers would attend but for the most part it was his parents and his sister. Rafael continued riding with his friends at the farmers pit area adjacent to the property with the big house on it.

Rafael became the best rider of them all. He was also one of the youngest. He found that riding with the other boys allowed him to have to work harder to beat them. This equated to them pushing Rafael to be the better rider he had become.

For the last few weeks Rafael had been racing and continually finishing in first or second place. The other rider who was tactfully a dirty rider continued to place first and was forced to move into the expert class. The bully rider, Billy Ports, had been racing several weeks before Rafael showed up and finally made the transition to the export class.

This left Rafael to race without being bullied on the track by Billy Ports or AKA, "Pork Belly." It was funny because he was not a large kid but the play on words by twisting the name around fit his personality and riding style.

Rafael was not intimidated by Pork Belly. He was more concerned about his bicycle. He did not want the other rider to damage it. He was afraid of not getting it repaired in-between moto's.

Rafael had good fortune in the last few weeks. He won all of his races and was automatically moved up to 10-11 expert class. He was excited; he had a conversation with his father last week about moving up to the expert class. Maximo sat with his son alone under a shady tree and had a talk with Rafael. He wanted to express a few particulars that needed to be discussed.

Maximo, speaking to Rafael in Spanish, "Son, one day in the future, hopefully in about twenty years from now, you will know what it's like to be a father. I am proud of the young man you are becoming. You are still the size of a child but demonstrate characteristics of a man. But, there is always room for growth. Why am I saying this? You are entering into a sport that is far more competitive than I could imagine. Although you see all the teams on the sidelines, you are the only one out there peddling your bike. You are the only one who has the ability to make decisions when you are racing. I wish I could run alongside of you when you're riding to tell you what to do. I don't care if you play football (soccer) or baseball. If this is what you want to do, I will support you. You're about to race in the faster class today and I am a little concerned. That dirty rider has a problem with Latino's and other nationalities other than his own. He is a young man influenced by the wrong people. He makes it very clear with his racial slurs towards other nationalities as well. There is no filter or consequences for him I suppose. Not a nice thing to do. Listen to me closely. He is not like this on his own. He was taught to be this way. I don't care what he says to you or about our people, ignore the words, they are only words. Just remember, words are power. Words will hurt and causes people to react without thinking. I don't want you to make this mistake. If he or anyone else has something to say, remember that your reactions are noticed more by others ten times as much. People will remember you more of how you react. If you react correctly, the other person will be recognized by their true intentions. Please don't get trapped. I pray that you make the right decisions. You are a nice young man. Not because you're my son. That only makes you perfect. You're a nice young man because of the decisions you make. Be careful out there today and stay safe. Winning isn't everything, this is just a race.

It's nice to win. It's significant to win fairly. People will love you when they see you being a fair sport. Everyone respects a gentleman. Everyone loves a competitor that is fair and down to earth, honest and trustworthy. You are that young man. Prove it to these people as you have to me."

Rafael was beside himself. His father was a rugged man with a soft heart. His father came out of his shell for the first time that he could recall. He had no words for his father. He simply looked at him and shook his head. After this talk they walked back to their spot together.

As they were walking back, a well groomed and neatly dressed man approached them. He introduced himself as Harry Hartle. He expressed that he was the owner of a bicycle shop in the area. He wanted to know if he could talk with Maximo. Maximo looked at him and agreed to speak with the man but insisted Rafael listen.

The man smiled and replied, "Of course." He said that he has noticed Rafael over the past few weeks and he wanted to discuss a possible sponsorship. It was not a full sponsorship but limited. He continued to explain that he likes to sponsor kids with partial sponsorship before giving them a full sponsor.

The full sponsorships include an entire uniform from head to toe including a large discount at the bicycle shop and off-season practice sessions. Rafael was gleaming from ear to ear. Maximo explained that he would like to discuss this with his son and requested some time to think about it. Harry agreed and wished them both the best of luck.

As they continued to walk back to their little spot at the track, Rafael asked his father why he didn't say yes.

Maximo said, "If you win today, you might have several sponsors to choose from and you can make them compete over you."

Rafael looked at him and said, "Dad, I really want to win but these kids are bigger and faster."

Maximo looked at him and smiled shaking his head. It was time.

Rafael made his way to the staging area. He pulled his lane. He was lane five, right in the middle of the pack. He thought to himself, oh great. Most of the other riders introduced themselves and Rafael was cordial in return.

Pork Belly made references to Rafael as the "Crisco Kid" and other epitaphs in this manner. Some of the riders laughed and others just shook their head.

One rider next to him looked at Rafael and said, "He's jealous. His mother can't cook Mexican food."

Rafael and some of the others laughed as they pushed their bicycles to the starting gate.

On the gate and ready for his first expert race, Rafael was nervous not knowing what to expect. The cadence was called and the gate dropped. Rafael was off screaming down the first straight making his way to the left hand turn.

They bunched together into the turn and Rafael was surprised. He was in second place with Pork Belly behind him in third. They entered the first turn over the jump and into the next turn all jockeying for position.

Into the next turn there was a loud smash. It happened. Pork Belly smashed into the back of Rafael on purpose trying to slide him out of the way. There was some crunching but Rafael was able to make it through the turn. Rafael noticed there were some strange noises coming from his bicycle. He continued to ride and finished in second.

As they crossed the finish line, the entire pack coasted further out of the way before the first place rider turned around and bumped firsts with Rafael as to indicate nice job. As they were continuing to slow down, Pork Belly rammed Rafael again hitting the back of his leg and knocking him down.

The announcer made a comment of the poor sportsmanship and one of the track officials came running down to help pick up Rafael. Rafael pulled himself up and slightly limped back towards his parents.

He was met halfway by his father. Rafael was being assisted by a track official who was carrying his bicycle because the back wheel was completely bent. Rafael passively walked on. Pork Belly attracted a large crowed of angry spectators around him based on his actions.

Rafael made his way back to the car. Immediately Maximo went to work on his bicycle. An unknown man offered some assistance to Maximo. Maximo looked at the man with a look of discontent on his face.

The man said, "I can help you with this. I know how to make this easy."

Maximo and Rafael watched as the man walked away to only return thirty seconds later with a back wheel.

Maximo said to the man, "We can't accept this."

"Sure you can. This is an old wheel that we keep just in case of this type of thing. Besides, my son was the one who came in first."

Maximo shook the man's hand and thanked him. The man said nothing as he smiled and walked away. Maximo looked at his son and said, "Remember, people remember good sports. This man was an example of what we discussed earlier."

Rafael agreed that the man's actions were far more empowering than any moves he had seen on the track.

Rafael continued to race on this day to finish in third place. He was fast but the other riders had the experience. Rafael was in first place in the last moto, but he carried to much speed in the turns, slipping and sliding, which allowed the other more experienced riders to pass him.

And what about Pork Belly? He was disqualified for the day and asked to leave the track. Pork Belly's father completely embarrassed himself and his family. Pork Belly's father protested that his son's brakes didn't work correctly. Nobody believed it and he was not making any friends. He was finally escorted off the track by an off duty police officer.

Feeling happy of how he raced, Rafael asked his father if he could possibly upgrade his bicycle parts a bit.

His father told him, "Let's see what next week's race entails. You might be into something more intricate.

Rafael looked at him very confused. He said nothing and enjoyed the view from the back of the car, finally drifting off to sleep.

Chapter 17

It's mid-September and Team Panther is recognized as one of the best factory BMX Teams. Among all the factory teams Team Panther is a driving force. Reggie has been promoting his new bicycles, frames, and racing accessories. He called his team Manager Carl and his team Leader Tony for a 10 AM meeting in his office.

Carl's office was just down the hall from Reggie's and he simply walked down the hall. Tony was working at the factory and made his way to Reggie's office five minutes early. Tony and Carl walked in around the same time to the open greeting of Reggie.

Reggie's office was not too high tech for the time period. It was very simple and somewhat organized. He had large filing cabinets all lined up with some papers laying on the top. There was some poster sized photographs turned around on an easel deliberately so both Tony and Carl could not see what was on them.

Reggie possessed a large desk decorated with pictures and stacks of papers neatly pushed to one side with an in and out basket and some documents stuffed inside of it. His office overlooked the mountains with several highways intersecting his view.

He was in a traditional office building totaling five stories. His office was on the top floor with a small staff, including himself, Carl and a woman who answered phones and helped him organize mail, itinerary, and his affairs in his absence.

Tony and Carl walked into Reggie's office as he stood looking out the window with profound excitement. He was too anxious to hold back the news of what he wanted to express to them.

He walked towards them from the window and announced, "Team Panther is competing in the World Championships right after Christmas this year."

They both looked at each other with disbelief. Tony stood up and pumped his fist with exultation.

Carl smiled at Tony and then looked at Reggie, "Well, I guess this is job security!" Carl knew how much work would be involved with this endeavor.

Reggie continued with his presentation saying, "We have the opportunity to pick up some new riders and possibly win the world championship. Can you imagine if Team Panther won the World Championship? Think about what that would do for us as a company. Look at the possibilities this opens for us collectively. Think of the young lives we could touch. What if some of our riders win, they would be considered the best in the world until the next year's season begins. This is our opportunity to show the world who we are and what we stand for. We have the ability to change tradition. And it starts with you Tony. You are the man to beat at this time. I want you to train hard and be the same man you have always been. You are going to be a distinguished part of our future and I want you to know that I will never forget your efforts. I promise that you will be compensated."

Reggie walked over to pictures and turned both of them around. On the poster board was an insignia of Team Panther's new logo. The poster board showed artist concepts of the new uniforms. Reggie talked in detail about the uniforms and continually asked for both Tony and Carl's input.

They interjected with their ideas but it was clear, Reggie already had his mind made up. Tony was overwhelmed with emotion and was astonished with all the work Reggie put into this project for the team. Tony thought to himself about the logistics involved. Reggie had to procure rooms for all the riders including airfare and feed everyone. More than he wanted to think about.

At the end of the meeting Reggie expressed to Carl that they need to have a meeting later in the day to discuss all the logistical support and itinerary of the upcoming event. Carl got up and walked to his office knowing that Reggie wanted to have a heart to heart meeting with Tony.

With the door shut Reggie walked over to Tony and sat in the seat Carl was sitting in. Reggie looked at Tony and asked, "Well you excited as me?"

Tony quickly answered, "I feel like I want to jump out of my skin. I'm stoked!"

Reggie sat comfortably in the chair and talked firmly but softly at the same time with Tony. He started by saying, "Tony I am more excited about this than you think. I look forward to possibly picking up more sponsors and displaying our new bikes. You are the number pro. You are the man. I want you to do well in this series. I want you to prepare. No more working at the factory. Your job now is to train. I don't want you getting hurt before the race begins. You're in good shape now; I want you to peak on the day of the race. I'm guessing it will be a two or three day event. There is going to be one full day of qualifiers and the next day for all the main events. Tell me what I need to do to ensure you're at the top of your game for the Worlds?"

Tony sat back and thought about Reggie's words. He sat there for a few moments before speaking. He finally answered, "I need to know, it's going to be indoors?"

Reggie answered, "I never told you all the particulars as I am going to do with Carl, but yes it will be indoors. I don't know if they are going to truck in dirt or race on the concrete. My speculation is that it will be racing on concrete. I overheard talk of an electronic starting gate and starting ramp of some sort."

Tony quick to speak stated, "Well, this makes it easier. I know that I'm not the only pro preparing. I need to find a warehouse with concrete floors for me to practice my sprints and turns both sharp and long. I need to figure a way to pedal as much as I can. If I could find this place and practice, this will give me a nice fuzzy feeling inside.

Reggie answered, "Did you want a man to assist you in your training or do you need me to do anything for you?"

Tony answered, "Maybe another rider or someone who understands what I am doing. They need a full understanding of what it is that I'm doing.

Reggie looked at him, "Agreed."

That was it. Tony's new job was to train. He was a pro and was being paid to be a pro even as he trained. He thought to himself how to start his training. He knew he was going to have to practice his gate starts and his sprints. It didn't matter what kind of track he raced. Speed wins.

Technical abilities increase your chances of winning. He wanted to start sooner than later. As he got on his bicycle and rode towards the bus stop knowing he had some arrangements to figure out, he thought of where he could practice on concrete.

Later in the evening Tony was as home watching television when his phone rang. It was Reggie.

"Tony, good news, I have some good information for you. The race is going to be in Indianapolis Indiana. You're going to be racing on polished concrete with wooden jumps. Also, found a place for your training. There is an old military barracks not too far from you. The old armory has the same type of floors. I'll be at your house in the morning with Carl. We want to come get you and take a look at this place. It might be advantageous to possibly have some of our other riders practice with you from time to time."

Tony Agreed and was excited about this new challenge.

The next day Reggie picked up Tony and headed towards the old army barracks. Just as advertised, the place was abandoned with an old armory standing far off the road. There was a security service protecting the property but Carl had made all the arrangements for Tony to practice.

They checked out the old armory. It was in good repair and a wide open space for sprints and makeshift turn. Reggie looked at Tony and asked, "Is this what you expected?"

Tony shook his head no and answered, "I'll make this work. I'll need some cones for the turns."

Reggie looked at Carl, "Pick up some cones today and get Tony some transportation down here every day. Put this on the schedule. If he needs help, show up late. I'll understand."

Tony made a routine of racing one race on the weekend. He practiced every Wednesday night at the track. They had an electric gate and he used this time as his workout. He would do sprints every day except for Sundays. He was committed and motivated. This is what he would do. He had a plan and he was going to make it work.

Reggie asked Carl to come into his office. Reggie was very clear and precise with Carl. "I know Tony is going to start practicing but we need to be fair. Go to all the magazines and promoters and give them the particular of the track. It's going to be on polished concrete with wooden jumps ranging from three to five feet tall. Make sure they all know the jumps are all table-tops. I don't want one single person screaming fowl. I want them all to have the ability to train as Tony. Make sure we get this out today. Get the pictures of the arena from their promotions department. We got all the pictures in this morning. All the Magazines and BMX industry is awaiting information. Get the cost out along with the hotel specials incorporated with the race fees. Protect ourselves and our brand. Everyone will have an equal chance of winning and practicing. Get the practice schedule out for times and classes. How the other teams practice is their business. Get this out today. Next week Tony will start his sessions at the Armory and we want all the teams to have one weeks' notice before we send Tony and our team on their training bender."

Carl looked at Reggie when he was done and asked, "Anything else?"

Carl smiled as Reggie laughed, "Make sure you call me before you go to lunch." They both laughed as Reggie's phone rang.

Chapter 18

Dominic was excited about his new opportunity with his new sponsor, Power Shot BMX. That Monday morning he made his way out to the pits to meet with his friends. Like clock-work, his friends made it out to the pits around 10:30 AM.

Dominic was making his way around the track pushing harder than he ever had. Pete, Rex, Jimmy and Larry made their way around the track and met with Dominic at the end of the course. They approached Dominic to find him sweating and winded from his practice session. They were happy for their friend who is now and expert rider and sponsored.

The friends chatted for a while waiting for Dominic to catch his breath. They made their way to the start of the track where they were met by a bunch of older kids who looked to be sixteen to eighteen years old. They were riding their bicycles and hanging around the starting area smoking.

The boys all made their way to the top of the practice course. One of the older kids asked, "Hey, who are you guys?"

Dominic answered, "We build this track and were just riding it."

One of the older kids clambered, "This is our track now!" The older kids starting laughing, acting like the punks they were portraying. These punks were the epiphany of your everyday run of the mill bullies. It was clear that these older village idiots wanted trouble. It was unknown what kind of trouble they craved.

Dominic looked at his buddies and made a head gesture to the left as to say lets go. It was five younger kids and only three older punks. As they rode off, so as to not cause any trouble, one of the punks smashed his font tire into the back of Dominic's bicycle causing his back tire to instantly lock and not be able to turn.

Immediately Jimmy rode off and the other kids stayed. Dominic looked in disbelief at what had just transpired. His back rim was bent beyond repair and his bicycle was only a few months old.

He asked the kid, "Do you plan on paying for this?"

They all laughed and one of them said, "You're lucky we don't take your bike."

Dominic now understood the severity of the situation. In that very instant, he understood the fight or flight principal. All the while he kept thinking of where Jimmy went.

His other two friends petitioned, "We don't want any trouble, we just wanted to ride and have a good time."

It wasn't long before the punks took advantage of the situation. They thought it would be fun to torment the younger kids and intimidate them. They first demanded that the kids first give them their money pushing them down on the ground causing them pain. Then they demanded that they give them their bicycles or they would beat them until they were unconscious.

Dominic's life flashed before his eyes. They were not that far into the woods. They knew that neither he nor the other boys would give up their bicycles. This was their livelihoods. At this moment in time he made the decision to fight. Simply fight.

As he lay on the ground in pain, he found a very large rock. He decided he was going to smash at least one of the older kids in the face and take his chances. One of the older kids kicked Dominic several times for making him wait to give up his bicycle. Every time the punk tried to grab it, Dominic would hold on to it for dear life. Dominic didn't know if his friends would gather the guts to take on these guys but he had no time to discuss it.

Dominic made it to his feet. As he got up, he smashed one of the kids in the side of the face instantly splitting his head wide open and knocking him out as blood spewed from his head. It was as if it was slow motion.

Pete, Rex and Larry were perplexed. They could not believe what just happened. As the bully lay on the ground, one of the older punks tried to help him by putting direct pressure over the wound. As he did this, Dominic and Rex rushed the other punk.

They punched and kicked him, then made it to their bikes and tore off down the trail. Dominic pushed his bike as hard as he could with his friends close on his tail. As they emerged from the trail he noticed his father standing at the front of the entrance to the pits making his way towards them.

They started screaming to Angelo, "Mr. Carlucci, we are being chased by someone." His other friends made their way out of the woods being chased by the other two bullies.

Jimmy had made his way to Dominic's house and got hold of Mr. Carlucci. He explained in great haste what was happening. He immediately made his way to the pits. He knew where it was being from the area and knowing his way around town. It was nearly three blocks from his house.

Angelo made his way into the woods noticing Dominic pushing his bike. Angelo asked with great concern, "did they hurt you?"

Dominic replied, "a little, I'm ok."

Angelo nodded, "They're not."

As the punk kids came around one of the turns, Angelo knocked both of them off their bikes. The other boys were screaming and yelling with satisfaction.

Angelo grabbed the biggest kid by his throat and asked, "How old are you?"

The punk didn't answer. Angelo pushed the kids face into a tree. The bark of the tree push imprinted into his face. Angelo asked again, "How old are you?"

The kid replied, "Eighteen douche-bag."

Angelo answered, "Good."

He continued to rub the kids face into the tree and caused him to bleed. As the punk turned around, Angelo punched him in the face knocking him out. Meanwhile, the other punk was making his way towards Angelo.

Angelo yelled out to him, "Please tell me your eighteen also." The punk quickly answered, "I'm old enough to kick your ass!"

Angelo answered, "Perfect."

The punk kid tried to fight with Angelo. This lasted nearly thirty seconds. Angelo over-powered the punk, striking him several times in the face before he fell to the ground. Angelo repeatedly kicked him to ensure he wouldn't get up. Up the trail he noticed another bloody boy making his way down the trail.

He approached the kid noticing the blood. Angelo asked, "What the hell happened to you?"

The kid replied, "F-U old man."

Angelo looked at the poor kid and noticed a very large gash in his head. Angelo told him with concern, "You need a hospital. Why don't you let me get you an ambulance?"

The kid answered him, "Why don't you mind your own business and die."

Angelo told him, "You made it my business when you picked on my boy."

Dominic was in shock. He never saw his father angry nor did he ever see him hit anybody, including himself. Angelo waved for the boys to come over.

Angelo quickly asked, "Which one of these morons hit you?"

Dominic pointed to the one kid with the half black and blond hair.

Angelo picked the kid up and asked, "How are you going to pay for my son's bike?"

The kid spit at Angelo. Angelo threw the kid to the ground and punched him in the face a few times. He took the kids wallet and told him, "Now I know where you live."

Angelo reached into the kid's wallet and was amazed of the amount of cash. He had nearly one thousand dollars. He asked the kid, "Where did you get this kind of money?"

The kid answered, "Cutting grass."

Angelo reached in and took all the money and told the kid, "Now you know what it's like to be robbed." He looked at the kid's license, "You live over twenty miles away from here, what are you doing here? Buying or selling?"

He kicked the kid again. He continued, "Buying or selling?"

The kid replied, "Selling."

Angelo grabbed a large stick off the ground. He told all the dealers this message. "If I ever see you here again, I will kill you myself. Not hurt, stab, or wound, but kill. Get on your bikes and peddle away from here and never come back. If I see you ever again around here, you are going to wish I finished the job. You need to peddle your asses back from whatever rock you crawled out of. Seriously. Never show your faces again. This was only a warning. Consider yourself warned. Or do I need to call the cops?"

The young adults pleaded not to call the cops and they simply got on their bicycles and rode off. Angelo looked at all the kids and said, "All of you to my house now." He took Dominic's bicycle and placed it in the back of his truck.

All the kids were at Dominic's house and Angelo called them to the back of the house. He began," I want to talk to all of you. Obviously you met some drug dealers in the woods where you hang out. It was just a matter of time before something like this happened and you meet idiots like this. I don't know how old these kids really are but, I could be in serious trouble if they are under eighteen years old. I don't want any of you bragging of what just happened. I'm not proud of what I just did. I never want to hear about it nor do I want any of you to remind me. I don't want to hear about it from any of your parents. I just want this to go away. I want to explain some things to you kids. The idiots you just met would have beaten you up, taken your money, bikes and whatever they felt and left you there with no remorse. They are druggies. Their only concern is for them. You mean nothing to them and they don't give a crap about you. You were an easy target for them. They took advantage of it. Had I not been around, God only knows. You all need to stay away from that site for a while. Play and ride around here. I'll do something at the plant for you if needed. I can't have this on my conscience."

There was an eerie silence. Finally Dominic spoke up, "What about my bike?"

Angelo laughed and shook his head, "I have money to cover it." He then showed the thousand dollars he took from the punks.

Dominic spoke again, "What are you going to do with all that money?"

Angelo answered, "Fix your bike for one. Son, I don't know. Maybe give it to charity. Honestly, I don't want it. This is poison money and I don't want it in my hand now as we speak."

The other boys were still shaking. As they sat there speaking a police car pulled into Angelo's driveway. He told the kids, "Stay here."

He met with the police officer for some time. They laughed and Angelo made his way back to the boys. "Well, it seems the boys picked on someone else before you and robbed him, his mother, and another passerby at the grocery store. They were just picked up and they had drugs on them. I have to go to the police station. Remember, I don't want any discussion about this." Angelo pulled Dominic's bicycle out of the truck and drove off to the police station.

Angelo arrived back at the house later that afternoon. He sat with Dominic and Jimmy who was still hanging around. Angelo asked, "Who cracked the kid with a rock and gave him forty-four stiches?"

Dominic answered, "Me dad."

Angelo continued, "You kids had no idea who you were messing with. These ding dongs will probably go to jail for a few years. You realize they robbed and beat a woman and her son taking money and other valuables. They were on a spree of robbing people. They were doing this for drug money. Let me explain. They needed money to buy more drugs. They were selling drugs and lost some of them back in the pits where you kids ride. The police found the drugs with one of the police dogs. These guys are very dangerous individuals and had no regard for your lives. You kids are lucky I happened to be home early for lunch when Jimmy showed up. Drugs do many things to people. You get hooked and catch a high. Before you know it, it catches you right back. You change. You become dependent on drugs as if it was food. They need it and crave it. Druggies will do anything for it. They will mow you down as if you were a blade of grass with no concern except for their self-gratification of getting high. Life for them means nothing, your life or their own. You are simply an obstacle that is in their way of their next fix. Drugs do nothing but drag you down. These bastards are going to jail for a very long time. I didn't press charges but did admit I had a confrontation with them. I gave the police the money I found on them. Of course I didn't admit to taking it off them. But I felt it was the right thing to do by giving it back. Dominic, I want you to know that if you ever have an issue or concern in life where you feel that you're spinning out of control, you call me. I won't be mad. I'll be happy you called me for help. I'll be there for you. I don't care if it is drugs, alcohol, or gambling. You call me. I'm not proud of what I did. I would do it again for you, son. I would lay my life down for you. This is not your fault but just remember, the choices you make now will reflect in you for the rest of your life. I'll be here to make sure you make the right decisions. I don't ever want you to fail."

Dominic understood the severity of this situation. He had to ask, "Dad, where did you learn to fight like that?"

Angelo looked at him, "I didn't grow up in the best of neighborhoods son. That's all I am going to say. If you say anything to your mom…."

Jimmy asked, "Mr. Carlucci? Is this over? I mean, what happens next?"

Angelo answered, "Nothing Jimmy. The police have it now. We are done with this I hope. They told the police that they don't remember anything and didn't say much. They only admitted to the crimes they committed."

Dominic looked at his bike in disgust. Angelo looked at Dominic and said, "I know son. Hey get your bike in the back of my truck. Let's take a ride to your new sponsor. Besides, you have a regional race this weekend before school starts."

Chapter 19

It's Saturday morning around 5 AM. Angelo wakes Dominic up, "C'mon son! It's the big day and we have a three hour drive to North Jersey for the District G regional race."

Dominic jumped out of bed and grabbed his shorts and a T-shirt and threw on a pair of flip-flops. Angelo yelled out to him from the other room, "Don't forget another T-shirt and socks. I don't want to smell you all the way home after the race!"

It was the norm to wear a pair of shorts under your uniform racing pants. When you were done racing you simply pulled off your pants and wore shorts in order to stay cool afterwards. Dominic made his way around the house gathering his belongings as his brother and mother staggered out of their bedrooms toward the kitchen.

Angelo had the family car packed and Dominic's bike secured on the back. Dominic was proud of his bicycle. When he and his father went to the bicycle shop, Power Shot BMX, the owner Brent Lock convinced Angelo to make a few upgrades. Angelo bought Dominic a new number plate, new brakes converted from side to center pulls, and different pedals. Dominic's bicycle was complete. There wasn't much more he could do to upgrade. He was primed.

They all gathered into the car and made their way north on the NJ Turnpike to exit 11 and then north again on the Garden State Parkway. It was a short drive. For Dominic, he and his brother slept the entire time as their father drove. Maria dozed on and off during their three hour drive to the BMX track.

They arrived at the track around 8:30 AM. Both boys awoke, and to their amazement, they were at the track. It seemed like five minutes for them. Dominic was amazed about the size of the downhill portion of the track. It wasn't a long track, but it had its difficulties. It was rocky combined with flat turns and sudden downhill drop into a sharp right hand turn with a berm and hay bales for protection. The track was closed. They had arrived before Power shot BMX. They set up at the second turn as described by Brent Lock.

Angelo registered Dominic for both the eleven expert class and the 11-13 open. Dominic was excited. He was anxious to ride the track. It wasn't long before Power Shot BMX arrived as a convoy. Angelo already had the spot set up and they simply pulled in, nearly ready to go.

All Dominic's teammates made their way to registration with their parents as the rest of the pack set up their camp. As this was happening, the announcement that practice would begin in five minutes came across the loudspeakers. Dominic made his way to his bicycle and donned his racing gear. New racing pants, jersey and helmet. He was ready and looked the part.

He was the third group to make his way onto the starting gate. He watched as all the riders before him made controlled skids into the first turn. He noticed all the local riders had front brakes. He made his way to the starting gate. The gate dropped and he was the second rider into the first turn.

He noticed that he carried a lot of speed and could not compensate washing out to the outside nearly hitting the other riders. He continued the rest of the track half speed and became more familiar with the rocky compacted dirt. The downhill section was fast and bumpy.

He would need to control his speed into the last turn or he could seriously hurt himself based on the backside of the berm. It was boulders with no protection. He knew it was a disaster waiting to happen.

He made his way back to team camp. He recognized for the first time that he would need to utilize front brakes in the first turn. He discussed this with some of the older riders. They all agreed that they needed to try it. Dominic attached his old brakes to the front of his bike and adjusted them as such so they wouldn't skid on him. It was a balancing act for him to overcome.

Dominic made his way to the gate and waited for the cadence. The gate dropped and again he was on second with an older kid in front of him. He started skidding his way into the turn and utilized his front brakes and tapped them as needed to stop him from drifting to the outside.

He nailed it. Instantly he figured it out. He would pull the front brakes before the rear slowing him down enough to set him up for the exit of the turn. He was feeling confident.

The moto's were posted and Dominic was ready. He knew that there were two heats for his class and he would have to race a main. Both his open and his normal class had mains. He was going to have a long day of racing.

Dominic took a few more practice laps and made his way back to his team. He felt assertive about the track. He was ready and he took a break awaiting the call over the loudspeaker for his moto to start getting staged. Nearly an hour later it was time. The races were going to start 11 AM sharp.

Dominic made his way to the staging area and sized up the other eleven experts. There were riders from other states and a lot of number one plates with different letter designee's at the end of it. He was in lane one for his first heat.

This was not an optimal gate position but he was confident he could pull this off. The group of riders set up on the gate, the cadence was called, and the gate dropped. Dominic like normal was in front. There was no jump to negotiate and he was first into the turn.

Like he practiced, he pulled the front brakes first and then the rear transitioning into the controlled skid throughout the turn. He emerged from the turn in first place.

He could hear the roar of the crowed and the announcer calling his name, "Dominic Carlucci in front being chased by….." He made his way down the second straightaway pushing as hard as he could. There again were no jumps in the second straightaway and ninety degree left hand turn into the downhill section.

He made his way through the turn and noticed that as he started towards the downhill section that he had a commandable lead. Down the hill he went faster than he could pedal to berm right handed turn and across the finish line in first place.

He made his way back up the hill with the rest of the pack he just raced. One of the kids asked him, "When are you turning 12?"

Dominic answered, "In January."

He stopped and watched as the next group of 10-11 experts made their way down the track. He knew that four of those riders would advance to the main and he had the possibility of having to race them.

He made it back to the team, sat in his chair, pulled off his racing pants and waited to watch the twelve and thirteen year olds knowing he would have to race them in the open.

Dominic watched in amazement at how fast the thirteen year olds were flying around the track. He sat back and thought to himself about how he had to race them. He made his way to the staging area for the open race.

He was towered by the other riders in his moto. For the first time he was intimidated. He felt very small next to some of the older kids. He lined up on the gate and waited for the cadence. The gate official shouted out, "Ok guys."

The cadence was called and the gate dropped. Dominic was stuck in the middle of the pack. He made his way to the first turn and realized he was in fourth place. He made it through the first turn and the sudden sense of reality sunk in. He was a small fish in a big pond.

The older riders were much stronger and had more power than he. He raced as hard as he could down the second straight and maintained his forth position. This part of the track was the challenge. He pedaled as hard as he could down the third straight and down the hill as fast as he possibly could. He was being pressured for his position.

Knowing that the first four riders advanced to the main, he focused. Into the turn he could feel the other rider next to him on the outside. He made it across the finish line in fourth place.

He continued the race all day long finishing first in his age bracket of 10-11 experts. His main was the same result. He finished in first place pulling away from his group by the second turn. Dominic continued to finish in fourth place all three moto's of his open class.

His main was less spectacular. He was the only eleven year old to make the main. All of the other kids were twelve and thirteen. He made the valiant effort to only finish in sixth place.

He was not discouraged, but also knew he was the youngest rider in the open and he was racing all expert riders. Dominic was congratulated by both his family and his sponsor for finishing in first place. This would be the last point's races in the state.

As the last race made its way down the course, Brent Lock spoke to his team. He conveyed how proud he was of them. The team finished in second place for the day. He made mention of possibly going to Indianapolis for the world championships. Dominic looked at this father. His father winked at him.

He asked, "Can we go?"

Angelo replied, "I have another surprise for you Monday."

Chapter 20

The weeks continued for Rafael. The season ended and Rafael finished in 125th place overall in his district with the combined number of points with all the riders in his district. He continued to ride his bike at the pits with his friends and was becoming more technical and obviously a better rider than all his friends.

Rafael was never offered another sponsorship. He accepted Harry Hartle's partial sponsor. He was excited that he was going to attend his first team practice on Wednesday night. They all met at the same track he had been racing.

Wednesday night had arrived. There were other riders than just his team. It was open night. The track was open to all riders and well organized. There were many teams and new riders trying to ride for the first time.

Maximo and his older son, Carlos, escorted Rafael to the team pit area. Rafael walked with his father, brother and his bicycle towards Mr. Hartle. Harry yelled to his team, "Everyone gather up."

He introduced his newest member Rafael Santos. All the riders said hello to him and he felt a sense of joy. Harry also told Rafael, "We have another surprise for you. OK guys roll it out."

There it was. His new bike. It was awesome. It was an amazing BMX racing machine. It was constructed with an aluminum frame, aluminum handle bars and cranks. The wheels were thinner and all aluminum.

Rafael was literally jumping with joy. Harry Hartle continued, "Raf, here are some things you need to understand. You were racing on a bike that was too big for you. You were also pushing a lot more weight. This bike is much lighter and more your size. The cranks are shorter allowing you to spin much faster. The pedals are a little smaller and you might need to get familiar with them. You're running the same gear, 44x16. This is subjective at this time. Let's see how this works. You will be faster but remember you are going to need to practice the turns with the thinner tires. You'll be fine son."

He then yelled over to one the older riders, "Hey brad, give young Raf a hand adjusting his handle bars and get him a team number plate with a 125 number."

Raf looked at his brother and father and asked, "Ok, when did this happen?"

His brother answered, "Last week when we went over to formally except his offer. Remember when you were sitting on this bike? Well I wanted to help Dad do something nice for you. I mean, I am constantly tormenting you anyway."

Raf was still rambunctious. He answered, "Isn't that what brothers are supposed to do?"

They all laughed as Harry called his team to the center of their camp for a meeting. He went over the agenda for the next few weeks and made mention of the worlds in Indianapolis. Harry also mentioned some races for them to ride in but no points would be awarded. It was more of a fun ride for them all to keep in shape and enjoy the sport.

Rafael made friends with some of the older riders and listen to them give him advice on the starts. He walked his bike to the top of the starting gate and lined up behind a bunch of older riders watching what they had described.

Rafael finally lined up and pedaled about five times and coasted. He wanted to become more familiar with his bicycle. He noticed instantly he carried more speed. He also noticed that in the turns he had the bite but easily could washout if he was not careful. He pushed his way around the track noticing the differences between both bicycles.

He finally made the decision to go for it. He was on the gate and noticed one of the riders from his class. It was the kid who gave him the wheel when Pork Belly smashed him up. Rafael made his way to the rider and he acknowledged Rafael instantly.

He commented on his bike, "Nice scoot. How do you like it?"

Rafael laughed, "My first hour with it. Trying to figure her out."

They both laughed and lined up for the start. Rafael pushed his way off the gate and realized he was in front. He was into the first turn and he started to slide to the outside. He sat back and coasted. He realized he needed to ride his bike some more at the house to learn how to negotiate the turns.

As he was riding around the track the other rider caught up and said to him as they were riding, "I can see you're going to be a force to be reckoned with." He laughed and rode on.

Rafael concentrated on his gate starts for the rest of the practice. He was nervous and didn't want to mess up his new bicycle. He had a completely new style bicycle and needed some time to familiarize himself with the drastic changes.

Rafael made his way around the track picking places to speed up and see how his new bicycle performed. He was impressed. He was able to accelerate without delay. It was almost effortless.

School had started a few weeks back and Rafael knew his time would be limited between school and his riding time. He also knew that it would start to get dark sooner and his afternoons would diminish. Time was a commodity for him. He enjoyed having two new bicycles in the last few months.

He knew it was not cheap, even with the discount. He looked at his jersey with his jeans. He asked is father what he could do to obtain the racing pants.

His father answered, "Win and get them for free. I would buy them for you, but I think when you are ready, you will get them for free, you'll have to earn them."

Rafael laughed and said, "I'd rather have them now."

Maximo smiled, "In time son. I know you'll earn them and don't forget about the new helmet."

Rafael nodded his head and understood he needed to earn this as well.

Time flew that afternoon and Rafael asked his father, "What am I going to do with my old bike."

Maximo looked at with a blank stare, "I don't know, maybe give it to your brother Juan."

Juan was the second born child. He thought his older brother already dibs on it. Besides he was nearly seventeen years old and probably was already hounding their father for a car of some type.

The end of the day was near. Harry called the team over for a final meeting. "OK guys, we will meet here every Wednesday night for practice. Raf, congrats on your new bike. Ride it and get used to it. I want to see you racing the whole track next week."

He continued to discuss all the riders and what they needed to do for next week. Harry also discussed the world championships again but not too much in detail. Several riders helped him pack up the tent and other items into the back of his pickup and trailer he was pulling.

On the ride home Rafael asked his father, "Papa, what about the world championships? Maybe we can go?"

Maximo quickly answered, "Son, its right after Christmas and its bad timing. I promise if they have one next year, I'll take you."

Rafael thought about it and decided his father was probably correct. His brother thought it would be fun to poke at Rafael, "You get a new bike and you already think you're a world champion. You're lucky I don't give you a weggie."

Rafael quickly replied, "One day, one day. You'll see me on the podium."

Chapter 21

Its mid-September and Dominic started school. It was pleasure for him to see all of his old friends. He made his way to home room and noticed the difference from his previous school. His new school was both seventh and eighth graders.

He noticed that he had grown taller than some of his friends he had not seen since the beginning of the summer. He also noticed that some of the girls no longer looked like girls but more resembled young ladies. He was enthusiastic; he liked seeing his old friends and was adored by many of his peers.

It wasn't long before the end of the day arrived. He had a total of eight periods and was out of school by 2:30PM. He took the bus home and arrived at 3:05PM on average. He was getting anxious. He was not allowed to ride at the pits and had several conversations with his father about going back down there. His father arrived home nearly 6PM every day.

Angelo arrived on Wednesday greeted by his wife Maria. She took him aside, away from Dominic and had a conversation with him. She started, "Angelo, we need to do something about Dominic. He is making me crazy. I want to strangle him at times. He's a good kid but he is persistent. He keeps bugging me about riding his bike, here, there and everywhere, promising me he won't go to the pits. I believe him but, please talk with him."

Angelo looked at his wife and noticed the frustration in her face. He replied, "Honey, I know what to do. He will leave you alone and he will be in plain sight."

Maria looked at him with concern, "What are you up too? I know that look Angelo. You're up to something; you're going to tell me."

Angelo laughed before she did, "This is my best work yet, trust me."

She looked at him smiling, "Let me guess, you're going to build a boxing ring in the basement."

He looked at her with adoration, "This is the reason I love you so much. Your gentle approach and sense of humor about things I have done. I'll tell you this, you're close."

She answered softly, "what are you up to sweetheart?"

Angelo smiled and made a phone call.

The next day Dominic left for school early in the morning. It had become the norm for Angelo to drive Dominic to the end of the block to the bus stop on his way to work. Dominic arrived at school and it was a normal day just like any other for him.

This was until he arrived home. He noticed that his back yard was being transformed. There was tractor moving dirt with both a back hoe and front end loader. His property had a very large back yard and it backed up to a forest.

Because of the property location, it enabled the ability for a make shift track with large jumps and tall berms. He had his own private track with a makeshift starting hill and a smooth track with enough room to race all his buddies at the same time. Dominic was beside himself.

He thought to himself, "I have my own private track."

He got on the phone and called Jimmy and Larry. He told them to call Pedro and Rex. He urgently expressed that they needed to get to his house in the back as soon as possible. They all arrived within fifteen minutes.

They were stunned. It was like a dream come true. His work companion Oscar was running the tractor pushing dirt into corners making berms. Dominic came over and was thrilled to see Oscar.

Dominic's first questions for him made him laugh. Dominic asked, "Did you bring any food from home?"

Oscar sat in his seat and laughed, "No Dom, I'll be back tomorrow to finish. Figure out what you want to do back here and I'll finish it up. Maybe I'll ask my wife to make some Mexican food for you." He laughed when he was done speaking.

Oscar finished up for the day. It was nearing 5 PM and Angelo showed up to give him a ride back to the plant. He left the dump truck and the front end loader at the house. Dominic had three straights with 2 huge berms.

The track was smooth and all he and his friends needed to do was figure out the type of jumps to put in. There was a sandy area in the very back of the property that was easily moved from the woods to the track. The boys walked the track for hours discussing what they wanted to do.

The last period bell could not have come sooner. It was Friday and Dominic was on his way home to see what progress was done with the track. When he arrived, he was excited to see that Oscar dumped large piles of dirt in the middle of all the straights. Dominic came home, said hello to his mother, and made his way outside.

His friends arrived soon after he got home. They all were in the back speaking to Oscar. Oscar moved the dirt as they directed and within an hour the track was done. Oscar grabbed a tamper machine and started packing down the track to make the dirt hard.

The boys all grabbed shovels off the truck and moved the dirt around allowing for a smooth transition onto the jumps. The turns were already completed by Oscar. It was nearing dinner time and all of Dominic's friends left for their houses. They all had to eat and complete their dreaded homework.

As Dominic came into the house his mother told him that she had a surprise for him. He noticed that Oscar brought over four empanadas for him. He immediately ran outside as Oscar was driving off. He jumped onto the dump truck driver's side running board and high fived Oscar.

Dominic yelled back to him as Oscar was making his way out of the back yard, "Tell your wife she made my day. Thank you, thank you, thank you!"

Dominic made his way back into the house as his father arrived into the driveway. He thanked him as well.

Dominic told his father, "Oscar brought me food."

Angelo laughed, "He likes you son. He wants to come watch you race next year. He asks me continually during the summer. He enjoyed working with you. You made an impression. How is the track?"

Dominic answered quickly, "It's awesome. I take it you don't want me at the pits any longer? I'll stay here."

Angelo laughed, "How's your mom taking it."

Dominic stated, "She hasn't said much."

Angelo laughed.

Angelo walked in the house behind Dominic. Maria looked at him and said, "You realize all the neighborhood kids are going to come here every single day?"

Angelo answered, "I'd rather them be here and safe than in the woods alone."

Maria looked at him, smiled and kissed him on the cheek. At that time Dominic's little brother walked into the room and said, "I want a bike." They both laughed.

The entire weekend was taken up with the boys moving dirt and fixing the track. It was a project for the boys and they were proud of what they accomplished. The track was awesome and Dominic was envied by his friends. They earned full rights to ride whenever they wanted. They all rode for hours and hours. They rode into the darkness, something they could not do at the pits.

Dominic continued to ride every day. His friends sometimes could not make it to his house. Nevertheless, Dominic was motivated. He rode until he couldn't stand from exhaustion.

He remarked continually about the worlds. His father timed him as he made his way around the track. Dominic was on fire. He rode his track everyday month after month. As the weather changed and the leaves fell, Dominic continued to ride.

The cold did not hinder his riding. He was only limited by the amount of daylight. His friends all agreed that he was becoming untouchable on the track. They made small changes to the track only improving it.

Dominic continued to progress both technically and with velocity. Dominic was fast. He was a force. Occasionally older kids would come over and ride with Dominic. They pushed him to ride harder and faster. The older kids were much stronger than Dominic and this motivated him further.

Dominic was peaking with his riding skills and needed to find his way to the next level. He was unsure about the sport and never raced outside New Jersey.

Some of his teammates occasionally visited his home to practice. He was given pointers by the older riders and they also give positive inputs of how to improve the track based on his age and technical ability. Again, Dominic would push these boundaries.

Chapter 22

It's mid-December and Reggie is preparing for the World Championships and his family's Christmas Holidays. He is thoroughly stressed and things are happening faster by the minute. All the preparations have been made, the entire program is in place, and the race agendas have been checked and ready.

All he has to do is make his way to Indianapolis and complete some minor items. There are no hindrances; it's going to happen and its only two weeks away.

Reggie left his office early this day and started heading home. He finally had some time and made it a point to stop and complete his Christmas shopping. He was going to leave the day after Christmas for Indianapolis with his entire family.

He thought to himself, *"How can I put on a world-wide event like this and forget to buy Christmas gifts for my family?"* He shook his head and laughed to himself as he drove off to the mall.

More than several hours later, Reggie sat in his recliner at home alone watching TV. He was fighting off the urge to fall asleep when his phone rang. He picked it up and it was Tony.

Reggie asked, "Are you OK?"

Tony laughed, "I'm fine but my bike isn't. Is there a way I can get some tires? They are Bald and I need a little meat on them. Riding on the concrete wore them down pretty good. Also, riding on the polished floors with new tires is horrible. Make sure the guys ride a little on their tires before they get on this surface."

Reggie was elated, "Awesome Tony. This is good news for us all to know."

Tony continued, "I know that there are some skate parks with other factory teams renting time for their team. You did say it was the polished concrete, not the type in the skate parks or driveways?" Reggie thought about it and answered, "I am positive we made it well known. If other factory teams are practicing, then I am one hundred percent positive that word has gone out. How's your training going?"

Tony quickly replied, "I am ready. There is nothing more I can do to prepare. I am in good shape and I feel strong. Just get me some tires."

They both laughed at Tony's reply.

The next day Reggie made it a point to make sure all the riders were shipped the tires Tony requested. Reggie personally contacted every rider by phone to ensure them what was expected of them and to bring their report cards. Some of the riders were not surprised. Others were terrified.

Many riders did not understand Reggie's objectives. Although he championed his brand, he cherished young men and women. He continually wanted to better youngsters and give them the positive attitude to succeed.

He loved his BMX team and the characterization it portrayed, but it was the young adults and children that represented his brand that he treasured. It was a group of individuals that embodied one entity and that entity was Team Panther.

Reggie continually worked with all the members of his team and respected every last person who represented him. He gave everything to his cause. Reggie understood that this is a ride of a lifetime for these youngsters.

Reggie was given a gift. Not a factory sponsorship to riders, but a gift to touch young lives. The ability to ensure these youngsters understood choices and free will. Reggie was given the unique opportunity to mold these young lives into something special.

He had the capability to give them the ability to take ownership in their choices and the paths they decide for themselves. Reggie was given the benevolence and knowledge of choosing one's destiny. He was given full authority to craft these youngsters into positive and productive individuals.

Reggie understood that our past could predict our future. Choices we make now will ultimately affect us as we progress in our lives. We make supplementary choices that influence other lives. It's like a domino effect.

Reggie wanted to give direction to these youngsters and make them understand they have all the power to be successful. BMX is his love, but he would simply walk away if it negatively spattered others leading to their destruction.

Reggie continually spoke about the ability he possessed as a gift. He made it a point at every meeting to close positive and uplifting. This was business 101 and taught at every management school or seminar.

Reggie lived it. He knew in his heart that young minds are continuously watching. They watch everything we do, everything we say and watch every reaction we make. He was not a rescuer of souls, but craftsman of character.

He had the gift of molding uncertain, indecisive decisions into conclusive irrefutable results. Reggie is by no means a philosopher, but a life coach. Not self-appointed but self-educated.

He faltered and fell as much as anyone else. Flourishing in life, he simply had the ambition to safeguard others from the same miscalculations as himself. Reggie had the uncanny ability to find a positive in any contrite situation.

Reggie never looked at life through blinders. He never had tunnel vision. He always knew of his surroundings and walked with a purpose. Reggie always had a game plan in his head. His peripheral vision was better than twenty-twenty.

His life experiences gave him the advantage in any situation. This was the reason he was successful. This was the reason people trusted him. His word was his bond. If you shook Reggie's hand and he looked you in the eye, there was no need to scribe your names on a piece of paper making it legal. Legal documentation was a formality, not binding. Reggie's trust and word was all anyone needed. This was Reggie's character.

Reggie called Carl into his office. Carl sat and awaited Reggie's instruction. Reggie looked at Carl with minor concern, "Seriously, we need to make sure we have every single report card from our student racers. Make sure you follow up this week with another phone call to the parents. No report card equals no race, at least with our Team Colors."

Carl looked at Reggie, "Wow. You mean it. We might lose some good riders."

Reggie answered instantly, "Fine. Simple detailed instructions, I didn't ask for anything else."

Carl muttered, "What if they haven't received their report cards?"

Reggie, "Let's see what happens. I have a feeling we will be seeing about a half dozen report cards."

Chapter 23

It's the day after Christmas and the weather is San Antonio, Texas couldn't be nicer. It's nearly sixty degrees and not a cloud in the sky. Rafael is enjoying the school break and time with his father. Maximo has the entire week off between Christmas and New Year's.

His family is embarking on a weeklong vacation back to Mexico to visit family. Rafael is ambivalent about the trip because he will not be able to spend time riding his bicycle and enjoying his time away and alone at the pits with his friends. It's about a day's drive back to Hermoso Mexico. He is looking forward to spending time with his grandparents.

Rafael and his entire family arrived later in the evening. It was a nice day with a bit of cool air blowing across the plains. He and his family were greeted by their grandparents and distant cousins. It was going to be a long week. He saw a tent pitched in the backyard with an extension cord ran from the house to the flap entrance of the doorway of the tent.

He thought to himself for a moment of what this was for. Like a jolt of lightning, Rafael looked up at his father and shook his head NO. Maximo laughed shaking his head Yes. All the kids now understood why they had brought the sleeping bags. Not for the ride but as a makeshift bed. Rafael longed to be back home in San Antonio, Texas riding his bicycle and hanging with his friends.

He and the family gathered on the back porch area eating and drinking soda's, relishing in the festive atmosphere. Rafael could see that his father was really enjoying himself. Rafael enjoyed being around cousins he just met for the first time.

He also liked the fact that he could talk to his brothers and sister in English without anyone understanding him. It wasn't long until the dusk turned to night. It was nearing midnight; he and his siblings were growing tired. They all swallowed the fact that they had to sleep in the tent. They joked and called it their bivouac oasis.

As he and his brothers entered the tent, they all took notice that their sister was headed indoors. They protested to no avail. There were a total of four people in the tent. Rafael, his brothers and a cousin were going to share this sanctuary.

In typical boy fashion, it didn't take long for the first boy to break wind. Then a symphony of flatulence filled the air with its pungent aroma of their butts. Within an hour the entire bivouac oasis was more like a fecal matter manor.

The louder the flatulence, the louder the laughs. Finally the boys subsided and fell asleep. Nearly three hours later their cousin woke up and headed into the dark abyss only guided by the lights from inside the house. He stumbled just outside the tent before he started to urinate.

It seemed liked he was peeing for an eternity. The others were awakened by his bathroom exhibition. They all yelled out to him to move away from the door. He was so tired or didn't care what they said to him. He finished and made his way back to his sleeping bag.

Like clockwork, all the boys had to pee. They gathered up together and made a single line peeing all at once. Again, like boys do, the oldest Carlos peed on Juan and called it an accident. They were running in the darkness yelling and peeing on one another.

The lights in the house came on and Maximo made his way to the tent. All the boys acted like they were sleeping. Maximo believed them until Rafael started to laugh and all the boys joined in.

Maximo spoke to them, "Its three-thirty in the morning! Be quiet or I'll send your grandfather out here to sleep with you."

They all laughed and promised to sleep. As Maximo walked away he asked, "Who wet the ground out here? Who spilled their drink?"

They were in hysterics laughing. They were laughing so hard they couldn't answer.

Finally the older son, Carlos spoke, "Are you bare footed dad?"

Maximo answered, "Yes."

They were nearly laughing themselves into their own demise. Finally Carlos answered while still laughing, "Our cousin spilled his pee." Maximo stood there for a moment before he figured out that he was standing in pee.

The night subsided and they all fell into their nocturnal slumber to only be awoken a few hours later by their cousin again. He took Rafael's shirt and walked outside. As the boys lay asleep they were awoken by what sounded like wild pigs just behind the tent.

Within the next few minutes they knew exactly what the sound was. It was not wild pigs snorting; it was their cousin making poo. The smell would stay with them for a while this time. As their cousin made his way back in, they remarked, "Dude, what's up with that? We know you didn't wash your hands."

One of the brothers asked, "What did you wipe yourself with?"

They looked and noticed Rafael didn't have a shirt. The laughter was immeasurable. One of the brother shouted, "Raf is the kind of guy who would give you the shirt off his back and let you wipe your butt with it." This rant continued for nearly thirty minutes.

As the sun started to appear on the horizon, the boys made their way inside the house. The smell of bacon and chicharon awakened them. Not to be over-powered was the smell of sun baked poo. The crew made their way into the house together. They all joked for their cousin to go wash his hands.

Maximo was already awake and dressed. Rafael asked his father, "How much longer are we staying here?"

Maximo answered, "A few more days son, why?"

"If we stay much longer I'm going to need more shirts." They all started laughing.

Maximo answered him, "Your mom packed plenty of clothes for you."

They were in hysterics as Rafael answered his father, "Not if our cousin keeps using them to wipe his butt."

Again, shattering laughter. Maximo looked at them, "What the heck are you guys doing out there?"

Rafael answered, "Not us, him." He pointed to his cousin.

Maximo walked outside behind the tent and observed what the boys were laughing about. Maximo was impressed how the shirt was laid over the top as to disguise it. But the smell gave it away. Maximo came inside shaking his head.

He looked at them and said, "Could you imagine what would have happened if I allowed your sister to stay out there with you guys?" He continued, "Your mother would have every one of your heads." He looked at the boys, "All of you, especially you Hector, go wash your hands. Now."

After nearly three days of visiting, Maximo decided it was time to head home. He enjoyed the time with his family but he understood that his children were bored. Besides, Rafael was going to need some new shirts. They made their way home by nightfall.

As they were getting out of the car, Maximo yelled over to the boys, "Who wants to go camping?"

They all laughed except for his wife Florencia. Although she was very proper, she waited to enter the house away from the family before she broke down in tears laughing about what transpired in Mexico.

Maximo walked in and Florencia could not hold back her laughter. She looked at Maximo and broke out in hysterics. He understood and looked at her with happiness. They both broke down in tears laughing, trying to talk about the boys' escapades.

Chapter 24

The big day finally arrived. Dominic woke up early Friday morning. He had a big day ahead of him. He was exhausted from the airplane ride that only lasted nearly two hours. It wasn't the ride, it was the late arrival. He and his entire family got to their room at nearly midnight.

It's now 8 AM and he and his family headed downstairs for breakfast. This was his Christmas present. Dominic didn't ask for anything other than this opportunity. He received some gifts. Of course it was all BMX related. He received new handlebar grips, shoes, and a new Bob Haro number plate.

Dominic was excited; he could tell that his Dad, Mom and brother were excited as well. They are on the road trip of a life time. They were there to cheer him on in the BMX World Championships. There was talk of who the fastest riders are in the country. It is rumored that California and Florida riders are favored because of the weather and practicing conditions.

Dominic didn't care; he practiced harder than anyone he could think of at the time. He felt good and was positive about his conditioning. He was excited to see the track and practice. It was a two hour window for him to familiarize himself with the track and the layout. He was ready. They all went downstairs to eat and then made their way over to the Arena Center for practice.

It was going to be a long day. Although he was not riding at first, Dominic wanted to watch from the grandstands as the pros made their way out to the track. He watched how they negotiated the course. It was nearing 10:00 AM and Dominic made haste to the room to gather his belongings and make his way to the track.

Dominic grabbed his bike and his gear. His father and brother grabbed his racing bag with his helmet, racing pants and other items he might need. As a group, they walked over to the area for practice. They were greeted by an attendant who asked for their tickets they had purchased before the event.

Angelo displayed all the tickets for Friday's practice and they made their way inside. The track was closed but it was totally different then Dominic expected. The course was laid out with traffic cones and wooden jumps.

Dominic locked his bicycle to a pole near where he and his family were sitting. The track opened up first for the pro's only. The pro's made their way around the track slow at first getting acquainted with the unfamiliar surface. It wasn't long before they cracked the throttle and made their way around the track at full speed. Dominic was amazed of the speeds they were generating.

It was unbelievable. It was like watching them ride and glide over every obstacle as if they were not there. It was if he was watching two things at once. He was amazed.

Dominic could see the excitement on both of his parents faces as the pro's made their way around the track. More amazing was the fact they were using an electric starting gate held up with magnets. Some of the pros were balancing at the gate with both feet on the pedals and timing the starts. It was as if they were shot out of cannon.

After hours of watching everyone practice, it was his turn. Ages 11-13 were able to take the track. Racing the World Championship had some differences than the races in New Jersey. The biggest difference was the age groups.

All riders except for the opens, including the Pros, would only race kids their age. There was a five year old and younger class. There were some other minor differences but none that affected Dominic. Like the pros, Dominic made his way around the track getting familiar with the surface.

It was slippery but manageable for him. He lined up on the gate and noticed he was one of the smaller riders. He was also the youngest. He was ready. The cadence was called and the gate fell. Dominic was off. It was a wooden start ramp and he made his way down onto the concrete. He made it down the first straight over the wooden jump and into the first turn.

He was in third place and it was tight. He was unfamiliar with the riders being so close and not falling into him. He made the ninety degree left hand turn to a straightaway only to have another tabletop jump in front of him.

He pulled up before the jump and allowed for his bicycle, hit the ramp and timed his body to pump over the obstacle as if it was something getting in his way. These jumps were no issue for Dominic. He owned them and he had been riding for only fifteen seconds.

After the jump he stopped pedaling and coasted the track. He was feeling good about it. Some of the riders did the same. There were a few more turns and jumps but nothing he was concerned about. He noticed that he had beaten some single digit riders older than him.

As he came across the finish line, one of the riders asked him, "How old are you?"

He answered, "11 Expert."

It's funny in the world of BMX. Everyone has an age. For example; if asked how old you were, you always answered with your age and your class. Example: I'm 11 expert or 11 novice.

Dominic made several practice runs that day. He was not getting fatigued. He was in shape, but he knew not to overdo it. He made his way back to the staging and pit area. Angelo, with his family in tow met him.

Dominic told his father that everyone is using hairspray to better their grip on the tires. Angelo answered, "I know son, and I was talking with some people in the stands. They drove here; I gave them some money to pick us up some belt spray. I gave him the exact make and described the color of the can. I told him to pick up four cans and I gave him the money. Hairspray is sticky and then gets hard. Belt spray stays tacky."

Dominic thought to himself, *"My father is always one step ahead. He's a genius."*

Chapter 25

The next day came in a flash. Like clockwork, Dominic and his family ate breakfast and made their way to the arena. After a short wait in line, they made their way inside. Dominic made his way to the spot he claimed the previous day.

He locked up his bicycle and waited for his practice slot. It wasn't long before he would be back on the track. Angelo applied the belt spray he obtained from the man he spoke with the prior day. He put the belt spray on Dominic's tires before he was about to take the track.

Dominic's riding was brilliant. He made his way around the track with ease. He even stopped practice early and headed back to the stands.

His father asked, "How do you feel?"

Dominic answered, "I feel good, and I'm ready Dad."

Angelo winked at his son and his brother patted him on the back. He sat in the grand stands for a few hours and watched the other riders make their practice runs. He was relaxed and didn't have the weight of the world on his chest. Dominic knew this is what he trained for and he was ready. No excuses from now until tomorrow night when the race ends.

There was a sizeable amount of fanfare on the opening day. Team Panther sponsoring the event had all their riders take a victory lap followed by the traditional speeches. There were more Team Panther signs and posters hanging everywhere in the arena.

It was nearly over-whelming for Dominic. This was his first year racing and he was at the World Championships. He trained as hard as he could and no excuses were permissible. He was ready and he knew it. If he lost to any rider, it's simply because they were faster.

After a short round of parades and speeches, the most famous announcement, "Motos are posted." He waited because he knew it was going to be pandemonium getting to the moto board. There were thousands of riders and he had over an hour before the races commenced. Nearly an hour later Angelo and Dominic made their way to the moto board. There was a considerable line but they managed.

There were four heats of eleven experts. There were exactly thirty one riders which translated to a semi qualifier and then a main event. All the Semi-qualifiers and main events were going to be run on the next day. It was going to be a long day on Sunday as well.

Dominic decided not to race the open class. He was eleven years old and he would have to race the thirteen year old experts. Dominic accepted the fact that they were faster and much stronger than him. He understood that he was eleven and would not be twelve until just after the New Year.

He spoke with his father about racing the open. Angelo was very supportive saying to his son, "If you feel that way son I understand. You might not make the semis or the mains but it would be good experience. If you don't want to run this class, I get it. Besides, you don't want to get hurt if you fall or make the mains in your age group."

Dominic felt relieved that his father felt the same way he did about racing the open.

Dominic had to wait nearly two hours before he raced on the first day. He was in moto number fifty-five. He enjoyed watching all the little kids racing making their way up to his class. He made his way to the staging area. He found his moto group and sized up his competition.

He said very little and his father stayed with him to apply the belt spray just before he made his way onto the starting gate. Some of the other riders where doing the same using hairspray. He was in lane three. He lined up and waited for the gate to come up. He blocked all of the other distractions out and concentrated on his start.

Just as he practiced, the cadence was called and the gate dropped. Dominic flew off the gate leading within the first ten feet. He made his way over the first jump and distanced himself from the pack. Dominic looked strong. He didn't think about it, he was concentrating on keeping his tires firmly on the ground. He kept thinking to himself, "No mistakes."

He made his way halfway around the track and he could hear the announcer calling the race. He could hear that he was way out front. He made his way to the last ninety degree right hand turn and noticed that he was alone up front.

He came across the line pulling both his front and rear brakes to slow down. As the other riders crossed the line they all bumped fists. There were riders from all over the country. One rider in his heat had a number one plate. He asked him what state he was from.

The rider looked at him with a blank stare in his face. One of the other riders with a big number three on his plate answered, "He's from Sweden and doesn't speak English."

Dominic smiled at him and bumped his fist. It was a friendly gesture and he was overwhelmed of all the single number plates in his moto. He made his way to watch the other moto's in his class.

They all looked fast. There were a couple of riders he was impressed by. They were like lightning on the track and some had tires that looked bigger than his. He pondered about it and decided it was no big issue. He was going to race his race and that was final.

He sat in the grandstands with his entire family. When the pro class lined up on the gate, it was mayhem. They were so fast and smooth. Some of the pros didn't touch some of the jumps. They bunny hopped over them. It was just an obstacle in their way and it was a mad dash to the end. There was very little separation and the action was nonstop.

He was impressed when Tony Scholls of Team Panther took the track. He was the only pro who was able to pull away and distance himself.

Dominic thought to himself, "Maybe it's because the racers in his moto were slower. Then common sense kicked in. There are no slow pros." Tony was on fire. He had the number one plate for a reason and it showed.

Dominic raced his second moto and came in first again. He didn't hold back when he rode. He wanted to make a statement. He trained hard and wanted to win like a champion and be a good sport. He was not a dirty rider and never used duplicitous tactics when riding.

As he made his way back to the stands, he was approached by a man who asked him where he was from. Dominic answered, "New Jersey sir."

The man asked, "How long have you been racing?"

Dominic answered, "This is my first year, but I have been practicing hard. I love this sport. I enjoy riding. It's the best."

The man replied, "OK, catch your breath and have a good race, nice talking to you."

In like fashion, Dominic won his last race and made his way back to the stands to meet his family.

His father met him halfway asking, "You want to go back and get some food and a shower?"

Dominic asked if he could stay and watch the pros. Angelo nodded his head in agreement knowing the entire family felt the same way except for his wife. She was exhausted.

It was nearly 11 PM when they made their way back to the hotel. Dominic's mother prepared sandwiches for them prior to their return. She left early and didn't want to deal with the crowd as the arena dispersed. Dominic, with his father and brother in tow, walked into the hotel room, kissed his mother, ate his sandwich, took a shower and was sleeping before his brother was undressed and running the water.

The next day was suddenly upon them. Like clockwork again, they ate at the hotel and left for the arena. This time it was different. There were a lot less riders and the races started at 9 AM. Dominic only took a few practice runs and made his way to the bleachers.

As he was approaching, he noticed that the same man he was speaking to the day before was speaking with his father and mother. As he approached, the man waved at him and walked off rapidly with a purpose.

Dominic asked his father, "Who was that?"

Angelo answered, "A man asking about you and your racing."

Dominic thought nothing of it. Dominic sat and watched the races.

Moto's were posted and he was riding a quarter final and a semi qualifier. He had to finish in fourth place or better to qualify for the semi final. He had to finish fourth in both races. If he qualified for main event, he was guaranteed eighth place in the world for eleven year old experts.

Dominic made his way to the staging area. He sized up his competition and was amazed. He was the only rider with a triple digit number plate. All of the riders were amiable. There were no malice remarks and like him, they were all accompanied by a parent or a sponsor.

He made his way closer to the gate and his father applied the belt spray. He was in lane eight. This was the worst gate assignment. Dominic didn't make a dispute about it. He just thought to himself, *"I need to finish fourth or better."*

They all lined up and the cadence was called. The gate dropped and Dominic made his way out front. He was not clearly in the lead but he was in first by the first jump. He could not make his way to the inside because of the other riders. He made the decision to stay on the outside and make the turn and see what position he was in. He noticed as the turn approached he would be in first but way to the outside.

As they came around the turn he was leading on the outside, but there was another jump and another left handed ninety degree turn. He made the turn with no incident and was in second pulling his way in front of the first place rider but was cut off when making the long right handed turn.

Dominic could see that he was in a solid second place and basically laid back content for second place and qualify for the quarter final.

His father met him halfway. As he was walked up to his father he recognized Tony from Team Panther. He waved at Tony as Tony made his way over to him.

Dominic was shocked. Tony introduced himself to Dominic. He didn't need an introduction; he knew who he was already. Tony asked, "You look like you're on fire out there. How long have you been doing this?"

Dominic, still winded answered, "It's my first year Tony."

Tony replied, "Wow, nice job! Hey, after the quarters and semi's, stop by our pit area. There are a couple of people who want to meet you."

Dominic was beside himself and asked Tony, "Can I get your autograph?"

Tony smiled, "Stop by after your main and I'll give you my home phone number." Tony smiled and walked off.

Dominic finished first in his semi qualifier. He was able to pull away from the second place rider and he rode strong. It was time for the Main Event for the eleven year old experts. Like clockwork, Dominic was escorted by his father to the staging area and made his way to gate position six.

He made his way up to the starting gate and positioned himself for the gate start. Dominic was finally starting to feel the butterflies. This was it. He knew what he had to do. He positioned himself and noticed that some of the riders where standing on both pedals as he was only using one foot. He dismissed this for now and readied himself. The cadence was called and the gate dropped.

He was in the middle of a tight pack of riders. He pedaled as hard as he could. After the first jump he noticed he was in front but that drastic first turn was going to play havoc on his position. He positioned himself into the first turn and again, he was in second.

He was able to pedal a few cranks before the jump and make up some momentum. He and the first place rider were unable to distance themselves from the pack. They were a solid bunch making their way around the track.

Finally on the long curved right handed fourth turn Dominic inched his way in front. He squeezed the rider to the inside but gave him enough space to negotiate the turn. Just like his track and the pits by his house, if you hold the rider to the inside, he won't have the momentum to pedal, allowing the outside rider to make a run into the straightway.

Dominic was able to pedal a few more cranks before the last right hand turn. Dominic executed this to perfection. He could hear the crowd cheer louder as he took the lead. He was able to pull ahead of the second place rider and make the right handed turn to the finish with enough momentum to carry him to victory.

He could not believe it! He was the eleven year old World Champion and this was his first year racing! He bumped fists with all the other riders as he made his way to his father who was running towards him. He never felt such a bear hug in his life.

He was a real World Champion. He noticed all the riders had a bicycle manufacturer jersey and he was wearing his Power Shot BMX jersey and matching pants.

A few riders asked again, "Where are you from?"

Dominic, catching his breath said, "New Jersey."

Some riders patted his shoulders and some simply rode off. One of the riders who did not place in the top five threw his helmet on the ground in disgust.

Dominic was making his way back to the pit area to lock up his bicycle. He noticed the same man with whom he spoke earlier approach him with his hero Tony Scholls from Team Panther. The man walked up to Dominic shook his hand.

"Hello World Champion! My name is Reggie Stokes, CEO and President of Team Panther. I'm sure you remember Tony?"

Dominic, in shock answered, "You're Reggie Stokes, the man who sponsored this event?"

Reggie replied, "That would be me." Reggie looked at Tony and nodded his head and said, "Why don't you tell this young World Champion what we're doing here."

Tony handed Dominic a Team Panther Jersey and said, "This is for you."

Dominic, surprised said, "Thanks Tony. Did you sign it and put your phone number on it?"

They all laughed, Tony smiled and answered, "No, I didn't sign it, this is for you. As the team captain of Team Panther, we're offering you a Factory Sponsorship."

Dominic fell back onto his seat.

Reggie interjected, "Don't say yes right away. There are some conditions and strong commitments you need to agree to." Reggie continued, "Just a few things to consider. First thing I need is your report card. You're going to be on tour next year and gone from your family for about seven weeks. You can only race expert. That means when you turn twelve years old next week, you're going directly to the expert class, no novices. You're a factory rider and we only sponsor expert riders and pro riders. Also, you're going to have to ride one of our factory racing bikes. You're going to wear what gear we give you.

There are some other stipulations but this is for your parents and I to discuss. I'll be in New Jersey in three weeks; I'm going to meet with you and your parents to discuss the particulars. Oh, there is a contract you need to sign. Welcome to the Family."

Tony winked at him and gave him a piece of paper and whispered, "I'm home after 9 PM Pacific Time. Give me a shout."

Dominic opened it to discover Tony was a man of his word. On that paper was his home address and phone number.

Dominic made his way back to stands with his father and watched the rest of the races. As icing on the cake, Tony finished first in the Main Event and won the World Championship Pro Open. After the races ended they made their way back to the hotel room with an eight foot trophy.

Dominic looked at his father and asked, "How are we going to get this on the airplane in the morning?"

Angelo replied, "I don't know son but I'll pay whatever we need to get that trophy home."

As they entered the hotel, there was a representative from UPS in a booth assisting all the guests of the hotel with their shipping needs. This was common practice after any large event at the Arena. It all worked out. Dominic spoke with his family for a short time as to what his options were with Team Panther.

Angelo explained that he needed to speak with Reggie before any arrangements were accomplished or established. It was late and they had an early flight in the morning back to Philadelphia International Airport with their eleven year old expert World Champion.

Chapter 26

Nearly three weeks later, Reggie Stokes was celebrating his triumph and successful World Championship. All his and his staff's hard work successfully produced the World Championships and it was recognized by both racing organizations of this period. Reggie could now rest.

He completed all the post interviews including magazines, TV, and newspapers. Reggie was more victorious because his factory team won the World Championship. The formula was simple: all the factory teams submitted a specific number of riders and their places were tallied. Team Panther finished first.

Reggie called his manager Carl, Team Captain Tony, and the rest of his staff into his office. They discussed all the particulars of the event. After all the bills were paid, Team Panther audited the unreserved monies. Not only were they the World Champions, they were profitable.

Reggie was pleased and his calculations were in the amount of what he projected. Reggie spoke to his staff and thanked everyone for their untiring efforts enabling the success of this event. He spoke of next year's event and a national tour. He continued speaking about his new line of bicycles and racing gear.

Reggie adjourned the meeting and asked Tony and Carl to remain behind. The staff exited the office allowing Reggie to speak directly to Tony and Carl. He first turned his attention to Carl. He asked Carl if there was anything he would like to share about the event.

Carl basically shook his head and simply said, "For me it was fast paced but no complaints from my end."

Reggie asked Tony. Tony replied, "No Reggie, I had fun. I was more worried about racing. We had our pit area with beach chairs and Carl. I like having a mechanic to assist us. Other than that, to me it was fun."

Reggie smiled and asked Tony, "It's even more fun when you win, right?"

Tony laughed and shrugged his shoulders as to indicate his approval.

Reggie quickly got to the point, "We have to make some decisions. We need to let some riders go and we need to discuss our new prospective riders."

Reggie continued on this subject. He started, "We need to let some riders go for several reasons. One of our riders has not been racing as much as we agreed. He has not contacted us and didn't show up to the Worlds. He never called to explain. I would think as a factory rider he would contact his sponsor of his status. We have two other riders who have not progressed in their scholastic studies. We have given more than a fair warning and they have not progressed. I spoke to both individuals' parents some time ago and they have not progressed. We need to discuss some potential new riders. Let's discuss the riders we are losing. Have any of you spoken to them or have conversations?"

Both of them shook their heads no. Reggie further explained that he was going to call the parents this week and end their sponsorships. There were some interruptions by a phone call and some type of document signature. Finally Reggie returned to the conversation at hand.

He was adamant about sponsoring Dominic. He started with Tony, "Did you have any contact with Dominic?"

Tony laughed and replied, "Oh Yes."

Reggie looked at him and asked him to continue.

Tony continued, "He called me a few days after the race. He was star struck I think. He seemed giddy and nervous. We talked mostly about BMX but he also showed interest in sports. He was very polite with nice manners."

Reggie stated, "I have to go to New Jersey next week for some business regarding clothing and then to New York for more clothing such as gloves and shoes. I am going to meet with his family, is there anything I need to know?"

Tony and Carl looked at each other and shook their heads no. Reggie then discussed a female rider from Oklahoma who placed third place in her class. She was in first place and fell, got up and chased all the riders down placing third.

Tony interjected, "I had a chance to speak with her. She is one tough cookie. I like her as well. She is an honor student so you won't have to worry about school issues."

Reggie looked up on the air indicating a sign of relief.

Reggie picked up his phone and put it on his loud speaker. He dialed the phone and called Angelo at work. Angelo picked up the phone and Reggie began to speak, "Hello Angelo, Reggie Stokes here with Tony and Carl."

Angelo greeted them and Reggie continued, "I would like to talk to you about Dominic."

Angelo was very professional and made it a point that he could talk as long as Reggie needed. The conversation progressed as follows:

Reggie: "How is Dominic in school?"

Angelo: "He does well. Normally A's and B's."

Reggie: "Well as you know, we would like to offer him a factory sponsorship. I personally take our riders studies seriously."

Angelo (laughing): "Reggie, he won't need to worry about you if his grades diminish. He needs to worry about me and his mother."

Reggie: "Good, good, good. I don't want to always be the bad guy. We are very interested in him. We would like to bring him on with a full factory sponsorship. He will be coming out to the west coast and riding out here for nearly the entire summer. We will be driving out to New Jersey in this period. We can discuss all the details next week when I'm in town."

Angelo: "Sounds like a plan. Are you coming alone?"

Reggie: "I plan on it."

Angelo: "Dominic wants Tony to come. He wants to show off his practice track in the back of the house."

Reggie: "No, I'll be there on my own. I want to sit with him and explain the entire package I'm offering. I want him to hear it from my lips. I have a few stringent principles he needs to understand."

Angelo: "I agree it would be nice to see you. Let's try to set it up over dinner. My wife is a remarkable cook."

Reggie: "Food, sounds like a good plan. I'll call you in a few more days from now. I will be there next Tuesday. I will confirm what time or possibly Wednesday."

Angelo: "Sounds good Reggie. Thank you so much."

Reggie hung up the phone and looked at Tony and Carl, "Well we probably have a new rider. Carl let's get a bike together for this young World Champion. Tony, is there anything I or Carl need to know?"

Tony replied, "Let's get him the complete sealed bearing hubs and the skinnier wheels. He will need 170 Millimeter size cranks with 43X16 gears. He will need a sealed bottom bracket and three piece crank set.

He will also need the smaller handle bars and smaller goose neck that is lighter and let's not forget the center pull brakes for both front and rear brake set ups. Reggie, this bike is going with you correct?"

Reggie shook his head yes.

Chapter 27

It's nearing the end of January and the hour is drawing near. Reggie
Stokes arrives at Dominic's house. Dominic has completed his homework
and the smell of his mother's cooking is permeating the entire household.
The smell of fresh garlic and basil is overpowering in the fresh tomato and
cucumber salad.

The lasagna is cooked to perfection and there is an overabundance of
desert. It wasn't long before Angelo arrived home, slightly early, from
work. Within the next few minutes the doorbell rang and there stood the
statuesque figure of Reggie Stokes and another man in trail. Dominic was
beside himself in inordinate anticipation of the figure being Tony from
Team Panther. To his misperception it was Carl the Team Manager
accompanying Reggie Stokes.

Reggie walked in and was greeted by Dominic's entire family. Carl
walked in behind him and was received kindheartedly as well. Both made
their way into the Carlucci home. Reggie made it known of how he adored
the way the house was set back far into the woods and he admired the
privacy.

It was dark and he could just make out the neighborhood. Reggie was a
gentleman and made thoughtful remarks of how pleasant the house
smelled with the aroma of Maria's culinary masterpiece. Reggie was
impressed of how neat and clean the house looked.

It was not ultra modern by any standard but it rendered the sentiment of
tranquility and a sense of calm. Reggie appreciated the fact that the
Carlucci's were not putting on an act but simply being themselves. He
understood the extra preparation of food being prepared, but he felt a
presence of peace and relaxation.

Reggie and Carl spoke with the family in the den for nearly an hour. They spoke about the World Championships and how the team performed. There were various topics such as sports and how fans differed from East Coast and West Coast. Reggie discussed in general what he was doing on the East Coast, specifically in New York City with the new clothing line.

He was discussing how it was ready to be revealed. Finally Maria called everyone to the table and she presented the best Italian dish Reggie and Carl had ever seen or tasted. Reggie raved over the salad dressing that was home made. He praised the lasagna. Reggie, in his true form, was a gentleman and carried himself with a command presence. They all dined for nearly hour. Carl extolled the fact that he would never have a meal like this again.

There was wine, coffee, salad, fresh fruits, and other Italian delights. Reggie made it a point to extrapolate that he couldn't move after eating like this. He jokingly warned Dominic not to eat like this too much or he would be way too fat to race by the time he was fifteen. When they completed eating, Reggie took notice of how both boys assisted their mother by clearing the table. He said nothing but took notice of their discipline.

It wasn't long before the moment of truth was upon them. Reggie spoke to Angelo for nearly an hour at the kitchen table accompanied by Carl. Dominic and his brother were in the den watching TV and chatting alone. Finally Reggie and Carl entered the den with Dominic's parents. The TV was shut off and Reggie was sitting in the chair next to Dominic who was sitting on the edge of the couch.

Reggie began to speak: "Well Dom, you know why I made my way down here?"

Dominic shook his head yes.

Reggie smiled and continued, "It was for your mom's cooking. No, seriously we needed to have a discussion together. I'm going to talk to you as a young adult and all I want you to do is listen. Your father and I spoke in detail of what I want to offer you. So here it is in detail. You have a gift. You are a young and a talented athlete. You were blessed with a nice home, amazing parents and an ability that you don't know you possess. I came here to offer you a full factory sponsorship with Team Panther, the number one factory team in the world. We proved it a month ago when we won the World Championship as the number factory team. I want you to be a part of it. You see, normally I come into family homes to rescue certain kids. You have no idea of some of stories I could tell you. But fortunately, that is well behind us now. You are very fortunate."

Reggie smiled for a while looking at both Maria and Angelo. Reggie pulled out a document from his briefcase. Dominic noticed that it was very official looking and had his name on it in big letters.
Reggie looked at Dominic and continued, "OK Dom, here is what I am offering you. I am offering you a full factory sponsorship with the following conditions. As a factory team rider you are expected to race a full season in your state of residence. The only exception to this rule is this summer when you are racing at the national level. As a factory team, we like when our riders have a state number plate with their ranking on it. Moreover, we as a team like it more when you have a national number distinguishing you from the other riders on a national level. As for now, you are authorized to race the number one plate in New Jersey, but on a national level you are to race your sanctioning body number. You have not raced enough nationals to be nationally ranked, but that will come this summer. You can no longer race as a novice. You are to race as an expert rider and only as an expert rider. The only other class you are authorized to race is Professional. In time I trust. You will race with only our uniform. You are allowed to sew patches of sponsors you obtain throughout the season, not patches of products you adore, use or like. This is a true factory ride for you and if you are sewing on patches of products, it's because they use you as their endorsement. Any items placed on your uniform must be authorized by me before doing so. You may receive some patches from a Team Panther representative instructing you to sew this new patch on your uniform. We may send this to you in the mail. You may also have a local bike shop like Power Shot BMX on your uniform, but it must not be bigger than Team Panther. It must be at least one half the size of our lettering." Reggie could see that Dominic's head was ready to explode.

He continued to speak calmly and held himself at the highest professional level. Reggie smiled at Dominic and continued, "Relax Dominic, I'm almost done. It gets better trust me. You are expected to come out to California this summer and race on tour with Team Panther. It is nearly seven weeks and it entails the entire summer break from school. You will stay at my home and sometimes Tony's. He requested you stay with him and train. We will tour our way back to New Jersey and you will be back home and continue to tour ending in the state of Maine if you decide. You must maintain a B+ average in school. I just made three phone calls last week ending three sponsorships because of poor grades. It didn't bother me. They all had been warned. They chose not to make school important and it ended in their termination of a factory sponsor. I have no doubt that you will propel in your studies. I support higher learning and always give way to students and their scholastic achievements. You are going to keep yourself in a race conditioning program. As I can see you have an awesome practice track in your back yard. This summer the team is going to make a stop here at your home and use your track to practice. So keep it groomed and race ready. I'm sure your father has all the resources to assist you. Last but not least, you must ride one of our factory racing competition bikes." As Reggie said this, Carl rolled a brand new Team Panther bike into the den. Carl had made his way out during Reggie's discussion.

Team Panther's bicycle was top of the line. Dominic had a really nice bike but this one was special. Carl pointed out something more special about this bicycle. Carl looked at Reggie for approval to convey the special characteristics of his new bicycle, "Dom, you see these pads on your frame, handlebars and gooseneck? These were the pads Tony raced with last month when he won the pro open. He signed them and wanted you to have them. Tony wrote on them and it says, "From one champion to another, enjoy the ride" signed Tony Scholls. You have the same gears you had been using with all sealed bearings and the latest technology."

Dominic was speechless. So was his brother.

Joey piped up, "Dad, I want to race too." Laughter filled the room.

Reggie pulled out a mountain of paperwork and had Dominic sign them as a formality instilling the importance of making a promise. Dominic signed nearly twenty documents before he was done.

When complete Reggie asked, "What size shirt and pants are you?" Reggie explained that he was going to send a new team jersey, pants, gloves, and helmet along with some other goodies. They all talked for nearly an hour before Reggie made it known that he had a long ride ahead of him.

As he walked out of the house he yelled back, "Dom, I almost forgot, call Tony and give him the good news. He wants to hear from you."

They all waved goodbye and Dominic made a beeline to the telephone to call Tony. Before he got to the phone his brother asked, "Can I have your old bike?"

Dominic instantly replied, "No, only if you race."

Angelo kissed both his sons on the top of their heads and told them to get ready for bed. He allowed Dominic to call Tony and they talked for nearly twenty minutes. Dominic was still confused about what had just happened but he was delighted.

Chapter 28

Its early May in Texas. Rafael is gearing up for his BMX season. He turned twelve years old and He had been riding his new bicycle for the past few months with his friends at the gravel pit. He had grown slightly and increased in strength. He mastered his new bicycle. Rafael had become a riding machine compared to his friends. He was quick off the start and his center of balance allows him to pedal in specific areas of the track that his friends could not.

It was Saturday afternoon and the race season had begun. Rafael is racing his 125T series plate. Out of all the riders in Texas or in the league series, he finished number 125th in the entire state with all the points totaled with all the riders. Impressive considering it's his first year. Although Rafael is fast and technical, he has not mastered the starting gate. The weather was still not insufferable in the mid-afternoon. The sun was blistering and Rafael's family came to watch. Rafael was accompanied by his parents, sister and his older brother Juan. Carlos had to work and promised if he was done early he would drive directly to the track.

Rafael performed his usual ritual except this time he had a team with whom he could practice. His family set up their demi-camp site next to the team's location. There were many parents with who children were part of Mr. Hartle's team. Rafael was wearing his team jersey HBS BMX. This was a play on words. The name of the bicycle shop was Hartle's Bike Shop but the team name was Hartle's BMX and it was shortened to represent Hartle's Bicycle Moto Cross.

Nevertheless, Rafael was excited and ready to race. Many of his last years competitors were in his class. In the sanctioning body for this race he has to race 12 and 13 year old novices. He looked around to his astonishment; Pork belly was nowhere to be seen. There was a relief.

Rafael practiced for nearly an hour before taking a break and waiting for the moto's to be posted. It wasn't long and the announcement was made. All the riders made their way to the boards to check their positions and motos. There wasn't a vast turnout of racers but he still had to wait for moto twenty three.

There were a total of seven riders in his class. Rafael sat with his new team and parents quietly watching as the races started. As he was watching, he noticed his friends Tommy and Bobby showed up to watch. Rafael asked his father if he could give them a ride home with them. Maximo nodded yes not thinking of the tight squeeze in the car. They sat with his family as the day prolonged. Rafael enjoyed his friends being there and was getting eager to race. Finally he started making his way to the gate.

While in line at the staging area he was able to size up his competition. He could tell that his bike was nicer than most of the racers he was going to race against. There was one kid who was exceptionally tall. Rafael approached him as he was pushing his bike towards the starting gate and asked, "You're twelve years old?"

The kid looked at him and replied, "Are you a Mexican?" Rafael said nothing as he was instructed by his father; he shook his head in disbelief.

Rafael was moving forward and one of the riders whispered over to him, "He's kind of new, he thinks he is some type of superhero just because he is so tall. Good luck, I know you're fast. I saw you in practice. I hope you kick his butt."

Finally Rafael made his way to the gate. He pulled the chit for lane two. He was ready. The gate was not electric and still required two men to lift it, hold it and drop it. The cadence was called, "Pedals up wheels on the ground."

Bang, the gate dropped. Rafael did not pull the best start but this was his routine. He made his way off the gate and pedaled up and into the first jump propelling him into the lead. Once out front Rafael looked considerably smaller than the rest of the riders but he made up for it in his speed.

He was able to make it over the jumps with little or no hesitation. Once out front, Rafael was able to maintain his lead. He was pressured by the tall lanky kid. There were no questions; Rafael was going to win his races.

Rafael won all three motos and finished first overall for the day. All the riders in his moto were very amiable with Rafael. The tall kid rode off back to his spot on the track and said nothing to anyone. Rafael did not mention the incident to his father. He followed his father's advice and ignored what the kid said to him. It did not bother him.

Besides, he was right. Rafael was a Mexican. He laughed to himself as he thought of it. Likewise, he finished second to a short Mexican kid.

The day lingered on until the eighteen and older classes arrived at the gate. Rafael stood there studying their every move. It was as if he recorded the race in his mind and rewound it over one hundred times in his mind.

Rafael was motivated to become faster and better. After the race ended, there was another team meeting. The subject was practice. Once the school year ends, there was going to be practices on Wednesday nights. Rafael was excited about it. He could tell that his father did not have the same enthusiasm.

As everyone packed up, Maximo asked his family and Rafael's friends if they would like to go eat some Tacos. Florencia looked at Maximo with confusion. Maximo had the perfect remark for her penetrating stare.

He remarked, "Flor, it's a long day and I know you're tired. I appreciate you wanting to go straight home and start cooking. Let's just stop and get some tacos. You could use a break, it has been a long day. Besides, Raff's friends don't get to eat Mexican like us. You won't have to cook, clean, and deal with the mess."

Florencia looked at her husband and answered, "Why not my love. Honestly, I didn't want to cook anyway and tacos are cheap. Let's stop at Texas Taco Loco on the way home and eat in the back on the picnic tables."

Maximo kissed his wife on her head as he hugged her. Rafael and his siblings made the unmistaken ooooh sound. Maximo answered all of them at once, "You know why I kiss your mother, because we love each other. You kids are lucky to have parents who love you as much as we love each other. Now let's get to the car before I start kissing all of you." They all ran to the car making the 'yuck' sound and giggling.

As they sat eating tacos in the shade, Bobby asked, "Raf, how long did it take you to learn Spanish?"

Rafael laughed and answered, "It took me six months to learn to speak English. I came here with my family when I was young and only spoke Spanish. It wasn't hard but it still took me nearly a year to speak correctly."

Bobby laughed and replied, "Maybe you can teach me to speak Spanish one day."

Maximo laughed and replied, "Come by tomorrow and I'll teach you."

Everyone laughed as Maximo spoke. He had a strong accent but he spoke correctly. They all sat around the table chatting about various subjects.

Finally Tommy asked, "Mr. Santos, what do you do for a living?"

Maximo answered, "I fix air conditioning and heating on the military base. I also do other small repairs when asked. I have been there for a few years."

Tommy asked, "Could you fix our air conditioner at home? It broke last year and I live alone with my mother."

Maximo answered, "When I drop you off at home I will come inside and check it for you."

Altogether they nearly ate thirty tacos. Maximo drove his family home. He spoke with Florencia, "Do you mind if I go and take a look at Tommy's air-conditioner? It is starting to get hot and I feel bad for him if what he is saying is true."

Florencia replied, "Sure honey, you're doing a nice thing for him."

Maximo dropped off Bobby first and then he went inside with Tommy and Rafael. Maximo made his way into the small two bedroom apartment. He brought a small tool bag with him. Tommy introduced Maximo to his mother and explained that he was going to take a look at the air-conditioner.

She looked at Maximo and stated, "My landlord refuses to fix it. I don't have any money to pay you."

Maximo looked at her, "You don't need to pay me. Our kids are friends. Let me see what you have first."

Maximo took off the cover of air conditioner in Tommy's living room and immediately saw the problem. He walked out to the car and came back with a bottle and hoses and some type of round thing with a wire on it. He changed something and ran the air conditioner. He charged it up and it worked perfectly. She was very appreciative and offered to pay him when she could.

He looked at her and said, "It's my good deed for the day. God bless you."

On the way home Rafael asked his father, "Why did you go out of your way to help them? You didn't know them."

Maximo answered, "Raffy, this boy Tommy. He has no father in his life correct?"

Rafael shook his yes and said, "His father is gone and never calls. He doesn't say much about it and I don't ask."

Maximo continued as he drove, "This young man has no concept of a father figure. He appears to be a nice boy and he treats you kindly. I wanted to repay him with an act of kindness. I am guessing his mother works hard for very little money. I understand this concept too well. This is what I was doing before moving to America and educated myself with a trade. I am using my trade to enact kindness and feed our family. God teaches us grace is a gift undeserved. I gave her a fraction of my potential as a gift. God will repay me ten times over. I have faith in this concept. Besides, I want Tommy to see someone doing something nice for him and his mother. I am no saint or guardian angel, instead I was blessed with a gift and I wanted to share it. You have a gift. I'm not talking about racing your bicycle. One day you will figure out what it is and I want you to share it as I just did. There is nothing wrong with showing kindness to someone. I don't expect anything in return. If I did, this wouldn't be grace. I would be better off asking her for money. Son, remember, when you find your gift share it with the world. You'll feel better about yourself and you'll find the lost faith in humanity."

Chapter 29

Reggie made his way from his car towards the office. He was greeted by Tony who was on his way into the building. Reggie was caught by surprise. Keeping his composure, he invited Tony into his office as he walked into the building complex towards the elevator.

Reggie extended his morning salutations to his staff and made his way into his office. Reggie was feeling anxious for Tony's surprise visit. As they both entered the office, Reggie asked, "Tony, I have all day for you. What's wrong? Are you OK? What is it that you made your way here this morning?"

Tony replied, "I just wanted to talk about the upcoming season. I have been doing a lot of thinking and I need your feedback."

Reggie explained that he was always going to be there for Tony and he wanted to have this conversation. Tony asked Reggie about the tour dates and what details he was willing to share.

Reggie replied in detail, "Ok Tony here is the agenda. I want you do understand a few things as we progress from this point further. I might own the team name. Understand this Tony; this is your team also. You're the leader of all these young men and possible new young lady. I trust one hundred percent in your decisions and vision for Team Panther. We are the number one World Factory BMX Team. Like any other business man, I want to capitalize on the name we collectively build four ourselves. I simply applied the tools; you and the rest of the team are the instruments. Tony, you are the glue that holds this team together. People respect you and want to emulate you and the funny thing is they don't know you personally. If they knew you, they would love you. I know I do. You're the veracity of all athletes. Let me explain. Nobody walked up to you and gave you anything. You overcame certain obstacles but nothing unbearable.

You didn't grow up in a horrible home beaten everyday by your drug addicted parents. Just the opposite is true. You had a nurturing family with a remarkable hardworking mother who loved and cared for you and your brothers dearly. You took on a sport that was unpopular in your community and brand new. You overcame the adversity of getting to tracks, finding rides and gaining respect. Look at you now. You're eighteen years old and you're a World Champion. I want to grow this product line and I want you to be a part of it. I need to know what the youth is thinking. What are the changes and how do we keep up with change."

Tony gasped for air after Reggie was done speaking. He looked at Reggie smiling, "I just wanted to talk about the summer events. You have me like, Whoa!"

Reggie quickly responded, "Good, I'm not done yet. Here is the first bit of good news I have not shared with the staff or team. Nor, do you ever say anything of it. I am looking at another World Championship in the same venue at the end of this year. Also, next summer, possibly Japan. Japan is still in the works but we need to start now. I am looking at bids on a new factory bicycle frames. This time they are going to be made out of aluminum. All this is subjective but we need to crush this season's races in order to be successful. You see, nothing is done on a whim in business. We need to plan, organize and set up goals and achieve these goals in order to be successful. We can make simple changes instantly but long term planning is crucial. We can tweak things along the way, but overall we need a good solid game plan that fits our business model. Our team is our model. It enables us all to change with the times and be relevant."

Tony listened and hung on to every word Reggie said. He was getting a lesson on real business issues. He was now starting to understand how his BMX future was being financed. Tony was deductively connecting the dots per say. With no company, there is no sponsor, no tours, nothing.

This is the reality of any business. But no business is going to pay him a salary to work out, race and be productive. Tony had concerns about what happened as he aged and his racing career ends. He asked Reggie about this circumstance.

Reggie shook his head in disbelief and answered, "Tony, you have at least fifteen competitive years of racing left. Let me ease your mind. If you suddenly woke up this morning and couldn't ride a bike, you would still have a job. As long as Panther is here and making money, so will you. For now, I need you to be the champion that you are. Not for Team Panther, but for Tony Sholls. I want you to feel good about what you're doing or your life will be miserable. Let me ask you Tony, when you were practicing every day before the world championships, did you like it? I know you probably felt tired and pain at times. But it was a goal that secured your success. Right now, we are back in training mode as a company. What we do now enables us to be the champion of this sport. In other words, what is it that we can sell and be profitable? What is our next product? As a company we need to secure finances and produce a product that the public desires. We stand on quality and performance."

Reggie continued, "We need to be the best all the time. I know technology will change and so will we. In the years to come, you are going to be that person who steers this ship towards success. With success come rewards. This is why I'm personally grooming you. I am making a long term investment in you. I want the public to know the Tony Sholls I know. For now, you race and be that champion. Take advantage of your youth and live it in its entirety. Later in life, you will be successful. I will not let you fail. If you fail, we all fail. This is Team Panther, not Team Reggie. Young man, you're going to be revered. You're going to be successful and financially secure. I hope I eased your heart of any concerns."

Tony felt relieve. He felt as if a load of bricks had just been lifted off his chest. He finally understood the faith and friendship Reggie whole-heartedly poured out to him. He looked across the desk and asked Reggie, "Can we talk about our new recruits?"

Reggie, "Sure who do you want to talk about first?"

Tony said, "Let's talk about the young lady you want to sponsor."

Reggie quickly responded, "I don't think this is going to happen for several reasons but let me give you the big ones. First thing is that her parents are not very receptive to letting their daughter go cross country alone. Moreover, compound this notion of her being alone with a dozen guys in an RV all day and night for a month. I understand how they feel. Secondly, I have a sense that she was offered a sponsorship with another team. Not positive but she has not returned my calls. Kind of strange."

Tony shook his head to indicate his approval of Reggie's concerns.

Tony asked, "Since we are on this subject, what about Dom in New Jersey?"

Reggie's eyes lifted up and looked directly at Tony, "Are you kidding me? What a quality family and polite young man. He is more excited about Team Panther than I was. I sent him a complete uniform a couple of months ago and he is ecstatic. He has been racing all the practices and locals in New Jersey. His school threw him a surprise party.

Reggie continued, "When he showed up to school after the Christmas break, the principal had arranged a back to school seminar which was nothing more than surprise to announce to the entire school that Dom was the 11 Expert World BMX Champion. Imagine how that young man feels. He is popular, his picture is in the newspaper and he was well received by his peers. He is coming this summer and some of it is being spent with you Tony."

Tony sarcastically, "Great!"

Reggie laughed, "You're his hero Tony. Take this young man under your wing and mold him."

Tony thought about it and answered, "He is a nice kid. Besides he invited me to his house already."

Reggie chuckling, "If they offer you dinner, don't say no and don't eat three days before go. The food was out of this world. His mother is the best Italian cook. Spectacular cuisine."

Tony asked, "When are we all getting together for the tour?"

Reggie pulled out a map and a calendar and showed Tony visually what to expect. Reggie pulled out markers, "Tony, we are going to go with a ten man roster this season if all our riders have a good report card. I suspect no issues but you know how that goes. We are going to make our presence in Van Nuys and Corona CA. as a team before we make our way across the states. We are going to follow the national schedules of the NBL and the NBA. We are going to cross all the way like last year except we have more resources and support than last year.

Reggie leaned closer to the maps, "We also have the finances to support our cross country venture. We fixed up our RV and had the air conditioner serviced. You guys won't die this time. Also, I scheduled many seminars and product lines to promote. You also have a job as the team leader to champion our brand and make the public want it."

Tony interjected, "Van Nuys is a fast track, and this will be a good test for our new rider. I want to call him and surprise him. I know how he feels. You said I was his favorite, the more I think about it, you're right. I want to influence this kid as you did for me. I will make him faster and give him all the knowledge you gave me about being a champion. He won't be my assignment, he will be my friend. I look forward to hanging out with this kid, but I will need time for me. What I mean is, I am seven years older than him"

Reggie answered, "Of course Tony. I need it from this place sometimes as well."

Some time had passed during their discussion. Tony thanked Reggie for his time and made his way to the door.

Reggie yelled out, "Where are you going?"

Tony, "To the plant. I am scheduled to work."

Reggie answered, "Wait up, I'll go with you. I want see what they're up to anyway. They're probably wondering why you're so late. Plus I know you want a ride and lunch."

Chapter 30

I wake up at 10 AM Frankfurt Germany time. I look at my clock and stop myself. There is a 6 hour time difference from the East Coast.

Later that evening, I pick up my cell phone and call my angel. I use my cell phone because I have international calling and it's free. Free is good.

My wife picks up the phone and says, "Hello sweetheart."

Although we have been married for many years, I still love the terms of endearment she uses. I asked her how her day was and what her plans are for the afternoon. She laughed and replied, "Its already afternoon here." She told me that she and her mother have a day planned with the kids. They planned on going to the mall then the local fair down the street.

I listened to her talk about the nights events. When she was done I told her I would be in very late, possibly early morning. She understood my job and how the airplanes are susceptible to delays due to weather, mechanic issues and etc...

We talked a short while before I hung up. We conveyed our love to each other as she blew me a kiss on the phone. My plane departs at 6 PM and it's a seven hour flight plus the time difference. It was going to be a long day. I figured I would eat breakfast, try to take a nap and finally make my way downstairs for my flight and meet up with the rest of my co-workers.

As I sat and ate my breakfast, my mind started to wander back to my BMX days. There were many fond memories. There was none better than my first trip on the airplane on my way to California to meet up with Reggie and the rest of the team.

I remember boarding an Eastern Airlines L1011. It was too big to fly in my thoughts. It was like a city block long and about ten seats wide with two isles. It was just an enormous airplane. I thought to myself, how cool would it be to fly one of these? It is surreal. These things are too big to fly. It's not possible, but they get off the ground. I was always astonished about how airplanes flew and how they stayed up in the air. I recall myself asking these tasking questions.

I remember flying nearly five and half hours direct from Philadelphia Airport to Los Angeles Airport. I landed in Los Angeles and was immediately met at the gate area by Carl. He was very professional and offered me lunch.

I almost forgot about the three hour time difference. We made our way to the car and we were off to meet up with Reggie. I recall all the sights. I compared them to what I have seen on TV.

I asked Carl, "When do we get to see all the TV stars?"

He laughed at me and told me that they are everywhere and keep looking, I'll see them. I had no idea what I was doing, but there I was looking for unknown stars.

I remember driving for nearly an hour before we made our way into Reggie's office. I was suspecting an extravagant office with bicycles everywhere, with riders in and out of the office talking about BMX, living and breathing BMX.

I expected to see pictures of bicycles and products everywhere. I was looking to people questioning Reggie about the team with graphs and charts of strategies of how to win the next championship race. Instead, I walked into a professional business complex surrounded by palm trees and shiny cars. The offices where all glass and filled with men and women wearing business suits.

I recall walking into Reggie's office, he looked up at me from his desk and yelled over to me, "There he is!"

He introduced me to his staff that was working in the office. Men and women dressed accordingly. He introduced me as the eleven year old World Champion but now twelve years old as he laughed.

It felt good. I remember that feeling. It never went away. I still feel it inside of me at times. I only pray my children could feel this sense of gratification. I recall Reggie sitting at his desk with his short sleeve shirt with the Team Panther Logo on the upper left hand side of his shoulder with the oversized collar.

It was 1980. I was overcome by all the attention I was receiving. Reggie made me feel like I was a movie star. It was like I had just won an Oscar. Truth be told, in Reggie's eyes, I did.

He paraded me around the office introducing me to friends outside the office of Team Panther. There were several other companies in the office complex not just BMX. I was surprised at first, but the novelty quickly faded. He brought me into his office and sat me down and started asking me questions. I felt welcomed and nervous at the same time.

After a few hours watching Reggie work he asked me, "Do you want to go to the factory to see how our bikes are made?"

I quickly answered, "Yes, Yes, Yes."

He made his way around the desk grabbing his briefcase and belongings. He said good bye to the office staff. He and I were alone on our journey to the BMX factory. Again, I remember being shocked when arriving at the factory. I was about the size of my father's plant but there was only one building.

There was no big factory puffing smoke and no BMX track or kids handing out riding their bikes. Simply, we walked into a very nice office area with several offices and a waiting area. We walked down a hallway and Reggie opened the door revealing what resembled a machine shop.

There were people bending pipes in a machine and another man welding tubes together. There were a couple of ladies putting stickers on the bicycles and Tony Scholls packing the boxes. It was a factory but cleaner. Again, my mind was blustered.

I fully remember every aspect of the factory to this day. I quickly understood my role as a team member. I remember the talks my father had with me as a young man. I completely understood my father's and Reggie's loyalty to the workers.

It was me racing and representing Reggie's brand that made others want to emulate our team that enabled the sales of the bicycles creating jobs. I, for the first time, understood my father when he stringently enforced loyalty to his customers and his staff.

For the first time in my life, Reggie showed me what my father had talked about for years. I never really understood him until I saw it with my own eyes as an outsider. It's like the old saying, "Tell me I hear you, show me I understand."

Everything my father told me at my young age started coming to fruition. I remember growing up all of a sudden at my young age. I felt as if I was hit with a ton of bricks and set me back in my stance. I get it. I finally get it. I've been in California for only three hours and got hit with reality check.

I was so proud of my father after witnessing the Team Panther plant. This experience made me instantly recognize how wonderful my father was as a human and a man people respected. I started to understand why he had a loyal workforce and why he made them feel important.

Tony came over and greeted me for the first time. This was the first of many greetings we would have in our lifetime. He looked jacked, as if he pumped iron all day. My first thought was that of my father's plant. Men working all day with bricks made them muscular.

But I think back and knew it was from his rigorous training he instilled on himself when the work was done. He asked me if I was ready for the, "big push?" I looked at him not knowing what any of it meant.

I didn't want to appear unhip to his vernacular and replied, "Absolutely, let's do this."

I had no idea what he was talking about. But he patted me on the shoulder and winked at me. I felt like a million dollars. Reggie prodded me along and we made our way back to the car. We were headed to his house.

As I lay in my hotel room bed thinking of my first encounter with Reggie in California, I couldn't help but think of all the positive aspects of my life from this one day out of my life. It is one of those things that do not go away. I remember it as if it were yesterday. I laughed to myself and drifted off to sleep recalling the fondest memories of my childhood.

Chapter 31

Its mid-June and Dominic is ready for his adventure to California. School is out, the weather is pleasing and BMX season is in full swing in California. Tomorrow is the big day for Dominic. Although he is excited about his trip, the anxiety of being separated from his family is sitting heavy in the pit of his stomach.

He packed his bags several times, ensuring he did not miss a thing. His bicycle was packed securely in a shipping box he obtained from Power Shot BMX. He had enough clothes for two weeks before he had to do laundry.

Experiencing an unsettling feeling about his trip the next day, he noticed his mother sitting alone in her chair in the living room slightly weeping.

He approached his mother and asked, "What's a matter mom?"

She looked at him and answered, "I'm going to miss you son. Please take care of yourself and make the right decisions. This is an opportunity of a lifetime and I don't want you to miss a thing. Take full advantage of what this trip has to offer. Promise me you'll do that. You're my oldest son and I will miss you for the next seven weeks."

Dominic hugged his mother and answered her, "mom, don't worry about me. I'll be fine. I promise to make you and Dad proud."

She smiled and answered with a slight tremble from her sobbing, "I'm already proud. Always have been."

The night came and went in an instant. Dominic awoke to the smell of breakfast. He jumped out of bed and made his way to the kitchen. He ate breakfast with his father and mother discussing the day's events before leaving for California. They ate together joking about Joey missing breakfast as he slept.

Angelo looked at Dominic and said, "Well, it's that time. Let's get the truck loaded and ready to leave."

Dominic gathered his belongings and started on his way to the truck with his two suit cases with Angelo carrying his bicycle. They eventually got to the truck together after his farewells with his mother. She watched as her son and husband climbed their way into the truck. You could tell she felt saddened that her oldest son was leaving for the next seven weeks. She waved goodbye from the window as Dominic and his dad departed.

Dominic and Angelo arrived at the airport at 10:30 AM for a 12:05 PM flight. They parked the truck in short-term parking, and walked to the ticket counter.

Angelo presented the ticket to the Gate Agent and she handed the ticket back to him and said, "You're all set. He is in seat 20A. It's a window seat. He will be traveling as an adult. Go to security upstairs and go to gate B-15."

They did as she instructed, and sat at the gate awaiting the airplane's arrival. Angelo looked at Dominic and said, "We need to have a talk son. A mature talk. A man to man talk. I don't want to scare you, but I feel we should have a discussion."

Dominic looked at his father, "Ok Dad, what do you want to talk about?"

Angelo answered, "Don't say anything I just want you to listen." You have been given a gift beyond comprehension. One day you're going to look back at this day and it will forever captivate you. This is a one in a million opportunity for you. Relish it, embrace this moment, never forget the feeling you are experiencing right now. Remember this instant in time.”

Angelo continued, “You about to embark on a journey many people consider an adventure. I want you to go to California and enjoy the moment. I know you’re going to race and make your way across the country with a passionate group of talented riders like yourself. You might not win every race, but you and I know you won’t give up. You understand that you’re going to be racing kids your age and one year older. Don’t get upset if you lose. Don’t over-celebrate when you win. Enjoy the moment just the same. Win or lose, just give a hundred percent. Reggie is not going to care if you lose if he knows you are giving one hundred percent. Understand, he wants you to win, but all champions lose sometimes. I am not expecting you to win every race. I want you to give your all and not give up. Stay healthy and be yourself.”

Dominic sat for a few moments taking in what his father said and finally answered his father, “I know it’s going to be different in California and the riders are faster, but I want to win as much as possible. I want to be the one to beat.”

Angelo smiled, “I know son, but remember, you’re already known for your win in Indy. Everyone will know who you are. Reggie will make sure of it. Here is one thing I want you to take with you and remember while you’re gone. At first, people will judge you on the track. Be personable, talk with people and get to know them as they approach you. Champions are produced on the BMX track; legacies are made in person. A champion will be remembered for his achievements; a legend will be remembered by how they acted after the fanfare. No matter what you do, have fun, enjoy the moment, make new friends, show respect, and be a champion off the track. You’ll be remembered more by how you act. Your actions are not a statistic but a quality. Go out there and tear up this circuit. Do it with class. I know you have it. If you feel mad about something or if you feel like you’re cheated, act accordingly. Act with respect. I know that you’re a nice kid. You have a compassionate heart. Do everything in moderation. Show people your true side. Go out on the track and vent. Again son, Class. Everyone cherishes a champion who has class."

Dominic was excited about his father taking the time to share with him. He finally began to understand all the life lessons his father had given him over the years. Dominic was curious of why his father was having this talk.

He asked his father, "Dad, why this intense conversation about the way I will act? Do I act correctly?"

Angelo answered with a slight laugh, "You do son, but what if? Let me give you an example. What if you pass someone and they purposely kick your tire and make you fall. You come in last place in that moto. I know you're going to be upset. It's how you act at that point that the world will recognize you by your actions. If you get up finish the race and punch the kid in the face afterwards, what would people say? How will that affect your racing every time you're matched in a moto with those riders? Or after you get up, you brush yourself off and simply ride through the finish line and back to your team. People will see that you're not an aggressor. This is the act of a true champion. Next moto get far enough in front of him so he can't touch you. People notice these small things. When they add them all up, what do you have? A champion! The people will know by your actions what it is to be a champion. Plus, Reggie will not let you falter. I'm pretty sure about it."

"Dad, what about girls," Dominic asked.

Angelo nearly spit his coffee out of his mouth. He answered, "Son, don't fall in love already. You're too young. You have a lifetime ahead of you for this. Why are you worried about girls?"

Dominic quickly replied, "I like girls."

Angelo smiled, "Well that's good; remember the respect part we just discussed?"

Dominic shook his head. Angelo continued, "Good. Show them respect and you'll never go wrong."

Dominic blurted, "So treat them like you treat mom?"

Angelo was shocked as he answered, "I would say yes. But remember, I'm married to your mother."

They both laughed. It was at this point that Angelo realized that his baby boy was developing into a man and like many kids his age, he was curious.

The plane had long arrived and the gate agent started making the pre-boarding announcements. They talked for a while longer before Dominic's row was called and made his way to the podium.

Angelo called out to Dominic, "Here son." He handed Dominic $200.00 dollars. He said, "Don't spend it all at once. Use it on tour and buy things you need and not want."

Dominic was excited and promised to be responsible. Dominic made his way down the jet-bridge as his father sat a quietly and waited for his airplane to push off the gate.

Long after Dominic's plane departed and took off, Angelo sat in the airport seat pondering over his conversation with his son. He asked himself if his son would be okay. He contemplated how Dominic would find his new endeavor. He sat there just thinking. Finally, he jumped up and made his way to the pay phone to call his wife. They talked for a few minutes and Angelo made his way back to the truck before leaving for the plant.

Chapter 32

Reggie pulls into his driveway with young Dominic by his side. Dominic is in awe of the size of Reggie's house. It was like a mini fortress. It had an electric gate opened by a pass-code Reggie punched in like a phone keypad.

They made their way down the long driveway to an open area nicely landscaped and manicured. As they rounded the bend into the front of the house, Dominic could see the Team Panther RV with the trailer sitting next to it. Both the RV and the Trailer were both opened. It looked as if someone was working inside of both of them.

Reggie parked directly next to the trailer but far enough away to ensure his new Jaguar would not be scratched. As both Reggie and Dominic emerged from the car, another tall figure appeared from the trailer.

Reggie yelled over to him, "Hey, how we making out?"

The figure answered, "All set boss. Spare tires are in place. Generators are tuned up and the engine oil is changed. I just picked up some other goodies from Camper World about two hours ago. Air Conditioning seems to be acting funny, but it's cold inside the Puma Palace."

Reggie gave him the thumbs up and entered his front door. Dominic asked, "What is the Puma Palace?"

Reggie looked at him with a delicate laugh as he answered, "A Puma is smaller than a Panther, and we call the RV the Puma Palace because the team wants me to buy a bigger RV so they can call it the Panther Palace. I know their M.O. Tony was joking about the size of the RV compared to the size of the some of the more established teams and he made the reference to the RV as a Puma Palace and it stuck."

Reggie walked into his home and yelled out, "Family! I'm home!"

His wife and four kids made their way from all areas of the home. He had a two story home with about six bedrooms and bathrooms. They all hugged him and Dominic felt as if he was home. He saw the love they had for Reggie. It was nearly the same thing in his home. He introduced Dominic to his family.

"Family, this is Dominic from New Jersey. Dom, my family. You won't remember all the names but you will as we get on the tour this week. My wife is going to meet up with us later this month in about three weeks in Texas."

He introduced his children. Dominic found it easy to remember Reggie's wife's name and simply called her Mrs. Stokes. His oldest son was in his early twenties and would be one of the drivers. He remembered his name, it was easy. His cousin had the same nick name; they simply called him "G." Dominic thought it was funny that he traveled all the way across country to find someone else called "G." His cousin's real name was Geovanni and Reggie's son was George.

Reggie yelled out from the garage, "Come on Jay, food is ready."

Reggie's son was grilling and had dinner ready for him as he arrived.

Dominic asked, "Reggie, our drivers are going to be G and Jay?"

Reggie laughed out loud along with his family. He answered, "I guess so. Maybe we should call Carl 'C' when he is driving. You know what Dom, that's his name only when driving. It's his alternative alter ego when behind the wheel."

Everyone laughed and continued on eating. Reggie reminded everyone that they had an early day tomorrow. The rest of the team is flying in and Tony set up gate practice for the entire team at the local track.

Dominic asked, "Is it OK if I call home and tell them I'm OK?"

Reggie answered, "Of course Dom. I called your father the minute you arrived. Carl called me from the airport and said your plane arrived. I figure if you were not on the plane I would have a lot of explaining to do."

Dominic was relieved. He called home and let his family know how he was doing and how he loved the California weather. He told them that Reggie had a pool in his back yard and he was going swimming as he winked at Reggie.

It is 6 AM California time and Dominic lay in bed wide awake. He could hear the pattering of feet in the kitchen. He arose and made his way to the kitchen. A women dressed in a maid uniform was startled at his presence.

Dominic said, "Hello my name is Dominic."

She looked at him with a blank stare in her face and replied, "Hola."

Dominic was confused and made his way to the hallway bathroom. As he made his way out, he noticed Reggie sitting at the counter drinking coffee and reading the paper.

Reggie looked over at Dominic, "I know it's like 9 AM for you Dom. Have some orange juice and a bagel. You're gonna need some strength today. Tony is going to work you guys for the next three days."

Dominic laughed and sat quietly admiring the day. It was nearly 7 AM and Reggie was dressed and outside with Jay in the RV.

Dominic asked, "Need any help?"

Jay answered, "Sure son, come on."

Dominic helped Jay store all the gear and guided him back to the trailer and lowered it on to the hitch as if he was with his father at the plant.

It wasn't long before Carl showed up with the rest of the team with Tony driving another car. There were a total of ten racers and Reggie's small staff. Reggie greeted all the racers and asked them to make their way into the house and get changed as Tony and Jay loaded the bicycles and the rest of the gear.

In no time, the bicycles were loaded and all of the riders were lined up facing the RV side door entrance. Reggie came out of the RV and made the following speech.

"Hello everyone. For some of you, this is not new. For the rest of you, we need to have this talk. My number one rule is this. Respect one another. You will be assigned an area of the Puma Palace and it is your responsibility to ensure your chores are completed with no excuses. The next and final rule, be considerate. Some of you will nap while we make the tour, others will be wide awake, and some of you might be full of energy. Remember our drivers. If they need anything while behind the wheel, we all make it happen. If a driver is taking a nap in the back, leave them alone. It's going to be a long journey at times and it might be boring for some of you. Respect each other. Let's make this fun. Enjoy the views as we head out. Look out the window and enjoy you country."

Tony then stood in front of everyone. He started his discourse, "There is one rule all of you need to hear and we as a team take it very serious. The first person to use the bathroom is responsible for cleaning it. The only exceptions are the drivers and Reggie. This includes me, whoever uses it cleans it. I am the inspector. It will be clean, tidy and smelling good. All the cleaning products are under the sink area and you will use them. If you don't want to clean it, you'll wish you did. Does anybody have a problem with this rule?"

There was an eerie silence. Tony continued, "It's a long journey and we will keep ourselves and our Puma Palace clean. Trust me guys; there is no room for grunginess on the road. We will make a few camp-overs and we will cherish the Puma Palace when we need to use the can."

After the speech, the assignments were established. They were handed out one by one. Some people were given floors to sweep and mop every day. Others were given windshield cleaning duties every day. Dominic heard his name called. He was given trash duty. Every stop they made, Dominic would gather all the trash and throw it away or change the bags as needed.

When camping, he was responsible for throwing all the trash away. He had a helper if needed, but he was the trash king. There were only three trash containers in the RV. Trash containers were up front with the drivers, another in the back by the table and the other in the bathroom. Dominic felt as if he got off lucky. He had no grass to cut or dishes to wash or clothes to put away.

Everyone made their way into the RV. For now there was a pseudo spot taken by everyone, but no rights to the specific territory. Dominic knew as time passed, people would find a spot and make it their home. The team was in route to the track that was only ten minutes from Reggie's home.

As they arrived, Carl was already there with buckets of water and some track officials. The team gathered at the trailer to claim their bicycles as G handed them out cautiously. The team was dressed and ready to race minus their helmets.

The two track officials came over to welcome everyone and explained they were only there to operate the gate and that Tony was in charge. With that said, Tony ordered the team to the starting area and the team was grouped into four groups. Everyone geared up and everyone was practicing their gate starts.

Tony made it a point to iterate the importance of the gate starts. Dominic pushed his bicycle to the starting gate. He was paired with 14 and 16 year old riders. The gate dropped and they raced to the first turn before shutting down and returning to the gate. Dominic was not used to being last out of the gate. He made several gate starts before Tony critiqued his starts.

Tony approached Dominic on the gate. Dominic was nervous. He thought to himself, what if he was going to have to race Tony, the World's fastest BMXer off the gate.

Tony looked at Dominic and said the following, "Dom, first things first. You need to start with both of your feet on the pedals. Forget everything you know about starting. I'm gonna show you how I start and I want you to learn it. This is going to be the future of BMX starts. You're one of two riders on the team who use the old traditional one foot start. Watch what I do."

Tony got on both pedals and worked with Dominic for nearly twenty minutes before he was able to balance himself.

Tony continued, "Now I want you to anticipate the cadence. Think of it as a count. You have to time the snap. You're gonna snap back and pump forward pulling your bike towards you as you launch off the gate. I want you to do this every start from here on out. Don't race into the first turn. After ten feet, turn around and come back."

Dominic made nearly thirty starts before he finally got his timing nearly perfect. His snap off the gate was clean and he could feel the second pedal come around more quickly. He knew he was getting it.

Tony approached Dominic after working with some other riders. "Ok Dom, step two. When you come out of the gate, don't rock back and forth. You're losing momentum. Keep pushing forward not back and forth. The more you push forward the more ground you cover. The more ground you cover, the more you move in front of the other riders. Just remember, snap out push forward. You see this horn; every time you rock back and forth I'm going to blow the horn to remind you."

Dominic made several starts and he did as Tony instructed. Tony blew the horn a couple of times, but Dominic quickly adapted his starts.

Finally Tony called Dominic back over, "Get back in your group and stay with them. Race into the first turn as normal. I think you got it."

Dominic did as instructed. Right away he could see the difference. He was not beating the other two riders; they were older, stronger and faster. But he noticed that he was much closer and he felt more comfortable about his starts. He would be the first one in New Jersey to use the new two pedal starts.

The team continued to practice their starts for the rest of the day. As the sun started to set and the team was well fatigued, Tony called the team over, "Were going to race half-track sprints. After the second turn coast it out. Make your way back to the starting point. I only want to see how some of you negotiate the rollers (a type of round jump) and the table top (longer jump).

Dominic made his way up to the start gate. As instructed he pumped off the gate and made his way through the first turn. Like before, he was in third place behind the older riders. He rolled over the first jump nearly the same as the other riders. Racing towards the second turn, he was able to stay close to the ground on the table top pumping down the back side gathering more momentum. He was able to pedal a few turns before entering the second turn. As he finished, he could see Tony clapping at him.

Tony shouted, "Yes Dom, Yes Dom. That's how you pump it out. That was perfect. Remember Dom, the jumps are just obstacles in your way. You own them. They don't slow you down. Pedal when you can." He looked at the other two riders, "You guys are lucky. He was gaining. I know he won't beat you but he has the jumping skills." They high fived Dominic and Tony called it a day.

As they arrived at the RV, Carl was cooking burgers and hot dogs for the team. They were all exhausted.

Tony yelled out, "Chores!"

The seasoned riders with the team knew exactly what this meant. They jumped up and started grabbing bikes since it was their chore. Dominic looked at Tony.

Tony gabbed, "Get the trash Dom. Chores Dom, Chores."

Dominic laughed and started gathering all the trash and dispersing it into the large green can near the RV. Dominic made sure every bit of trash was thrown away including any articles on the ground. Everyone had something to do. It was a rat race at first but he knew it would get better. This was too fun and Dominic enjoyed the camaraderie with his teammates.

Tony addressed the team before they got into the RV. Tony exclaimed, "Remember, respect. I know you're tired. Tomorrow is another day. Tomorrow's activities, gate starts, jumps and executing passing techniques with Phil and I. Friday night, we race here at this track. When we get back to Reggie's, I want you all showered and into bed. We will be up by 8 AM and back out here by 10 AM. I want to be done by 5 PM so we can enjoy Reggie's pool." There was laughter and Reggie pointing at Tony with a huge smile on his face.

The team practiced the entire day on Thursday. Dominic was gaining his rhythm with respect to his gate starts. He was more impressed that Tony introduced a turn technique and made Dominic lean on him in the turns. It was a technique used when being squeezed up high by another rider inside of you.

Tony and Dominic were beginning to become closer friends. Tony was highly impressed with Dominic's skills and his bearings. Dominic was a polite individual and his demeanor impressed Tony.

Tony yelled, "Chores."

The team immediately started working on their chores. They finally finished their chores nearly 30 minutes later and made their way back to Reggie's house in the Puma Palace. After exiting the Puma Palace, Reggie was standing at the pool with a hose. He insisted that every rider be hosed off before entering his pool. He really didn't care, but he found it funny how the kids just sat there and took their hosing by Reggie.

Reggie yelled out, "None of you are allowed in until I clean you off."

It wasn't long before his wife yelled out of the house for him to stop playing around and let the boys swim. The team enjoyed the pool and enjoyed the cool water after riding all day.

Chapter 33

Rafael woke up in the morning and made his way to the bathroom. As he arose from his bed and walked a few steps, he fell flat on his face. He looked down and noticed someone tied a string on his leg to his bed post. He heard the uncontrolled laughter coming from his brother Juan.

He looked at Juan and asked, "Why Juan, why?"

Juan still laughing, "You know why. It's payback from when you kicked out your back tire on a mud puddle getting me soaking wet. Payback brother."

Rafael shook his yes understanding what had transpired. He thought to himself that he probably had it coming. He untied his leg and walked out of the room towards the bathroom. Rafael turned around and said, "This is it. You got me. No more or else."

Rafael was sitting at the table eating breakfast with his mother and sister when Maximo returned from outside the house. He looked at them both and asked, "You ready to go son?"

Rafael answered. "Yes."

It was race day at the local track. Rafael was riding the expert class and he was excited about this race. He finished school and many of his friends were going to the track to watch him. Besides, BMX was becoming very popular and more and more riders were racing. Rafael called his friends Tommy, Bobby and Austin. They said they were all going to be there.

It was nearly 11:00 AM and the race was ready to start. Rafael was surrounded by all his friends and family in his pit area and surround by his sponsor when Pork Belly walked by and shot his middle finger at them. They all looked at each other with be wilderment and all started laughing out loud.

Maximo was the last to laugh, but could not contain himself. He looked at his wife and shot the ring finger at her. Florencia was startled and shocked at first, but she found the humor in his gesture and started laughing herself. Within seconds the entire Hartle BMX team was laughing and giving each other the finger.

This went on for nearly 30 seconds and the novelty quickly died off and the gestures ended. Rafael was wondering what the other people surrounding them were thinking. Some witnessed Pork Belly give them the finger and others were simply laughing along with them.

There was a quick team meeting followed by the familiar announcement, "Moto's are posted." Being part of a team and being sponsored has its advantages. Rafael simply waited for the team designee to return from the moto board.

Within fifteen minutes, Rafael had his moto and some of his competition. He was racing in the 11-13 open. Of course, Pork Belly was in this moto. Rafael made his way to the gate with his gear in hand. It was nearly one hundred degree's.

It was hot and like many other kids, Rafael was going to dress a few moto's before he was to take the gate. Dressing in the staging area is best described as putting on helmets, gloves, and some riders wore shoulder pads. Rafael took the gate and won his moto. He didn't win by much, but from the drop of the gate and his third pedal, he was leading the pack and continued to push further forward until he reached the finish line.

While sitting in the shaded area awaiting his 11-13 open moto, another strange happening occurred. A young adult walked by their camp. He was dressed all in black with a kilt or some type of skirt. He had chains hanging from different articles of his clothing. He had a face painted white with black lipstick and his eyes were blackened.

He had several different hair colors and it was all spiked with some type of dog collar. The entire team stared in puzzlement at the young man. He took notice that he was being stared upon.

For some reason he looked directly at Maximo and asked, "What's a matter papi? You never did anything different in your Viva."

Without missing a beat Maximo answered him back, "Sure, I had sex with a parrot and I thought you were my long lost son looking for me."

At first there was a strange silence followed by colossal uncontrolled laughter. Florencia nearly fell off her chair as she laughed. Rafael was shocked by his father's response. The rest of his family was in awe of Maximo's comment.

The entire BMX Team was in hysterics. Not only was the team laughing, all of Rafael's friends that came to watch him race were bent over with laughter. People came over and high fived Maximo. All of a sudden he was a hero. Florencia finally gathered her composer, looked at her husband and said, "I think the heat is affecting you." She continued laughing and Maximo sat back as if nothing had transpired watching the older kids taking the track.

Rafael made his way to the starting gate to race the open class. There were a few older riders in his moto. He did not know who they were but was sure they were fast. The gate dropped and they were off. Rafael could see that he was in first or second place. It was going to be a race to the first turn. As they made the turn he was still side by side of the older rider. He pedaled as hard as he could.

He could hear pig sounds coming from his pit area over the sound of the announcer and cheers. There was oinking, squealing, and snorting. It was loud as if someone handed the crowd a megaphone. He didn't think much more about it. He was trying to get in front of the rider to his left.

There was a second left hand turn and he was in second place. He finished the race in second and noticed Pork Belly was in last. He rode past Rafael and the first place rider purposely hitting them with his elbow as he flew by them. Rafael and the first place rider looked at each other at laughed at first. Rafael asked the rider how old he was and the class he races.

He answered, "I'm 11 year old expert." Rafael looked at him with astonishment shaking his head. The rider smiled and answered, "No, I'm 13 expert turning 14 next month."

Rafael smiled and replied, "You had me going for a minute, and I was going to ask you what you ate." They both laughed and walked towards their respective camps.

When Rafael returned to his camp he asked, "What were all the squealing and other sounds you guys were making?"

One of the other riders answered, "It was to let Pork Belly know we were cheering for him in last place."

Rafael laughed, "You guys are killing me. I almost fell from laughing so hard." He continued, "Who started the pig chanting?"

One person answered, "Your dad."

Rafael, shaking his head, "What?"

They laughed, "No, we did. Your father sat back and laughed along with your mom, sister and your friends. They seemed to enjoy it."

Rafael was surprised and looking into the air with bewilderment. He thought to himself about how his parents were coming out of their respective shells and they were not uptight. He was proud this day.

Rafael continued to dominate the 12 year old expert class this day. The classes had changed and there no groupings of ages except for the open class. He continued to finish in second behind the faster 13 year old rider.

Pork Belly continued to receive mockeries from the Hartle BMX camp. In typical Pork Belly fashion, he had the fortitude to stand and want to argue with the team for making catcalls at him. The more he protested towards them the louder the dispersions continued. It was a no win situation for Pork Belly.

He lost his races and was being ridiculed by his peers for acting the way he did both on and off the track. Pork Belly had no class and his actions had turned on him. It was such a mockery that enticed other spectators to join in with sound effects.

As the race ended and everyone was packing up their cars and trucks, Harry Hartle the BMX Sponsor approached Maximo. He shook his and hand and asked, "Are you going to be here next week?"

Maximo answered, "Sure, this was the most fun we had in weeks."

Harry smiled and replied, "Yes this was uncharacteristic of everyone today. I wanted to ask you if you wanted to bring some food next week. I am going to bring my grill and supply the burgers and hot dogs. Other kids are bringing in drinks, chips, and other varieties of snacks. I was wondering if you wanted to bring something?"

Maximo looked at Florencia. She answered, "I could make tacos."

Harry laughed and answered, "Perfect. Just bring tacos with whatever you fill them with. I am excited about this myself. Rafael brags of how good a cook you are to the rest of the team."

She smiled and kissed Rafael on the top of his head. He had just arrived at the time of Harry explaining what good a cook she was.

He looked at his mother and asked, "What's this for?"

Harry looked at her and Maximo as they all smiled. Rafael looked at them and remarked, "I'm going to help load the vehicles." He shook his head as he walked off confused.

Harry thanked Maximo and Florencia again as made his way back the vehicles.

Chapter 34

It's late Friday afternoon and Team Panther arrives at the Van Nuys race track. The team arrived with great pageantry and many spectators looking at them. Reggie already warned the riders on the way over on how they were to act.

It was just after 5 PM and the races started at 7 PM. Reggie wanted to get the trailer off-loaded and get his team set before entering the track. It was the same track they had been practicing for the past few days. The riders knew the track well and were very familiar with its bumps, jumps and inconsistencies.

The trailer was off-loaded in a very precise and organized fashion. The bicycles were lined up carefully and neatly. The props and signs were all off-loaded in a well-organized manner. The grill was set up and the coolers were aligned with military precision.

The awning was pulled out and the night lights set up. Team Panther was ready for business. The tables were displaying all the latest products and a representative from Reggie's main office was there to answer any questions.

The entire team took the track at once. There were many other race teams there on this day. The tour was getting ready to start and this was the first race before the nationals started the next day. The track was packed. There were many riders and teams present. It was nearly a mini national. There were many riders wanting to test their skills and teams profiling their new riders. It was a jam packed event.

Dominic took the gate for his first start of the day. He noticed many kids asking how old he was. He would reply, "12 expert." In typical fashion there were few twelve year olds who wanted to warm up and do gate starts with him.

Dominic simply did his own thing. He took a few gates and did not race hard on the entire track. He was saving himself for the race. During his first gate start he noticed that all the riders were using the two pedal start technique. He was happy that he practiced this way of starting. It really gave him the advantage over his prior method of dragging his foot behind trying to find his pedal.

Dominic leaned on the gate trying to time his snap off the starting gate. The cadence was called and Dominic shot off the gate like a bullet from a gun. He wasn't the oldest rider on the gate but he was in a group of older riders into the first left hand ninety degree turn.

He noticed how the riders in California differed from the East Coast racers. The tracks in California were more technical and the riders were the same. There seemed to be less fear.

Dominic didn't want to admit it. He was East Coast and considered himself an ambassador for the East Coast. He continued to ride a few more gates starts. He purposely practiced a few gates with some bigger and older riders to see how he performed.

In typical custom he made his way off the gate fine but was out powered by the older and stronger riders. He could feel himself being leaned on as he had practiced with Tony and Phil. He was ready for the race and was excited to see how the night time lights affected him.

After nearly an hour and two burgers later, the moto's were posted. There were no opens on this night due to the amount of riders. Dominic was racing twelve expert class and he was ready. He rode his number 87G plate from the New Jersey District Series.

He did not have a national number because he had to participate in five national races. He did not meet this criteria but he was OK with that number. He was in moto forty six. He had to wait for all the novices to race before the expert classes. It was a matter of preference of the track officials.

They could run the novice and then the experts immediate after. This day Dominic would have to wait. He watched as the little kids started off first and then they made it to his age group. He noticed the novice class was fast.

He looked to one of his teammates and asked, "Am I this fast?" The older kid looked at him bewildered and answered, "Bra, they can't touch what you bring. You smoke bradder." Dominic loved the accent of his Samoan teammate and smiled at him.

About thirty minutes later Dominic made his way to the staging area. He met up with some of the riders in his class. He was surprised; a couple of the racers knew who he was.

One of the riders asked, "You're Dominic from New Jersey. You won the Worlds last year right?"

Dominic shook his head yes and answered, "I was eleven then."

The riders laughed a bit as he quietly made his way up to the starting hill. He was nervous. He was starting in gate one. It was a nice starting gate but the turn was steep and he needed to watch for slipping and sliding into the other riders as he made his way into the first turn.

Dominic was at the gate as the race announcer called off all the riders. He was surprised when the announcer called his name. The announcer said, "Lane one racing out of the Team Panther Camp from New Jersey and the eleven year old expert World Champion, Dominic Carlucci."

The announcer made his way through the list and every rider was a sponsored rider announcing who they were and achievements of some of them. The announcer even knew some of the nicknames of the riders. For Dominic, it just became real.

No excuses or reasons why he didn't win. He understood that if he wanted to be the best, this was the first steps of being a champion. As he stood up on his pedals, out of the corner of his eye he could see that all the riders were doing the same.

The announcer made the cadence, the same as in New Jersey, "Pedals up wheels on the ground."

Bang! The gate dropped and Dominic looked like he was shot out of a cannon. He made his way to the first pseudo jump almost pedaling over it without stopping. He pedaled right up to the first ninety degree left hand turn. He was in first place. He could see Tony giving him the pump fist as an indication to keep pedaling. He had to hold his line; there was a rider outside of him in the higher part of the turn. Dominic started to pedal and made his way in front of the rider. He could hear the cheers of the crowed as he made his way around the track.

The announcer called the race with great excitement, "Dominic the New Jersey factory Team Panther rider out front followed way too closely by the number one rider and local Richey Timms followed by the number one rider from Nevada. Here they come to the second turn."

It was a another ninety degree left handed turn to a straightaway with a large jump to a long one hundred and eighty degree left-hand turn. The announcer continued, "New Jersey rider still out front. Richey is trying to run him down. New Jersey Dominic pulling some distance over the tabletop. Into the left turn New Jersey rider still in front. Dominic Team Panther rider pulling more distance out of the turn now. I didn't know New Jersey had fast riders this young. This kid is on fire folks! Over the jump for New Jersey followed by Richey and the number one Nevada rider. Dominic Carlucci into the long right hander now. Smooth folks, very smooth. Pedaling now, he is checking out folks."

After the long right-hand one hundred and eighty degree high bermed turn, there were a series of table top jumps and sharp fast ninety degree right hand turn with a short straight and then the finish line.

After the moto, Dominic pulled his brakes followed by the other riders. The second place rider rode up to him and shook his head at him indicating yes. Dominic understood this as a sign of respect and tried to catch his breath.

One of the other riders commented, "You're fast dude, wow."

Dominic moved to the side of the track to see the next class of his peers. He watched as the 12 experts raced. He knew he would have to race some of them in the mains. He watched very closely as he coasted back to his camp. Tony immediately made his way towards him as soon as he saw Dominic.

Tony, high-fiving him stated, "Those guys have nothing on you. You're smoking around that track. Keep doing what you're doing. Don't worry if you're in second. Choose your move. Pick the time you're gonna pass and do it. You looked phenomenal out there."

Reggie made his way up to Dominic, "Do you know who you just beat?"

Dominic answered, "No idea Sir."

Reggie answered, "He was the twelve year old kid to beat at the Worlds last year. He has a birthday coming up in a couple of weeks. You just beat him at his home track and it's one of the most technical tracks on the circuit that we know of."

Dominic felt good about it and simply sat down and grabbed a cup of water from the jug hanging from the Puma Palace.

Soon Tony was at the gate and the air was filled with excitement. Everyone wanted to watch the pros. The gate dropped and the pros made their way down the track into the first turn. Tony was barely in front. This was typical of the pro class. They were all evenly matched off the gate. It wasn't until further down the track that the skills and technical abilities spotlighted who the more advanced pros really where.

Tony was pulling away after the second turn. Not by much, but still out front. He was so smooth and lightning fast. He was amazing. Dominic wanted to be like Tony. He wanted to emulate him on the track. It was ironic because the rider in second place was the same factory team that Dominic just raced and defeated.

Tony went on to finish first in the moto. Dominic was excited when everyone was cheering and clapping for Tony. He was proud to be his teammate and his friend. Phil was in the next moto. He also was a pro. He finished in first as well. Only a few Team Panther riders did not finish first in their moto's this day.

Team Panther was on the prowl. Reggie built a team of true champions. Reggie was living well this day. All his racers made it to their mains and his business at the track was soaring. He sold out of many of his products and would have to get more before tomorrow when the first National of the series commenced at the same track.

Dominic finished his moto's with two first places and a third. He nearly fell when an inside rider lost his grip and crashed into Dominic. Dominic managed to stay on his bicycle but was passed by several riders. He made it up by passing two riders before his third place finish.

In the Main Event Race he was tested. Dominic was unable to pull away from the pack. He was closely pursued by the pack of riders tugging at his heels. Although he finished first this day, he understood the definition of competition and competitiveness. He was a champion, but only because of his hard work.

He thought to himself, if these riders worked as hard as he did, would they be able to out race him? Dominic's eyes were opened this day. He knew he was fast and possessed skills. It wasn't all natural. He had athletic abilities, but his riding skills were polished and defined by his character. Only because he worked hard was he a champion. He had much to prove to himself before anyone else.

Dominic wanted to live up to his father's words. Dominic continued to reminisce on the conversation he had with his father the day he left. One thing stuck in young Dominic's mind, his father's words, "Champions are produced on the BMX track; Legacies are made in person. A champion will be remembered for their achievements; a legend will be remembered by how they acted after the fanfare and well after the fact. No matter what you do, have fun, enjoy the moment, make new friends, show respect, and be a champion off the track. You'll be remembered more for how you act. Your actions are not a statistic, but a quality of a true champion."

He remembered these words and even wrote them down. He paraphrased what his father stated and he kept a piece of paper in his helmet with these words inscribed on it. He watched his new friend Tony. He took sharp notice of how he acted on and off the track.

No doubt, Tony was a true champion on the track. Off the track he was the same. He signed every autograph, replied to everyone who acknowledged him, and he was always positive. Never did he display negativity. It was human to become frustrated when you lost a race or something went wrong, but Tony did this with class. His dignity was overwhelmed by his stature.

Dominic was praised this night. It wouldn't be until tomorrow that his real metal would be tested. He was excited and couldn't wait to call his parents. He won a first place trophy in California. He couldn't wait to show everyone back home. Many of his teammates finished first this evening.

Not all, but most of them. Tony yelled "Chores" and the organized chaos began. In a short time all the chores were done and Team Panther was on the road. Reggie reserved their spot for the next day and ensured it by roping it off with the Team Panther Logo sign in the middle. It wasn't long before the drive to Reggie's house took its toll on Dominic and he simply fell off to sleep.

Chapter 35

It was early Saturday morning as the team arrived at the Van Nuys BMX Track. It was a typical California morning, sunny, hot and not a cloud in the sky. There was as slight breeze and it was only 9 AM. Team Panther was pulling into the reserved spot. Carl and 'G' got out of the RV to guide Jay into place. Tony called everyone to the back of the Puma Palace.

He gave a very short speech, "Okay guys, here we are. This is the first stop of the tour. We are always under the microscope. How we act is how we are perceived. Remember, act professional, show manners, and don't be a fool. If you can't act right, you don't belong here. All of you are champions and this is why you're here. If you want to prove it, now is the time. Prove it with you skills, prove it with your manners, and prove it to yourselves. This is the big time. You all made it. It's going to be long trip cross country. Let's have fun and make it memorable. We are a team. Let's make a team effort to win. Let's make a team effort to show class. Let's make a team effort to show respect. I am proud to be here with all of you. You're my team. You're my friends. There is no other place I want to be than here with you. Let's make our presence known on and off the track. Let's make each other proud. You're all champions. Again, you're all champions." Tony smiled as they all joined hands in a tightly bunched circle. As they moved apart, Tony belted, "Chores!"

The RV was parked and the team jumped out of the Puma Palace and started performing their chores. Reggie was already outside awaiting the team. He had arrived and hour earlier with his family. This would be the last time he would see them for the next few weeks.

Reggie was greeted by many different authority figures from the local track and other bicycle organizations. He was king for the day. He took notice of how all the chores were being performed like clockwork. His Panther BMX display was in place along with posters and signs.

It took nearly twenty minutes before the team was standing around with their bicycles ready for practice. Practice was called by age groups. The four to seven year olds were first, followed by the eight to eleven year old riders. The twelve to fifteen year old riders were next to take the track. Finally the sixteen year old riders and older followed by the pro riders.

Each age group had nearly thirty minutes to practice. This allowed for nearly seven to eight gate starts. It was exciting for the team and Dominic. He never saw so many BMX racers in his life. The place was packed. He waited for his age group and finally took the track.

He warmed up by riding sections of the track before taking the gate. He was impressively fast off the gate and was being noticed by many riders. Many riders were curious about Dominic, how old he was and his class. It was a given if he was wearing a factory jersey, he was an expert rider.

Dominic continued to practice until the next group of riders was called. Dominic sat in the Team Panther Camp area with the rest of the team and simply watched practice. He was overly impressed with the older riders. He never saw so many fast riders in his life. It wouldn't be long before the pros took the gate.

Immediately everyone recognized the pros were on a whole different level. Dominic thought the sixteen and over class practice was fast. The pros were blazing. They rode around the track effortlessly as if they were gliding. They made it look so easy.

It was amazing, when Tony took the gate, spectators stopped to watch. Tony was shot out of a canon into the first turn. He was remarkable. He was the fastest by far. Nevertheless, other pro riders were riding right next to him. Tony had the unique skills of coming out of the turn first. He had to be flawless, one mistake and he would be passed. The pro class was this tight. That one extra pedal would make the difference.

It wasn't long after the pros finished their practice that the famous words were echoed over the P.A., "Moto's are posted." Dominic waited and Carl came back with all the Moto information.

When he got to Dominic he mimicked, "Dominic, moto number 52, lanes 2, 5, and 8. You're going to have a quarter, semi and a main. There are Sixty-two riders in your class. Good luck."

Dominic thought to himself, "I can't imagine if I had to race the open." He wanted to, but Tony insisted that he only race his class at first. Tony had his reasons and Dominic didn't mind. Besides, they had the best view at the track. They also had plenty of shade from the awning.

Dominic sat with the rest of the team drinking water and eating hot dogs. He made his way inside the Puma Palace to use the bathroom. As he exited the Puma Palace there was a line to use the bathroom. He looked at everyone with bewilderment.

One of the older riders called out, "Dominic was first, he gets to clean it. Thanks Dom." Dominic realized he now had trash duty, stacking duty of the bicycles and now he had to clean the bathroom.

Dominic sat in his chair thinking about the bathroom. He couldn't help himself. He got up went inside the Puma Palace and opened the bathroom door and took a look around. He thought to himself, this isn't bad. Actually this is easier than cleaning his bathroom at home. He shrugged his shoulders and made his way back out of the Puma Palace.

Tony looked at him and asked, "You questioning yourself about how bad of a job the bathroom is aren't you?"

Dominic nodded, lifting his shoulders with his head tilted to one side.

Tony continued, "It's not that bad. It takes only five minutes to get it clean. You'll see that as the tour goes on that others won't mind cleaning it and it becomes less of burden to worry about. Others will fanatically not want to clean it, but they will. I'll make sure everyone gets a turn. Unfortunately, you're first and there is an inspection. Don't worry about it, it's nothing." He smiled at Dominic and they both sat in the chairs watching the race.

Nearly forty minutes later Dominic was pushing his bicycle to the staging area. He lined up with his group. He noticed a few riders from yesterday. They all said hello to Dominic and bumped fists.

Dominic asked one of the riders he raced yesterday, "who's the guy to beat in this moto?"

The rider laughed and answered, "You Jersey. You're the one we are hearing about."

Dominic looked at him and replied, "Really, I'm nervous about everyone."

The rider laughed at him and nodded at Dominic to start moving towards the gate.

Dominic was on the gate in lane two. He was surprised to hear the gate operator call him out by name. The operator shouted out, "OK guys move back. Come on Dom, you too." The gate was up and the call was made, "Pedals up wheels on the ground." Bang, the gate dropped.

Dominic flew off the gate. He made it over the first jump and into the first left turn. He was first. He could feel the pressure. There were riders outside of him pressing him. Dominic kept thinking inside his mind, "I need to keep moving. I have to pedal."

After the turn, Dominic continued to pedal as hard as he could. He looked strong. He could hear the announcer calling the race, "Into the second turn, the Factory Panther rider from New Jersey in front. He is starting to pull some distance on the second place rider from Nevada. Dominic Carlucci still out front into the third turn."

Dominic was holding a tight line at the bottom of the berm. He was able to get a few pedals in before the jump and the last turn. The announcer calling the race remarked, "New Jersey rider Dominic

Carlucci of Team Panther takes the win. Folks, he was the eleven year old expert world number one last year in Indy."

Dominic made his way to the side of the finish to watch his competition. He was in the second moto of riders and wanted to watch the next two races. As Dominic was making his way back to the team, he was met halfway again by Tony. He could see the excitement on Tony's face.

Still out of breath, Dominic asked, "How do I look?"

Tony answered, "Like a champion. Dom, you're fast, really, really fast. You're smooth over the jumps and untouchable out of the gate. Keep riding your race. You'll be fine. You have a long day. Go take a break."

Dominic continued to watch all the races and cheered on his teammates. It was time for the pros. There were over forty-five pros racing. It was amazing watching them race. The track seemed short as they made their way around it. It looked effortless. Tony's moto was on the gate. The entire team was standing cheering him on. The team was parked just outside the first turn.

The gate dropped and they were off. Tony was in lane eight and had to make his way over. Into the first turn Tony was neck and neck with another rider. He held his line and continued to pedal. The entire moto of eight pros were tightly bunched together. Tony was not in the lead but he was in a tight second place losing by only a wheel.

As Tony described to Dominic, he held his line into the second turn and took advantage of getting a run of the high side of the berm. As they both reached the third turn, Tony was now in the lead by a tire length. They both came out of the third turn together and Tony was able to slowly pull away.

Tony finished first and the crowd cheered. Dominic made his way over to Tony who was clearly catching his breath. As they walked back, Tony began to speak with Dominic.

He gasped for some air and conveyed, "Remember what I told you, and pick you opportunities to pass. Be patient and wait. If a possibility to pass or make a move presents itself, take it. Be careful, calculate your move. Think ahead of what you want to do. I knew that I was going to make my move in the third turn. I made up my mind. If I could not pass him, second is ok for me. I only want to make it to the main, then its game on."

Dominic continued to finish first in all his qualifying moto's. As the afternoon lingered on it was time for the quarter finals. Dominic only needed to finish fourth or better to continue on. He made his way to the gate with a group of different riders. He was in lane five.

The gate dropped and Dominic made his way off the gate. It was not his best start but he was in the front bunch of riders. He made it around the first turn and heard the sounds of crunching and carnage behind him. He was out front and was pulling away from the second place rider.

The entire pack fell behind him. It was a mad dash to gather up their bikes and finish in third and fourth place in order to continue on. Dominic made his way across the finish line and watched from the side as the others finished the race.

He asked what happened. One of the riders answered, "Some dummy in last place tried to cut the inside and slid into the pack taking them all out." Dominic shook his head indicating he understood what had just happened.

The day turned to night and it was time for the semi-finals. If Dominic finished in fourth or better he was guaranteed eighth place for the day. Dominic grabbed his gear and his bicycle and started walking to the gate. He was quickly escorted by Phil the other team pro.

As they walked Phil gave Dominic advice, "Listen, don't do anything stupid. If you find yourself in fourth place it's ok. Don't worry about the points. You'll make it to the main. That's all you want. I know you are in lane seven. That's ok; stay outside if anyone is tight inside of you. Pick your moves. Lean on them if you get squeezed in the turn. Just finish in a transfer spot, fourth or better." Dominic was nervous, this was a big race. There were more people in his class than at the World Championships.

Dominic positioned himself into the gate and Phil gave him the thumbs up as he stepped back and allowed the gate officials to take charge. They understood the importance of the teams escorting their younger riders. The call was made, "Ok fellas, get ready." The cadence was called and the gate dropped.

Dominic had a horrific start. He came out of the gate near dead last. He miss-timed his gate-start and was basically left hanging at the gate. He quickly got pedaling and was in third place out of the first turn. He remembered what Phil and told him and he held his line into the second turn. Dominic was able to pedal off the top of the turn and move quickly into second place.

He thought about making a move to pass the first place rider but reluctantly held off. He could see Phil out of the corner of his eye giving him the relax gesture and he was holding up two fingers in a piece sign. He understood that he was going to hold second and transfer into the main event feature race for his age.

Dominic coasted easily in second place and rolled up to Phil. Phil looked at him and said, "I know you could have passed the other guy for first. It was a bit risky and you were far enough in front of the pack to coast in for an easy transfer spot. The guy you passed for third is another rider to watch. He is a ranked rider here in Cali. Catch your breath and relax for your next race."

Dominic was sitting in the Team Panther camp waiting his main posting. Tony was finally at the gate and this was his semifinal. He won his semifinal. It was not by much but he won and would be going to the main event. Phil did not make it because he flat out got beat and finished fifth. Phil himself admitted that he was hot and cold. When he was on he was superfast and other times he had to push.

Dominic was in the staging area when Tony clutched his shoulder by surprise. Dominic was excited to see Tony and jumped a mile when Tony grabbed him. Dominic put on his helmet and gloves before he said anything.

Tony leaned down and said, "Dom, this is it. Show this crowd who you are and why you're on this tour. You can beat these guys. Relax at the gate and time your start. I'll be waiting for you just over there at the finish line."

Dominic gave him the thumbs up and pushed his bicycle to the gate. He was in lane four. Not a bad lane but he was in the middle of the pack.

Dominic lined up on the gate and readied himself. Nervous and ready the cadence was called and the gate dropped. Dominic flew off the gate like he was stretched on a rubber band. He was in the middle of the pack off the start and watching from afar, one could see he was strong and pulling into the lead.

He was first into the turn and being pressured hard on the outside by an Arizona Rider. The announcer called the race, "New Jersey Panther rider in front being harassed on the outside by the Arizona factory rider. Here they come into the second turn. Arizona pushing a little on New Jersey, Nevada in third and the rest of the pack behind them. These three riders have checked out. Out of the second turn, Nevada having a run on New Jersey. New Jersey shuts it down and says no. New Jersey standing on his pedals now. Strong race folks. Who is this kid? Into the third turn, New Jersey pulling a few bike lengths."

That was it. Dominic was going to win if he doesn't fall or do anything stupid. Dominic finished in first and the crowd cheered. Tony grabbed him before he could stop.

Tony was jumping up and down saying to Dominic, "That's how we do it! That's right Dom. Strong, very strong. You're the next force. You're Dominic the Dominator!"

Dominic was patted on the back by the other riders as they passed. He was exhausted. He was so excited about the win. He understood why Tony would not let him run the Open Class. He was on fire. It was hot and he was drenched with sweat.

He made his way to the team camp and sat in his seat with all the congratulations from his teammates. Many of them made the mains but only a few finished in first. It was only Dominic and Bobby Durant that finished first. Bobby from Texas was a sixteen year old expert and another one of those fast riders.

Tony's main event was on the gate. The gate dropped and it was a mad tear to the first turn. Tony was clearly in the lead. The second and third place riders were not giving up and pressed Tony the entire race. Tony won by only a half of a bike length.

Dominic ran over to meet Tony half way. This was the last race of the night. Tony high fived Dominic and there was a large crowd around Tony. There were more flashes going off than the fourth of July. Dominic felt like he was in the presence of a movie star.

Tony was doing interviews and signing autographs. Tony finally arrived back at the Puma Palace. He dropped his bicycle off and made his way to the trophy area. There was an announcer who called off each class winner.

Dominic received his five foot trophy to a large crowd clapping. Carl was standing waiting for Tony. Tony received his trophy and a check for $800.00. Dominic was flabbergasted. He could not believe that Tony made that much money in one day. Carl quickly grabbed Tony's trophy and made his way back to the Team Camp area.

As Tony arrived he called the team over. He told them, "One more day guys. We get to do this all again in the morning. The races start at 8 AM with no practice scheduled. We're sleeping in the Puma Palace and we need to sleep. No horse play. Dominic, go clean the bathroom now. Next person after him has it tomorrow. Anyone wanting to call home, come with me. We need to wait for Dom first."

Dominic cleaned the bathroom in about five minutes. It was not long and it was easy. It was cleaner than when the team arrived. Dominic was able to get to a pay phone and call home. He called the house and his mom answered. He said hello to his mother and immediately his father picked up the other phone.

He explained to both of them how his day went. His mother was crying and his father was excited to hear his voice. They were both surprised and happy for him. They both were asking a bunch of questions. Finally he asked how his brother was doing.

His mother answered, "His being punished for fighting."

Dominic laughed, "Who Joey? He's like only ten years old. Can I talk to him?"

They both agreed and they exchanged their "I love you's" to each other.

Joey grabbed the phone and said, "Hey big bro, how is it out there?"

Dominic laughed, "What did you do?"

Joey answered, "I punched out Jerry Laugherty for calling our mom a bitch."

Dominic asked, "Joey, what did you do or say to make him want to call her that? Tell me the truth."

Joey replied, "We were playing football and one thing led to another calling each other names and we started fighting."

Dominic expressed his love to his brother and begged him to calm down.

The next day was a smaller turnout. Tony won his pro class and won another $500.00. Again, Dominic placed in first. At the end of the day Tony gathered the team and conveyed how proud he was of their performances and their attitudes. He then yelled, "Chores." It was business as usual.

Chapter 36

It's one week later and Rafael is preparing for Saturday's race. He is excited because everyone adores his father. Rafael was proud of the fact that his father emerged from his guarded shell. Normally Maximo was reserved and quiet.

Never had Rafael seen his father this way. Rafael had the car ready and simply needed to help his mother carry out the spread. It was neatly packed in a cooler. They had a propane stove that was going to be used to refry the meat.

They arrived at the track and Harry Hartle had their area already set up. It was to be the Hartle BMX Camp. As Rafael and his family made their way into the camp, they all took notice that they were all wearing Parrot hats. This was not the 1985 Jimmy Buffet Parrot Head hats, it was something that one of the parents found in a store and thought it was funny and purchased all the hats on display.

She sold out of them as soon as she showed it to the team. Not only did the team make the purchases, but some of the spectators that set up next to the Hartle BMX camp. Maximo looked on smiled and shook his head with a gesture of amusement.

Florencia on the other hand, lost her composure and broke down in tears of merriment. She thought it was more than hilarious that these people went out of their way to support her husband. She was proud of Maximo. She was crying with jollity that her husband had created a new bond with these people.

As Rafael and his family made their way into the camp, everyone was asking about the tacos. Maximo answered, "We have everything we need. Let me know when you get hungry and we'll cook you up some food."

As Rafael grabbed his bicycle he noticed that there was a small parrot sticker on his number plate. He looked at it for about 30 seconds and then started to laugh. His father took notice and shook his head smiling ear to ear. Florencia did not see it right away and Rafael took off towards the starting gate with all his gear on ready to start his practice.

It wasn't long before the heat of the day kicked in and all took cover to shade. The tent provided just enough protection for all participants to feel somewhat comfortable. It wouldn't be long before Maximo, Florencia and the rest of the Santos family, they were in for the second surprise.

Rafael had made several practice runs and patiently waited before his moto was to race. Rafael was on to the starting gate. As he made his way up, another team member's family handed out whistles. It was not a typical whistle. When blown, it made a pig suey sound. But the Santo's family had no idea what to expect.

The gate dropped and Rafael flew off the gate. He was in first place being cheered on by his teammates. As he passed, a few seconds later he could hear the horrifically loud sounds of the suey whistles. He realized that pork belly was in his moto but well behind him.

He tried to pedal and not laugh at the same time. Finally he gathered his composer and finished his moto in first place. As Rafael arrived back to his team, he was catching his breath and laughing at the same time. He looked at his mother, "Did you buy those whistles?" She broke down in tears with laughter. Rafael never saw his parents have some much fun.

Finally it was time for the tacos. Maximo fired up the propane burner and reheated the tacos. It was every man for himself as soon as Maximo was finished with the meat. Everyone was craving the tacos. All who participated glorified Florencia for the well prepared meal she and her family provided.

It was a happy day for all. During the feasting, the whistles were all going off but there were no racers on the track. It was easy to figure out. Pork belly walked by and the adults lowered their standards to make fun of him. They even interrupted their meal in order to blow the whistle.

Many around the Hartle camp took notice and were laughing with them. It was as if the race didn't matter. They were simply enjoying the afternoon making fun of pork belly and wearing their parrot hats. It was a sight to see.

As if it were planned, the Goth kid walked by the camp and took notice of the hats. He understood the meaning. It was more ironic that he was not alone. He had other Goth kids with him. As they walked by the laughter began to amplify from the Hartle pits. One of the other Goth kids looked over with anxiety.

One of the parents belted, "Hello son."

The Goth kid answered, "Whatever."

Maximo sat quietly and they made their way by. He said nothing and didn't want any more interaction with these kids. Maximo was happy sitting down watching the races and eating his tacos. He liked making fun of pork belly. This kid was not a nice person and his family was the foundation of his behavior.

The day finally ended and Harry called a meeting of the riders and their families. He pronounced, "Ok everyone, in about a month or so there is a national event in Waco. I would like all of us to make it to this race. There is going to be many factory teams and some of the fastest professional BMX racers you'll ever see. I want us to participate as a team and let's see how we do. It's about a three hour drive and it's a one day event. It's the BMX tour and this would be a great opportunity for our team racers to see how they compare with national circuit riders." There were some questions about the day's events but it was agreed as the date drew near, the final count would become more defined.

The team packed up and the race day had ended. On the way home Rafael asked his father, "Why do those kids dress like dead people?"

Maximo explained, "I don't know exactly why but I can only offer you my opinion. I don't know these kids. Maybe they're rich, maybe poor, I don't know. It's my judgment they are looking for some type of attention, either positive or negative. Maybe they are rebelling against their parents for some reason. They need acceptance and this is their way of getting it. Maybe they just come to the track dressed like that as a joke. I have no answer for you son. But if what they are portraying is a true personification of their inner person, they are hurting. I don't want to believe that people dress like this because they don't like the style of clothing in mainstream department stores. This is like saying; I smoke pot because I don't like the smell of cigarettes. It doesn't work like that. Possibly they look at us as being the weird ones for dressing the same. Nevertheless, society creates norms. This doesn't mean that our norms become concrete pavers that allow us to walk through life. We need to accept that everyone is different and show respect even if they don't deserve it. This is the grace GOD teaches us about. This is what your mother and I are trying to instill into you kids. It's fun to make fun of them when they provoke it, but left alone to their own accord, respect them. Maybe it's a phase of life and they will outgrow it. "

Rafael answered, "Dad, they are not nice. They use horrible language and act crazy. They sit around all day smoking cigarettes and cursing. They show no respect when they do this, especially in front of younger kids and adults."

Maximo interrupted, "Why do you think they are here? They could hang out anywhere they want, but they chose this place. I'll tell you. It's full of people and they crave the attention. Simply ignoring them will make them want to leave.

Rafael listened to his father and they drove back home. Rafael wanted to ask a question, he started asking something and quickly fell to sleep.

Maximo looked at his wife and asked, "Do you think he heard any of what I said?"

Florencia answered, "I'd say ninety percent. But I'm tired also. She smiled and closed her eyes as Maximo drove homeward.

Chapter 37

It's nearly a week later and Team Panther was still in California. Tony called the team together for a meeting. He started by saying the following, "OK guys we leave in the morning for Corona. If any of you never raced downhill before, you're in for a treat. Corona is the steepest and fastest downhill track on the circuit. A couple of things to remember, we are not changing our gears. Whatever gear you race, do not change it. You may think that you are going to spin out of the gear going down the hill. It's OK, there are some uphill sections and the track will flatten out. Many riders are going to make this mistake. We're going to practice Friday afternoon. We have a friend of mine that will drag us up and down the hill. Trust me; it's a long walk up to the starting gate. Besides, there is no Sunday race, only Saturday for this one."

The team arrived Friday afternoon as predicted by Tony. The team set up and Tony called, "Chores." So it begins. Team Panther was going to camp overnight in the Puma Palace. This was the second night with the team sleeping in the Puma Palace and camping out. After a short set up, Tony had the team grab their bicycles and walk them up the hill.

As they walked up the hill he began to hear the murmurs and complaints of how steep it was and tiring. He ignored it because he knew his friends would be there shortly with the tractor. The entire team made it to the starting gate area.

Tony called them into a huddle and gave direction, "As you can see guys, the first straight is a massive downhill section with a drop off. As you enter the first turn, hug the inside and allow your bike to slowly move and drift towards the berm. Hold any line you have. You will not go over the berm. Although you're going faster than you ever have before, you can hold the turn. As you come out of the turn, it's a bit of an uphill climb but you will be carrying a ton of momentum. Pedal if you can. Make the right hand turn at the top of the turn and now your normal gear ratios come back into play. There is a downhill straight, pedal again and set up for a left hander for ninety degrees. As you come out of the turn, there are a few jumps but not very big. It's a slow long incline. It bears a little right and then another right ninety degree turn. You can see the straightaway. It has a whoop section into a one hundred and eighty degree left hand turn with a straightaway with a small jump and you cross the finish. I want all of you to simply glide down this hill and get used to the speeds. You can hold the turn. Matter of fact, Phil go first and show everyone since you know the track. Watch what he does, guys."

Phil made his way down the hill. He was flying and didn't even pedal. He came into the first long sweeping left handed turn that was about two hundred degrees. He did not fall and everyone could see from afar that he negotiated the turn with no issues and flew up the hill into the next turn without pedaling.

From this point he had to pedal to make it around the track. Tony sent the riders down the hill one at a time. He started with the older riders and insisted they glide. Everyone watched until it was their turn.

Dominic admitted that the size of the hill was alarming, but he did not say much more. He glided down the hill as instructed. It was rocky and the drop off came very quickly. The first turn was the most difficult but after that it was nothing more than pedal as hard and fast as possible. No different from any of the other tracks.

One by one the riders took the track. Tony was the last to come down and he made his way over to the team. Tony started with his instructions, "As you all can tell, once the downhill section is over and you come out of the first long sweeping turn, its business as usual. Don't be apprehensive of holding back fellas. Let it happen. You'll all be fine after you get used to the sound of the wind and the amount of speed you are carrying."

After he was done speaking with the team, a farm tractor with a hayride looking cart being pulled behind it pulled up to the Puma Palace. Tony sat and talked with the man driving it for a while.

He looked at the team and shouted over, "OK, bring all your bikes here and I will show you how to load them properly so we can all fit comfortably as we make our way up the hill."

All the bikes had the handlebars locked on to the wooden rails hanging outside the buggy. Everyone loaded their bikes on both sides and the tractor made its way up the steep hill. It would be more correct to say mountain but nevertheless, it was a steep incline to the top.

Once at the top, all the riders made their way onto the track. One at a time they took the course pedaling some to get used to the speeds and rocky surface. Dominic's turn was next.

As he readied himself Tony grabbed him by the shoulder and whispered in his helmet, "You need to get in top gear instantly, your class is fast and they have no fear. Now, own this track."

Dominic flew off the starting area. There was no gate yet, he simply picked up his feet and pedaled as hard as he could down the first straight. As he pedaled the drop came quick. He settled his bike and pedaled as far as he could before taking the first turn. Dominic made it look easy but he had some control issues coming out of the turn carrying speeds for which he was unaccustomed.

The team practiced until dark. Every rider was pedaling and tamed the track. It was impressive to see Tony and Phil take the first straight. They looked like a streak coming down the hill. It was amazing to witness. Tony called the team to the RV.

He yelled to them all, "You need to clean yourselves. You smell like ten day funk!"

To their amazement, Tony had a garden hose with a sprinkler head on it. This was to be the shower. At first the riders enjoyed playing in the cool refreshing water, but it was getting dark. They cleaned themselves with soap and washed their hair. Afterwards, they changed in the Puma Palace into shorts and t-shirts.

The team then had to hang their bathing suits on the makeshift clothes line. Tony reminded them, "This is going to be our shower at times, especially as we make our way cross country. Get used to it. This is going to be the norm from here on out guys as we continue on this tour across the country."

The team divided up the Puma Palace. There were tents being hauled and stored in the trailer. Some of the riders wanted to sleep in the tents and others elected the Puma Palace. The air conditioning was not turned on and Reggie drove home.

It was nearly a three hour drive for him. It was fun for most of the boys. There was the expected cackling. Dominic found the only one man tent and called it his own. He had his pillow and a sleeping bag. It was hot that evening so he slept on top of his bag. The rest of the team quickly fell off to sleep.

The morning came quickly as the other teams pulled up their RV's and tractor trailers. It was nearly 8 AM and the moans of waking kids filled the already increasing heat index of the day. They were all awakened to the smell of bacon, fried onions and eggs. All the riders awoke and made their way to the grill.

Jay and 'G' were cooking. They had a jug full of iced tea with ice and another five gallon jug full of ice water. There was coffee made but only Jay, G, and Tony drank it. Tony yelled, "Chores" and the team pressed on with their assigned duties. Within ten minutes the site looked nearly perfect. As Reggie arrived with his wife and kids, he was pleased to see the organization of his team.

There was no tractor to pull the team up the hill this day. Most of the racers took four or five practice runs. They really needed to pull a couple of gate starts.

Dominic made his way to the gate; he was impressed by how tall it was. It was an inclined start and the gate needed to be higher for the support of the weight. Dominic dragged himself up to the gate and waited for the cadence. Like normal he was off and nearly in first place.

This was only practice but he wanted to see how he would react in the turns with bigger and stronger riders. He was outside, not familiar with this track, but he handled himself well. He was confident. He took a couple more gate practices and decided he would wait for his moto.

It wasn't long before the moto's were posted. Dominic's race class had nearly thirty riders and he would have to race a quarter, semi and a main for his trophy. He started to understand the points system and the more first places in both the moto's and the qualifiers (semi's and mains) he collected, the more he accumulated points.

Dominic reached the staging area already a little winded from the climb. There were many other riders doing the same as he. Finally he was staged with his group. He recognized some of the riders from Van Nuys.

Some of them joked with him and others simply nodded as to indicate hello. There were many questions of the gearing in the staging area. Some of the riders were bragging of how tall they made their gears. Dominic said nothing and remembered what Tony had told him.

Dominic entered his position on the gate. He was in lane six. He readied himself and waited for the call. The cadence was called and like a rocket Dominic shot out of the gate. He was out front but other riders quickly caught him because of the taller gears.

Dominic was able to dig into the first turn and set himself up for the second turn at the top of the small incline. He made the right hander and he was able to distance himself. He was so far out in front during his heat races he was able to coast parts of the track. This continued every time during his moto's.

Dominic finished first in his quarterfinals. During the semifinal Dominic needed to finish fourth or better like last time. He made his way to lane two on the gate and waited for the cadence. The gate dropped and they were off.

Dominic again pulled the early lead but, the three other riders were able to get around him on the outside because of the gearing. Dominic at first panicked. But he remembered what Tony and Phil told him. Be patient, they will run into problems after the second turn.

Sure as expected, after the second turn Dominic made his move. He passed the third place rider with ease. The rider could not pedal throughout the track with any ease. It was as if his was pushing concrete.

He easily ran down the second place rider and passed him in the third straightaway. Dominic effortlessly caught the first place rider and passed him so quick, the rider never saw him coming on the outside.

By the time Dominic made it to the finish line, he was nearly a full straightaway in front of them all.

Tony made his way over to Dominic. He looked at him and said, "I told you to be patient. This is not a normal track. You may have to do this in the main. Don't worry you can get by them. They won't let you slip by so easily this time. Be ready for anything including them cutting you off."

Later, Dominic was at the gate for his main. He had lane eight. This was a good thing on this track. He could hear his team at the bottom of the track cheering him on. Dominic took notice of Tony in the announcer booth talking with people. He also was in the main with Phil.

The gate dropped and Dominic flew off the gate. As the drop approached, he timed the drop and pushed his bike down as hard as he could and was able to gather a few extra pedals. To his amazement, he was into the turn in first place. He would stay in that position and finish first for the day.

The other riders who decided to keep their same gears made their moves and finished behind Dominic. Dominic could hear the announcer as he made his way down the second to last straightaway. The announcer, "Out of New Jersey and the Team Panther Camp, Dominic the Dominator Carlucci making his way down the whoop section. Ladies and Gentleman, this kid is only twelve years old. Around the last turn and pedaling for the line, The Dominator finishes first."

Dominic coasted back towards his team. He was high fived by his teammates in his camp and the other riders in his moto fist bumped him and patted his back. Dominic made it a point to acknowledge them all as a sign of respect.

Reggie ran up to him and proclaimed, "We have a champion. Dom son, you looked fantastic. You truly took command of this track. You were awesome."

Dominic was happy that Reggie came out of his shell. Many of Dominic's teammates finished first this day. Tony crushed the track and had to make a few passes on the track himself to gain the first place position. He also won $6000.00. Phil placed third this day and the team was going nuts. They had the best pro rider in the country and Tony promised them all pizza and ice cream if he won.

He made his way back to the Puma Palace. It took some time. It was getting dark and he had several interviews to accomplish. Tony showed up and immediately yelled, "Chores."

Too late they were nearly done. They all wanted pizza and they were hungry. He agreed to expedite their clean up. Tony explained to the team that tomorrow was laundry day. He further explained how they were going to accomplish this task with precise organization.

The team ate six pizzas and drank twenty five sodas. Reggie made it a point to the team that they were going to a hotel and needed to act accordingly. He explained that they are making their way to Oklahoma for the next race and they had a few stops on the way.

Chapter 38

Rafael was helping his father load the car for this Saturday's race. It was a bigger than usual weekend at the track. It was a regional championship and it was also a double point's race. Like clockwork, Maximo had the car loaded and ready before his wife packed the cooler with the day's lunch and snacks.

On this day, Florencia's cuisine consisted of burritos and enchiladas with various sauces. She finished packing the coolers and called for Rafael. Rafael brought the cooler to his father who was waiting at the car.

Rafael asked his father, "Why is this so heavy?"

Maximo grabbed the cooler and replied, "It does feel heavy. Your mother is up to something."

Rafael, his mother, father and sister arrived at the track just after 8:30 AM. Rafael immediately made his way to the track to get some practice. Maximo and his wife finished unloading the rest of their gear. They were at the front of the Hartle BMX camp.

They had a nice area at the edge of the track just outside the first turn. Many other riders showed up soon after. Harry Hartle made his way over to Maximo giving him salutations. Harry was wearing his parrot hat along with many others.

Maximo thought it was funny at first but he started feeling bad for the young man he made fun of. He pondered what he had said for many weeks now. He decided to allow the fun and camaraderie to continue, but would not partake.

He simply said nothing and enjoyed watching his son race and spending time with his family. He enjoyed the feeling of being accepted but did not want to do this at anyone else's expense. Not even a Goth punk individual. He had an unsettling feeling inside that continually churned when he thought about it.

It wasn't long before Pork Belly made his way by the camp. He was with his father and together it looked like a bowl of jelly and a soup sandwich pushing a rope. It was that ugly. There was silence until Pork Belly shot his middle finger at the Hartle camp. Immediately there were the sounds of pig whistles and chanting in his direction.

Maximo sat up front with his family. He shook his head indicating no. He was in disbelief that Pork Belly was this dumb. If Pork Belly simply walked by and said or did nothing there would have been silence.

Rafael was enjoying the day with his family and had a big day planned. His class would have a main event. The pressure was on for Rafael. He had riders in his class he never heard of or recognized.

Finally Rafael was at the gate. The team stood up to watch as the gate dropped. Rafael was in the lead into the first turn. No Pork Belly sounds. He was in a different moto.

Rafael made it around the track in first place. But, there was a lot of competition heating up. He was pushed harder than he was accustomed. He knew if he made one mistake he would have gotten passed. As Rafael pushed his bicycle back to his camp, he could hear the sounds of the pig whistles. He knew that Pork Belly was in the next moto.

The heat of the day was starting to make its appearance. The mercury starting rising as many spectators took shelter in the shade. The team had an awning and cover that provided shade for everyone. Maximo and his family started eating.

Rafael had a small bite because he didn't want to feel too full when he was racing. As they were sitting and eating, Rafael noticed one of the Goth kids approaching from afar.

Rafael looked at his father and mother and said, "Oh boy, here it comes."

Maximo looked to his right and nodded at Rafael. He said nothing and continued eating his lunch. Florencia could see the figure of the Goth kid getting closer to them. It wasn't long before the kid was upon the camp. One of the other riders shouted something out to the kid.

Immediately someone else yelled, "Shut up- and don't provoke him, you dummy."

The Goth kid stopped within two feet of Maximo and started yelling back. He used some fiery language, enough to offend anyone in ear shot distance. This went on for a few moments.

Maximo heard enough. He stood up and raised his hands over his head. He turned to the.Goth kid and starting talking with him. Nobody could hear what he was saying and they spoke for a long time. There was silence. It was as if the crowed was in shock.

Maximo in his broken English asked, "What's a matter with you?"

The Goth kid replied, "Nothing old man."

Maximo answered, "Look, I don't want to argue with you or have a conflict. Let's just talk for a few minutes.

The Goth kid looked at him with some confusion and asked, "What's there to talk about?"

Maximo answered, "Probably nothing but let's have a conversation." The Goth kid looked at Maximo saying nothing. Maximo continued, "I don't know if it bothers you or not, but it bothers me that many people make fun of you. I don't want to have any issues with you. I don't want others to have an issue with you either. I just don't understand why you allow the hecklers to get under your skin. As you reply it's like fueling a fire. You understand what I mean."

The Goth kid answers, "Happiness is over rated."

Maximo answered him back, "Is it? I would like to help you find happiness. Seriously, forget about the sharp tongue and poison these people are spewing. I seriously want to talk with you. Let's take a walk away from here so nobody can hear us."

The Goth kid answered, "Honestly, you scare me. I'm afraid."

Maximo could see in the kid's blackened eyes and white face and the real concern in his brow. Maximo shook his head and said, "I understand. Let's sit here then."

The Goth kid agreed reluctantly at first.

Maximo looked at his daughter Julieta and made the move sign with his hand. She got up and Maximo invited the Goth kid to sit. Florencia was shocked but she knew her husband and understood his faith. Many around were staggered at Maximo's gestures. Maximo and the Goth kid spoke for a long time.

Rafael came over and got his bicycle and made his way to the staging area. The conversation lingered on for a while.

Finally Maximo asked, "What is your name?"

The Goth kid answered, "You can call me Valac."

Maximo shook his head in disbelief. He answered the Goth kid, "Valac is a demon. I can't call you that. I don't think of you as a demon. But I am willing to call you by your real name and continue our nice conversation."

The Goth kid answered, "Very good papi, Valac is the president of hell. I like this name because I feel this way."

Maximo answered, "You feel this way inside or does someone else make you feel this way?"

The Goth kid was confused and stared at Maximo for a short time. He could see the kindness in this man and was reluctant to leave. Maximo asked him to stay for a short time longer.

Rafael was on the gate and in normal fashion took the lead into the first turn. The Goth kid stood there expressionless as he watched Maximo and his family cheer on Rafael. After Rafael had returned and found a seat for himself, Maximo kissed him on the forehead and turned his attention to the Goth kid again.

Out of nowhere the Goth kid turned to Maximo and said, "My parents named me Christopher."

Maximo immediately answered, "Nice name. Christopher, are you hungry?"

Christopher said nothing.

Maximo looked at his wife and in Spanish asked for a plate of food. Florencia returned with a generous portion of food and a can of soda. Maximo handed it to Christopher and said, "Here, try my wife's cooking. She cooks very good."

Christopher asked, "Why are you giving me something to eat?"

Maximo answered, "You're too thin and I hear your stomach growling. Please eat something, I insist. My wife is an amazing cook. If you never had Spanish food or don't like Spanish food, you can at least try it and say you've had it."

Christopher the Goth kid ate the entire plate and sat in the seat drinking the can of soda. Christopher looked at Maximo and Florencia and said, "That was the best Spanish food I ever had, thank you."

Maximo was shocked and answered, "You're welcome Christopher."

Christopher then spoke to Maximo again, "You know, I have to get going, I have some friends waiting for me. "

Maximo answered, "Ok Christopher, we will be here next weekend. Make sure you show up. I'll have my wife make you a plate of something else for you to try out."

Christopher left and did not hang out at the track. People were shocked at how Maximo interacted with the Gothic kid. Many asked, "What did you guys talk about?"

Maximo simply answered, "Him."

Rafael continued to win his last moto. The next moto was a show in itself with Pork Belly. Pork Belly was last in all his motos and decided to let his bicycle go as he rounded the turn. His bicycle went on for several feet and finally came to rest in the middle of the other straightaway.

The first place rider hit his bicycle and ruined the rim. Pork Belly sat and argued with the Hartle BMX team and blamed them for him losing by heckling him as he rode. It was uncontrolled laughter.

He yelled, "Shut up you A@@ Holes." At this point many spectators were laughing. Finally a track official came and got Pork Belly and made him retrieve his bicycle. As he lifted it, he noticed that his back rim was busted. He shot his finger at Hartle BMX and was heckled by the rest of the crowd as he departed.

Rafael finished first in his main event. He was happy. He had to pass one rider in the second turn to win his first place. He was happy and his family was ecstatic about his win.

On the way home Rafael asked his father, "Papa, what did you and the vampire talk about?"

They all laughed as Maximo was driving. Maximo replied, "We talked about a lot. His name is Christopher. I promise to tell you one day. He actually speaks with excessive intelligence. This kid is not stupid. I don't know his story. He is seventeen years old and a senior. I don't want to say more. I ask one favor, act kindly with him. Don't worry about how he looks. Be polite." Rafael looked at his father with confusion. He agreed to do as his father asked.

Later that evening Florencia asked, "Why does Christopher dress like the devil?"

Maximo answered, "He is looking for attention. Something is going on with this kid. I don't know what it is but we talked about various topics and he speaks very well as if he was well educated. I personally think there is a parental issue but maybe next week we will talk some more."

Florencia laughed and asked, "Should I pack an extra plate for next week?"

Maximo laughed and replied, "My Love, you pack for an army every weekend. But yes, I want to see what happens with this young man."

Chapter 39

Its Sunday morning nearly eight o'clock in the morning. Tony began knocking on everyone's hotel door waking up the team. Dominic nearly jumped out of his bed when he heard the pounding on the door. Tony yelled to everyone, "Let's go girls, get up and take a shower. Hopefully you all took one last night, if not you're nasty. Come on out to the Puma Palace for a moment and you can get back to your rooms to get ready for our next trip."

Everyone made their way to the Puma Palace. Tony explained the laundry situation and how it was to work, "OK look at me. Here is how we are going to do laundry. We will do laundry every week either on Sunday or Monday. We will be clean. I don't want to smell funky drawers."

Tony held up two netted looking bags. He continued, "Look up here everyone. I am going to give you all two bags. These are yours to keep. You are to place whites in one bag and colors in the others."

He held up a bag and a white T-shirt. He continued, "This is a white T-shirt, this goes in this bag, this is color." He then placed his uniform shirt in the other bag.

Tony continued his instruction, "We are going to the laundry. Not all of us need to be there. I am going to give every one of you a piece of cloth that has your name on it. This is how we are going to identify your clothing bag. This system works and all your clothes will smell nice and clean. I will choose a few riders to assist me in cleaning the clothes. Eventually on this trip I will allow you to do this without supervision. Until then, I'm stuck on laundry duty. Wear shorts and a shirt. If you have sandals or flip flops I would wear them in order to be comfortable. Don't steal any towels, especially if you're from New Jersey."

When Tony was done with his details, the team started making their way back to the rooms with their bags. Tony yelled out, "Dom, Erick, Terrell you're the first ones. Guys get your stuff in the bags and bring all your other items with you. We are leaving in a twenty minutes. We have an eight hour drive once the clothes are done. Also, we are short one rider. Young Jose is done. He decided this was not for him. He was only seven years old fellas. Our youngest rider with us is eight years old. He will learn how to do laundry as well." Larry turned and looked at Tony and gave him the thumbs up and continued on to his room.

Nearly thirty minutes later the team was at the Puma Palace with their suitcases and their bags with dirty clothes. Tony ordered them to load up and store their suitcases. This was like clockwork for them. This was a proven science and Tony perfected it.

They loaded up, Jay and 'G' were in the front with Reggie at the dining table reading a bunch of papers. Jay was driving and 'G' was holding the map giving direction. They drove for nearly five minutes until they pulled up to the laundry.

Tony had the team gather their belongings and bring them in to the laundry. He made them all leave except for Dominic, Erick, and Terrell. He showed them how to load the washer and put in the detergent and bleach in the whites.

When it was time, he showed them how to put in the fabric softener. Nearly forty minutes later he loaded the huge dryers and they needed to wait another hour. Nearly two hours later the laundry was complete and Tony called the team back in to the laundry.

Tony handed the bags to their respective owners. The team made their way back to the Puma Palace and placed their clothes orderly in the respective suitcases and backpacks. Dominic and the boys made their way back to their suitcases and continued to fold their clothes and put them away.

Tony called out, "OK, we have about an eight hour drive to Flagstaff, Arizona. When we get there, we are going to set up camp in Kaibab National Forest. I know some of you want to sleep in the tents. That's ok. We will have running water and bathrooms nearby. You will shower tonight before we go to sleep. The bikes will stay in the trailer. In the morning we will be moving on to Oklahoma and this is about twelve hours. We will wake up when we smell the bacon."

While at the laundry, Dominic was able to call home. He spoke with his mother and father at the same time. He conveyed that he was doing laundry and that he was on his way to Flagstaff, Arizona. He continued speaking with them for nearly ten minutes.

Angelo and Maria expressed their love for him and how proud they were that he was on this adventure. Dominic said goodbye to his parents and made his way to the Puma Palace. The RV pulled out and it was on its way.

It was fun looking out the window and taking selective pictures. Dominic bought a camera with the money his father gave him. He didn't spend all his money on the camera but he purchased a Canon and good amount of film. He wanted to document his trip and have someone take his picture while racing. He figured that he would develop them when he returned home.

All was well on the way to Flagstaff. Dominic was impressed with the size of the Colorado River. Most of the team killed time playing cards and debating sports. Dominic continued looking out the window and was amazed of the country side.

The team finally arrived at Kaibab National Forest. It was beautiful where they were going to set up camp. The moment they arrived Tony allowed the team to get out of the Puma Palace and stretch their legs. No one used the bathroom in fear of having to clean it.

Reggie, Jay and 'G' were the only ones who used it and they would not have to clean it. It was a mad dash to the trees for everyone including Tony. He insisted they move a far enough distance from the Puma Palace in order to not smell anything from all the team peeing in the woods. As they returned he called, "Chores."

Dominic awoke in his tent to the smell of bacon. He immediately ran to the bathroom and cleaned himself up. He packed up his tent and readied for breakfast and his chores. The team ate breakfast and made their way back on the road. It was 7 AM and they had nearly a thirteen hour ride to Oklahoma City. It was not determined if they were going to drive straight through or stop and camp one more night. Reggie would make the decision as they drove.

The team was going to camp in the Puma Palace for a couple of nights and on to a hotel for a few more nights in Oklahoma City. Team Panther decided to camp at Choctaw, Oklahoma. It was a nice place and it was not far from the track. The race was on Saturday only and Sunday was laundry day.

It was a long ride. Tony addressed the team as he gathered all their attention, "Alright guys this is what's up. I don't know if any of you use the bathroom; it needs to be cleaned every day. So with this said…" Tony went into the bathroom to the roaring of claps, whistles, and laughter. He came out and addressed them all again, "…You guys can't hold it in for twelve hours. If you pee on the seat or miss, you will clean up behind yourself. I will check. I don't mind cleaning the bathroom but you will not pee on the floor or seat. If you don't wash your hands when you're done, trust me, you will be sorry." Everyone was laughing and the line for the lavatory began.

Tony sat with Reggie for a long time and talked. After an hour or so, Reggie called Dominic over. Tony and Reggie were sitting at the table and they moved over to make room for him.

Reggie started, "Dom, you are doing better than we thought. You obviously are a quick learner and clearly you prepared yourself. I just want to talk with you and get to know who Dominic is. So, what is it you want to be when you get older?"

Dominic thought about it for a few minutes and answered, "I don't know. I want to go to college but I have no idea yet. I might want to take over my father's business one day but I am not sure if it is for me or not. My parents are very adamant that I go to school. I won't have a choice. I think I want to be a pro rider in BMX if I am good enough."

Reggie and Tony both laughed. Reggie replied, "I want you to be a pro rider but, if you had a college degree I could market you more so than Tony." Tony sat there and shook his head up in down yes with a nod.

They talked for a while about Dominic and his aspirations, his favorite music, favorite foods and goals. Tony spoke to Dominic, "Dom, I went to college. I went for two years. I don't have a four year degree but I actually took some time for academics. There is nothing more important than education. Ask Reggie. One day I will not be able to race like I do. It's inevitable that one day a young man like you will come through the ranks and take over my short reign I am holding. After BMX I have to figure out what I want to do. I'm not going to be a BMX champion when I'm sixty years old. I will only be a former BMX champion with these vivid memories. Maybe I will be involved with BMX somehow, but it's not a guarantee. With an education a person becomes more marketable and it becomes easier to find a job making more money. Let's face it, we all get old. Could you imagine your father racing BMX?"

They all laughed. Tony continued, "Dom, figure out what you want to do one day. Not now, you're too young. Promise me you will go to college and get a four year degree or more. There is nothing more I want than to see you be the number one pro rider one day. But with an education someone will gather you up and give you position in an organization that allows you to further your career. I know one day this will end for me. I am one accident or injury away from retirement. It's always on my mind. I am blessed to have Reggie, I know I have a job for life with him, but one day Reggie will retire and even sell his company if the price is right."

Reggie looked at Dominic, "What Tony said is true. I don't know the future and I can't predict what is to come. I enjoy what we are doing right now. I want this to last forever. Maybe it will. But it is true, one day Tony will have to retire and decide what he is going to do next. I have a strong feeling it will be BMX related, but I am as dedicated for my riders as they are for me."

Dominic was surprised how he spoke with him. He felt like an adult in an adult conversation. He has heard this speech before from his parents. He never thought about it much but he also knew that he had time to figure out what the future brings.

It was very clear that Tony and Dominic have become close and good friends. They hung out together in the Puma Palace all the time. They were buddies.

The Puma Palace finally arrived at their destination. It was getting dark and the team was ready for food and their chores. The Puma Palace pulled into the spot they would be camping for the next few days and Tony called for the chores. It was a peaceful evening for all and the team was allowed to sleep in for a short time before the smell of bacon filled the air.

Chapter 40

Another week has flown by and Rafael awakes to his mother and father's laughter. Rafael made his way out of his bedroom to see what was so funny. Evidently his older brother Carlos fell asleep on the sofa. His younger sister Julieta found humor applying make up to him as he lay motionless, fast asleep.

He was adorned with glitter blue eye shadow, rose colored blush, red lipstick not applied with any care, and his eye lashes were long and full. They all agreed to not wake him and let him sleep. Carlos would soon find out what had transpired as he laid in his slumber. During the morning's rant of laughter, Florencia was able to gather and pack the cooler for the day's events of racing.

Rafael was making a name for himself for being an extremely fast BMX racer. His friends continually pushed him at the pits. He constantly rode hard and was on a winning streak. Rafael was adored by many different people. His BMX team respected him and he had many friends in all aspects of his life.

Maximo loaded up the car with his wife, daughter and Rafael. As they were driving to the track, Rafael asked, "Dad, do you think the vampire kid will show up today?"

Maximo laughed and replied, "I don't know, but if he does, be nice to him."

Rafael looked at his father and shook his head yes.

Rafael and his family showed up at the track and unpacked the car. It had become a collective occurrence, and little words were spoken. Everyone knew what they were supposed to do and all the tasks were completed within ten minutes.

As soon as they were done setting up their little piece of the world, Rafael grabbed his bicycle and headed towards the starting hill for practice. Harry Hartle made his way over to Maximo. He sat directly next to Florencia and Maximo.

He asked, "So, I am just curious. Is this the last week we stop wearing our parrot hats?"

Maximo answered, "If you want to wear them, then wear them. The kid is making conversation with me and I am trying to figure out what he is doing. I don't know if I want to trust him, but I think there is something going on and he seems to open up for me."

Harry answered, "I understand, but he looks horrible. It's almost funny but not really. It's virtually creepy. If you can knock down any walls by all means go ahead."

Maximo smiled at him and continued to watch the riders take the track.

It wasn't long before the moto's were posted and Rafael was on the gate. In typical fashion the gate dropped and Rafael was leading the pack with Pork Belly in last place. As they came out of the first turn, the entire team was blowing their pig whistles and making the suey sounds.

The announcer began to laugh as he called the race. One would think this was cruel to pick on a twelve year old kid, but there are those special exceptions and Pork Belly was one of them. He acted like such a fool, it had become expected to make fun of him.

It seemed the day had almost dwindled away before Christopher the Goth kid made his presence. There was something different about this day. He wasn't so Gothed up. He had the black eye shadow and the clothing with all the trimmings.

He lost the white face make up. As he walked by he acknowledged Maximo and pleasantly said, "Hello."

Maximo called over to him, "Christopher, come and eat something."

Christopher approached Maximo, not realizing Maximo had put his hand out as a gesture of friendship. Christopher shook Maximo's hand and returned the Maximo's gesture, "Hello."

Maximo asked, "You want some food?"

Christopher answered, "If it's not a problem sir."

Maximo was shocked. Christopher had manners and was acting polite. It was as if the kid had changed overnight. They talked for a few minutes before Rafael had his last moto race. Again, Rafael finished first and everyone blew their whistle for Pork Belly. Christopher understood what was going on and even he began to snicker. He even smiled.

Maximo and Christopher talked as Christopher was eating. He truly liked Florencia's cooking. Maximo broke the ice, "You don't eat much Mexican food?"

Christopher answered, "My family is very different. They are traditional and routine. They don't do anything that is not considered proper."

Maximo looked at Christopher and replied, "Really, tell me about you."

Christopher looked at him with a blank stare. He was shocked that anyone wanted to know anything about him. Christopher finally rebutted, "You really want to know or do you want to make fun of me some more."

Maximo quickly replied, "Christopher, the race is over for us. Our son just won first place and we could get up and go. But I honestly want to talk with you. You interest me. Not just the way you look, but the little things you say. You may find it hard to believe, but I find you to be a smart intellectual with some type of twist and I can't put my finger on it."

Christopher was silent for a few moments before he uttered back at Maximo. Finally he asked, "OK, what do you want to know? Let me guess the first one. Why do you dress like that? What's up with the spiky hair?"

Maximo said nothing. There was silence for almost a minute. It felt like an hour. Maximo finally answered, "At first I was wondering about all those things, but honestly tell me about you. How do you do in school? How are your grades? What interests you?"

Christopher continued to finish his papayas. Maximo waited as any gentleman was expected. He made a motion to his wife to get a drink from the cooler for Christopher. Christopher finished eating and was polite and thanked Florencia for food. He told her, "My family would never allow me to sit here and eat with you."

Maximo interjected, "Christopher, please tell me why."

Christopher replied, "Sir, I'll be honest with you but you won't like it."

Maximo answers, "Please, just be honest with me. I will understand."

Christopher said, "OK here is the truth. My father feels that anyone other than white Anglo Saxon Americans should not be in this country. He also believes that Mexicans should be cutting our grass, cleaning our pool, and cleaning our house."

Maximo shook his head in disbelief, "I asked you to be honest. I will not judge you on what your father believes. This is not fair. But tell me, how do you feel?"

Christopher answers, "My father forgets that the true Americans were Native Americans. I know we took what was theirs. I don't want to be my father and I guess this is why I rebel by wearing these clothes. I want him to feel as I do when he looks at me. But the problem is, I love my parents and I am hurting my mother. I wish my father would snap out of it and get a reality check."

Maximo thought about what he just heard. Basically, Christopher was acting out against his father and did not want to be who he has become. Maximo patted Christopher on his back and said, "Listen to me my friend, it's ok to be different. But sometimes we take things to the extreme. Sometimes it becomes dangerous. Let me ask you, what do you like, what are your hobbies?"

Christopher smiled, "I like playing piano. But, I was classically trained and the formality of it all is boring. I want to wear something different and shock the audience with my playing. A very prestigious college accepted me. I am so tired of wearing a tux on stage. I want to wear this, what I have on and walk out. I can still play the same music. What would the audience think then? I have many thoughts going through my head and I can't get my ideas on paper fast enough. I want to add something different to a concerto that I like, for me."

Maximo answered Christopher, "So make it happen. I am a firm believer that you need school first. Become educated and obtain all the knowledge your professors give you. Then make it yours. Besides, a college education is good tool to have when looking for a job even if its music."

They talked for a while of the type of music Christopher enjoyed. Surprisingly, Christopher enjoyed the typical classical music of the renaissance age and baroque periods. Maximo finally came out with the big question, "Christopher, why? Why all this?" Maximo then pointed to his face and his clothes.

Christopher quickly answered, "Honestly, I don't know. I guess to be different. My father crawls out of his skin when he sees me like this."

Maximo answered, "I don't know what is happening in your house but, respect your father. One day he will be gone and you're going to miss him. You will miss him. You don't have to believe as he does, but you can make a difference. Go to school, dress normal. Dress however you feel you want. Just remember, first impressions are lasting ones. People at this very track have judged you and I can tell you that just sitting here talking with you for this short time, they have you all wrong. You don't deserve it. But you bring it on."

Christopher answered, "I'll make you a deal, and I'll dress what is considered normal if you have these talks with me."

Maximo shook his head yes and stated, "I have an idea. Do you want any ice cream? I am taking my family out for ice cream. It's at a Latin part of town. Even if you dress like this, you'll be the one shocked. They have a piano, organ or some type of keyboard devise. You can play for these people. Latin people will dance to anything. I can drop you off at home."

Christopher laughed, "Ok but, maybe I should wash my face. I don't think I need it any longer."

Maximo and his family continued to pack the car. Christopher came back about fifteen minutes later. They were shocked. He almost looked normal except for the clothes. Florencia looked at her daughter and in Spanish said, "He is very handsome. I like when he doesn't look like the devil."

They jumped in the car and made their way to Rivera's Helado Hacienda. Rafael didn't care what he said. He wanted ice cream.

They arrived at Rivera's Helado Hacienda. As predicted, all eyes were on Christopher. As they made their way to an open table, there was a few Latino's playing music. Christopher looked at Maximo with a bewildered look on his face. He never heard this type of music.

They sat and ate ice cream for a short time before Maximo asked, "Christopher, why don't you play something, whatever you want to play. It might be fun. It might even be a shock to these people."

Christopher quietly sat and watched the Latino's as they finished. Christopher silently made his way to the piano. It was very old, but it worked and sounded good. It was in tune and Christopher sat behind the keys alone. The place was silent. He started to play and within thirty seconds he captured the audience. His playing was phenomenal. No doubt, he was a concert pianist. He was playing a piece from the Nutcracker Suite. He won the hearts of all the onlookers. He won the audience over with his marvelous playing.

When he had finished, there was a long applause with some people standing. Someone yelled something out in Spanish. Maximo walked over and translated for him, "They want something in Latin."

Christopher replied, "Give me the music and I will play it."

Maximo replied for him, "Dale un poco de música para tocar (give him some music to play). Someone ran a book over to Maximo. It was a book of sheet music of Popular Latin Music. Maximo turned to a song title he knew and Christopher started playing. It was amazing. He played the song better than anyone had ever heard before. As he played, a man came up and started singing. It was surreal. This Gothic man has just won over the Latin community and he was mind-blowing. When he was finished and the applause ended, Christopher simply walked back to the table and sat down.

Maximo said, "Christopher, you just made fifty new friends. These people are very simple. Music is one thing that makes them feel important. It's an escape for them."

As Maximo and his family sat speaking with Christopher, a man approached them and asked Christopher, "My name is Eddie Rivera. I own this place. Every Saturday night we have a group come up and play. I pay them a small fee and it brings in customers. They sit and listen. While doing so, my business profits with the food and ice cream. I was wondering if you would like to come by Saturday night and play some music like you did before I gave you the music book. It's not much, but I can pay you $25.00 to play for an hour."

Christopher sat back in his chair completely astonished by Mr. Rivera's proposition. Christopher replied, "I would like to think about it."

Mr. Rivera answered, "No problema. If you want, just show up. You decide."

They departed and made their way home. Maximo asked, "Christopher, where do you live?"

Christopher answered, "I live by the old farm off of Long Pasture Drive."

They made their way toward Christopher's house. As they turned down Long Pasture Drive, Rafael remarked, "Dad, this is near where we ride our bikes at the farmer's pit."

Christopher said, "Yes, I live in the big house off that road."

As they approached, Maximo was surprised. The house he lived in was a mansion. Christopher asked, "Sir, just let me out here and I'll walk up. Like I said, my father has issues with many people. He is judgmental and I don't want any drama with him."

Maximo complied with Christopher's wishes and let him out of the car near the big gate. Christopher looked back at Maximo and waved.

As they drove home Rafael said, "Oh my goodness. His family lives in the house I was telling you about. He must be rich. I can't believe it."

Maximo replied, "I told you not to judge others. Now you understand. You thought he was a freak of some type. In reality his family is obviously wealthy and he is a nice boy. Be nice with him. He might need a friend like you. He will stop by next week at the track and who knows what happens from here. Florencia, burn my hat, I don't want to wear it any longer."

Chapter 41

It's Tuesday Morning and the team was heading toward Oklahoma City for the next national. Reggie was contemplating setting up camp in Albuquerque, New Mexico. He knew he could drive straight through with two drivers, but he wanted to relax on the way out. He had a long schedule ahead of them and he sensed that the scenery and the outdoors would be enjoyable for the kids.

Moreover, it was a long tour and he did not get to spend time in a beautiful countryside like the one he was witnessing often. He wanted to enjoy the views as he had done in the past. The overwhelming beauty cleansed his soul. The therapeutic sensation of the open surroundings of the trees and distant snowcapped mountains brought an inner peace and revitalization of self-preservation. He wanted to stay one more night but he knew that the kids were anxious to race and get to the next venue.

The team loaded up the Puma Palace and headed towards Oklahoma City. Along the way Dominic was continuously taking pictures. He utilized the money his father gave him for a camera which he used to document his trip. He used the camera to document his trip along with his racing. He had taken many rolls of film for both his racing and his trip across country.

Tony sat next to Dominic and asked, "I remember my first trip. I was like you. I wanted to take pictures of everything. It's a big country and it amazes me how spread out it is."

Dominic nodded and continuously took in the views. Tony and Dominic talked for hours before Reggie made the decision to camp in Albuquerque.

The team arrived at the Sandia Park area. They had time to stretch and unload their bicycles. Tony decided to take the team for a pseudo ride. It was to get the tension and anxiety out of their system. It wasn't long before they were all back at the Puma Palace and camp was set up.

Reggie called the team over as they sat eating burgers and hotdogs. Reggie spoke, "Ok people, we are leaving in the morning for Oklahoma. We are going to stay at Choctaw, Oklahoma then to a hotel for a couple of nights. I want all of you to take a proper shower and smell nice and clean. Remember to act accordingly and be respectful. This is going to be a lot of fun."

Like clockwork the team left in the morning. They arrived in Oklahoma late in the afternoon. Dominic noticed that they had traveled down route 66 and he made it a point to take several pictures because he had heard of this historic route.

The team was going to camp out one more night but Reggie decided to stay in the hotel for the next three nights. The hotel they stayed in had a pool and it was refreshing for the team to enjoy some down time. Dominic did not room with Tony as he desired. He was rooming with Eric who was two years older. Dominic was friendly with Eric and enjoyed his company.

After the night's events of swimming and eating at the hotel buffet, Tony explained to the team that they would be sleeping in late and would meet at the RV at 10AM. They would go out for lunch and then to the track for a Friday practice.

The race was on Saturday. Ironically the entire team was in their rooms by 9PM and all were sleeping by 9:30PM. The road was taking its toll on the team. The long lumbering sleep refreshed everyone.

In the morning, everyone was at the Puma Palace on time except for Reggie. He came down last minute as usual. He apologized to the team and explained that he was on the phone with the track officials. Team Panther was scheduled for a 5 PM practice.

The team ate lunch and slowly drove to the track. Although they were scheduled for 5 PM the track officials allowed them to take the track early. It was noticeable that as they moved across the country, many teams started falling off. Many of the riders from the west coast did not make it to this national. There was still an impressive amount of riders at the track.

Finally Team Panther took the track. Before long the starting gate was in operation and they all were very eager to get some gates. This track was not as technical as other tracks. There were only a few jumps and the turns were semi flat. It was lengthy but it was a sprinters track. It was a matter of getting in and out of the turns.

The berms were not very high and the track presented many opportunities for passing in the straights. The team made many gate starts before they huddled at the Puma Palace. Tony gave his observations of the track to the team. He described and pointed out all the opportunities for passing. He described in detail each and every aspect of the course.

The team departed for the evening. They went back to the hotel and enjoyed the pool and buffet as they did the previous night. They all met at the RV in the morning close to 7 AM. The team made their way to the track.

As the RV pulled into their designated spot, it was apparent that is was going to be another scorcher. Tony came out of the Puma Palace and yelled, "Chores." The team was very progressive at this point and it took very little time to set up the display and ready the camp.

As the day progressed, it was obvious that this was not going to be the biggest turnout but still very sizeable. Nevertheless, there were many riders and the day would go into the twilight finishing near dark.

Dominic got his moto number and like always, he sat and watched the races. He and Tony sat for approximately an hour and a half before Dominic made his way to the starting gate. He would have a main event and needed to qualify in fourth or better.

As he staged, he was approached by many riders in his age group. He recognized only a few other riders from past races but basically all new faces. One of the racers asked, "Are you Dom from New Jersey?"

Dominic answered, "Yes."

The rider then remarked, "We have a couple of riders here who were talking about taking you out in the turn." As he said this, he nodded towards the riders to indicate who they were.

Dominic replied, "It's not the first time. They need to catch me first."

The rider laughed and said, "They think they are fast. They're experts, but only race around here. They know you're the one to beat." Dominic thought to himself that he keeps hearing this but does not get it.

Finally Dominic was on the gate and ready for it to drop. The cadence was called and like a bullet, Dominic was out in front. There was a little jump that he simply pedaled over and made his way into the short berm, first ninety degree left hand turn. As he exited he noticed that one of riders he was warned about tried to smash into him but he was already distancing himself from them.

There was another right hand ninety degree turn. Dominic made the turn and checked out. No contest. He was pulling way out front. He was strong. He had one more turn. Another left handed turn to a right handed turn. Both turns were forty five degrees. He crossed the finish line and realized how far in front he was.

The announcer commented, "Well folks if you're not convinced maybe now you are. New Jersey does have some fast rides. Dominic

Carlucci is back at his team's camp eating hotdogs and his moto is still racing. This kid is twelve years old folks."

Dominic made his way over to Tony and Reggie. They were talking to someone who looked important. Dominic asked, "What do I do? I was told these two kids were trying to take me out. I could tell that if I was any slower out of the turn it might have happened.

Tony replied, "If this happens, there will be serious reckoning. "

Dominic answered, "OK, but I think there are some issues with these guys."

Later, Tony was on the line. As soon as the gate dropped, he was gone. Like Dominic and many other strong riders, once out of the first turn the race was over. Tony darted away from the pack. He received a standing ovation as he raced around the track. He was the number one pro in the country and everyone one knew him. He was faster than ever. The track was so straight that Tony was able to use his strength and sprinting ability to pull away from the pack.

Dominic was at the gate for his second moto. He was far to the outside and knew that he had to somehow make his way to the inside. The gate dropped and Dominic was in front instantly. He was making his way to the inside but could not completely close the gap.

He knew he was going to take the first turn and make his moves as needed. As Dominic made his way into the turn, one of the riders he was warned about crashed directly into his back wheel with no intent of making the turn. Dominic and the entire pack went down.

The last place rider slipped through and was now in first. Dominic instantly grabbed his bicycle, pushed it and jumped on it. It was too late. His back wheel was caved in. He now finished in last.

He noticed out of the corner of his eye Tony and Reggie running over. Dominic looked over to them and showed him his bike. Reggie asked, "Are you OK?"

Dominic shook his head yes and walked his bike to the finish line in order to gather the points. He knew if he finished first in the next moto, he would qualify for the main.

Reggie and Tony were furious with the official in the first turn. The announcer commented, "I don't know folks. You call it what you will, I call it dirty. The OKC bikes' rider didn't even try to turn, he made a b-line into the Team Panther rider from New Jersey. Now you have the owner and the number one pro in the nation arguing with the track officials. I know what I saw."

As Dominic pushed his bicycle to the finish line, many spectators clapped for him. Still at the first turn, there was a gathering of all the officials. Reggie was furious, yelling and moving his hands all over the place. Reggie's rant lasted for nearly fifteen minutes holding up the racing.

Dominic could hear Reggie yelling, "What's right is right. I would not have this conversation with you if one of my riders' did this to someone. They would be off the team and on the plane home already. This isn't right. You know it."

Dominic was in his camp while Reggie was still protesting the actions of a rider who deliberately ran into him. As Reggie walked over to the Puma Palace, Dominic's bicycle was already repaired. He had a new wheel installed and he was ready for the next moto.

The announcer was muffled but he was talking with another official. Finally he announced, "Ok dokey folks, here is the result of the last race. Number 202 of the OKC Bikes is disqualified for the day. Johnny LeGraf is disqualified. The race will not be rerun and the positions will be as finished."

There it is. Dominic needed to place first in order to qualify. As he sat in his camp, he did not react. He simply sat and watched the other riders and knew what he had to do. Finally he made his way to the staging area.

Tony walked with him. It was almost intimidating to see. Many people wanted his autograph as he stood with Dominic. Tony stared down the other rider who was talking with Johnny LeGraf. Tony looked at him and said, "Don't be stupid. I'll do the time. Come near the track when my boy is on it and you'll deal with me first. I promise you. Leave him alone. He did nothing to you except smoke you on the track. Grow up."

Dominic was on the gate and Tony stepped back as the cadence was called. Dominic was in lane 2. The other rider talking to LeGraf was outside of him in lane 8. Dominic checked out instantly. He made his way out of the first turn and the race was over. He put a large distance between him and the pack of racers behind him.

The main event was the same way. Dominic jumped in front and cleared the track. No one was going to catch him. Tony finished first along with every rider from Team Panther except for Phil. He finished second behind Tony. Everybody received a first place trophy.

Dominic watched as the sun lay heavy in the sky making its way down. Someone with a clipboard approached Dominic and asked, "How do you feel about dirty riders?"

Immediately Reggie shouted, "Dom, do not answer her son." Reggie approached the lady and talked with her at length. She left and Reggie called Dominic over.

Reggie and Tony took Dominic away from the rest of the team and Reggie began to speak, "Dom, you need to understand a few things. Put on your big boy pants, open your ears and just listen. You are becoming famous. From here on out, everything you do will be noticed. I was proud of how you reacted to that idiot who tried to take you out. He nearly succeeded. You acted like a true champion. You did the right thing jumping back on your bike and finishing the race. That problem might appear later but you know how to respond. Many BMX magazines are going to start interviewing you. You need to be careful what you say. If someone wants to interview you, call me or

Tony. There a few things they are not allowed to ask and we want to protect you from saying anything that could rebound and have a negative effect on you."

Tony put his arm around Dominic's shoulder and quietly said, "Don't worry about that simpleton who tried to take you out. It's not going to be the last time this happens. You did the right thing. The first time this happened to me, I punched the rider out and then found his car and punched out all the windows. This solved nothing. Most of my winnings from that day were used to replace car windows. I almost got arrested. But, he never did this to me again. I was almost labeled as a hot head. Keep your cool and let us take care of business. By the way, you were smoking today. You're on fire Dominator."

Tony smiled as he walked back with Dominic. He now understood that his nickname was going to be Dominator. He didn't know if he liked it or not but it better than other nicknames he has heard in the past.

Chapter 42

It was late Sunday morning, Tony came out of the Puma Palace and sat in one of the fold up chairs and looked over the track. Team Panther camped overnight at the racetrack. There were other RV's and camp sites set up. Team Panther was not the only team and individuals who decided to camp out.

Dominic exited the tent and saw Tony sitting in the chair. He pulled up a chair next to him and asked, "What's up? You normally don't sit outside alone?"

Tony laughed and answered Dominic, "I had to get out of the Puma Palace. Everyone is snoring and farting. It's a big gas blast in there. I can't do it anymore. I needed air. You have the best gig with your own room and nobody to bother you."

Dominic rebutted, "It does get hot at night."

Tony and Dominic were talking for a while. Approximately thirty minutes later the RV door opened and Phil walked outside. He saw Tony and Dominic sitting outside. He looked at them and said, "It's a mess in there. We need to get some air-fresheners and ear plugs when we stop later."

Tony and Dominic started laughing. All three of them were sitting under the awning talking. They talked about various subjects. They varied from sports to music. Tony and Dominic had nothing in common when it came to sports.

Tony was completely West Coast sports and Dominic was East Coast teams. They both liked two different genres of music. But when it came down to it, they were nearly best friends. As all three of them sat discussing their various topics, several spectators and riders who camped out that night at the track approached Tony for his autograph.

Phil laughed, "What about mine?"

One of the young riders asked, "Who are you?"

Both Tony and Dominic started to laugh again. Phil assessed the situation and he also laughed.

It wasn't long before all the riders were up and making their way to the shade where Tony, Dominic and Phil had been sitting. It was nearly 9 AM and the sun's heat was already beginning to scorch the terrain. Tony noticed everyone was awake.

Tony approached Carl, "What time are we heading out?"

Carl answered, "Were going to make some lunch and start our four hour journey to Waco, Texas."

Tony called the team over as Reggie walked out of the Puma Palace. Reggie began to speak, "OK guys, here what's up. We are going to move out of here around noon. We are going to make our way to Waco, TX. We are going to stay at Lake Waco. I have a very good friend who owns property on the lake. When we get there, we will unpack for our camping adventure. We will be somewhat isolated. On Monday, we are going to do laundry. After we're done, we have a seminar and bike specialist demonstration. You guys are being featured and will demonstrate specific skills you possess. Continue to behave and have fun."

Carl, Jay and 'G' started up the grill. It was almost time for lunch. This was kind of special. There were scrambled eggs on a burger with cheese and all the condiments. The team ate lunch and broke down their camp. It was nearly 1 PM and Tony called the team to the Puma Palace.

It was refreshing for them to feel the cold breeze of the air-conditioning suddenly batter them. They loaded up and headed towards Waco, Texas. On the way, Tony and Dominic continued to jovially hack at each other. Other Team riders would chime in but it was apparent that Tony revered Dominic.

It was nearly a four hour drive to Lake Waco. As the team traveled down route 35, the air-conditioning suddenly stopped working. It was beginning to get hot inside the Puma Palace. Only the air-conditioning from the front of the vehicle from the engine was working.

Reggie spoke up, "Ok fellas, this is a little set back but these things happen. I will find someone to fix it for us. Just open the windows and enjoy the nice Texas heat."

Within five minutes there were rumblings about the heat. Dominic looked at Tony and asked, "Let's make them think you farted!"

Tony smiled and answered, "Nah, that's wrong in this heat."

Tony got up looked at Dominic as he fanned his face with his hand, "Oh man Dom, no you didn't in this heat. You're wrong. I can't believe you did it."

Dominic was speechless. Tony stole his joke and turned it on him. Dominic tried to defend himself but it was too late. He was getting blamed for something he didn't do. The entire team was beating him with their pillows.

Jay yelled back as he was driving, "If I smell it up here I'm stopping. I'm not here to smell your asses. Dom, I don't care how fast you are. If I smell it, I'm booting my foot in your butt."

Tony chimed in, "Jay relax, you're not booting anyone's butt. We are on the road in Texas in the middle of nowhere."

One of the riders yelled out, "Look, Beverly Hills in fifty miles."

There it was a sign for Beverly Hills. Dominic yelled out, "Hey Jay, I thought we were in Texas. You must be lost, we're back in California."

Jay laughed as well and shouted, "I'm gonna kill you Dom."

'G' turned around and shouted, "We're almost there guys."

Finally they reached their destination. As predicted, they arrived to an uninhabited area of land next to the lake. It was surreal at first but the reality set in. This was home for the next few days. The Puma Palace stopped and parked sideways facing the lake. Tony yelled, "Chores." The camp was set up in record time. Dominic had his tent up next to the lake enjoying the breeze coming in to cool him down.

Carl and Jay broke out the grill and started cooking dinner. It was quiet and a sense of calm overwhelmed the group. Tony shouted, "Get your bikes. It's bike maintenance time. Don't ride them. Clean them and fix whatever you think is wrong. Take advantage of this time to work out any issues you have with your bikes."

Dominic was happy that he was able to clean his bike. He never thought he would allow his bicycle to be this dirty. He cherished his bicycle and took extra time and care to ensure it was clean. In like fashion, Tony pulled up next to Dominic and began cleaning his bike showing Dominic some tricks that he used to clean inside the spokes next to the hub.

It was getting dark and the lights on the RV strung around the outside were shinning bright. It was also getting breezy and rain was in the forecast. Tony laughed and said to Dominic, "You might want to rethink sleeping outside tonight. It's going to rain."

Dominic looked around and understood that he had a decision to make. He entered the trailer and found some new tarps still in the packaging. He asked Tony, "Hey give me a hand spreading this over my tent. Get some of those big rocks and put them around the perimeter. This will make it nice and cozy." Tony and Dominic waterproofed the tent.

Later that evening the heavens fell out. The lightning was so formidable it was nearly daylight throughout the night. It was loud as if it were three feet from Dominic's tent. He thought nothing of it and simply rolled over and continued to sleep.

It rained harder that night than Dominic could remember. Still, he was dry. There was no water entering his domain. Finally daybreak broke through the ominous clouds. Dominic awoke. When exiting his tent he noticed that he was directly in the middle of the biggest puddle he had ever seen.

He was on high ground surrounded by a lake of water. There was laughter from his peers. He knew he was going to get wet as made his way towards the Puma Palace. The water was nearly knee deep.

He made his way to the Puma Palace as everyone laughed at him walking across the puddle. He said nothing and finally made it to his seat. He took his breakfast sandwich and starting eating it as if he had no cares in the world.

Tony laughing, "You realize you have to pack up your site?"

Dominic answered, "Not today."

Tony laughed knowing he was right.

Reggie came out of the Puma Palace stretching, "How are our guys that slept outside?" He noticed there were a few older riders who decided to camp out in the trailer and make it their demi home. He looked over at Dominic's tent and asked, "Did we pack a canoe to get Dominic off his island? He is the luckiest kid in the world. Imagine if he set up five feet closer towards the RV? Boy, he would have had to send up flares."

Everyone laughed and Dominic continued to eat. Dominic didn't mind. They were making fun of him because he was well liked. Reggie continued to speak, "Carl, we need to make our way downtown. Is Brian coming to get us soon?"

Carl answered, "He should be here around 11 AM.

The day's event was normal. Reggie's friend showed up with his van. The laundry was getting done and all the errands were complete. Reggie arrived to the campsite close to 6 PM with the rest of the team who were done with the laundry detail.

Reggie grabbed a large box out of the van and called for Dominic, "Dom, come get your new home!"

Tony walked over with Dominic. Reggie bought a large four man tent. It was a lot larger and allowed Dominic to stand up inside.

Dominic asked, "Why so big? Do I have a roommate?"

Tony raised his eyebrow at him indicating it was him. Dominic was really excited. He was going to room with his hero and new best friend.

That evening was no different than any others. Dominic and Tony were in their new home. Dominic found it very comfortable to sleep on his sleeping bag. It was perfect for him and he loved it. Tony slept on a blow up mattress. It was nearly 2 AM when Dominic made his way out of the tent to relieve himself.

From out of nowhere there was blood curling scream. It sounded like the soundtrack from night of the living dead. Dominic was screaming with sounds of snorting and wheezing from the distance. Phil ran out of the Puma Palace and instantly put on the lights. Tony ran out of the tent and the rest of the Puma Palace occupants emptied into the darkness.

There was still screaming and snorting from the woods. Finally everyone observed Dominic running out of the blackness with a small animal pursuing him. It was a wild boar running Dominic down. The boar was nearly three feet from Dominic when out of the darkness a large object struck the animal and it stopped instantly in its tracks.

After a long silence, Tony could be heard laughing loudly and hysterically. By this time Reggie came out of the Puma Palace with a flashlight. No doubt, it was a wild boar. It wasn't extremely large, but still a wild animal. By this time the entire team was outside in the middle of the night to see what had happened.

Reggie asked, "Son, what were you doing out in the middle of the night?"

Dominic answered, "Reggie, I had to pee. I walked away from the site to be polite so nobody would hear me or smell it. I saw this cute little animal next to me. Before I knew it, I was being run down by one of the three little pigs."

They were all laughing. Reggie tried to talk but couldn't, he was laughing as well. Dominic observed his best buddy Tony laughing at him. Tony called him back to the tent.

"Common brother, we'll pee in teams from now on."

Dominic found the humor in the situation and yelled out to Reggie, "I got the bacon, who is going out into the woods to get fresh eggs?"

Chapter 43

It was July 19^{th,} 1980 and the sun was hammering Waco, Texas. It was the day of the national. Hartle BMX was en route to the race track. It was nearly 5 AM and Rafael was sleeping in the car as he, Maximo, Florencia, Christopher and his sister Julieta were following Harry Hartle and the rest of the team to Waco, Texas.

This was a national event and part of this year's tour. Rafael had the opportunity to gather triple points and a national ranking. He was the most favored on the team to win. Rafael had no idea of who his competition would be on this day. He was excited about racing other riders; it had become more mundane racing the same individuals week after week. This would be a textbook opportunity to assess his skills.

Rafael's friends Bobby, Austin, and Tommy were coming to the race to be spectators. They were traveling with Tommy's father. It was odd, but for some reason, Maximo had taken a liking to Christopher. Rafael didn't seem to mind and he found Christopher interesting.

This day was much different. Christopher was dressed normal for the first time. He was wearing dungaree shorts with a light blue t-shirt. His hair was cut and he appeared like a normal young adult. Florencia continued to declare that he was an attractive young man.

Maximo arrived at the Waco, BMX facility. Rafael was surprised by the number of riders and the factory teams. There were tractor trailers, RV's, campers and vendors everywhere. It was a bigger deal than he imagined.

Harry Hartle set up his team camp area and called for a meeting. Harry explained the day's events and what he expected of his riders. He wanted them to have fun but he truly wanted them to win. It was a hot day. They all knew this day would not be over until early evening.

Rafael took the track and was astounded by its technical areas. The first straight had a large rolling jump into the first turn. The first turn was a 180 degree left turn with high a berm. There were several jumps in the second straight. The third turn was a right handed 180 degree turn with a high berm.

Next was a short straight to a left 90 degree turn to a long straight with two jumps. Rafael was excellent at jumping but he had a sinking feeling that he was slightly out of his element. Rafael made several gate starts and was shocked by how good the out of town riders were able to move off the gate so fast. He knew at this point that he had his work cut out for himself.

It wasn't long before the recognized announcement, "Moto's are posted." Rafael and his father made their way fighting the crowd to the moto board. Rafael was stunned. There were over thirty riders in the twelve year old expert class. He was not racing the open on this day.

He never had this many riders in his class before and did not expect the amount of riders he witnessed today. He sat in the camp area speaking with his father and Christopher. Rafael explained the system to Christopher. Rafael took a liking to Christopher. Beyond all the eccentrics, Christopher was incredibly intelligent and possessed life knowledge and incomparable street smarts.

Around the corner of the first turn were all the factory motor homes. Team Panther was a prominent force in BMX and always drew a crowd surrounding their camp area. It was not uncommon for younger riders to sit and wait for Tony to emerge from the RV.

On this day it was different. The air-conditioning was acting up and Tony sat outside enduring the heat. Tony and Dominic sat under the awning waiting to race their moto's. Dominic and Tony talked about their week and the exhibition they participated in during the week.

Continually out of the blue Tony would laugh out loud for no reason. When he did this, everyone understood he was reflecting back on Dominic getting chased by the boar running him down.

Tony was laughing when Dominic remarked, "I hope it happens to you. That was crazy. I'm afraid to pee in the woods. We don't have wild pigs in New Jersey, yet."

The races were underway. It was time and Dominic grabbed his gear and walked himself up to the staging area. He met up with moto racers and introduced himself. One of the riders looked at him and said, "So you're him. The one I'm going to smoke."

There was some laughter and one of the riders looked at Dominic and replied, "Let me introduce you to Pork Belly."

Dominic thought to himself, "Oh great, I can't get away from this plaque."

Dominic shook hands with the other riders and slowly crept into place before he was finally on the gate. He was on the gate directly next to Pork Belly.

Dominic looked over to his right and said, "Don't try anything stupid. That's all I'm going to say. I have a very protective team and I just want to race and nothing else."

Pork Belly replied, "Don't get in my way then."

Dominic knew that he needed to get in front of this guy and distance himself.

Dominic is in lane six and it was a full gate. The sun was burning through his clothes. It was so hot, Dominic felt like he was standing in the middle of an oven. The gate pulled up and Dominic readied himself on both pedals ready to get started. He noticed Pork belly was using the old one footed start and recalled how much better he had become using the two pedal starts.

The cadence was called, the gate dropped and they were off. He had a good start and was in the lead on the outside with a few riders inside of him hanging on his left shoulder. The group of riders reached the first jump and Dominic was able to distance himself by pedaling over the jump and pump through into the first turn.

It was a 180 degree left handed turn. He was pedaling out of the turn and he noticed Pork Belly shoot to the inside and crash into a bunch of riders. It was a domino effect. Pork Belly crashed into a few riders including Rafael who crashed into Dominic.

After all the commotion, Dominic was able to control himself. He fell down and grabbed his bike and pushed it until remounting his bicycle and start pedaling. He was in third place. There was a home town rider in front of him and Rafael was in second. Dominic tried to run them down into the second turn.

Dominic was able to make up some ground but remembered Tony's instruction about qualifying for the next round. Dominic finished third.

He regrouped with all riders after the moto and asked Rafael, "What happened? Why did you run into me?"

Rafael answered, "I was hit by someone else and I was knocked into you."

Dominic was clearly upset and rode off to his camp saying nothing.

When Dominic made it to his camp he dropped his bike and was still upset. Carl grabbed his bike and noticed he had several spokes missing. He put a new wheel on his bicycle. One of the other riders helped adjust his front brake.

Reggie walked over to Dominic, "Young man, I saw what happened. Relax, this happens."

Dominic answered, "How does that group over there know about my pig experience?"

Reggie asked, "What? What are you talking about? Is the heat making you delusional?"

Dominic answered, "No, I hear pig whistles and people yelling suey and junk like that. Did you say something?"

Reggie laughed, "No, but I heard it too. I will find out what's going on young man."

Dominic waited patiently in his camp for his next moto. He was excited when Tony took the gate. Everyone was cheering for him. Tony won his heat race. Dominic was happy for his friend. Finally Dominic was getting ready for his second moto.

He met up with all the riders and they commented about Pork Belly being an idiot. Rafael made his way over to Dominic, "Hey, just so you know, I didn't run into you on purpose."

Dominic answered, "Okay, I hope not. Let's not have this happen again."

Rafael shook his head in agreement.

Dominic was on the gate with both feet on his pedals. The gate dropped and like before, Dominic was in first place over the first jump and into the first turn. He pedaled through the turn and was clearly out in front. Dominic made more distance over the two jumps in the second straight.

He was coming out of the third straight and he could hear the sounds of crunching. Dominic was so far in front that he could have coasted to the finish line. He did not know it and raced to the finish line. As he crossed he noticed that the rest of the moto was still fighting for second place.

Pork Belly struck again. Like before, Dominic heard all the pig calls. He was clearly upset.

He made his way back to the Puma Palace. Tony met him halfway and noticed he was clearly miffed. Tony asked why he was so upset. He explained the pig sounds. Tony could not help himself and started laughing.

At the Puma Palace, Tony was explaining to Reggie why Dominic was so upset. Reggie was laughing and finally agreed to talk with the Hartle BMX group. Tony and Reggie both made their way over the Hartle Camp.

Reggie introduced himself and everybody already knew who he was along with Tony. Dominic made his way over a couple of seconds later. He walked up with a few other teammates. They were in shock. There was Reggie speaking to a few people and he was speaking Spanish.

They said to each other, "Reggie speaks Spanish?"

It was clear. He did. As Reggie spoke to Maximo, he began to laugh harder and harder. Maximo was explaining the Pork Belly fan club. As Reggie spoke to Maximo and the rest of his family, he explained what happened to Dominic and they all nearly fell to their knees laughing.

Dominic was standing at the Hartle camp in complete shock. He knew there was something going on but he wanted in on the joke. Maximo called Dominic over and patted him on the shoulder. He tried to explain to him what the joke was but he began to laugh too hard.

Nobody could explain it to Dominic, it was too funny. Finally Christopher approached Dominic and explained the complete story of how they use the whistles for the rider in his moto they call Pork Belly. After a while Dominic began to laugh.

Maximo called Dominic over again, "You have some luck."

Again he began to laugh. Christopher turned to Dominic, "Don't even ask about the hats, that's another long story and I don't want to remember. Maximo and his family are good people. Rafael is a nice kid. Get to know him."

Tony took some pictures with the team and signed a few autographs and returned to the Team Panther Camp with Dominic almost crying form laughter. Dominic continued to finish first in all his moto's including the quarterfinals, semifinals, and qualified for the Main.

Dominic was on the gate with Rafael. Pork Belly did not qualify. Dominic looked over to Rafael to the inside of him, "If I hear pig whistles this time. I'm going to go crazy."

Rafael laughed and made himself ready. The Cadence was called and the gate dropped. Dominic was gone. He pedaled into the first turn and literality checked out. The announcer, "New Jersey rider Dominic the Dominator Carlucci out front being chased by Texas rider Rafael Santos in second. Third place rider from Nevada looking to make a move on second. Out of the first turn New Jersey rider making some distance. Here he goes, New Jersey pedaling over the jumps. Rafael Santos in second but losing ground to first place. The New Jersey rider is checking out folks. Team Panther is proud of this young man. He is making it look easy. Jersey is checked out. Second place rider Rafael Santos being stalked by the Nevada rider. Fourth place rider from Oklahoma and fifth place rider from Alabama holding on. Folks, the race here is for second place. Down the last straight for second is… I don't know. It's too close. Okay, I am told its Texas rider Rafael Santos."

After the moto, Rafael and Dominic walked up together to the Team Panther camp. Rafael stood and talked for a while with Dominic and Tony. Maximo came running over to greet his son. He was proud of his son and hugged him. Reggie walked over like a gentleman and shook Rafael's hand and then Maximo's.

Reggie and Maximo spoke for a while in Spanish pointing at the Puma Palace. It wasn't long before Maximo returned and made his way into the Puma Palace with a tool bag and some hoses. Maximo was the hero of the day. He fixed the air-conditioning.

After Maximo was done with the Puma Palace, Reggie invited the Hartle BMX team over for burgers and hotdogs. They all came over and were eating as Tony took the gate. Tony went on to win the Pro purse of $5000 this day. He returned to his camp with everyone eating burgers and empanadas. Tony arrived to all the fanfare. He grabbed an empanada and sat down. He grabbed a cold drink and tried to catch the rest of his breath.

This was to be the beginning of new adventure. Dominic had a new friend and competitor. As they sat there eating and talking, the cool breeze of the air-conditioner could be felt on their backs as riders entered and exited the Puma Palace. It was a fun day. Dominic won first and so did his best buddy Tony.

He made a new friend and finally had food that reminded him of his buddy Oscar back home. Maximo invited the team to the ice cream store three hours away before they made their way back on the road. It was getting late and the sun was beginning to set. Reggie asked them to stay for a while. They were all in agreement; they would try to meet up in Birmingham for the next race.

Chapter 44

It's Sunday morning and Team Panther is packed up and ready to embark to Birmingham, Alabama for the next National. Dominic completed his chores and is in the Puma Palace with refreshing cool air-conditioning. Reggie called for a team meeting in the back of the RV.

Reggie conveyed that they were going to make their way to Shreveport, Louisiana. He wanted to ensure that everyone understood the dangers of camping in the southern region of the USA. He tried to explain about the types of snakes and other creatures living in the woods.

But he couldn't contain himself. As he spoke and tried to collectively hold in his emotions, he continually began to laugh. Reggie was recalling the incident of the boar chasing Dominic. He finally broke down in laughter followed by the rest of the team. Dominic was a good sport and took it in stride.

Reggie finally collected his emotions and communicated the information about the various poisonous snakes, insects, and other animals. He referred to the animals in the forest as locals.

Reggie stringently instructed Tony and Dominic to secure their tent. He instructed them to zip up all the enclosures and check their beds before climbing in them when they go to sleep. They both agreed along with the other riders who elected to sleep in the trailer.

Reggie yelled out to Tony and Dominic, "Ok guys, you're all set now. It's like hog heaven out there." There was some laughter in the Puma Palace but everyone understood the sincerity of Reggie's meeting.

The team arrived at the Red River National Wildlife Reserve area. They had arrangements for a KOA campground in the local area. The team arrived at their camp site and in usual fashion Tony shouted, "Chores."

It was business as usual. Tony grabbed the tent and found a nice shady place behind the RV on a flat area. Within a couple of minutes Dominic was assisting Tony. He completed his chores and was making his nest inside the tent. Tony was continually laughing at Dominic.

Finally Dominic rebutted, "Come on man, what's so funny now?"

Tony laughed and answered, "Dom, I can't get that incident out of my head. I never saw a white boy run so fast in my life with their junk in their hand."

Dominic laughed at his remark and answered, "Come to my high school this fall."

Reggie gathered up all the riders and informed them that they were allowed to ride their bicycles to the pay phones. He cautioned them about being professional and courteous to the other campers. He also reminded them that it was laundry day. Dominic made his way to his bicycle along with Tony.

They took their time riding to the phones. They both knew that the rest of the team would be a while. Dominic worked on his bike. He lubed all the cables and adjusted his brakes. His bicycle was always in perfect shape. He was commended for taking care of it. After a while Tony and Dominic pedaled leisurely to the payphones.

Dominic called his house and his father answered. Tony waited silently as Dominic continued to speak with his father.

Dominic asked, "How is everything going in New Jersey?"

Angelo laughed, "Well, not too bad. Your brother got into another fight and you mom is ready to kill him."

Dominic answered, "Another one? What did he do this time?"

Angelo answered, "Not too sure. He really didn't want to tell me. But your brother lumped up the other guy pretty good."

Dominic asked, "Who was it?"

Angelo answered, "J.B."

Dominic began to laugh, "Can I speak to him?"

Joey grabbed the phone and said his hellos. Dominic asked, "Joey, what's going on there? Why are you fighting with J.B.? You're bigger than him and he normally doesn't bother anyone."

Joey answered, "The whole thing started over hotdogs and fruit pies."

Dominic continually laughing, "I don't even want to know."

Joey and Dominic talked for a while about the tour and the exhilaration of it all. Dominic continued to talk with both his father and mother on the phone at the same time. Maria couldn't stop crying. Dominic assured her that he would be home soon.

Maria cried out, "You were only supposed to be away for seven weeks and I just found out that it's nearly nine."

Dominic answered her, "Mom, I will be there soon. I miss you guys but I am doing really good racing. I made new friends and people know who I am when I show up at race tracks. I feel like a rock star. But in all seriousness, I miss you all."

Angelo answered, "Well son, when you get home, we have a surprise for you. Oscar and I pulled some resources together and we want to show you something when you get here."

Dominic was jumping out of his skin. He tried to get his father to tell him what it was but he would not budge. Dominic told his father and mother, "When I get home, please, please, please, no hotdogs or hamburgers. Maybe something different to eat like lasagna or anything mom makes."

Maria starting to cry again because of the beautiful comments Dominic expressed towards her.

Dominic talked for nearly twenty minutes before he hung up. Tony was shaking his head at him. Tony expressed that he felt the same way about eating hamburgers and hotdogs all trip. He assured Dominic that Reggie is full of surprises, especially when he makes money at the tracks. He is very generous and continually brings happiness and a sense of dignity when he acts on impulse. Tony continued to assure Dominic that surprises are coming.

Dominic waited as Tony grabbed the phone and called home. This was a life changing event for Dominic. He listened to the one sided conversation from Tony not hearing the party on the other side of the phone. Dominic found out that most of all Tony's winnings were being sent home to care for his family.

Tony had no father figure in his life except for Reggie. He had two brothers who also helped with money and sometimes his other siblings. Tony's mother was very sick with cancer and she had no health insurance.

She was given assistance with health programs but Tony was doing all the groundwork on keeping his mother as healthy as he could. She wasn't terminal but she was showing signs of incapacity and was slowing down. She was in remission but had to continue progressive treatments to keep her condition from relapsing.

Dominic understood now, Tony wasn't racing for pride, glory, or recognition. He was racing to keep his mother alive. Dominic couldn't imagine riding for this reason and for every pedal Tony cranks is for his mother's life. Dominic wanted to cry but kept his composure.

He acted as if all was OK. He listened as Tony said his goodbyes to his mother and brothers. As Tony hung up the phone he noticed the swelling in Dominic's eyes. At first he said nothing and rode off with Dominic towards the site. As they neared and the Puma Palace came into sight, Tony stopped and sat on a bench along the side of the dirt road under a shady tree.

He looked at Dominic and said, "Well, I guess you know. I only ask you keep it our secret. Only Reggie knows and no one else. If they find out, I know you said something." Dominic promised to keep their secret.

As they both sat on the bench. Dominic began to weep. He asked, "Tony, how do you go on? Does it bother you to do this in order to take care of your family? I mean every time you take the track you are reminded of home."

Tony looked at Dominic and laughed again, "Dominic let me be perfectly honest with you. My first love is always going to be family. But I love riding BMX. I love it. I have such an opportunity to better myself for the future. Besides, if I had to work for a living and take care of my family, we would starve. I make more money riding than I ever could working at a bike shop or building houses or something like that. Yes, there are times I think of my mother when I ride, but I ride because this is fun. I know many people think that I enjoy the publicity, but with the notoriety comes responsibility. Reggie explained this to me in detail. BMX was not Reggie's first venture working with youth. When you're ready to understand, maybe Reggie will tell you about his other ventures. He is a brilliant man with an open heart of gold. It's obvious Reggie is well off financially. He made most of his money in real-estate. Reggie would go into rundown urban areas, buy buildings, houses and apartments. He then set up educational programs and hired those same kids and adults into his organization. He provided them with skills and they would become carpenters, electricians, plumbers and stuff like that. There is a lot more to the story I'm leaving out. But Reggie would take kids out of horrible situations and befriend them giving them a fighting chance to be something they could never imagine."

Dominic interjected, "Like a BMX racer?"

Tony answered, "Yes, like a BMX racer. Reggie is respected and revered by many. There are some jealous people out there as well. Reggie eventually sold off some of the properties and invested some of it back into the community and some of it he kept. As he should, it's how he makes a living."

Dominic now understood what Reggie meant that day in his house when he said that he used to rescue kids. But this tour was no rescue mission. This tour was totally about his products and his branding. Dominic began to understand.

Dominic asked, "Tony were you one of those kids?"

Tony laughed, "No, my brother was. My brother asked Reggie to come out to the local BMX race on a Saturday. Thus, a long story short, this is how I met Reggie. I was nearly your age. I think I was actually fifteen. From there it was history as they say."

Dominic shook his head up and down indicating that he fully understood. Dominic asked, "What about your mom?"

Tony looked at him, "We all die one day Dom. She is doing well for now. Hopefully for the next thirty years. But I know it's inevitable, she will pass away young. I have prepared myself for this situation. When it happens, it happens. There is nothing I can do about it. She won't be suffering any longer. As for now, she is doing alright and she is not in pain. My mother is a devout Baptist and has a strong faith in God. She believes that when it's her time to pass, she will go willingly. I promised my mother to rejoice in her passing. She made me promise. I know she is going to heaven. She brought us up in a loving Christian environment. As far as my winnings; I give part of what I make to my family, some I keep, and some I donate to causes I choose. This brings me happiness."

Dominic enjoyed their talk. He not only became best friends with Tony this day, it was also his hero. Tony stood up and said, "oh, by the way. You've done it."

Dominic answered in horror, "Did what?"

Tony said, "Follow me."

They rode back to their campsite arriving at the Puma Palace as the rest of the crew was laughing and high fiving Dominic. Dominic was confused, Reggie walked over with the latest and greatest BMX magazine and there was Dominic on the front cover.

The title under his picture read, 'The Dominator of the Tour Series.' Inside, the article was about the up and coming BMX Stars. Dominic remembered when he was asked all the questions from the reporter in Van Nuys, California.

It was only a matter of time once he proved himself a champion before they published any articles about him. It was not long; it was a short paragraph of Dominic being from New Jersey and how well he was performing on the circuit.

Dominic looked at Reggie and asked, "Now what?"

Reggie quickly answered, "Opens."

Tony pumped his fist and said, "He's been ready."

Dominic understood that he was now going to race in the open class. There were older riders that would push his skills. Tony reminded the riders, "You guys know what this means?"

Dominic interjected, "I don't!"

Tony explained, "The first time your picture is in a magazine, we as a team get to put makeup on your face like a movie starlet. It's a sort of initiation."

They all clapped in agreement. Some of the others shouted out, "I remember my first picture."

Tony and Reggie expressed this is the first and last time this is to happen. Dominic sat back and let them all do what had to be done.

Dominic expressed, "I only have one question, why do you guys have women's make up?"

There was laughter. Tony looked at Dominic and said, "Someone give me some eyeliner."

Chapter 45

It's very early Friday morning, Maximo, his wife, daughter and Rafael are loading the car for their ride to Birmingham. They are going to camp overnight at a local campground for the BMX race on Saturday.

Rafael is excited. He recalls his last camping adventure. Maximo calls for his family. He explains the situation as they entered the car. He starts, "Ok, we are going to camp out tonight, then we are going to leave at 7 AM for the track. We will eat cleanup and leave. We will come back and sleep before going home Sunday morning. We need to get to the track before 8 AM. We have been invited by Reggie. He is the man who owns Team Panther, remember?"

Rafael is excited about the race. He is looking forward to racing in the nationals. The competition is extremely tight. He doesn't dominate the races as he does at his local track. All the factory riders are going to be racing and he is curious to see how he compares at this race.

This is one of the smaller nationals. Besides, he is looking forward to spending time in the camp of Tony Scholls and Team Panther. He is in disbelief of the upcoming events.

Team Panther is traveling directly to the track. The team is enjoying the scenery and singing Sweet Home Alabama as they cross into Alabama. Tony is dancing. He was known as a good dancer and when questioned, he called it popping. There is the typical horseplay as they travel.

This is the last stop for Tommy the nine year old expert. His parents are going to meet up with the team. After the race they are going to drive back home. They live nearly three hours from the track and it was originally agreed for him to end the tour at this track. He is going to meet the team again in Jacksonville, Florida.

The team pulls into the track and is met by some of the track officials. Immediately they tell Reggie he has to leave. Reggie was shocked. He asked why they had to leave. There are other teams already at the track and set up. The official basically told Reggie that he had to come back tomorrow at 7 AM.

Reggie was smart, he figured it out. There is the person from last year whose son was beaten by a Team Panther rider. He was in first place last year and was passed in the last turn by a Team Panther rider. He protested under the premise that his son was knocked and hit illegally by the Team Panther rider.

The protest was not valid and was dropped. This was the guy whose son came in second. Reggie reminded the track official in front of the entire team of what happened. They all laughed as he told the story.

The official became irate and shouted, "Move that piece of crap or I will have it towed."

Reggie responded, "I am here under the protection of your boss and I confirmed our arrival this morning with him. Call him and find out. We are camping here and we are not moving. If you want to call the police or whomever, feel free. I will contact both organizations about your actions."

There was nothing said after this argument. Reggie called over Dominic, "By the way, his son is a 12 expert rider. Please do what you do. Race clean and smoke this fool tomorrow. Don't forget your riding in the opens. Save some energy."

Dominic was excited and had never seen Reggie get mad. But he was very contained. Reggie walked off and headed towards the pay phones. As he walked off Tony belted, "Chores!"

It's nearly 7 PM, Maximo and his family made it to the track to meet up with Reggie. Maximo had his camp site set up and drove over to the track to meet up with Team Panther. Team Panther was sitting under the awning and enjoying the nice evening.

It was cooler this evening for some reason but it was relaxing. Maximo parked directly on the side of the Puma Palace. He and his family came out of the car with large aluminum trays filled with food. The team was excited. Finally, new food, no burgers or hotdogs this evening for dinner. Tonight was a feast consisting of tacos, burritos, and empanadas.

Reggie was very cordial with Maximo and his family. The team enjoyed listening to Reggie speak Spanish. It was funny to them all. Florencia asked if anyone wanted some pork shoulder. There was instant laughter. Dominic shook his head knowing he would have to endure his misfortunes of being chased by a boar.

The team sat eating their newly discovered Mexican food. Dominic was sitting next to Julieta. He spoke with her the entire time. He found her fascinating; she was only ten years old and spoke two languages. She had a sense of street smarts about her.

She was no stranger to life. She had an uncanny ability to sift through nonsense. As he sat speaking with Julieta, Maximo made it a deliberate point to sit next to Dominic as an outward sign of protection for his little girl. Dominic understood Maximo's body language and did not want to portray any signs of disrespect.

As Dominic politely excused himself, Julieta punched her dad on the arm as both Reggie and Florencia laughed. Maximo also cracked a smile knowing the disposition he portrayed.

The night went on till finally Maximo and his family departed for the campgrounds. A few hours later as Dominic and Tony lay in the tent, Dominic asked, "So what do you think of Julieta?"

Tony immediately answered, "I think she is young and her father is protective. I like you and want you to live until you're thirteen. Leave that little girl alone."

Dominic answered, "I did, and I was only talking to her."

Tony rolled over and murmured, "Leave that little girl alone."

The next day arrived and the team was eating breakfast. A track official entered the camp of Team Panther and asked to speak to Reggie. They walked off into the distance and spoke for a while. Reggie came back and called the team together. He started, "Well guys, It's going to be one of those days. For some reason we are not welcomed here. Why, I don't know! Ride clean and keep your wits. I have a feeling this is going to be a busy day for us. Some of the other teams are catching some grief as well. Dominic, remember our talks, you have to race this track as a so-called prodigy. I want all of you to race today and make ourselves scarce. We will camp overnight and leave at first light."

The track was horrible. It was only two turns and three straight-aways. It had one jump in the second straight and one more in the third. It was sort of long but not technical. It was going to be speed in the straights that wins the race.

The moto's were posted and Dominic would have no Semi. Only the first through fourth place advance into the main event. The open class he was racing would have a semi qualifier and a main event race. It wasn't long before Dominic was in the staging area awaiting his turn to race.

As he sat quietly some riders came up to him asking him if he was Dominic from New Jersey. He politely answered, "Yes."

One of the local riders made it a point to tell Dominic that he was no longer a champion and he was going to prove it today. Dominic shook his head up and down saying nothing.

Dominic was at the gate awaiting the cadence. The cadence was called and the gate dropped. Dominic flew off the gate towards the first turn. A man stepped out with a red flag stopping them. He could hear the announcer asking what happened.

The man whom Reggie warned about replied, "Number 87G jumped the gate." There were some boos from the crowd. Immediately Tony ran over arguing. He could be heard shouting, "He didn't jump the gate. He had a pretty good start and you are only doing this because he was in the lead beating your son. You're wrong. You know you're wrong. Now you're going to penalize him. He is still going to finish first."

At one time in BMX, if a rider jumped the gate they would make him start backwards. The rider would have to turn his bicycle around and jump back on it. Thus, the penalty would be for him to have to turn, jump on his bicycle and then pedal off the gate.

Tony ran over to Dominic, "Listen, this is no different than you having to pass everyone. Make sure you turn and wait a second. Let the gate clear and then take off. If you move off early again they will give you a DNF (did not finish) and this is worse than 8th. Make sure you pass them when the time is right. Remember; pick your place to make your move."

The riders lined back up on the gate. Dominic was turned the wrong way. He sat there until Tony motioned him to turn and go. The gate dropped and Tony hesitated. Tony gave Dominic the sign to go and he turned around and took off.

Into the first turn Dominic was picking up speed. He used all the leverage he could find. He passed the last place rider and made a move over the second jump. He was able to catch the fifth place rider at the second turn. He pedaled on the outside into fourth. He knew this is all he needed.

He could hear the announcer, "Local rider Henderson out front followed by 22X and close behind him number 3US in the third slot. Number 87G New Jersey rider closing the gap and challenging on the outside for third. Henderson still out front closely followed by 22X out of Texas. Now in third 87G Team Panther rider. Folks, he started backwards and is moving way forward. Can he chase down second? 87G challenging for second. Will he make it? Over the jump, Team Panther rider passing 22X now chasing down local rider Henderson. They are running out of real estate. And it's going to be #1 Henderson followed by 87G, 22X ….."

Dominic was happy with second place. He waited for the next race to watch his competition. His new friend Rafael finished first. They walked back to Team Panthers camp.

As he approached, he could hear the official talking loud enough for him to hear, "I told you those New Jersey riders are slow. First place son, way to go. This is an easy day for you."

Dominic said nothing. Rafael laughed, "What's next, they penalize you for going too fast?"

Dominic raced his open race and finished first. He was waiting for his second moto. He moved into his gate position one waiting the cadence. He was still going to race as he always does. The gate dropped and he flew off the gate. There was no red flag and he was out front. He negotiated the turn and was struck in the back tire by Henderson. Dominic continued to ride.

He could hear a strange sound from the back of his bike. It was a couple of broken spokes. He raced through it and finished so far in front he had to wait for the rest of the group at the finish. As he waited, Henderson crashed directly into him. Both Tony and Phil ran down to see what happened.

There was some commotion but Dominic said nothing and did not react. Phil yelled over to the official, "Did you see that?"

The official returned an answer, "See what?"

Phil then reacted, "You guys suck. This is the worst sportsmanship I ever witnessed." He looked at Henderson and pointed at him, "I wish I was younger than eighteen. In my hood, we kill for less. You watch yourself boy, watch yourself."

Dominic continued to finish in first place in all his opens. He was shocked by how tight the competition was in this group of riders. He was pressed, shoved and could not distance himself. The last moto was the best revenge.

Dominic was on the gate and waited for it to drop. He pedaled off but not as fast as he normal. He was in first place out of the turn and pedaled hard off the top of the turn. In second was Henderson. They made it to the first jump dead even. Dominic jumped the second jump as high as he could. This shocked Henderson.

He looked up to see where Dominic was going to land. As Dominic landed, Henderson moved over and lost his balance. He fell and Dominic continued to ride as normal and finished first.

Dominic was walking back to his Team with Tony and Phil next to him. There was an announcement that Dominic was being disqualified for un-sportsmanship. Reggie and Tony made their way to the protest area only to be greeted by a mob of officials.

They all confronted Reggie and told him that there was a review going on as they speak. Reggie made it a point that Dominic had every right to jump as high as he wanted before landing. There were no hindrances or interferences, Dominic did not even touch the other rider and he was well within the rules.

Dominic was exonerated and awarded first place, but they awarded second place to Henderson. Although unfair, Henderson made the mains. Dominic was on the gate. The cadence was called and Dominic was off the gate first.

He was pursued very tightly by Rafael. They both came out of the first turn and Dominic was stronger and started to pull away from Rafael. Dominic finished first. Rafael finished second. Henderson finished in fifth. There were no protests and Reggie was disgusted with the entire day.

Dominic finished second in his open main. He was beaten by a thirteen year old expert. Tony finished first and won $3000.00. Rafael was so excited to be hanging out with Tony. Phil did not make the mains and was blanked for the day.

After the last race, Reggie called the entire team over including Rafael and his family. Reggie started to speak, "I want all of you to know, I am proud of you. Don't let one individual give you a bad impression of Alabama. This man has to live with himself for being a jerk. Many people I spoke to from Alabama were the most polite and hospitable people I ever met. This is a beautiful state with breathtaking views. Dominic, you scare me son. Terrell, nice pass at the end for first place. The 16 experts all know who you are. We are going to leave in the morning for Jacksonville. We are going to stop in Atlanta, for a few days and stay at a hotel with a pool."

Everyone was cheering. He continued, "I'd like to thank Maximo and his family for joining us. It was nice having you. Thank you for the food. We all enjoyed it. We will keep in touch."

After his speech the team sat back and watched as Carl wheeled out the grill. There was silence. Jay and 'G' laughed.

Tony spoke up, "Interesting day today for all, I'm sure. There are going to be times like this in life when you know it's not fair. There is nothing we can do about it. You need to accept the fact it's happening to you and it's your turn. You have two choices, fight back and lose or learn from it and you'll never have lost at all. Chores!"

Chapter 46

Its late morning on Friday, Team Panther is traveling down I75 South headed towards Jacksonville. The team is sluggish from their early morning rise and breakfast. They are enjoying the comfort of the air-conditioning in the Puma Palace. It's not afternoon yet and the thermometer is reading nearly one hundred degrees.

Like any situation, when one gathers a dozen teenagers together there is going to be shenanigans and practical jokes. This time it was Phil's turn. He has been the silent assassin along the trip. He did not say much but he was the biggest and the strongest of all on the team. He was big, muscular and an all around good sport.

Phil fell asleep across the back of the Puma Palace taking up two sitting positions. The younger riders performed the shaving cream in the palm trick and it worked as advertised. Allen the eighteen year old expert piled a heaping handful of shaving cream into Phil's hand as he slumbered.

Darren the ten year old expert wiggled a string in Phil's ear. In textbook fashion Phil plastered himself with a full helping of shaving cream. There was an uproar of laughter from the rear of the Puma Palace. It was enough for even Reggie to get up from the front table where he was sitting with Carl and Tony to see what transpired.

He witnessed Phil wake up in a vacillated state of confusion. Reggie, Tony and Carl found the humor in the practical joke and enjoyed a good laugh. As Phil entered the bathroom to cleanup, there was more of an uproar. He was going to have to clean it. Phil protested that he didn't use the toilet.

Nevertheless, Tony laid down the law. Tony replied, "It's your turn Phil." Phil laughed and understood the rules. Phil might have had the last laugh. He used the bathroom for all its glory and left the door open as he exited. It only took a few seconds before the entire Puma Palace windows were ajar.

The riders enjoyed their time together. There were practical jokes and esprit de corps throughout the Team. They shared respect for one another and many times a good laugh. Tony was the master of his craft. Not only was he the best rider in the United States, he was a motivator and leader.

He carried himself with a command presence and people genuinely enjoyed being around him. His personality was characterized as a shy individual, but he had a motivational switch. He was positive and led by example. He never expected anyone to something he could not do himself.

He was knowledgeable in the art of rationale. He had a gift of knowing when to push and when not to push. He was gentle but inside he was a lion. He protected his pride and was a professor of motivation. Tony was received by many and giving in the same respect.

As they rolled into Jacksonville, Tony called the entire team to the back of the Puma Palace. He started, "Ok fellas, we are in FLA. Like Texas, it's hot and muggy. I know you're going to be hot, sweaty and may feel miserable from the heat. But, we all need to drink plenty of water and look after each other for the signs of heat stroke."

The indications of heat stroke were briefed several times in the Puma Palace. The entire team was given instructions by Carl. He described how to treat it should it happen. Tony continued, "Remember it's not just us we need to look after. If you see someone else experiencing the signs of heat stroke, help them."

It was nearly 4 PM and the team immediately started the chores as the RV parked in its assigned parking area. Reggie was off instantly to meet with the track officials. He was always on the move and motivated.

The team was all set up and the heat of the day was scorching. It was nearly one hundred degrees and not a cloud in the sky. The team was allowed to practice but there was no operational starting gate at this time. The track was well maintained and all the turns had high berms. Dominic found the track to be his favorite so far. Every straightaway had several jumps and the last straightaway had a whoop section. He was able to jump across all three jumps that tightly made up this obstacle. He felt good about this track.

The team camped out that evening in the Puma Palace. They all joked about showering under the hose. Tony and Dominic originally planned on sleeping in the tent but the night was balmy. The team made room for them to sleep indoors enjoying the air-conditioning.

As the morning arrived, the team woke again to the smell of bacon. It wasn't long before they were all on the track making gate passes with their respective practice age groups. Dominic was racing both his class of twelve expert and the open class.

The afternoon rolled on and finally the moto's were posted. This time it was different. The Pros were the first ones to race. This was a big turnout. There were nearly fifty pros and there were going to be quarterfinals, semifinals, and the main event.

Dominic was going to have a semi and then a main event. The open class was large. Dominic was going to race quarterfinals, semifinals, and the main event in addition to his normal heat class.

Tony was in moto number one. He was on fire this day. It was a large turnout and he led every lap when he was at the gate. He was unstoppable. He was revered by many on this day. Dominic was in the staging area readying himself for his first race. He took notice of some of the riders.

He was beginning to see the same faces at every track. He was polite and joked with many of the familiar faces. Many of them knew who he was before he introduced himself. One of them even joked about his picture on the magazine cover. He was cordial and joked about it himself.

Dominic was at the gate awaiting the cadence. As it was called the gate dropped and he was off. He was surprised. He was nearly unable to pull away from the pack as he did in the past. He thought to himself that this race was more like an open class and racing older riders.

He was challenged and had to push harder than he ever had in the past. He finished first in all his twelve expert class. He finished first and seconds in his open class. He could feel the heat blistering him and figured it was going to be a long day.

Dominic finished in first for his age bracket and was gathering notoriety. He made it to the main in his open class. In unorthodox character, he was in second place trying to pass the first place rider. Dominic was hit from behind and finished last in the main event for the open class.

He could see Tony running over to him. As he approached he asked, "Are you ok?"

Dominic answered, "Yes, I'm fine. This is the worst. I finished last."

Tony laughed, "It's ok how is the ground? Is it OK?"

They both laughed. Dominic grabbed his bike and glided through the rest of the track to finish the race.

Later that day after the racing was completed, there was much fanfare surrounding Tony. He won again. He was holding up a check that showed an $8,000.00 grand prize. Dominic was happy for his friend but he was exhausted.

He joked that he drank the five gallon bucket of water by himself. As the sun was setting late in the afternoon, 'G' was manning the grill. He was not cooking the normal burgers and hotdogs but polish sausage and chicken.

Dominic was drained of all his strength. He never raced that many moto's in one day. He was upset that he finished last in the main. Tony and Phil approached him. Phil stated, "Yo, don't be sad little guy. You made it to the main and fell. It happens to all of us. I didn't make the main today. How do you think I feel?"

Dominic shook his head almost too exhausted to speak. Tony looked at him, patted him on the back and said, "You're a loser, get your crap out of our tent. LOSER." They both laughed together.

As Tony and Dominic were speaking Reggie approached them. He started to speak, "Dominic, awesome race. It was pretty. You are the next big thing. I'm telling you that you are going to be the next Tony one day. There is nothing wrong with eighth place in the open class today. You made it to the main and acted like a champion when you fell. You did not react nor did you get angry. This is part of racing BMX. You're not always going to win. There is always going to be someone faster than you. Wait till you go pro, and I am telling you are going to be a pro one day. There are going to be times that you will win and times you will lose to the same person. It's a fact."

Dominic felt better about what Reggie said and understood his thought process. He was more excited that Reggie wanted him on the team for the next few years.

Dominic rode over to the pay phone and called home. He spoke to his mother and father. He conveyed the day's events and some of the week's hijinks. His parents were both laughing with him. His father told him that they had a surprise for him.

As Always his mother began to cry. Angelo continued, "Son, next week we are going to meet you down in Charleston, West Virginia."

Dominic was filled with excitement. It's been nearly seven weeks since he saw his parents and brother. Dominic asked to speak to his brother again.

His father laughed, "Well, he's in his room. I have to go get him."

Dominic asked, "What did he do now?"

Maria interrupted, "He was fighting again."

Dominic laughed, "Again, what's up with my brother?"

Angelo quickly answered, "He needs me to straighten him out. He was playing baseball this time. He got mad at one of the boys. One boy threw the ball at him. Your brother, in all his wisdom, picked up the bat and chased him down hitting him in the back and legs a few times leaving giant marks and welts."

Dominic replied, "He is coming with you correct?"

Angelo answered, "Yes, but I'm going to keep him on a leash. He is something."

Dominic said his goodbyes, thought back for a few moments and laughed. He was recalling Waco and Birmingham. How would Joey have acted? He and Joey were very close. He knew he could talk with him about his latest outburst. He pedaled slowly back to the Puma Palace.

He was in his shorts when Phil came around the corner with the hose and doused him with water. Dominic sat there in his shorts, t-shirt and flip flops enjoying the refreshing feeling of the cold water hitting him. As he sat taking on water he yelled out, "Someone get me the soap!"

Chapter 47

It is Sunday morning and Team Panther is ready to leave from Jacksonville for Charleston, West Virginia. Reggie is on the pay phone discussing a deal for a future venue. Reggie never stops. His only down time is when he is traveling with the team inside the Puma Palace. Cell phones were not invented yet or he would have one surgically attached to his ear.

It was undetermined if the team was going to drive straight through to West Virginia or stop overnight on the way. It was a decision to be made by the drivers Jay and 'G'. It was going to be nearly a ten hour drive. With stops for food, it was going to be a twelve hour excursion.

There was horseplay on the way up I77. The younger riders were trying to find ways to occupy themselves. They were playing games of who could find the most exotic cars, biggest trucks, and unconventional amusements. As they drove, Reggie made the decision to stay overnight.

He informed them to stop at the next food sign exit. There was a sign, "Best Chicken in the South." Jay exited off the interstate and pulled into the parking lot. The team got off the Puma Palace as Reggie made a direct path to the pay phones.

The team stayed overnight near Lake Norman. It was a fun evening. The night temperature was in the mid-seventies. Tony and Dominic set up their tent and it was camping as normal. That night was different.

There was extensive chatter around the fire that evening. The team was in good spirits and excited that the tour was nearing the end. Dominic was almost sad. He was going to miss his buddy Tony. There was discussions and debates of who had the best sport teams, hunting and typical squabbles as these.

Reggie emerged out of the Puma Palace and sat with the rest of the team. He started off saying, "Well kids, I want to be the first to tell you. We are now the number one team on the tour. We have won the factory award and you are all part of it. Let me give you examples. Tommy and Larry left the tour as we made our way cross country. Tommy's National number is 2US for the nine experts. Larry obtained the 4US for the eight experts. I have the rest. Darren finished with a 1US for ten experts. Allen is too close to call. He is a couple of points between number one and three for the eighteen experts. Terrell secured 1US for the sixteen experts. Eric, you won 4US for the fourteen experts. Dominic, you already secured the 1US plate for the twelve year old experts. Tony, what do I say. You have the 1US for the pros. Phil, you get to clean the bathroom. Seriously, you finished near number twelve. Guys I'm proud of you. We lost a rider but it does not negate the fact that you are all champions." There was rejoicing and many jokes being told.

Reggie sat back and allowed his team to enjoy the fire and the good news. Tony and Dominic sat up talking for a while. It was getting louder as they spoke. It was noticeable that the woods were active with crickets and locust making themselves known. They continued to talk for a short while before they agreed to get some sleep.

The team woke up late and it was peaceful in the morning. Reggie agreed to buy them all lunch as they departed. The team made their way onto the highway and they were en route to the West Virginia BMX track. Dominic was excited to see his family. He was telling Tony about his town, his track in the back yard and the friends he has at home. Tony could see his excitement.

The team arrived at the BMX track early on Tuesday evening. In normal fashion, Reggie was out the door and meeting with the track officials. The track was ready and there were many riders on the track. It was a public track with many kids riding for fun.

After the chores were completed, Tony called for a team meeting. He was in and out of character. He was a complete goofball. He instructed the team to retrieve their bicycles and meet on the starting hill. The track was slightly rocky with a few jumps. Tony wanted to have a jumping contest. He referred to it as, "Evil Knievel jumping contest."

The team all took turn jumping and landing as long as they could on the first jump. Everyone took their turn. Finally it was revealed that Phil won the contest. He was the fastest to hit the jump and was able to launch himself out the farthest. The track was not very long. It was compact but fast.

There was a small downhill start to a jump and a 90degree right hand turn. A short straightaway to a 45 degree right hand turn with a short straight with a jump into another right hand 45 degree turn. A short straight later there was a left-handed 45 degree turn to a straightaway with a table top jump then the finish line.

After the goofing off it was time to get serious. The track officials wanted to test their new magnetic gate. They stacked the gate with all seven riders that were still on tour to see if it would hold. All the riders were using the two pedal start method and the gate worked flawless.

The track officials were very accommodating and were slightly star struck by Tony. Tony was screaming off the gate. Because of the steep starting hill, the gate dropped faster and many of the riders were able to time their starts enabling them to snap off the gate quicker.

For the next few days the team made the Puma Palace their home except for Tony and Dominic who elected to camp out as they normally do. It was late Friday afternoon and Dominic recognized the family car as it parked alongside the Puma Palace. Dominic immediately sprinted over from the track to greet his family.

As he raced up, his mother grabbed him and hugged him. She was crying with exhilaration to once again acquaint herself with her son. As she was hugging him Angelo came over and hugged both of them.

Maria asked, "Why are you so thin Dominic? Your hair is so long! What have you been doing?"

Angelo interrupted as he was laughing, "Maria stop. He has been on tour racing. He is in the best shape of his life. Buddy, lift your shirt up and show your mom your stomach."

Dominic looked as his father with confusion and lifted his shirt displaying a six pack of muscles on his torso. He was ripped and understood what his father was conveying to his mom.

Soon Joey came over and hugged his brother. They joked and laughed for a short time. Dominic asked, "So, whose butt are you going to try and kick today?" They laughed.

Joey replied, "It's not my fault. I did what I had to do bro."

Dominic didn't push the issue. He was happy to see his brother.

Angelo, smacking the back of Dominic's head said, "Hey, watch your mouth. Joey, no butt kicking's today."

Dominic was laughing knowing his father was coming out of his shell.

Angelo asked, "So, I hear you're a little faster than you used to be. I also hear that you like to sleep in tents."

Dominic answered, "Dad, I can't sleep in the camper full of people snoring and farting all night."

Angelo laughed and asked him, "Well, when do we get to see you practice?"

Dominic quickly answered, "I hope were done. We have been riding all day."

Tony came over and introduced himself to Angelo and Maria. They were taken by his manners. Tony was a gentleman and spoke eloquently. Angelo and Tony spoke for a while as Maria sat with Dominic and talked about the tour. Dominic gave detailed narrations of his trip.

He showed his mother a camera he purchased. He also pulled out about twenty rolls of film that needed developed. Maria asked, "Do you want to go to dinner with us? Then maybe we can get you a haircut."

Dominic answered, "Dinner sounds great Mom, but I don't want to cut my hair. I want to grow it long like the other guys do in California. I just want to see what it looks like before I do cut it. Please."

She answered, "I don't know Dom. I need to speak to your father."

Dominic said nothing. He knew his father wouldn't mind him growing out his hair.

Tony and Angelo approached Dominic and Maria. They were all talking when Reggie also entered in the conversation. Reggie was seasoned on dealing with people. It was evident as he conversed with the group.

Reggie continued, "Well, let me tell you about Dominic. He was a pleasure to have around. He acted like a young gentleman. Understand that he had much more than racing to perform on this tour. He has become a woodsman. He and Tony shared the tent you see over there behind the RV in the wood line. He and Tony have become inseparable. They are two peas in a pod. He has grown mentally and of course physically on this tour. I'm sure he will tell you about all our adventures and the experiences he has gained in our travels. He was a joy, a real joy. Nice work Mom and Dad. It shows with his demeanor. I look forward to next year and this December for the next World

Championship. Did you know Dominic is the number one rider in the USA as a twelve year old? He has a lot of defending to do come December."

Reggie patted Dominic on the back of the shoulder and said, "Ok, you need to go run off with Tony so I can speak privately with your Mom and Dad. There are some adult things we need to discuss. Don't worry, I'm not going to get you in trouble."

Dominic gathered his belongings and packed the back of the family vehicle. He was excited and sad at the same time. He was going to miss his best buddy this evening. After spending over two months together every day it was time to re-acclimate with his family.

Tony helped Dominic with his gear and told him, "Don't sweat it Dom. We still have New Jersey. I'll tell you what. How about in New Jersey I sleep over at your house."

Dominic was leaping for joy. Dominic asked, "I can't wait to introduce you to my friends. They will never believe that Tony Scholls is sleeping over in my house."

Tony replied, "I have a feeling you're going to be even more surprised."

Dominic begged him to explain what he just said. Tony would not budge. He held fast on any more comments.

Dominic and his family departed the BMX track and drove back to the hotel in order for Dominic to shower and change his clothes before going to dinner. As they drove to the hotel, Angelo began to speak, "I am very proud of you Dominic. I am happy about the report I got about you. You have no idea how I feel at this moment."

Dominic answered, "Hopefully like a big giant oversized steak. I'm craving for a steak dinner."

Chapter 48

Dominic was riding back to the track with his family. As they entered the track, Angelo commented on the amount of motor homes and people attending the race. Dominic quickly interjected, "Dad, this is nothing. This is actually small. Florida and California have huge crowds."

Angelo parked directly next to the Team Panther RV. As Dominic and his family exited their car, Tony ran out of the Puma Palace and shouted, "Chores!" There was laughter and the normal business of performing chores commenced.

Dominic protested, "You all waited for me to show up before you started. This is not fair. Tony I know what you're doing."

Tony was laughing as the rest of them started their chores. Angelo and Maria stood quietly as Dominic grabbed the trash bag and started policing the area including the inside of the Puma Palace. When he was done picking up the trash he then started to empty the trailer along with the rest of the team.

Reggie emerged from the trailer and began a dialog with Dominic's parents. They stood alone off to the side of the Puma Palace as the rest of the team completed the chores. Tony was summoned by Reggie and all four of them began talking. After a short time, Maria was almost crying with laughter.

Dominic approached and Tony held his hand up and pointed Dominic away from them. The chores were completed and the team sat quietly awaiting practice to begin. Dominic was in his shorts and t-shirt and slowly pulled his racing leathers over the top of them getting ready for the race. His parents approached Dominic and were laughing. He asked what was so funny but they did not answer.

It was nearly 8 AM and Dominic was making his way to the gate for practice with Tony. Without warning, Dominic was approached by all his New Jersey friends and fellow racers. They made a spectacle over him. They all missed him and Dominic was well liked. He introduced Tony but they all knew who he was and asked Dominic several questions. The questions were coming rapid fire.

Questions like, "Where have you been? How was the tour? Are you ready for the race today? Are you racing both races in New Jersey next weekend?" There were nonstop questions for both Tony and Dominic.

Finally Dominic made it to the gate. All his New Jersey friends his age and older were escorting him to the gate with Tony. They all wanted to see how Dominic was doing. As he lined up on the gate they were stunned.

There was joking about his starting position. His New Jersey friend directly next to him asked, "You're allowed to do that? I never saw this before."

Dominic laughed and waited for the cadence. The gate dropped and Dominic was gone. He left his friends well behind. Dominic gave it his all into the first turn and shut down. He coasted the rest of the way. He wanted to conserve his energy. He wanted to show his parents and friends how good he had become.

At the end of the track, Tony and Dominic were talking as Dominic's friends approached. They commented, "Dom, you are amazing. The tour has changed the way you ride. Wow, you are the real deal now."

Tony looked at him and said, "Dom, you have changed. You're the goods."

Dominic shook his head and didn't ask what he meant.

Finally it was race time. There was a strong turn out from Pennsylvania and New Jersey. Dominic was feeling home sick for the first time. His family was surrounding him and supporting his passion. There were only seventy-five moto's this day. The first to race were the pros.

Dominic along with his family and Team were standing at the fence on the first straight to watch the race. Tony was in the first moto. The gate dropped and the race was underway. Tony was leading by a few feet. After the first jump and the right hand ninety degree right turn, Tony started to pull away and there would be no catching him. He won his first moto.

Angelo along with his wife and son were amazed. They could not believe how fast the pros raced. It was incomprehensible at first and took time for it to sink in. There were three more moto's of pros taking the gate.

Dominic was in the staging area getting ready for his moto. Again, he had to finish fourth or better to qualify for the main event. He was approached many of his New Jersey friends. There were a few riders from New Jersey in his moto. They were joking and goofing off in the staging area.

Finally Dominic was at the gate. He blanked out the rest of the world and concentrated on the cadence and his start. He wanted to reveal how he had improved while he was gone. The gate dropped and Dominic looked as if he was yanked out of the gate. He was leading by a bicycle length after the first two pedals. He looked strong and he was untouchable.

He raced down the first straight, over the jump and into the first turn. As he exited the first turn he was pulling away from the pack. A couple of turns and jumps later, Dominic was at the finish line as the rest of the moto was only coming out of the last turn.

In normal fashion, he waited for his moto and bumped fists with them all. His friend from New Jersey finished in third and commented, "Damn Dom, you checked out on us. Whatever they are feeding you at Team Panther please bring me some. You are so fast. It's amazing to see the difference in you since the beginning of the season. Wow!"

Dominic made his way to his camp and he was greeted by his father and Tony. Angelo was very excited for his son. He hugged him on the side and said, "Dom, you're not the same racer I remember sending off to California. You look strong son. You are special. You look fast, strong and mostly smooth. You glide around the track."

Dominic was exceedingly exultant to hear his father say such things. Dominic remembered Tony telling him, "If you want to be faster, ride smoother." He finally understood what this means.

Dominic went on win all his moto's and his Main event. His father was so proud of his big trophy. Dominic laughed as his father was discussing the trophy. Dominic told his father, "Dad, I have a bunch more in the trailer. Some are bigger than that one."

Angelo laughed, "OK son, when the team makes it over to New Jersey we will offload the trophies."

Tony won the pro open and again he won $3000.00. Angelo asked, "Did Tony win a total of three grand over the entire tour?"

Reggie laughed, "No that was for this race only."

Angelo was perplexed. "Now I understand why he was training so hard."

Reggie replied again, "Wait until the World Championships this year. I'm trying to raise a $30,000 pro purse or close to it. Wait until you see this event. We'll talk about it later."

There was much fanfare after the race with Team Panther featuring Tony. There were many reporters, spectators, and other media representatives. Dominic noticed Jay pulling the grill into place.

Reggie shouted, "Listen up guys. We are going to camp out here tonight and leave first thing in the morning for New Jersey. We are going directly to Dominic's house."

There was cheering and jovial remarks directed at Dominic. Dominic was excited to hear the good news. Reggie continued, "Dominic, you're traveling with the team to New Jersey. You're going to sit upfront when the Puma Palace is close to your house. You're going to give directions. I'm going with your Mom and Dad and I'm taking Carl. You and your brother are traveling with the team. Joey, enjoy the trip. Remember, your brother has been doing this for nearly two months. Oh, another thing. These guys are all bigger than you." There was more laughter.

The team sat around for several hours eating and telling stories about the road. Angelo and Maria were enjoying all the stories being told. Darren the ten year old expert brought up the boar incident. He was quickly quieted by Tony and Phil.

Dominic asked, "Mom, when we arrive tomorrow night, will you please have some food you always make. I don't care what it is, it's always the best." Maria was touched by his comments and hugged her son with boundless satisfaction.

The sun was starting to set and everyone was content after eating hot dogs and hamburgers for the billionth time. The lights on the Puma Palace came on and Tony was still occupied with Reggie and Dominic's parents. Finally Dominic's parents approached him and kissed him on the top of his head.

His mother remarked, "We love you son. We'll see you on the road to New Jersey. It's only a four hour drive. Don't forget to shower."

Dominic quickly replied, "As soon as it gets dark we are all going to shower behind the trailer."

Maria remarked, "Do I need to ask?"

Dominic, "Only if you want the truth."

She kissed him again and said, "I heard you know how to do laundry."

Dominic answered, "Yes, please don't remind me. Monday is laundry day. I can't wait."

Maria smiled, "I'll help you guys, don't worry."

Joey grabbed his bag out of his family's car and made his way to the Puma Palace. Dominic shouted, "No Joey, we don't sleep in there." He then pointed to the tent.

Tony remarked, "Joey, nothing to be afraid of except the poisonous tic-turds."

Joey asked, "What's a tic-turd?"

Dominic and Tony laughed and informed him that they were joking.

Angelo kissed both his son's on the head and said, "I can't believe I get to say this, I'll see you at the house tomorrow."

Dominic's parents, Reggie and Carl were driving away in the car as the night grew darker. There was the normal hustle and bustle around the camp. Joey was amazed at how they worked together. It was like clockwork for them all. Finally Tony looked around the Puma Palace and their camp and yelled, "CHORES!"

Chapter 49

The Texas heat continued to batter the southern state. Rafael is at the pits with his friends Tommy, Austin and Bobby. It was not the normal all out trying to go faster and bigger. This time it was different. Rafael is now trying to stay close to the jump and find opportunities to pedal.

He and his friends have taken a new approach to jumping. Rafael's friends did not race his age bracket; however they raced an older class in the novice class. Practice benefits everyone. As they were exiting, Rafael noticed Christopher's home. It was enormous and spread over several hundred acres.

He made mention to his friends about the kid, Christopher who lived in the house they were passing. They all agreed it was beyond comprehension of how a person could live in a house like this and be despondent.

Rafael arrived at his house and noticed that Christopher was inside speaking with Maximo. He thought nothing of it. He said hello and continued to his room with a tall glass of water. Rafael was more interested in the air-conditioned temperature and what was on television.

The coolness of his home was a welcomed relief compared to the outside temperature he endured for the last many hours. Rafael could hear the conversing between his father and Christopher but could not make out exactly what was being said.

Maximo sat with Christopher for nearly two hours and spoke about Christopher's father. Maximo spoke very delicately with Christopher, "Christopher, your father is a proud man. I am proud to be Mexican. I am more proud to be a Christian man. I believe God put you here for a reason. I strongly feel that pride comes before the fall. Sometimes pride is not a good thing. Humility is the only resource we have that enables us to be mindful of whom we are. I don't judge but I enjoy research. Remember as we spoke a few weeks ago? Here are some things you need to remember about this great country. The United States was first settled by Asians well before Christopher Columbus. In fact, the Pilgrims were not the first white people in America. There were already white skin people living in New York, New Mexico, Virginia and Florida. There were Filipinos and Jews living in the United States before the European settlers arrived."

Christopher sat quietly saying nothing completely focused on Maximo as he spoke.

Maximo began to speak again, "If your father does not like someone because of their nationality or skin color, it is his sad analysis of life. It takes more energy to hold a grudge than acceptance. For me, it's far better to forgive and try to forget than to hold onto something that in time a person will forget why they are angry and continue to hold that anger for no reason. I can't say I understand how you feel inside, but he is still your father and one day you will miss him when he is gone. What legacy will he pass on to emulate. Is your father content of just being who he is and not caring of what changes he could bring to someone else's life such as yours? I know that one day I won't be here any longer. I want to leave this earth knowing people genuinely liked me. So Christopher, I can't help how your father is or why he feels the way he does. But I can try to help you and how you look at life."

Christopher finally opened up to Maximo, "I know I'm different. Not by the way I dress or act. I act out maybe because I want attention. But my father spends no time with me. He is always busy with his job and he constantly leaves for his business trips overseas. I can't even tell you exactly what he does for a living. I know my relationship with my father is pathetic. I have tried to reach out many times with him over the years. The only time he responds to me is when I dress like I did. Although negative, I still gather his attention. I know my father is prosperous with money. I don't ask. I wanted to go to college for music and I was accepted at Julliard. I just want to go to college and not return on my breaks. Maybe I could visit with you?"

Maximo shook his head yes. Christopher continued, "I need to escape. I feel like a prisoner in my own home. There is something that eats at my heart and I feel like I am crawling out of my skin. This is why I started playing piano. I would stay in my room every day for hours at a time rather than face my father and his tyrannical rants and racist judgments. I sometimes feel like I can see myself from across the room. It's a feeling but it feels so real. There were times I was so depressed I felt like sleeping all day and not getting out of bed. I never had the urge to hurt myself. My motivation for anything was zero. Sometimes I feel like the piano saved my life."

After Christopher was done speaking Maximo sat and looked at him for a few seconds and replied, "Well, the good news is, it's better a piano save your life than a paramedic. It's ok to feel sad at times. I have the best family in the world and I sometimes feel sad. Here is the problem with life, it doesn't end. Not even here on earth. Our physical bodies die, we live on. It has to be true. I can't think of it any other way. It's a part of me that I hold dear inside my soul."

Christopher smiled at him and asked, "How do I handle my father?"

Maximo shook his head and answered, "I don't know. Maybe I can come over to your house and cut your grass and you can introduce me to your father."

They both laughed at Maximo's quip. Maximo continued, "Here is my advice to you Christopher. Go to school. Get a degree in music. Continue going to school and get another degree or further your degree. It can't hurt. People can take everything from you except your education. Who knows, when you're done with school an opportunity will present itself and you will know what path to take. I always pray about it. My faith sustains me and I am satisfied."

Christopher asked Maximo, "So I guess I will try to figure my father out. What else should I do?"

Maximo looked at him and simultaneously they both said, "Pray about it."

Christopher continued, "I appreciate your kindness. I am glad you invited me over that day for tacos. You are one of the first people to ever extend kindness towards me. Speaking of tacos, is you wife cooking? It smells great in the kitchen."

Maximo yelled out in Spanish to his wife, "Christopher se va a quedar para la cena."

Christopher asked, "Did you tell your wife I was staying for dinner?"

Maximo replied, "Very good, I did."

Christopher smiled, "Good."

Chapter 50

It's Sunday morning and Dominic arises from his tent. He notices that Tony is already up and about the camp. As Dominic approaches Tony, he notices that there was a rain storm last night. Tony asks, "Did you hear that thunder last night?"

Dominic answers, "No, I didn't hear a thing. I was beyond tired last night."

Tony shrugged his shoulders laughing, "You missed the lightening as well."

Dominic was lethargic and still tottering as he walked. He sat down for a moment to gather his bearings. Dominic noticed there were many puddles and for the first time he realized that his body is giving tell-tale indications of fatigue. He asked Tony, "Why did I sleep so soundly?"

Tony looked at him for a moment, "You raced in extreme heat and your body needed to recharge. I do it all the time. How do you feel?"

Dominic answered, "Like a million bucks!"

Joey emerged from the Puma Palace looking like he didn't sleep a wink. Tony woke the rest of the team up for the morning chores. Jay and 'G' were still sleeping. The grill was opened and it was eggs, bacon and various cereals as normal.

Tony called for the chores and the Team was ready to depart for New Jersey nearly an eight hour drive. The Team made their way in the Puma Palace and they were off. They drove for four hours before Jay stopped to refuel and the rest of the team exited to stretch their legs.

It would not be long before Dominic was home. 'G' gathered up the team outside the RV before proceeding toward New Jersey. They sat outside for thirty minutes enjoying the sandwiches 'G' had them prepare before re-entering the Puma Palace.

Four hours later Jay called, "Dominator, get up here!"

There it was, the sign welcoming them to the Garden State. Dominic was excited. He was thirty minutes from home.

The Puma Palace entered Dominic's home town in New Jersey. He knew exactly where he was and how to get home. He gave Jay directions. As they entered his street, Dominic yelled, "Welcome to my house guys! We are here."

He pointed to his driveway and the RV made its way down the driveway. Dominic was excited to be home. Jay beeped the horn as they entered and Dominic's parents appeared from behind the house. Dominic jumped out of the Puma Palace and approached his parents and Reggie who was standing behind them.

Some of the neighbors, his aunt and uncle were there and he noticed they were cooking outside in the back yard. Dominic asked, "Mom, I thought you were going to cook?"

She laughed and replied, "Honey, your father is making you something very special and I know you're all going to love it."

Tony walked around the back first and nearly fell to his knees laughing loudly. Dominic peeked around the corner and he had to laugh. Angelo was cooking a pig over an open pit. Dominic asked, "I guess you know about it?"

Dominic was craving to show Tony his practice track. Tony and the rest of the team gathered their laughs about the pig roast and made their way to Dominic's track. They joked a little, but all were impressed. They discussed the turns and jumps. They all agreed that in the morning they would all take some gates and laps on his track. It wasn't long before nightfall was upon them and sleeping arrangements were being set.

Reggie got the spare room and his own phone to go with it. Many of the team was content with sleeping in the Puma Palace with the air-conditioner blasting and no generator running. It was plugged into the house electricity. Others wanted to sleep in the basement that was finished off as a game room.

It was cool. The couch pulled out into a bed and it was wide open. After nearly two months, Dominic was able to sleep in his own bed. He was relieved.

This week was a fun week for the team. They made many road trips to the Cape May Zoo, Philadelphia, Atlantic City, the beach for a day and finally his track. They all rode on the track for hours. Dominic realized some changes that needed done since he left for the tour. They all went to his pits for a short stint, and finally they were able to see the BMX track.

They enjoyed Maria's home cooking and a real Philadelphia Cheesesteak. They all agreed Dominic should weigh twice as much. Maria was a perfect host. She made so much food that the Team became spoiled for the past few days. It was a week for both Dominic and his teammates to remember. Like always, wherever Dominic was so was Tony.

The big day was upon them. It's Saturday morning nearly 6:30 AM and the team was departing for the track. The team was inside the Puma Palace and Dominic was sitting upfront showing them the way to the track. As Jay made his way out of the neighborhood, he was amazed at what was blocking the roadway.

There was an early model white Chevy Camaro and a 1974 primer colored firebird facing each other in the street power braking for nearly a minute with white tire smoke billowing from under them. It was a couple of teenagers who apparently found joy acting like a couple of reckless drunken imps. After the exhibition of acceleration, the Team was underway.

The team was able to set up near the track, but would have to walk from the parking area to the track to watch the races. Dominic was motivated and was ready to race. All his family was coming to watch him race along with all his friends. His local bicycle sponsor, Powershot BMX and all his BMX buddies were envious that he was best friends with Tony Scholls, the fastest BMX pro in the USA.

The team was able to take the track before it was closed for age class practices. Dominic enjoyed hanging in the Team Panther Camp with his parents and brother. He made a few laps and gate starts. He was ready to race. He was going to race all his old rivals from his home track and from the North. It wasn't long before the familiar announcement, "Moto's are posted."

Dominic would only have to finish fourth or better. There were only two moto's of 12 experts. Before the races started, he made his way over to the bleachers and spent some time talking with his family who commandeered an entire bleacher section along with Team Panther.

The team hung a giant banner marking their territory. Reggie jokingly pronounced it was a promotional banner. Nevertheless, it was in good taste and they were all receptive to anyone who wanted to join them to watch the races. It was long into the race before Dominic's moto was on the gate.

He could hear the announcer calling them out by name until it was his turn for the introduction. The announcer broadcasted, "Ladies and Gentleman. From your home town and from down the street, escorted by his team mate and the number one Pro in the USA, your very own homegrown hero, and the US number 1 World Champion and national number one 12 year old expert, The Dominator, Dominic Carlucci!" There many cheers and whistling from the crowd.

The gate was updated and held by electro magnets as the rest of the tour. The gate operator gave the cadence. The gate dropped and Dominic shot off the gate. He was leading before the pack of riders reached the bottom of the starting hill.

The first jump was about twenty feet down the straightaway from the starting hill. Dominic pedaled over the jump and still gathered more speed. Several feet in front of him were the woopdydoo section. A series of three jumps stacked tightly together. Dominic completely jumped over the entire section.

A few feet later there was a forty five degree right hand turn to a straightaway and a large oversized one hundred and eighty degree left hand turn. There were a series of a right and left hand bermed turns.

Dominic continued to distance himself from his moto. The announcer, "Around the left hand turn into the straight is the Dominator.

Approaching the table top section, the Dominator is over that portion. Into the left hand to right hand turn is Dominic Carlucci from New Jersey. Sit down Dom, you have plenty of room." Dominic was untouchable.

He finished the race and sat with his friends and family in the bleachers. He gathered some water and his friends were amazed by his speed and smoothness. They all remarked about how fast he had become. They were all talking and Tony came over to talk with Dominic. They all were star struck. Tony said hello to them and bumped fists with Dominic.

Tony remarked, "This is a long track. Not much technical stuff here. You pulled away in the straights. They can't touch you. This is why we practice sprints. This is why we practice. Enjoy your friends and family Dom. I'm proud of you." Dominic caught his breath and thanked him.

Soon Tony took the gate. Dominic told them to be ready for the fastest human BMXer on the planet. His friends and family were beside themselves. Tony lit the track on fire. He was so smooth and fast it was surreal. The speed he carried was amazing. The crowed was now standing and clapping.

It was the Tony show. Team Panther was well represented. Brent Lock, Dominic's local BMX sponsor leaned over to him, "So I now see how you got to be so fast. He is special. I'm glad you're on my team. I mean Wow. Oh, by the way, I have a new shirt for you. It's a Team Panther Jersey with our name on it as well." Dominic smiled and took the shirt and put it on.

Dominic and Tony both won their respective classes. Tony won $3000.00 this race. There was only one Team Panther rider who did not finish first but did finish with a respectable second.

Dominic received a mountain of attention along with Tony this day. Dominic's parents were beaming and proud of their son. He had become a BMX prodigy on tour. He was a champion with humble persona. They thanked Reggie for all he had done. Their son was growing up to be a fine young man surrounded by a respectable support structure of friends and family.

After the race day the team reassembled by the Puma Palace. There were friends, family and local sponsors surrounding the RV. Tony made the announcement that they were going to Craigmere in the morning for another race and that they needed to get back to the house and prepare for the next day.

He conveyed, "Mrs. Carlucci is cooking. She just left to prepare a special meal for us. Let's show her respect. It's our last night with Dominic and his family. Dominic, this is your last race with us. We have a couple of smaller nationals to race as we make our way back to California. Guys, I'm going to miss him as well. We will all meet again at the Worlds in December. But for now, we have another race in the morning. Chores!"

The onlookers were impressed by how seamlessly the team worked together to ready the RV. When they were done, they stood around and answered many questions about the tour. Reggie was his normal jovial self. His personality was magmatic and the team loved him.

He was the Godfather of the tour. He was always recognized and well respected by everyone. He praised the track officials everywhere he toured. He was the master of public relations. Reggie continued his praises and was magnanimous about how much he liked being in New Jersey.

He continued his rant about Dominic. He wanted the reporters and spectators to know how he had improved and was a genuine nice young man. There many questions about Dominic and Tony. Reggie joked about how they were very close and bunked together in a tent for the last few weeks of the tour. He wanted them to know that it was by choice.

He described in detail about how Tony's leadership is the glue that held Team Panther together. He further described the unsung heroes who drove the entire tour and Carl who managed nearly the entire schedule.

After the long day of racing was over, the team arrived at Dominic's house for the last time. It was nearly 8 PM and they were all famished. Maria provided one of the best meals they had eaten. She made lasagna with meatballs and sausage.

There were all the trimmings including spaghetti, fried garlic spinach, and homemade garlic bread. They all ate and assisted with the cleanup afterwards. Reggie assisted to the very end and then retired to his room and on the phone.

The team ate well and were all fast asleep by 9 PM. Reggie emerged from his phone conversations and sat with Angelo and Maria discussing the tour events. He ranted about how Dominic is going to be special one day. He discussed his many other ventures that allowed him to finance the tour.

Carl, Jay and 'G' were all sleeping. It was nice for Reggie to sit and converse without a large crowd. He even enjoyed a glass of wine as he sat with both of them. They talked for nearly an hour and Reggie felt the events of the day overwhelming him. He began to grow weary and was gracious for their hospitality all week.

As Reggie walked toward his room, he turned and asked the Carlucci's, "Ever think of coming to Cali for a short family vacation in October around the Halloween National?"

Chapter 51

We reached our cruising altitude of thirty eight thousand feet. I sat back in my seat and again began to regress about my childhood and my BMX days. The lasting memory was the BMX tour of 1980 and how it defined me, contributing to my success. My last race with the team that year was in Craigmere, New Jersey.

I had done so well as a twelve year old at my home track and I wanted to repeat the same destiny in Craigmere. This was an unusual track. It was built on the side of a mountain. It had only 4 turns and it was rocky. The last part of the track was fast and dangerous.

The start was a slight downhill to a flat left 180 degree turn. There was one jump and another huge 180 degree right hand turn that was completely falling downhill to a straightaway with no jumps and a left 180 degree turn to a small straightaway then a slight right handed downhill straight to a 90 degree right hand turn and small straight to the finish.

The last turn was murderous. If for any reason you did not make the turn and went over the berm, there was nothing but rocks and it was going to be painful. Hay bales were placed at the top but were only a hindrance before striking the rocks on the other side.

The ride up was short. Although it took us over three hours in the RV, I still call it the Puma Palace, to arrive at the track in the morning, it felt like five minutes to me. My mother made us all breakfast. It was not the usual eggs and bacon, although I enjoyed eating the eggs and bacon.

Let's be real, bacon rules and I can't imagine the world without bacon. That is, as long as it's not chasing you when you are trying to relieve yourself. My mother made a huge breakfast sandwiches with potatoes, bacon, Italian sausage, fried peppers, and fried onions on a huge Kaiser roll. It was the rave of the trip for breakfasts and probably contributed to most of us falling asleep after a large meal that she had prepared.

I remember pulling into the track area as I awoke and a huge crowd surrounding our Puma Palace as we entered the complex. I was so happy I got to get some sleep on the way. There was a large turnout on this day.

I remember sitting on the top of the Puma Palace watching the entire race from our vantage point. There was a lot people crammed in a small area. The one thing that was nice about this track was there was plenty of shade. There were the open areas as well.

This was my last tour of 1980. I would go on to Indianapolis but this would be the last time I would see all my teammates and friends for a while. I especially remember missing Tony and sleeping in the tent all summer. Don't ask me to go camping, until next year. I remember appreciating my bed.

Tony conveyed several years later that he enjoyed our time hanging out and sleeping in the tent, but he appreciated his bed as much as I did. Those were valuable times of my childhood. I recall these memories and I still laugh about the good times with Team Panther.

The day's events on this Sunday were normal and somewhat routine. Tony called for the chores as we arrived and it was like clockwork. My parents arrived fifteen minutes before we did and claimed our spot for the day's activities. As we were performing our chores I noticed my father pull a giant cooler out of the car.

It was the same one he used when he had cookouts with his crew from the plant. I approached my father and grabbed the other side of the cooler and helped him carry it towards the grill. The entire team was enthusiastic when we all looked inside.

My mother made Italian kabobs with several types of combinations of meats and vegetables. There were huge steaks and tons of ribs. I remember thinking to myself, "Now, this is how you BBQ." The team enjoyed the food this day and adopted my mother as the team mom. They all called her, "Momma C."

She was excited and more impressed by how polite the team was towards her. Reggie was joking about the food. He was more than thankful to my parents. He explained that the team needed a morale booster and this did it for them.

Reggie was joking that he was going to taste everything first to make sure it was ok for consumption. My mother had marinated eggplant and zucchini as side dishes. I remember when they started to cook, the entire track could smell the BBQ sauce and the garlic. We were envied by all who witnessed my father and Jay manning the grill.

The races went off this day without any glitches. Like normal, we practiced in age groups due to the large turnout of riders. I remember having to race a quarter, semi and a main event. There were many 12 experts racing this day. I did not lose one moto.

I finished first in every race. I was so happy to win and impress my parents. I recall the announcer calling my name and hearing the crowd cheering. My best friend Tony won this day. He did not win every moto but the last one counted and he finished first. He won about $2500.00.

I always remember him holding up the giant oversized checks and thinking he won that money. But in retrospect, he only won portions of it. If there was a $5000.00 pro purse, first place was guaranteed at least half. All this time I thought Tony was rich. But, he was very generous with us and always bought us ice cream and other goodies.

Our display looked extraordinary this day. All the trophies were displayed along with our number plates. Reggie was making a name for his product and he was effective at what he did with the marketing. He understood people and how to present himself. Throughout the day many reporters and photographers approached our camp.

Team Panther was the number one national team in the country and we were royalty at the BMX tracks. My sponsor, Brent, attended the race this day and was so proud of me for wearing the new shirt he designed with his bike shop name on it. I was sitting on top of the world this day and it still gives me goose bumps to this day.

It wasn't long before the inevitable had to occur. It was that time when the race was over and for the last time this season Tony called for the chores. Painfully I said my goodbyes as I gathered all my belongings and my teammate's phone numbers.

I hugged Tony and promised him I would be faster before the Worlds. He always joked with me and promised me he would call me when he got home. I remember Reggie giving me a speech on how he was proud of me and how to continue conditioning myself before the Worlds.

Tony helped me pack my belongings. My bike was placed in the bike holder and tied down. I had all my trophies in the back of our vehicle and we readied ourselves for the trip back to South Jersey. I told Tony to call me and let me know how he did in the last few races on his way back to California. He made good on his promises and called me frequently.

As we drove off I had tears in my eyes. I really missed Tony. We had become close over the past two months. I remember my father asking me what I wanted to do that week. I was slightly depressed but I replied, "School clothes shopping."

My brother sat quietly, not saying anything to me. He understood how I felt and was smart enough not to make fun of my feelings at this time. I remember one thing my father said to me that always made me strive harder to be a champion. He simply said, "Now that you have it, you need to keep it. That's your number one plate. Don't give it to anyone. Make them earn it. I'm proud of you. I don't care what your number plate says on it. They don't have what you have. Hold yourself to the standard you are right now. You'll surpass any champion."

I lived my life by my father's code. I only found that people respected me.

Chapter 52

Its mid-September and Dominic returned to school. He was very excited to see his old friends and their camaraderie. He was able to ride one of his bicycles to school. It was nearly four miles away and he rode often unless the weather was inclement.

He was well liked and respected for his athletic ability. His hair was starting to get long and he received much praise from the girls. This however did not help with his mother's thoughts about his hair style. He wanted to let his hair grow as most of the other kids he raced in California.

The school year passed quickly and before Dominic knew it, it was time for the World Nationals again. He was a good student. He took advantage of his time when he finished school. He had his practice track and a workout routine Tony outlined for him. Dominic rode his bicycle to his father's plant every day after school and worked with Oscar a few hours a day.

When he was done, Dominic would ride home performing long sections of sprints. His workout was strenuous at times, but he was motivated to prove to himself and others he was a champion. Dominic spoke with Reggie or Tony at least once a week. Reggie continually asked about his grades whereas Tony asked about girls and his workout.

It was the Christmas break and Dominic was starting to feel anxious about going back to Indianapolis. He was home late in the afternoon when the doorbell rang. A delivery man dropped off a large box addressed to Dominic Carlucci with the word Dominator under his real name.

He called for his father to ask if knew anything about the delivery. Angelo replied, "Sure do, you better open it up carefully. You're seriously going to like this."

Dominic cautiously opened his large box revealing a brand new Team Panther BMX bicycle. It was the newest Team Panther BMX frame with all the trimmings specifically for Dominic. It was the Tony Scholls race series frame that was a limited edition and personally signed by Tony. Each frame hand signed, not electric or stickers with his signature. Only one hundred were manufactured. Dominic noticed he had frame number 2. He knew right away that Tony had frame number 1.

His newest surprise was accompanied by all the latest and best products such as pedals, sealed bearings, newest cranks, wheels and forks. He received his Factory Number Plate just the day before and now understood why his father asked him not to put it on his bicycle.

Dominic and his father loaded his new bike in the work truck and traveled to Powershot BMX to have them assemble his newest gift. Dominic was well received at the shop by all who were there. They all knew he was on his way and wanted to see the newest limited frames. In no time, Dominic was riding his new bicycle and was ready to start his practices on his practice track with his friends.

It was early on Thursday morning, Dominic and his family were off to the Philadelphia Airport to catch their flight to Indianapolis. They arrived and in a few hours were seated on the airplane ready to leave for Indianapolis. The planed landed on time and Carl was at the airport waiting for them.

Carl remarked, "Damn kid, you're getting big. Looks like you're from Cali with that haircut."

Dominic laughed and replied, "Shhhh. My mom does not like my hair like this. My girlfriend told me she liked it." Carl laughed,

"Girlfriend?" Angelo smirked, "Yea, he is at that age."

Carl laughed and rolled his eyes at Dominic as they all amalgamated together in a friendly laugh.

They arrived at the hotel and Tony Scholls was in the lobby waiting for Dominic to arrive. As Dominic walked in Tony greeted him and they exchanged pleasantries and good-humored edicts towards each other.

Tony's first words, "Look at you getting tall, buff and looking like you just got off the beach in LA."

Dominic was excited to see his friend. He looked exactly the same. Dominic told Tony, "I love my new bike. I notice you signed my number plate. Thank you. My friends are all jealous of me. They can't believe that you and I are friends. Finally, I convinced them with the October's addition of Grind BMX with you and me eating in the pits at Craigmere."

Tony laughed and replied, "Oh yea, that food was off the hook."

Finally the entire team was assembled for the World Nationals. They all met in one of the conference rooms with all the riders and the parents. The team was down to seven riders and was going to stay small. It was as decision Reggie explained in detail to the team and the parents.

He described the track and the next year's activities regarding the tour. The team was excited and they were all going to practice tomorrow. He described some changes in the track but overall it was a positive meeting of how the product line had grown to an overseas market and the future plans of Team Panther and the BMX Products.

The next day practice was commencing. The gate was readied and Dominic was off. The track was almost the same as the year before. There were many cameras and banners as compared to last year.

Team Panther had the best pit area with access to a private bathroom and close to the starting gate. Dominic and Tony practiced together before the crowd started filling the arena. Tony was amazed how Dominic continued to progress and keep his stamina and technical abilities.

Tony and Dominic hung together the entire day even after practice. It was like two friends who have not seen each other for several years just hanging out picking up where they left off.

It's the first day of the World Championships. Dominic's new bicycle was better than he expected. He loved the fact that it was slightly longer and taller giving him a more tailored fit for his growing torso. He was amazed at how large his class was going to be.

He would have to race eights, quarters, semis and a main. In total, if he was to make the main event, he would have to race his three moto's and four more after that to make it to the main event. In total, there are six moto's of 12 experts. Dominic would be riding his US number 1 plate along with most of his other teammates.

Rafael was attending the race this year, escorted by his parents, brothers and his sister. Reggie made it a point to allow Maximo and his family complete access to the Team Panther pits. Dominic and Rafael's families sat together in the bleachers enjoying the race activities. Both Reggie and Angelo took a liking to the Santos family.

There were thousands of riders this year from several countries as the prior year. The announcement was made, "Moto's are posted." It was a mad dash for the moto boards. All the factory teams were given the moto's prior to them being posted.

Reggie again, understanding the pressures of owning a team and showing class by producing the moto sheets for them thirty minutes before the announcement. Dominic and Rafael were in the first moto's of 12 experts. They were in moto seventy-seven. It would be several hours between moto's.

Finally it was time. Dominic and Rafael were in their respective lanes. The cadence was called and the gate dropped. Dominic was off the gate first but this time it was different. He could not pull away as he once did in the past. The riders in his class were fast and from other countries.

Into the first turn Dominic was leading but heavy pressure from both inside and outside from riders he never heard of before and with names he could not pronounce. They raced over the jumps and into the next turn. Dominic was only leading by no more than a bicycle length.

Every pedal was going to be precious. He had to be smooth and make every effort count. Rafael was in fourth place and was pressuring for third place. It was a tight bunch and only a few riders were losing ground to the forward pack of riders that Dominic lead.

They raced the entire track before Dominic was able to make up some ground into the last turn. He won his heat race, but he was pressured way stronger than he had ever been in the past. Dominic was happy to see his other friend Rafael finish to fourth place.

In the pits Tony sat with Dominic and allowed Rafael to listen in. Tony started, "Remember how we practiced? Tight and squeezing you. This is it. This is what you trained for all this time. You just beat the number one rider from the Netherlands and Australia. These kids are the real deal. Remember what I taught you, pedal when you can and if all else fails, finish in fourth or better. Make it to the big show. First is nice but it only counts in the last race. The points are nice but you need to finish the race. You are better than these kids. You're that fine Italian sports car everyone hangs up on their wall, not a Chevette with an AM radio. Ride like you normally do and don't worry or make any mistakes if you get passed or get in trouble." Tony sat with Rafael for a short time to discuss his starting technique and how to negotiate the jumps.

Dominic finished first in most of his races this day. He did bobble a couple of times and was passed in the quarterfinal and the semifinal entering into the main event. Dominic remembered what Tony conveyed, relax take fourth or better and make it to the big show.

Late in the evening it was Mains. Rafael did not make it to the main event. He finished fifth in the last semi-final. He was impressive and Tony spoke with Maximo of possible suggestions to help with his racing techniques.

It was the last and final main of the 12 experts. It was a diverse group at the gate. Every racer was a factory sponsor and only two Americans qualified including Dominic. The crowd was standing and the entire Team Panther crew was in the bleachers with Dominic's family.

The gate dropped and they were off. Dominic was in the lead into the first turn. He was squeezed from the inside and the rider hit his leg disallowing Dominic to get on his pedals quickly. Into the second and third turn he was in second place.

As they entered the fourth straightaway, Dominic was able to get a full throw into the jumps and make his move. The first place rider from Australia was very clean but tried to hinder Dominic from passing.

Dominic was too strong. He was able to get over the last jump in the final push towards the finish line. Dominic pulled two bicycle lengths in front of the rider and finished first as the World Champion 12 year old expert. Team Panther was fanatical in the stands with exhilaration. Their teammate just won the World Championship.

Dominic made his way back to the pits where he was greeted by Reggie and the rest of the team. He was exhausted and it was late. Reggie reminded the team that there were a few more riders to go before they all left together as a team.

The event continued on into the late night hours. All of Team Panther's racers all made the main event. All except for two of the riders finished in first place. Tony was the last moto and the last racer left.

The spectators were all standing, ready to watch the pro main event. Tony won the event. He did not make it look easy. He was hounded the entire race and was able to hold off the advancement of the other racers looking for any opportunity to pass him. Tony was that good, he was the true champion. It was a paparazzi finale at the finish line. Tony won the World Championship.

After the race Reggie called the team for a meeting in the pits. He started, "I know it's late, you all are champions. Get some sleep and don't forget to show class as we enter the hotel. Some of you got a taste of what is coming next year. Some of you had new competition. Remember, you are only as good as people perceive you. You might have won first place, but now you have to act like a champion. Show respect to others and your prize will be magnified ten-fold. Nobody likes an arrogant Champion. People respect a down to earth person who treats them with respect who happens to be a world class champion. We are those people. Sign every autograph and say thank you and yes sir or ma'am. You are who people perceive you to be. Be that person."

Chapter 53

The winter break had come to an end and Dominic was living his normal childhood life. He was raced locally when he was able. He rode with his US 1 number plate. The local paper did a spotlight on his success and he had become very popular in town that year.

Dominic returned to school with notoriety after the World Championships. He had taken all the advice that was given to him by both his father and Reggie. He talked with Tony once a week about his conditioning and local events that showcased his success. Dominic was well liked by many of the students and relished in the fact that he was popular with the young ladies.

The months flew by for Dominic. He worked a couple days after school at his father's plant and was always teamed with his newest friend Oscar. He enjoyed Oscar's company and the fact that his wife normally sent a care package of food for him magnified his contentment.

Dominic and Oscar worked well together and when on the job, there was little spoken when performing their job related tasks. Dominic was familiar with what had to be performed and steadily worked with Oscar to complete the loading and offloading of the trucks. During their rides together, Oscar enjoyed his time with Dominic and kindled a little brother relationship with Dominic.

Meanwhile in Texas, Rafael was continuing his practice sessions with his friends. He had started to grow some and was becoming noticeably stronger. He, like Dominic, was popular in school and was a good student. He continued to ride his local track and was becoming very dominant in his class when the season began.

He did not work part time anywhere, but spent many hours with his father and Christopher. He enjoyed his father's attention along with his brothers. Rafael was excited when his father finally agreed to allow him to race at least five nationals in efforts to be eligible for a US number plate.

In the blink of an eye, the next year's tour was upon the factory race teams. Dominic looked in his helmet and saw the matted piece of paper he wrote his father's advice on stating, "Champions are produced on the BMX track; Legacies are made in person. A champion will be remembered for their achievements; a legend will be remembered by how they acted after the fanfare and well after the fact."

He held this to heart. He remembered his father's speech at the airport again this year. It's 1981 and it's a new season. Dominic had to retain his US #1 plate. Like clockwork, Dominic and Tony hooked up as if no time had passed. There were no new additions to the team this year.

The team had lost a few riders and Reggie did not backfill or sponsor any new riders. He made his investment in what riders remained. Phil, the other Pro, left the team on his own and did not want to tour this year. The three youngest riders, Tommy, Larry and Jose did not tour this year and gave up their sponsorship to race locally. There would be only 6 riders this season.

Tony and Dominic continued to live in their tent and only slept in the Puma Palace when the weather mandated. Like clockwork the team made their tour around the country. Dominic was one of the youngest on the team. He was 13 and the youngest rider Daren was 11.

There were the same old hijinks as the team toured the country. Dominic dominated his age class but the competition began to tighten up. He was still winning, but he was unable to pull away like he once did in the past. Dominic was strong and his conditioning allowed him to endure to the end. He would not slow or tire at the end of his moto's. The tour had new cities this year and the team was performing more riding demonstrations.

Tony and Dominic were up to their old practical jokes and the rest of the staff and team appreciated their respectable character and good nature. It was a long summer on tour and they both made it bearable. In Mississippi they held a protest against burgers and hotdogs with the team acting like they were picketing.

Reggie couldn't help but laugh. In return, Reggie promised them a dinner like they never had in their lives. He brought the entire team and staff to a restaurant that served dishes like rattle snake, alligator, buffalo and other exotic entrées.

Dominic and Tony made it a point to order the most exotic items off the menu and Reggie sat in awe as they finished their entire meals. They even ordered appetizers of different variety of meats. It was somewhat pricy but Reggie understood the hardships of being on the road and creating morale has no price tag. The team dared Tony and Dominic to eat specific types of foods and the waitress found the humor in the team's entertaining escapades.

It wasn't long before Dominic would meet up again with Rafael. He took notice instantly of how he had grown as well as his sister. In repetition of the last year, Maximo made himself known. Dominic took notice that Maximo and his wife had a food trailer and were selling authentic Mexican food from out of the trailer.

Dominic struck up a conversation with Maximo about how he worked with Oscar and his wife would make him care packages of food. Maximo and Florencia found awe-inspiring humor in Dominic and his addiction to Latin food. They gave him a free sample platter and were astonished at how much Dominic enjoyed the dishes.

It wasn't long before Dominic and Rafael were to race. Dominic won all his moto's but Rafael was nipping at his heals the entire time. Dominic knew if made one mistake, Rafael would have passed him.

Maximo and his family found Dominic and Tony to be quality people. They relished Reggie and how he was the master of controlling the kids on his team. Maximo and Reggie sat for hours talking. No one understood them from Team Panther, it was all in Spanish.

The entire tour was the same thing. Rafael raced national events and pressured Dominic in every moto. Dominic was strong and was able to fend off Rafael. Dominic was beginning to understand the rewards of practicing and working out on the off season.

He kept thinking to himself, "What if Rafael picked up his workout habits?" It was a matter of perspective and perseverance. Reggie adopted Maximo and his family at all the races they attended. In kind, the Santos family enjoyed being a part of the Team Panther camp.

The tour continued and Dominic continued to dominate his class. Tony was winning many of his races. He did not win every race like in the past but he was going to be the number one pro this year. Dominic was going to be US #1 for the 13 experts. Team Panther again won the Factory number 1 for the tour.

The tour ended for Dominic in New Jersey like last year. Reggie waited for this time to gather the team at Dominic's home. Reggie began, "Well guys, there is no secret, but I want to be the first to tell you all. There is no more World Championships this year. It's a new era in the sport and it has become big business. The tour is going to change as well. There is no set tour schedule, just a bunch of random nations. There is a pattern and we will continue in the RV as we travel. Things will change but we will be seen. Our product is more than successful. We are the number one factory team for the last couple of years. We will continue to do what we do. Just know that we will not have a World Championship. I am looking at the possibilities of going overseas for a few races. It's all in the works and you will all be contacted in advance. Get your passports and I will contact each and every one of you of the upcoming events should they come to fruition. Continue to practice and excel in school. Remember, no school is not cool and I will continue to check your report cards."

<u>**Chapter 54**</u>

The year progressed and Dominic continued to dominate his class. Dominic was asked to race in Hong Kong and in Great Britain. He was excited to race overseas and he dominated his class as a thirteen year old expert. He won almost all his moto's and won first place in both countries before returning home. He had become internationally known and was excelling in the sport.

He won the 14, 15, 16 and 17 expert classes for all these years. His final year of high school was in 1986. He would be turning 18 years old. Reggie and Tony sat Dominic down and decided they needed to discuss his role with Team Panther and the course he was going to take this year.

Reggie started, "Dominic, you have been a valuable asset to the team. You are a champion and have proven yourself both on and off the track. You have a decision to make in the next year. I want you to race one more year as an 18 year old expert. At the end of this season no matter how you place nationally, I think you need to think about turning professional. You are by all means a professional athlete and its time you take it to the next level."

Tony remarked, "My friend, you know you are ready now but you need to take Reggie's advice. I am willing to work with you and assist you in any endeavor you decide. It won't be too much longer and I don't know how many more productive years I have left racing competitively. I am not getting younger. The competition is multiplied from a few years ago. All the pros now have the same skills and strengths. It won't be long before you and I are neck in neck into the first turn."

Dominic was beside himself about their conversation. He agreed to wait one more season and see how his skills advance. His dream and aspirations were to be a pro BMX rider, but he was unsure of his decision. He knew that he had to sit with his father and mother at that time to decide his future. He had college to consider and what his role would be if he made the decision to race as a pro.

Dominic raced his final year as an 18 year old expert and won his national number one title. He had to qualify as a pro and needed to rethink all his possibilities. The team was only five riders. He and Tony were the only two original members of the team.

Reggie continued to build the team and product line. Tony and Dominic raced at many nationals and were flown in by Reggie to the city's they were racing instead of making the jaunt cross country in the Puma Palace.

It was more economical to simply fly them into the races and provide them with hotels and rental cars. Tony did not win the pro title in these years. He did however place in the top three every year and was more popular than previous years.

Dominic graduated High School in 1986 and a few days after his graduation he sat with his parents to discuss his future. Dominic was nervous and was having the conversation with his parents.

He asked, "Mom, Dad, here is what I would like to do. I want to race one year as a professional. I will always have these memories and I want to say that I raced all my life to accomplish this goal. I don't know if I will be competitive or be a champion. I want to take this opportunity to try it for one year and see what happens. I promise to further my education and graduate college. I don't know what I want to do but I want to say I was a pro BMX racer."

Angelo answered, "Son, I agree with you. One year and let's see what transpires. Your mother and I will pay for any college you are accepted to and will make any arrangements for you. You will need further education. This is not an option. I know you don't want to take over my business and I accept the fact that you want to move on.

However, your brother will take over the business and you will work for him if you decide to want to be a mason after he takes the reins. Joey needs to control his anger issues." They all laughed.

Angelo continued, "He only got in two fights this year in school. I guess he has my disposition. But, I am more controlled than he is at this stage of his life. He will have to learn the business and go to school for at least two years. He seems to take a great interest in what I have built for our family.

He is going to be fine when I decide to let him run the business. He is a good worker and I relish the fact he doesn't take any crap from anyone. You on the other hand need to take advantage of the opportunity of racing professionally. One year son, one year and you let us know what you want to do."

Dominic decided at that moment he was going to go to California and take Reggie's offer of turning pro. Reggie was experimenting with the new technology. His company produced aluminum frames. He and Tony were going to experiment with the new carbon fiber frame as a prototype.

Dominic flew to California and trained with Tony harder than he ever had in the past. He raced in California and was awarded the opportunity to race as a pro. His first race was exceptional. He qualified for the main event and finished third place. Dominic was awarded $350.00 for his efforts.

Tony finished second on this day. The first lesson Dominic learned that was he would not be able to pull away. Everyone is strong, all the riders are technical and they all have the ability to pass if he made the smallest mistake.

Dominic stayed with Reggie during the week and worked at the plant with Tony. Dominic earned a small wage but he was content on pursuing his dream. He and Tony practiced every day after work. Tony had the biggest pits he'd ever seen.

Dominic was impressed by how high the jumps were and the practice track with all the technical sections. Day after day they practiced. The local kids would show up to watch them jump nearly thirty feet across ravines. This was unheard of in these days and they were practicing the course as fast as they could ride.

Other days they practiced gates at a local track. Gate after gate after exhausting gate they practiced. This was where the race was won. Several weeks after they started practicing, Dominic noticed that he was able to beat Tony into the first turn one out of five times. Tony assured him that he was not letting him win, he was just getting faster.

From California, Tony and Dominic commuted to other Nationals. They flew together, shared hotel rooms and rental cars. Reggie continued to contribute and finance their tour. They were over eight races into the season and Dominic was in fourth place as a pro and Tony was holding second, but only a few points separated him from first.

It was a shootout and competition had intensified. When in Texas this year, many things happened to Dominic. He met up with his old friend Rafael. Rafael was a professional at this time and his parents were still selling food out of their trailer. The Santos's opened their house for both Tony and Dominic for the week before all three of them embarked to Florida for a few days to race in the nationals.

The Santos's cooked a feast for Dominic and Tony all week. Dominic finished first in his Main and was able to beat Tony. Rafael was attending a local two year college at the time and raced on weekends. Dominic also found himself interested in one of the local girls. It was a ton of bricks hitting his chest and he wasn't at his father's plant.

Dominic, Tony and Rafael continued to race together throughout Florida competing at all the Nationals in the state. Dominic was now frequently beating Tony and winning more often. Rafael was always in the main event. Rafael's sponsor's continually joked about having Dominic and Tony ride for them.

They both knew there was truth in their jokes. Tony and Dominic raced a few weeks in Florida and then headed back to California by airplane. Rafael drove home from Florida alone and continued with his life.

It wasn't long before the racing season was coming to an end and Tony was awarded #2 pro and Dominic #3. Reggie was ecstatic and could not be prouder of them. As they returned he called them into his office and asked them to ready themselves for an overseas National.

They were both going to France along with the other team members. Dominic was excited and called home later that day. The phone rang and his brother answered.

Dominic asked, "What are you doing home from school so early?"

Joey replied, "I got suspended but it wasn't my fault."

Dominic sighed, "Did you win or lose this time?"

Joey answered, "I won all three of them."

Dominic laughed, "OK I'll bite. What happened?"

Joey grabbed his breath, "I was walking to class and these three Spanish guys were making fun of me in Spanish. So I walked up calmly and started wailing on their faces. I was able to knock two of them out instantly but the third one took me some time before security broke it up."

Dominic didn't know how to answer his brother and simply asked to speak to his parents. Dominic spoke to his parents and gave them the good news about going overseas. They were happy for him and they were proud of his #3 plate as a professional. There was no mention of school or future plans.

Dominic simply avoided it and was contemplating what he wanted to do with his life. He liked working and fixing things. On the other hand, he wanted to work a job where he could still possibly race and have his evenings off. His thoughts were up in the air and had no idea of what he wanted to do or what he wanted as a career.

In the off season, Dominic made several self-paid trips to Texas. Many joked about the girl he liked and Dominic never denied it. Dominic was also in Texas visiting a University at his father's request. It wasn't long before Dominic decided to race one more year. He received the blessing from both his parents and Reggie.

The next year came as quickly as it departed. Again Dominic and Tony made the pseudo tour of the nationals and raced all over the country. Again they both rode and flew together. This year was different.

Dominic had become his nickname. The Dominator had started to dominate every race. He was the pro to beat in 1987. He was nineteen years old and in the prime of his life. He started to notice that he was beating Tony on a regular basis. They joked about it and Tony talked about passing the torch.

The end of the year was approaching and Dominic was in high contention for the number one pro position. He had the last few races and a Grand National to ride. If he could finish in first in these races, he would earn the #1 pro title.

The races continued and Dominic became the Dominator. He went on to win the title that year and had become the most popular person in BMX. His picture was splashed all over the industry's magazines. He was revered as a class act.

Dominic took the advice from his father, Reggie and Tony. He used all their principles and life's lessons to propel his image and relate to others. He always remembers how star-struck he was when he was introduced to Tony. He understood the industry and the role he was cast to play.

He knew he was always being watched by others. He calculated every move he made in public and in return he was praised with kindness. Dominic remembered the advice Tony once gave him, "Never turn on your fans and they will never turn on you. What you do is what they expect. When approached, always smile and tell them it was nice talking with you too. With kindness comes respect."

Chapter 55

Dominic woke in his family home in his own bed this morning. His father was awake on this Sunday morning. As Dominic arose he sat next to his father with coffee in hand. His father asked, "Well Dom, you're one year late. What are you going to do? Are you going to be the Dominator until the age of thirty or do you think maybe you should think about school?"

Dominic sat in his chair for a second with an anguished flush expression on his face. Dominic answered, "Well Dad, I promised you I would make a decision. I want to go to school in Texas. I thought this over many times in my head. I want to attend a four year school in Aerospace and Engineering. I have two years of the basic courses before entering in to the meat of my primary studies."

Angelo asked, "Texas? Is there a certain someone down there or is it the school?"

Dominic laughed, "I want to be honest with you Dad. It's both. The school is highly rated and maybe a girl. I don't know what will come of it or a relationship. Her family approves of me and I have been nothing but a gentleman. Who knows? Besides, in Texas I can race across the panhandle into Florida for all the Nationals. I still have to race on my weekends. I am going to try to work it out with Reggie. I need to let him know."

Dominic waited a few days and finally made the call to Reggie. He started, "Reggie how you doing? I need to discuss a decision I need to make. I hope you understand. You have been a part of my life since I was a child and I'm taking all your advice along with my father's."

Some silence on the phone and Reggie replied, "Go ahead Dom."

Dominic continued, "I want to go to college. I need to look more into the future after BMX. But, I still want to race on my weekends. I know it will cripple me a little in the points but I need to do this. I promised my family and I wanted you to be the first one I spoke with about my decision other than my parents."

There was a pause and Reggie began to laugh, "Dom, I thought you were quitting. Listen to me young man. You have made the most important decision in your life. I support your decision to further your education. You're not going to stop racing I hope. You are always going to be a part of Team Panther. I am so proud of you. You're doing the right thing. Good for you."

That was it. It's out in the open. Dominic was previously accepted by the school based on his SAT's taken his senior year of high school. He would attend college during the week and race on weekends. Dominic made the move to Texas later that next week.

His father made all the arrangements and Dominic was going to drive to Texas so he would have his Jeep and personal belongings with him. He was able to fit all his belongings in the back of his open air Jeep Wrangler along with his two bicycles that sat nicely on the rack.

It took Dominic nearly two days to drive to his campus. He left early in the morning. His drive was long and mostly uneventful. The most difficult drive was getting out of his neighborhood. It seemed another New Jersey driver found it funny to allow his passenger to relieve himself out of the car moving nearly 100 MPH being held by his friend who pulled him back in the car by the back of his pants.

After this unusual encounter, he realized he made the right decision to get out of New Jersey for a while. He arrived at the campus and performed all the enrollment obligations he needed to perform. He lived off campus and shared a house with four other people. He had his own bedroom and a full house including a basement to share.

Dominic continued to attend school and race on the weekends. He did not train as he once did but still rode enough to keep in shape. He practiced often and found a part time job at a local bicycle shop. He was recognized by many people who entered the shop and the owner developed a liking to Dominic.

He was trustworthy and a diligent worker. Dominic spent many hours with Rafael after school training or riding at the local track. One night a week there was a local race and another night for gate practice. The Santos family enjoyed Dominic and was proud of his accomplishments and his courage to take on college in the middle of his greatest success and he had become family.

Dominic continued to race and meet with Tony at many Nationals on the weekends to only hurry back to school before Monday morning. It was race day on Sunday and directly to the airport for a flight. Maybe time to shower at the hotel if possible.

This continued for many years. Dominic continued to perform well at the track. He was not going to accumulate the points to be number one but he was always in the top five along with Tony. Their friendship strengthened over the years and Tony was nearing the end of his career.

One day out of nowhere Dominic received a call from Tony. Dominic answers, "Yo big T. What's up buddy?"

Dominic knew something was wrong right away. A million thoughts went through his head. Was his mom ok? Was there another family issue? He always calls me and is happy. This time he was different.

Tony spoke softly, "Dom, I'm done. It's an end of an era for me. I want to retire. I'm approaching thirty years old and I want to enjoy the sport from the sidelines. Reggie helped me find a job working with the youth. I was able to use my Associates Degree to get this job. It pays

OK, but it's a new beginning. We are going to talk as we always have in the past. It's just that time. I wanted you to hear it from me first. I am going to announce it tomorrow. I am going to vacation at the Jersey Shore and will hang like we always did."

Dominic answered, "Ok, cool. I have a tent at the house. It will be like old times." They both laughed and Dominic congratulated him and wished him the best.

It wasn't long after this conversation that Reggie called Dominic a few days later. Reggie was a little shaken but held his emotions, "Dom, you're the man of Team Panther. Tony told you his decision. He is going to work for me with my youth program. He will be perfect. I want you to make school a priority. I also want you to continue your dream of racing BMX. You still have that gift. If not in college, you would be number one every year. I'm Ok with you sitting back and allowing school to be your priority. With that said, you will always be a part of Team Panther. Matter of fact, I need an address to send you a new bike. It's the dirt jumping series frame called 'the cub.' Its more rigid and made for jumping. Check it out for yourself. Also, continue to race. You are loved and respected by many. Tell the Santos's I said Hola and don't forget to send me your report card." Dominic laughed and gave his salutations to his old friend Reggie.

Dominic continued his studies and raced on the weekends and summers. He traveled with Rafael in the few surrounding Texas states. Dominic made his presence known at many National events and continued to place in the top five every year. Many times Reggie, Tony or both were present at the larger races endorsing Team Panther products and showcasing new product lines.

Dominic continued his friendship with Tony and Reggie. He found a peaceful sentiment overcome his persona when he was with his best buddies. He grew a fond friendship with Rafael and the Santos family. He enjoyed sitting with Maximo talking about various topics and current events.

Rafael and Christopher joined in their conversations many times when they were not attending their universities. It was like a big college campus at the Santos home. Dominic understood his gift and the gift of friendship while living in Texas. He never forgot to make time to call his family and speak with his parents.

He was often reminded of how lucky he was to have quality people in his life that demonstrated the knack of practicing what they preached. He surrounded himself with quality people and Dominic became a quality person with the same characteristics of his friends.

It's an easy decision in life. Do you become like those you surround yourself or do you choose your own path on your own terms with little or no direction? One needs to evaluate themselves and their situation. Does someone surround their self with quality people or flat line their entire existence? In life, you can't have too many friends.

Chapter 56

It's late spring in 1992 and Dominic is graduating from college. He has earned his four year degree and is employed working within his degree boundaries he earned while in school. His family, girlfriend, Reggie, the Santos family, his former employer from the bicycle shop in Texas and friends he has made while living in Texas came to his graduation.

It was a formal graduation with minor spoofs and awards. Unknown to Dominic he was awarded the best athlete and jokingly the nicest hair. He had continued to allow his hair to grow and agreed that when he graduated he would allow his mother to choose the hair style she wanted. After all, she and Angelo paid for his education. Dominic promised his mother that before he cut his hair, she would be there to witness it.

Dominic was still racing and currently number four in the nation in the pro class. Rafael raced but was not as serious as Dominic. After the ceremony commenced, Dominic sat with his surrounding company of supporters and spoke openly with them asking, "I am in a dilemma. More torn than a dilemma, I want to race one year seriously and try to obtain the number one ranking. Then, I want to start gaining more time towards my career. Also, I have made a commitment to my girlfriend for the last four years as well. I want her to finish college before we make any further commitments."

She leaned over and kissed him on the cheek as he continued, "Also, I need to figure out where I am going to live. I am twenty four years old and can't live a frat type of lifestyle. Also, I need a vehicle with air-conditioning. I am dying in my Jeep."

They all laughed and Maximo spoke up, "I'll make you a deal. When you are in Texas, you can stay in the basement. There is an extra room and a bathroom you will share with Juan. All I ask is you continue to grow in your career and show us the same respect you have over the last couple of years. We think of you as our child. Besides, Florencia enjoys cooking for you."

As if it were timed perfectly, Angelo and Maria asked Dominic if he liked their car they were driving. It was a 1990 Jeep Cherokee with very low mileage and a bicycle rack on the back. Dominic looked at them and exclaimed, "No way! Seriously, this is my new Jeep?"

They both laughed and threw the keys at him. Dominic went over to the vehicle and looked inside and noticed that it was air-conditioned and in perfect shape. He asked his father, "What do I do with my Jeep? It runs good, I have taken good care of it and there is nothing wrong with it. It doesn't have air-conditioning and it gets hot down here."

Angelo grabbed the keys from Dominic and said, "Here is what you do with this vehicle."

He took the keys and threw them to Maximo and said, "It's yours Max. My son doesn't need it any longer. Consider this a down payment on all the food Florencia has to cook in the near future."

Maximo made it a point to not want to accept the vehicle. Angelo insisted and told him, "I am not driving this thing back to New Jersey without air-conditioning. Please take it. Give it away. I don't care but it's yours and I want you to have it."

Rafael grabbed the keys and said, "I know what to do with it."

Maximo laughed at him and said, "I know, you always wanted a Jeep."

Rafael shook his head in agreement.

Tony and Reggie sat with Dominic the next day. Reggie began to speak, "Well Dom, this is it. You are going to make this your last run at the title or are you thinking of riding until you feel that you are no longer competitive?"

Dominic answered, "I don't know. I want to continue with my craft I obtained from college and on the same hand continue to race. I'm at the cross roads of what do I do?"

Reggie answered, "Race this season. I have you covered. Let's see how you do and continue your studies as you desire. You have a beautiful girl who loves you and supports you. This is going to be your biggest hurdle in life, not racing."

Dominic took in what Reggie had said and asked his closest friend, "Tony, what do I do after this season?"

Tony replied, "Rollout this season and see how you do. You need to start working on more conditioning and gates. You need to make a serious attempt to get out of the top five and back to number one. It's not easy anymore. Everyone is quick and they all have equal skills."

Dominic made the decision to race and working on his trade. He found a part time job near the Santos family home and was able to work part time on his trade and continue his race schedule. Dominic met with his form employer at the bicycle shop.

He agreed to help Dominic and assist with any training needed. He had access to the local BMX track and the ability to provide private gate start practice for him. In return, Dominic agreed to wear his name as a sponsor on his Jersey. For nearly a month Dominic trained almost every day and he worked on his trade. He took both of these seriously and worked harder than he did in the past. He was in constant communication with Tony and they would talk for hours.

The season began and Dominic started his races in California. Like the old Dominic, he began to dominate the pro class. He was winning and making the headlines. He was riding like he had in the past, only much faster and more recognized.

As coached, he spoke to every person who stopped him and signed every autograph. He was one of the few riders from Team Panther. Carl had set up a camp and the Puma Palace was still in commission. The Puma Palace was a little older, but clean and comfortable as in the prior years.

Tony attended almost every race that the team participated in. He was still recognized and carried himself with an encouraging attitude towards others. He was the poster child for Team Panther with Dominic nipping at his heals.

The 1992 season continued and Dominic earned his nickname. He was the Dominator. He was all the rave for this season. His picture was on every BMX magazine and promotional literature circulating in the sport. He was flying all over the country and would not be back in Texas for weeks at a time.

He often called his girlfriend who supported his efforts. She constantly joked about seeing his photo on every magazine and knew what he was doing while he was absent from her presence. Dominic made several appearances at the Texas bicycle shop and proudly proclaimed his support of youth sports. He was respected by his former boss and revered by many.

Dominic made several trips a year to New Jersey to race and spend time with his family. He enjoyed the time alone with his family and still assisted his father at the plant when he was home. He rode with Oscar as in the past. They constantly joked about him living in a Mexican home with endless taco's and empanada's.

The visits home were short visits but soothing to his soul. It was needed and he missed his family. He developed a support structure that enabled him to successfully obtain his aspirations and goals. Dominic awoke every morning with a sense of completion and a drive to perform. He was moving along with his craft and at the same time winning races.

The season was coming to an end and Dominic won the Championship. He completed several interviews and award dinners. He made good on his promises and made several appearances at the bike shop. He went as far as making visits to children with disabilities with his girlfriend who majored in early childhood development.

This was something they both enjoyed doing together. She was awarded a scholarship based on her grades from both High School and College. She was entering a Master's Program and wanted to finish in one year's time. She and Dominic spent as much time as they could together. Dominic was using his degree in Aerospace to earn extra income. He found another position working for a small regional airline in Texas and continued to race when he was able.

He sat with his girlfriend one late afternoon and asked, "Do you think one day we will ever be married?"

She looked at him and replied very quickly, "I have been with you for over four years; I hope I'm not wasting my time Dom."

Dominic pulled a box out of his pocket and handed it to her saying, "I don't know if we will be married soon, but I want you to have this as a promise that I will always be here for you and I want to marry you. I know school is important. When you're done, you decide when you want to get married."

She smiled and said, "Dom, are you asking me to marry you?"

He replied, "Look inside."

She looked inside the box and noticed a beautiful diamond ring with the traditional setting she always described. She hugged him and said, "Of course I will marry you. What did my father say?"

Dominic answered, "He kissed me on the top of the head and had tears in his eyes. He said nothing and hugged me."

She replied, "I guess he was happy."

Dominic asked, "Do you know of any good pastors?" They both laughed.

It was a new chapter in Dominic's life. He was stepping into bigger commitments and a new role soon. He had to make a choice about his racing career. He was going to keep racing, but make his career with his new employer more of a priority. Life was starting to make more sense. He was swallowing the dish life served him. So far, it tasted good.

He called home and proclaimed, "She said yes."

They were all excited for him. They loved his girlfriend and now his fiancé. He called Tony conveying the good news. He joked, "Oh boy, I'm not training two Carlucci's. One is enough."

Reggie sent his congratulations and spoke with Dominic for nearly an hour on the phone. Reggie was very supportive and gave his blessings. Dominic was in the crossroads of his life. He had options. He had more than one path and some of them converged. He did not have two paths to decide his fate.

He made the right decisions in life at an early age that allowed him several opportunities instead of only two. It's a matter of listening and making the right decisions. He had quality friends and family members to guide him on his journey into adulthood. Dominic's decision of what to do next was an easy one. Remember what he was taught by his friends and family, and then apply it.

Chapter 57

It was late October and Dominic had just returned to the Santos family home. He was greeted at the door by Maximo and Maria. Maximo was clearly upset about something but kept his composure. Maximo talking softly, "You need to call home. Your father needs to talk with you."

Dominic asked, "Is everything OK, what's the matter?"

Maximo simply handed Dominic the phone. Dominic lifted the receiver and called his home. Angelo picked up the phone. Dominic quickly asked, "Hey dad it me. Is everything OK?"

Angelo answered, "No son, I need to speak with you. Please sit down."

Dominic concerned and nervous answered, "Ok, go ahead dad. What's up?"

Angelo calmly, "Oscar was diagnosed with cancer. He has had it for some time now and kept it private and secret from all of us. He is in the hospital and they don't know how long he will hold on. You need to get here if you can."

There was a brief silence and then Dominic asked, "What kind of cancer Dad?"

Angelo replied, "Pancreatic."

They spoke for a short time before Dominic conveyed his friend Oscar's condition to the Santos family. Dominic called his boss at home and explained his dilemma. They allowed him to take the time off.

He spoke for a while with Maximo and the rest of the family. He joked about how good of a cook his wife was and the care packages she would send for him when he worked with Oscar. Dominic later asked his fiancé to come with him. She agreed and the itinerary was set for the next day.

Dominic and his fiancé were met at the airport by Angelo and Maria. They immediately proceeded to the hospital. Dominic was met at Oscar's room by his wife. She was so happy to see him and hugged him as he walked up. She expressed how happy Oscar was when they worked together.

She explained how he had been sick for a long time. Dominic introduced his fiancé to Oscar's wife and proceeded to Oscar's bedside. Oscar was awake and was lying in bed hooked up to several machines. He was in and out of consciences. Dominic knew he had a short time to speak.

He spoke to Oscar, "Hey Hefy, I want you to know that you were one of my heroes. You taught me a lot about being a man and being responsible. All this time you were sick and said nothing. I don't know what to say. You were a part of my life. You can't go yet. I want more of your wife's cooking. Seriously, I want you to know that I cherished our time working together. You are what people strive to be." Oscar grabbed Dominic's hand and slightly squeezed it and drifted in and out of sleep.

Oscar passed the next day. Angelo closed the plant on the day of Oscar's funeral. Angelo insisted and paid for the funeral. Oscar was not an employee but a friend. Many of Oscar's co-workers spoke about him on this day. Dominic was asked but could not find the words to speak without breaking down in tears and asked if he could simply be a pole bearer.

After the burial, the family met at Oscar's home. His wife joked about her cooking and sent Dominic home with a care package. His fiancé joked about his adoration for Latin cuisine. Dominic and his family departed from Oscar's home and drove back to his parent's home.

A couple days later there was a knock at the door very early in the morning. Angelo answered the door revealing two detectives wanting to ask him and Joey questions. He invited them inside and asked what had happened. There was a fire at a local union lodge last evening and they wanted to question Joey.

Joey was woken up by Angelo and asked to come downstairs. Joey noticed the detective and immediately became defensive. Dominic was awakened and listened in as they asked their questions. Joey did not answer any questions and demanded a lawyer. Angelo was highly upset as the detectives left. He sat Joey down and catechized him for information.

Angelo started speaking very angrily, "Joey, I will kill you myself unless you tell me what's going on and why they came here."

Angelo, Dominic and Joey were all sitting at the kitchen table as Joey began to speak. Joey replied, "OK dad, here is what happened. A couple of weeks ago some goomba's from the Union came on our property looking to talk with some of our workers about unionizing our business. Some of the guys called me about them being there and wanted them to leave. I asked them to leave and not come back. So, they left no issues. A couple of days later, they showed back up again. This time I wasn't so nice. I asked them to leave and they insisted that they be allowed to handout union cards. I walked back and got the forklift. I lifted their car off the ground and set outside of the property. I did not damage it nor did I hurt anyone. I did not threaten them with bodily harm. I did however tell them if they came back, I wouldn't be so nice"

Angelo answered, "That's it? Don't think I didn't know about the fork lift incident. I just didn't say anything. I know what goes on at the plant Joey."

Joey insisted he knew nothing about the fire of the Union Hall. Several days later Dominic was back in Texas and received a call from his father, "Son, how are you?"

Dominic answered, "Good dad. How are you and your arsonist son?"

Angelo laughed, "That is what I am calling you about. I just read the paper this morning. They found the cause of the fire. Someone threw a flare into the building. Did you know they were able to get a finger print from it? The flare was not burned up completely. They also have someone under arrest for arson. It's not Joey. I guess he was telling the truth."

Dominic sighed with relief, "Good. Take the forklift keys away from him."

Angelo laughed, "Nooo, he handled it better than I could have. I would have taken the dozer and pushed their car off the property."

Dominic asked, "You don't have an issue with a union coming in do you?"

Angelo answered, "No son, we have a pretty happy family here as far as I know."

Dominic's fiancé walked in halfway through the conversation. Dominic explained what transpired and they both had a good laugh.

She asked Dominic, "Are you getting ready for work?"

He replied, "Yes, you need a ride back to school?"

She looked at him with big puppy dog eyes and asked, "Can I drop you off? You are gone for the next couple of days and I would like to use your car. My car needs to go to the shop for scheduled maintenance."

He looked at her and said, "Of course."

Dominic was happy to be back to work. He sat back and recollected his thoughts of the past day's events. He realized that his brother was going to take over the business. His brother was respected by the workers and managers at the plant.

Joey had a temper problem, but he was imprecisely controlled. He made the correct decisions with adolescent behavior. This was Joey's demeanor and he wasn't going to change. Dominic realized his father accepted his brother this way and so would the next person that crosses his path.

We all have boundaries. Joey's was microscopic. However, before he reacted, he processed the consequences. He was highly intelligent and calculated. It's like the old saying, brilliance borders insanity. Joey wasn't insane. He had a short fuse, no fear and distinctly understood the consequences of his actions.

Chapter 58

It's now spring in 1993. Dominic married his long time fiancé. It was an outside wedding by a lake. Dominic originally wanted to be wed on his bicycle. The pastor agreed, but like always, it was her decision to be formal with no bicycles. It was a good gesture to want include his pastime, but Dominic understood how his wife felt about family and traditions.

Dominic's family made it to Texas, including aunts and uncles, many of his friends, BMX racers, and Reggie. Tony was his best man. His brother Joey made it a point to not even argue with anyone. He was well behaved. All of the Santos family attended. Christopher was the pianist and organist for the wedding. This was arranged by Rafael.

Dominic was extremely happy. His mother and Florencia did nothing but cook the entire time. It was like heaven, moms cooking Latin food. It didn't get better than this for Dominic. He even brought some of his food on the airplane.

The years continued and in 1995 Dominic had his big break. He continued to race the past few years but his career had become more a priority. His wife graduated college and was awarded her early childhood development certification for the State of Texas. They lived modestly in a one bedroom apartment and saved their money.

Dominic walked into the apartment in the late afternoon and called for his wife. She came down the steps and asked, "Yes honey, what's up? You sound excited."

He answered, "I was offered a job today with Global International Airways."

She was happy for him. Dominic worked very hard for this position.

He spoke uneasily at first then finally let it out. He looked at his wife and asked, "Can you help me make this decision?"

She answered, "Of course."

Dominic continued, "Well, they offered me the position in Philadelphia. They only have a position out of Philadelphia right now. I want this job but I don't want to go if you won't be happy."

She smiled and looked at him, "Honey, When do we leave? I have to get certified in New Jersey. I know we are going to live in New Jersey so I will figure it out. What did your parents say about us living with them for a few months?"

Dominic looked at his wife and said, "We are going to rent an apartment or a house. I love my parents but I can't live at home at this age."

So at age twenty-five, Dominic made the move to New Jersey with his wife. His father found them a beautiful condominium along a river for rent. Dominic enjoyed being home again. With his new position at G.I.A. (Global International Airways) he would be able to support his wife and himself until she had finished her New Jersey certification.

Maximo and Florencia were very happy for Dominic and understood that he had to go where his career took him. They supported his efforts of wanting to be successful in his career. They had a big celebration for both of them before they left.

Dominic continued to work and ride his bicycle and race competitively. It was getting harder and harder for him to stay in the shape he once was as a youth. He was still in excellent physical condition, but BMX condition was another layer of talent. Dominic understood he was not going to be a number one pro any longer and was widely recognized by many in his home town.

He knew he worked hard at his career and wasn't going to let anything stop him from his goals. Dominic achieved every goal he set. He made his goals tangible and reachable. Nothing out of the limits of what he knew he could achieve.

It was six months later when Dominic called Reggie on the phone. They were joking for a while and Dominic disclosed, "Reggie, I finally found the nerve and I clipped in."

Reggie laughing, "Nooooo. You are using clipless pedals. I know you are a purist. It took an act of God for Tony to talk you into changing your gears. Now you're clipped in? Say it isn't so?"

Dominic was laughing also, "It's a sign of the times. It's a new era Reggie. I can't believe it myself."

Reggie changed the tone of the conversation and Dominic could tell that something was amiss. Dominic broke the ice, "So Reggie, I know something's up. Give me the scoop?"

Reggie took a deep breath and came out with it, "Dominic, it has been an outstanding ride. But I am taking my last gate. I am selling Team Panther and all of its rights. I am retiring. There will be no more team. I can honestly say I have no regrets about moving on in my life. But, I want you and Tony to be a part of it. I have a new venture I am starting but I can't say anything at this time. I need a couple of months or maybe a year. Nevertheless, I need time. I just need to start over and clean. I am moving from California to the Florida Keys. I have saved and made enough money to buy a piece of property, build a house and not have to work if I desire. But you know me, I'm always up to the next best thing."

Dominic asked, "What about Tony?"

Reggie laughed, "He is coming down here with me soon if he wants. He is going to work for me in California for a while. I am selling all my businesses along with Team Panther. I only want to commit to one job at this point in my life. I promised my wife I would and I need to make good on my promise."

Dominic asked, "What about all my Team Panther equipment?"

Reggie answered, "Dom, Keep it. I also have a care package coming for you. I sent it to your parents' address. You will love it. We will always be Team Panther. Just remember that. Our legacy will always be a lasting one."

Dominic hung up with Reggie and immediately called Tony, "Hey big fluffy love, what's up?"

Tony answered, "How did I know it was you?"

Dominic asked, "So um, what's going on with you and Reggie? I just got off the phone with him and he won't tell me a thing."

Tony talking as if he had food in his mouth, "I want to tell you so bad but I promised Reggie I wouldn't. He needs time. I think he needs more than he thinks. So Dom, I can't tell. Don't pressure me."

Dominic sat back and thought for a moment. He continued, "Ok, you're right. No pressure. I'll let you go. I can tell you're eating and my wife is looking at me with her hands on her hips. I'll talk with you in a few days."

Dominic discussed his conversation with his wife about Reggie. Dominic was curious about what Reggie's next adventure was going to encompass. He pondered and obsessed for almost a week before letting it go.

Dominic knew Reggie and his demeanor. Reggie would not divulge any information until the right time. This was Reggie's career and he was the best. He did not give any hints or indications of what he was doing next. It was his way of doing business. Wait, confirm, commit and promote.

Dominic continued to work and put more time in at his job. He spent his days off with his wife and often visited his parents for dinners when he was home on the weekends and not working. He sometimes brought his bicycle to ride the track that was standing in the back yard.

He recalled the time he and Oscar spent together building it. He loved to eat his mother's cooking and it also allowed his wife a break from her everyday routine of cooking. Dominic made a point to reiterate how lucky he was to have a wife and mother that were the finest cooks. He also knew that it wasn't long before he would start to gain weight if he didn't continue his exercise programs.

Chapter 59

A couple of years have passed and Dominic is continuing with his career. He is traveling more often and at the same time receiving more time off. He enjoys what he is doing and his wife received her authorization to teach and work within her degree for early childhood development.

She had become a teacher and primarily worked with special needs children. It was another year of school but she finished with high grades and passed the time working as a tutor. Dominic on the other hand was working extra and even helped at the plant when his brother Joey asked him.

In February of this year, Dominic was blessed with multiple announcements. The major announcement was that his wife was pregnant. The second good fortune was that his wife's brothers were moving into town. They had made a venture to open a small business and Angelo offered to help them.

He gave them jobs during the day assisting them with the ability to work and save some money. This also enabled them to look for a storefront to open their contractor supply company. After a couple of months, Angelo offered to assist again lending them money to get started. Angelo was impressed by how hard they worked for him and was impressed with their work ethics. He opened up his wallet to assist them.

The family was ecstatic with the good news from Dominic and his wife. It was almost unbearable for him. His mother visited the apartment every day. His wife was only into her first trimester and already his mother was implanting herself into his everyday life. He and his wife both new she meant no harm and she was excited about being a grandmother.

Dominic's wife was working at this time and the timing was perfect. She was due at the beginning of the summer. This allowed her to work and lose very little time from her job. It was obvious that child care was not going to be an issue.

Reggie called at least once a month to check on Dominic. Every time Reggie called, the same questions from Dominic echoed the phone. In like fashion, Reggie answered the same, "It's still a work in progress."

Reggie called to congratulate him and was already asking if it was a boy or girl. Dominic joked, "I'll tell you if you tell me your big plans."

Reggie joked and never answered Dominic. Finally Dominic would give in and conveyed that it was a boy.

At the beginning of the summer, Dominic's wife gave birth to a healthy baby boy. He was nearly eight pounds and full of energy. The entire family from around the United States flew in to see the baby. Dominic now understood all the talks his father had with him as a young man.

He sat back and gathered his thoughts about what his life now meant. There were no more options for him. He now had to provide for his family. He and his wife were financially secure but he strived for more. This was Dominic's personality. He would do whatever he needed to ensure his family had everything.

A few weeks later Dominic received a call from his brother in laws. They asked him to come downtown to an address they gave him over the phone. He and his wife with baby in tow made the short journey to the downtown area. There it was, the store they always wanted. It was magnificent. It was thought out and every detail was curtailed with precision.

Dominic could see his father's hand in the smallest of details. More impressive was the basement. His brother in laws set up a makeshift bedroom for themselves. This allowed them to live in the store saving money on rent or mortgages. The older of the two brothers had a wife and a young child.

Still, the apartment was nicer than any apartment Dominic ever rented when he lived in Texas. It was brilliant. They were smart enough to make this work. It wouldn't be long before they were profitable and making money. The brother in laws wanted to bring their father into the business but he was reluctant.

He wanted to retire from his position before taking on another. Besides, when he retired he could collect a full pension with health care benefits. He promised the brothers he would go into business with them in less than a year.

Dominic was living a comfortable life. He had his parents and his brother, his wife and her brothers, and now her parents are making the move soon.

As they were alone eating dinner together he asked his wife, "So what do you think, do you want to buy a house? I figure if we do it now it would be the right time. Prices are down, we are both working and we have enough saved, I think."

She replied, "How much do we have saved?"

He rolled his eyes looking for an exact total and answered, "I would speculate somewhere around twenty thousand give or take a few hundred."

She shrugged her shoulders and smiled, "OK. Big kitchen please."

It took only four weeks. They found a moderate home on seven acres surrounded by trees in the middle of the pine lands. It was a three-bedroom home with a basement and an attached two-car garage with two and a half bathrooms. The house was only eleven years old. It was in perfect shape. It needed some paint and minor repairs but they were happy.

Nearly a month later they had their own home surrounded by trees and very it was private. Dominic joked about setting up a BMX track in the back yard. His wife did not find the humor of bringing in a back hoe and moving dirt around her pristine back yard. Moving day presented more surprises for Dominic. As he made the final walk through after settlement, his parents furnished the baby's room, the living room and bought them a new bedroom set.

Dominic stood looking at his new home and new furniture. He asked his parents, "Why did you do this for us?"

His mother answered, "Because we wanted to. Also, you never asked us to help you and we wanted to show our appreciation. Do you like it?"

Dominic had tears in his eyes of joyfulness. Before he could say anything, his wife answered, "We love it. Well, I love it and Dominic will learn when the wife is happy, life is happy."

Angelo laughed out loud and replied, "Amen to that."

Maria looked at him, "Oh, you have it so bad."

Angelo walked over and kissed his wife on her cheek, "This is the reason I'm happy. I cherish the way you understand me."

She looked at her son and replied, "Just remember, your home is what you make it. You have the makings of a beautiful start."

Dominic replied, "Yes I do Mom, Thanks for everything."

She looked at him and smiled, "I don't mean the furniture, I'm talking about the love your wife has for you. Only you can make her love you more. Keep working hard, show her respect and life will present opportunities you couldn't imagine."

<u>**Chapter 60**</u>

Another year rolled by in a blink of an eye. Dominic's son was getting bigger and now walking. He found it more tiring to chase his son around the house and stop him from putting everything into his mouth. Like most children at this age, everything goes into the mouth.

The house had to be child proof and not a second passed where both Dominic and his wife didn't have to be on their toes caring for their child. Dominic was working a different schedule. He was working more at night than on dayshift.

He didn't mind. He was up for promotion with the airline and he was excited to share the news when it occurred. He would not know for at least a few more weeks.

It was mid-morning on a Saturday. Dominic was cutting the grass and his wife came outside and waved him into the house. She was standing with the phone in hand.

Dominic yelled, "Tell them I'll call them back."

She shook her head and insisted he take the call.

Dominic answered the phone. To his surprise it was Reggie. Dominic somewhat out of breathe, "Hello Reggie, what's up?" He could tell instantaneously there was something wrong.

In a disheartening tone Reggie spoke, "My friend, I don't know how to begin. But, I want you to hear this news from me before you hear or read about it. This is hard for me to tell you so just listen to what I say."

Dominic could hear the tremble in Reggie's voice and he was becoming concerned. He had no idea what disturbed Reggie or why he was talking with a weep in his voice.

Reggie continued, "I just got this news about twenty minutes ago and I wanted to confirm this before I made any phone calls. I spoke to your wife and parents and now I need to tell you. Last evening Tony was helping a woman fix a flat tire. She had two children in the car and knowing Tony, he was being a gentleman. Oh boy this is tough. A man fell asleep at the wheel of a box truck on the highway and struck Tony. Dom, Tony passed last evening. The man driving the vehicle was over the legal limit for drunk driving. I don't know all the details, but Tony is gone."

Dominic simply said, "Thank you Reggie. I need a few minutes. I'll call you back. I need to digest this for a few moments."

Reggie answered, "I understand, I'll be home. Call me. I'm here for you."

Dominic said nothing else and hung up the phone. His wife emerged from the hallway crying, "Dom, I'm sorry."

Dominic hugged and kissed his wife for nearly two-minutes before finally breaking down into tears. Dominic never lost a loved one and Tony was his brother.

After nearly twenty-five minutes Dominic spoke, "He was not supposed to go out this way. His mother outlived him. I am lost in my emotions. I don't know what to do. I feel helpless for the first time in my life. What do I do?"

She kissed him, "You need to get to California. Call my brother; he is an expert in this area. It's his expertise."

Dominic shook his head yes and sat for a while on the porch blindly starring into the woods watching the birds fly from tree to tree.

It wasn't long before the news about Tony's death was broadcast in all the various medias. Dominic did not take any calls from reporters or outside individuals other than his family. He spoke briefly with his former sponsor Brent Lock but not in detail.

Dominic lost a part of himself this day. He felt as if a part of him had been torn away. Dominic made it a point to gather his composure and waited for the details of the funeral. Within a week Dominic was on his way to California.

Reggie and Carl greeted him at the airport. They embraced for a few moments and headed to the funeral parlor. It was surreal for Dominic and he was faintly scared of what this situation curtailed. Dominic held his composure as they drove to the church.

The attendance was bigger than expected at the funeral parlor. There were more old BMX racers than friends and family. Tony was cherished by many and was remembered for all his accolades both on and off the track. Reggie would not disclose if he funded the funeral but it was too perfect for it not to have been organized by someone of his caliber.

The church service was brief and more a celebration of his life. The cemetery and open grave was when the reality of mortality affected Dominic the hardest. Reggie made a heartwarming speech about Tony and how he was a leader, loved, and respected by many.

The final words at the grave were a recording of the gate cadence, "Ok riders set'ems up. Rider's ready! Watch the gate. Beep beep beep." The sounds of a gate smashing the ground were never heard. Tony would have holeshotted this moto. This clearly affected many of the former BMX racers who attended the service and knew Tony.

That evening Dominic called home and spoke to his wife. He told her about the funeral and the class of how it was performed. He talked to her for a nearly an hour before he told her he loved and hung up the phone. He was staying with Reggie and his family. He explained that with the baby, he felt that his wife needed to stay home allowing him the flexibility to travel.

That evening Reggie conveyed the event of how Tony passed. It was sad that the young children witnessed this tragedy. One day this will pass and they will hopefully forget it. They spoke about Tony's mother and how she was not supposed to outlive her son. Tony's siblings were deeply saddened and thought of Dominic as their other brother. Dominic could not hold back his tears but he felt comfortable with Reggie and let his guard down.

Reggie spoke with Dominic, "You know what Dom, I never understood why states take a hard stand on drunk driving. I fully understand it now. It's not the drunk who injures himself or herself when they drink, it's the innocent people they affect. This was a tragedy. We lost a good man today. He will be missed. We had a plan that was coming together. We were so close. I say about one more year."

Dominic asked, "Yea speaking of, what is this big announcement?"

Reggie laughed, "Good try Dom."

Dominic laughed. It was getting late and Dominic had an early flight to catch in the morning.

Reggie walked down the hall toward his bedroom turned around and said, "It's the end of an era."

Chapter 61

We're cruising at thirty-eight thousand feet for the last five hours. I recalled all my fondest memories of my friend Tony and how he affected my life. I have my private space in the basement that I consider my man cave. I have all my trophies aligned at the top of the wall.

I still have all my BMX bicycles and a few affects of Tony's. I had them for many years before I gave up the ghost and donated most of them to the BMX hall of fame. Although I was inducted, I sometimes go there to recall my memories of Tony and those glory days.

But that's what they have become. I am at the point on my life where I need to ensure my children make the right decisions. There is nothing wrong recalling pleasant memories of one's childhood, but I don't live in the past. Instead I allow the past to predict the future.

The decision I made when I was young has allowed me the life I have obtained. If it's true that one becomes a product of their environment, then I am a happy man.

Many things happened over the past many years. My wife gave birth to another child two years after our son was born. We now added a healthy baby girl to our family. Both of our children are excellent students and my oldest is closing in on his high school graduation. They are both above average athletically. My son has all the possibilities of securing a baseball scholarship.

My life turned out remarkable. I have no regrets of what I have done or became. As I sit back pondering on these thoughts, I hear the knocking on the door. I push the button and the door opens. The flight attendant asks, "Captain Carlucci, do you want some coffee?"

I answer, "Yes, that would be nice. Thank you." I worked my entire life to be a pilot and I now am a Captain of a Boeing 767 with over two hundred passengers and crew onboard. I sacrificed many long nights and weekends building flight time working for smaller companies and flying smaller aircraft for little pay. Global has been good to me over the last twenty or so years and I have no regrets.

As I was finishing my coffee we were called by Air Traffic Control, "Global 268, heavy descend to flight level two-two thousand and contact Washington Center."

My first officer answered, "Global 268 heavy flight level two-two thousand contact Washington Center."

We landed on time in Philadelphia and in typical fashion. We had to wait on ground-traffic to clear the alley in order for us to taxi to our gate. We arrived on time and I personally greeted each passenger as they departed the aircraft. I made it a point to do this so they would remember my face and meet the person responsible for their safety when in the air under my command.

I drove home and pulled into the driveway. We never moved or bought a bigger home. We made many renovations over the years and modernized it. We were both happy and besides, with a kid about to enter college we needed to be smart with our savings.

My wife Julieta greeted me at the door as she always has in the past. If she was at work teaching, I simply made my way in to a quiet peaceful home. It was nearly noon and I decided to take a nap since I was awake all night.

I awoke a few hours later to a full house of people. My parents, brother and my in-laws were there. I lurched myself up from my slumber and got dressed. I emerged from the bedroom and I was welcomed to the world by my smart aleck brother.

My brother's life turned out prosperous and the business was very lucrative. My father handed over the keys to his castle and Joey was successful. He still has a short fuse and sometimes flies off the handle, but he is business wise. He married a woman he grew up with in town. She is a stereotypical South Jersey Italian. She has him under control and they are blessed with three children.

I often ask my father why he doesn't retire. He always has the best answers. Once I asked him, "Dad when are you going to retire?"

He responded, "Describe retirement."

I answered him, "You know, wake up when you want, do what you want to that day. Decide what you and Mom are going to do that afternoon. You know, stuff like that."

He simply replied, "Then I'm retired."

He loves to work and he does not interfere with Joey and his business plans. Joey has grown the business tenfold and my parents enjoy a very comfortable life style.

My brother in laws and their father Maximo in turn have a very successful business. When Maximo and Florencia moved to New Jersey, they both joked about the cost of living. All joking aside they were correct.

Maximo added to the business and introduced a service center and on call repairs. Both Carlos and Juan repaid my father in full and now have three locations in the South Jersey Region. Their persistence and hard work rewarded them with a thriving business and they all enjoy a contented lifestyle.

My closest friend and fellow BMX rider Rafael continues to reside in Texas. He graduated from college with a Masters Degree in Divinity and is an ordained Minister/Pastor. He has a large congregation and several services throughout the weekend.

He performs one Saturday night service, two Sunday morning services and late Sunday service in Spanish. His Director of Music is Christopher. Christopher never disclosed if he or his father buried their demons, but Christopher obtained his PHD in Music over the years and works full time at the Church.

He and Rafael have been friends for many years and love working for the Lord. Rafael performed the marital ceremony for his sister and I. We were his first wedding ceremony and he was flawless. Both Rafael and Christopher married women they met in college and they were both blessed with children. Maximo jokes about Christopher being his favorite child.

I still keep in touch with all my friends from the neighborhood. We have been friends for many years. There was a brief period when all our lives were dormant from each other. We had to raise our kids, or simply became busy as life happened.

We still joke about who would win a race today. I tease them about having the track at my parents and threaten to take one of my bikes off the wall in my man cave and rip some gates with them. They all know I still have it and would crush them.

Tony's mother passed a few years after Tony. She finally succumbed to her cancer. It was a sad day, but at the same time joyful. She was a very strong Christian woman and lived her life the same. She made everyone promise to celebrate her death for two reasons. First and foremost, she wanted to be with God. Secondly of course was to reunite with her son.

I could hear my wife calling me over all the mayhem in the house, "Honey its Reggie on the phone."

Reggie still lives in the Florida Keys. Whatever project he has been working has taken him nearly twenty years to complete and has not told me what it was or any details. He has had other ventures after BMX.

He became a VP of a very prestigious marketing firm and flourished in his trade. He keeps in contact with me via email and phone. He has written many business articles and every one of them has been published. He has mentored many children over the years and never forgot his friends.

I picked up the phone, "Hey Reggie, how is retirement for real this time?"

He laughed and replied, "Remember the project I was telling you about?"

I quickly answered him, "Yes."

He asked me, "Do you want to know what it is? I am finally ready to go."

I answered, "Yes, I know it's not the Olympics, they were over a few years ago, but give me one second. I hear the kids making their way out the house."

I yelled to my children, "Oscar and Toni don't leave yet, CHORES!"

Epilogue

In gratitude to all the BMX riders over the years, I wanted to write a novel for several years about the sport. Although this is not an autobiography or factually correct in some instances, I wanted to glorify the sport and how much it meant to me as a young child.

I took you through a mystical journey of racing, compounded by life's lessons in hopes that young adults would be captivated by the sport. Many of the events are based on real people and real characterizations of mentors and sages alike. I want to honor all athletes who strive at a goal and achieve it or come close.

I want to dedicate my efforts in this fictional story to the parents who financially support any child even if not their own. The biggest sacrifice any parent makes is the support they provide for a child.

I still want to honor the BMX racers over the years that historically are recorded champions. I took the liberty of selecting specific years to convey a journey of hope and life lessons. In respect of those who raced and are champions, I limited my list to those who are professional in the sport of BMX.

I simply could not list every year and every age group. This would be a novel on its own accord. The list provided was copied from Wikipedia and includes only the NBA, NBL, and ABA. I want to give the UCI and USABMX honorable mention for their efforts of supporting the sport. The sport is global and an Olympic event.

National Bicycle Association (NBA)
Pro Nat.#1 Men*

- 1974 David Clinton
- 1975 John George
- 1976 Scot Breithaupt
- 1977 Stu Thomsen
- 1978 Stu Thomsen
- 1979 Scott Clark
- 1980 Anthony Sewell
- 1981 Scott Clark

National Bicycle League (NBL)
Elite ("AA") Pro Nat.#1

- 1978 Sal Zeuner
- 1979 Greg Esser
- 1980 Anthony Sewell
- 1981 Stu Thomsen
- 1982 Stu Thomsen
- 1983 Eric Rupe
- 1984 Eric Rupe
- 1985 Greg Hill
- 1986 Pete Loncarevich
- 1987 Pete Loncarevich
- 1988 Greg Hill
- 1989 Gary Ellis
- 1990 Terry Tenette
- 1991 Terry Tenette
- 1992 Terry Tenette
- 1993 Eric Carter
- 1994 Gary Ellis
- 1995 John Purse
- 1996 John Purse
- 1997 Christophe Lévêque
- 1998 Christophe Lévêque
- 1999 Danny Nelson
- 2000 Thomas Allier
- 2001 Jamie Staff
- 2002 Kyle Bennett
- 2003 Randy Stumpfhauser
- 2004 Kyle Bennett
- 2005 Mike Day

- 2006 Donny Robinson
- 2007 Kyle Bennett
- 2008 Randy Stumpfhauser
- 2009 Maris Strombergs
- 2010 Maris Strombergs

American Bicycle Association (ABA)
Pro Nat.#1 Men (AA)

- 1977 Title did not exist
- 1978 Title did not exist
- 1979 Stu Thomsen
- 1980 Brent Patterson
- 1981 Kevin McNeal
- 1982 Brian Patterson
- 1983 Brian Patterson
- 1984 Pete Loncarevich
- 1985 Ronnie Anderson
- 1986 Pete Loncarevich
- 1987 Charles Townsend
- 1988 Mike King
- 1989 Gary Ellis
- 1990 Gary Ellis
- 1991 Pete Loncarevich
- 1992 Pete Loncarevich
- 1993 Steve Veltman
- 1994 Gary Ellis
- 1995 Gary Ellis
- 1996 Robert MacPherson
- 1997 John Purse
- 1998 Christophe Lévêque
- 1999 Christophe Lévêque
- 2000 Wade Bootes
- 2001 Warwick Stevenson
- 2002 Danny Nelson
- 2003 Warwick Stevenson
- 2004 Bubba Harris
- 2005 Bubba Harris
- 2006 Bubba Harris
- 2007 Danny Caluag
- 2008 Khalen Young
- 2009 Randy Stumpfhauser
- 2010 Sam Willoughby

<u>**About the Author**</u>

Steven Cohen was born and raised in Vineland, NJ. He graduated from Vineland High School in 1985 and enlisted in the armed services shortly after his graduation. He served in the USAF, NJANG and the Army National Guard. He served his Country for 16 years and is a graduate of the New Jersey Military Academy, OCS Class 39, located in Sea Girt, NJ.

Steve is an Aircraft Mechanic by trade and holds both, Mechanics licenses and a private pilot's license. Steve has worked in the aviation industry since 1985 when he entered the United States Air force. He is currently employed by one of the largest airlines carriers in the world as an Aircraft Maintenance Supervisor. He currently resides in New Jersey and is married with children. He owns his own Photography business and hobbies include playing numerous musical instruments with the ability to read music.

"Determination coupled by the resolve to flourish is as close to reality as one concedes." ~ Steven Cohen

9 781935 795391